LIGHTS FALL

Nichelle Rae

ISBNs
EBook 978-0-9973586-0-5
Paperback 978-0-9973586-1-2

Cover art by ProBook Covers.
Edited by Tanya Egan Gibson.

Other Books by
Nichelle Rae

<u>The White Warrior Series</u>
Vol.I: Only a Glow
Vol.II: The Blaze Ignites
Vol.III: Steady Burn
Vol.IV: Doused
Vol.V: Embers under the Ash (available soon)
Vol.VI: Fire of the World (available soon)

Frost Burn

PROLOGUE

Megan was determined not to shed a tear, though her child's screams were a horrific reminder of what she had accepted nine months ago, and what she had to do next. The twit of a nun, also knowing what was about to happen, tried to hand Megan the baby.

Megan squeezed her eyes closed and turned her face away. "Get it away from me."

"But you have a daughter."

Megan opened her eyes and stared hatefully at the empty brick wall beside her head. "She's not mine," she declared through clenched teeth, as if they were bars keeping in her screams of loss and agony. "She's his."

"The gentleman from the state department is waiting downstairs. Don't you want to say goodbye?"

Megan's lips closed over her teeth, an extra layer of security against her screams, and shook her head. After her wailing daughter was mercifully removed from the room, she strained to hear her cries as they echoed down the hallway of the convent. A heavy door opened in the distance, its hinges groaning like a monster come to eat her child, and then closed heavily like the maw of the unfathomable beast.

The nuns suddenly started clucking amongst each other urgently.

"Lost too much blood!" she heard one say.

"Cannot stop the bleeding!"

"Get a doctor!"

Unconsciousness started creeping in.

Wait. Not yet.

"Lights fall," she managed to whisper.

The nun kneeled next to Megan. "We're going to fetch you some help, dear. Just hang on."

"Lights fall," she whispered again as a heavy darkness overwhelmed her into a deepness she knew she would not escape.

"What dear? What did you say?"

"Tell her," Megan managed as strongly as she could, "lights fall." Oblivion surrounded her like a lake and she was sinking quickly into the black. "Make sure she knows that…" With the last of her strength, and only by sheer will, she managed "…forever." Her chest fell as her final breath escaped.

1

"Go around back, Bay!" Jefferson cried.

"Fuck off!" I replied. "I can catch him!"

"Kennedy! No!" Ignoring him, I headed straight down the alley while Jefferson went around the back with a frustrated "God dammit!" lingering in the air.

Indulging in a triumphant little smirk, I picked up the pace. "Banner!" I hollered. "FBI! Freeze!" He ignored me. "I'm not going to tell you again!" He kept running. "Fine," I muttered.

The brick walls of the alley blurred as I ran at a speed that would have been called—had I let anyone witness it—impossible. People don't move at speeds over forty-five miles an hour outside of vehicles, so as always, I was careful not to be caught doing it. I was on Banner's heels quickly. I slammed my entire body weight into him and we tumbled across the pavement a few times, stopping with me on his back. I yanked his arms behind him and cuffed him. When he was secure, I ripped out a fistful of his hair making him scream.

"Well would you look at that," I said. "A DNA sample from our vigorous struggle. I better get this to my lab right away, huh?"

"You can't do this!" he screamed pathetically.

I tightened his cuffs. "I just did."

"I have rights!" He turned to look at me and I tensed for a brief moment. Banner's swampy brown-green eyes were empty. Sexual predators had one of two kinds of eyes—empty or evil. I'd seen a broad range of both in my eight year career, and neither was easy to look at. Empty eyes usually meant someone, at some point in their life, had turned them into what they were, often through some form of child abuse or neglect. The born predators, the hunters, they had the evil eyes.

"You're right," I acknowledged, struggling to stay professional and Mirandize him instead of bludgeoning him to death. "You have the right to remain silent. Anything you say can and will be used against you in court of law. You have the right to an attorney. If you cannot afford an attorney, one will be appointed to you. Do you understand these rights as I've explained them to you?"

"You bitch!" he screamed, spittle flying from his mouth onto the pavement.

My professionalism went out the window.

I seized his hair again, digging my fingernails into his scalp, and yanked his head so far back it was hard for him to breathe. "Bitch?" I asked, leaning really close to his ear. "You better fucking believe it. I'm also a well-connected bitch." He started wheezing. "And I'm going to make sure every single inmate at Hills Correctional knows your name and that you molested fourteen kids." His face started turning red. "I judge you'll last about a month. What do you think? Maybe less? Now, do you understand your rights as I've explained them to you? A simple nod will suffice." The man nodded once with what little room I allowed him to move. "Good."

"Kennedy!" Jefferson cried as he came up the other side of the alley, panting heavily with sweat spackling his brow.

I released Banner's hair and stood, sneering at the man before me. "Glad you could make it, but you're a little late to the party."

"You…" he panted, placing his hands on his knees, "are a bitch."

I smirked. "Well, like I was just telling our friend here, I'm not just a bitch. I'm the best in the city." I passed Jefferson and headed toward the street.

"Wait!" he called. I looked back over my shoulder. "Aren't you gonna grab him?"

I turned around with an over exaggerated look of confusion. "I'm sorry. I thought you would have liked to *pretend* you had a hand in arresting him."

"Fuck you," he sneered and reached down to pick Banner up off the ground.

My eyes narrowed. "Try not to strain yourself."

I indulged in watching his fleshy jaw clench and his beady eyes widen before I turned and continued walking the four blocks back to my SUV. Climbing in, I put the hair I'd palmed into one of the evidence bags I kept in my glove box and checked my watch. It was 10:30 pm, so Shia should still be in the lab. I was fairly certain he lived there. Porter, the executive assistant of my branch, would still be there, too. If Jefferson complained about me again, I was in for a long night, and I really didn't want to deal with it. I sat there and tried to convince myself I was going home. I tried to tell myself that the reports and crap could wait. But I looked down at the evidence bag with Banner's hair and sighed. I wasn't going home. I put my car in drive and headed back to headquarters.

I pinched the corners of my eyes and sighed. I realized I was tired, which was saying something because I didn't usually need to sleep more than once a week. I couldn't recall if I was overdue or not but figured I must be if I was this exhausted.

To stay awake, I turned my burning rage toward my pig of a partner, Jefferson. I'd managed to drive away all my other randomly assigned partners, but Jefferson was like a tick! Dug in and stubborn. I had pushed the limits of being unkind to him, treating him worse than any other jackass I'd been saddled with. He needed to go. It used to be that he practically drooled every time he looked at me. Every time he did, I'd imagined him holding a big, bloody, red steak in both fists and gnawing on it like a rabid animal. Spit and blood smeared his mouth and chin, and his hands were coated in a gory shine. His eyes were wide and intense, as if he could taste me through the meat.

A month ago, I got sick of his wandering eyes and inappropriate comments and clocked him. He ended up with a concussion from hitting the floor and a nice, plump shiner. There was still some ugly yellow bruising on his face from it. After that, he stopped looking at me lustfully and switched to hatred. I liked hatred better. Hatred kept his eyes off me and his hands from becoming too curious.

Porter told me at my discipline hearing that I could have just filed a sexual harassment report. Sure, I could have. But putting the man in the hospital got the message across quicker and more efficiently. And I was a quicker and more efficient kind of person.

I loathed dealing with partners because loyalty only went as far as your usefulness to the other person. No one was useful to me because I was always eight steps ahead of everyone. I was usually *eighteen* steps ahead of Jefferson. On top of his wandering eye, he was also slow in every sense of the word, and I did not have time to hold the hand of an idiot. People were only worth my effort and time if they got shit done. And no one could get shit done like I could. I solved a minimum of one case a week, mainly because of my sleeping oddity. While the world dreamed, I prowled the night looking for my quarry of child molesters, sex traffickers, and perpetrators of any other despicable sexual crimes the human race thought it was okay to inflict on each other.

I credited all my oddities for why I was so damn good at my job, and I credited my past for why I fucking *loved* my job. Locking up sexual predators was the life for me, no doubt. Partners just slowed me down.

———

The lab was surprisingly hopping at 11:00 pm. I had to stop quickly, jerk myself backward, and then do some other fast movements, some of them odd, to avoid the scurrying scientists—the "ants," I called them. Everyone moved with a sense of urgency, not seeing me until they were practically running me over. I spotted Shia in the center of the enormous glass wall lab – the "tank" for short. He was sitting at a table gazing into a microscope. I smiled as I made my way to him.

Shia was somebody that got shit done, which earned him high marks on the respect scale. In turn, he recognized me as someone who also got shit done, and always did what he could to make sure my lab work was completed before anyone else's. The guy worked as hard as I did, though he did need to sleep more than once a week. But I could forgive him a little sleep. He rarely got any as it was.

"I don't have time, Bay," he said, his voice sounding far away as I tossed Banner's hair sample onto his table. He briefly peeked at it from the corner of his eye. "What is it?"

"Serial rapist and child molester's hair sample."

Shia looked up at me, his shining blue eyes darkening a bit before he went back to his microscope. "And?"

"And I need you to process it."

"I really don't have time, Bay." He came out from behind the microscope and jotted something down on a clipboard to his right before indicating around the room with his pen. "As you can see, we have our hands full with a movie theater fire right now."

My eyes went wide. "Shit. How many?"

He put his pen down and went back to the microscope. "Seventeen dead that need identifying as soon as possible."

"Arson?"

"Not my department," he replied, adjusting the focal knobs. "I was told to identify the bodies, so that's what I'm doing."

"Come on, Shia," I jokingly whined.

"No."

"It's just a little itty-bitty hair sample. You know you're my favorite ant in the lab. Can't you just prioritize this real quick?"

With a sigh, he sat back and picked up the evidence bag. "You can't say I'm your favorite when you don't like anybody else."

I smiled. "Please?"

He pressed his lips together and met my eyes. "What am I looking for?"

"I just need DNA."

He looked at the bag again, flipping it over to look at the chain of custody label. "Matched against...?"

"The Farah Gordon case."

Shia looked back up at me with wide eyes. "The first victim?"

I gave him a self-satisfied smirk. "The first victim."

He nodded sharply. "You got it."

I grinned and ruffled his short black hair. "That's my favorite ant!" He rolled his eyes and stood to go to the table behind him. "Put a rush on it," I added.

"Aye aye, Captain," he said with a halfhearted salute, which looked more like he was flicking excess sweat from his brow, before he bent over the hair sample. I walked past him toward the opposite door from which I'd entered, where there was less ant activity.

As soon as I stepped into the bullpen, I heard an angry bellow coming from the executive director of my unit. "Kennedy! My office! Now!"

I sighed and rolled my eyes. Looking back into the lab, I saw Shia holding up a pad of paper with "2.07 seconds. A new record. Well done," written on it. He wasn't even looking up from his table. I smiled and headed across the bullpen toward Porter's big corner office.

James Porter was an attractive man with a narrow face and tan skin. His brown hair was speckled with white, mostly around his temples and ears, though he was only in his early forties. He was only my height, but I was tall anyway at 5'11". Currently he was the executive assistant director of the criminal, cyber, response, and service branches, all of which I'd been heavily involved in since I'd joined the Bureau, so I knew Porter well. I'd been thrilled when he got the promotion to head my unit and the three others—until he started trying to force partners down my throat.

Through the window of the office I could see Jefferson was already in there, and I deflated instantly. I knew this was going to be a long night. Sure enough, he exploded as soon as I entered.

"I can't work with this world-class bitch!" he yelled, the door still open behind me.

Finally, he was quitting! Relief flooded through me, but that was loud. I glanced out the open door toward the tank and saw Shia staring up from his work. That meant the entire bullpen was privy to this conversation. Maybe the entire floor. Shit.

Well then, I figured I might as well have fun with it.

I faced Jefferson and pressed my palms into the top of Porter's conference table. Leaning heavily over my hands, I peered at him with unconcealed distain. "I'm sorry. Are you still trying to insult me with that? I thought we already established I'm not a world-class bitch; I'm *the* world-class bitch. You'd do well to remember that." I glanced behind me again and saw Shia grin widely before looking back down at his work. I even heard a few chuckles from the bullpen.

Porter finally came to his senses and walked behind me to close his office door. "Jefferson, I understand that…"

"No! I don't want any therapy sessions. I want to transfer to a new department. I'll transfer to a new state if I have to!"

I sat down and crossed my ankles on top of the table, hoping my expression conveyed the boredom I felt. Porter had better not try to salvage this pig of an agent. I might quit myself if he did.

Porter sighed. "You've only been working with Kennedy for five months."

"It feels like twenty years!"

I tilted my head to the side and looked up at Porter. "I told ya, Boss. I don't play well with partners."

"You shut up!" he yelled jabbing a finger in my direction. "You're on thin enough ice as it is!"

I stared at him. This was not going as I had hoped. Our relationship had never been one of "like" really, but of tense mutual respect. He'd always given me the impression that he was on my side. After my discipline hearing for punching Jefferson, for instance, Porter had taken me for a cup of coffee so he could talk to me in a more casual setting than as my boss. He'd told me he understood why I'd hit Jefferson and even went so far as to say that he'd likely deserved it. But now Porter was defending him?

Porter quickly closed his eyes and started massaging his temples like he'd seen the betrayal on my face. When he opened them again, my heart sank, because I saw something familiar in them, a look I'd seen before in the eyes of my employers—all of my *former* employers. Porter was actually going to sack me. Well, I would be damned if I was going to walk away from this like a whipped pup. Porter knew me better than that, and right now I had nothing left to lose. I wouldn't go down bowing to them.

I kicked my feet off the table and stood, glaring at him. "I'm also the best field agent you've got, and you fucking know it."

Gazing at me with genuine regret, Porter seemed to have aged twenty years in front of me. He didn't want to let me go, that much was clear, so I didn't understand why he was. I couldn't help sneaking a glance at Jefferson, who stood against the window with his arms crossed, smiling like a cat that had just eaten the family canary. My eyes narrowed; he was enjoying this. My spine turned into a steel rod. I would not let him see how much losing my job pained me. He would not win.

I looked at my silently writhing director again. "Let me save you the trouble, Porter, so we can avoid any lengthy and false sentimental parting speeches. I'll go clean out my desk."

Porter deflated. "I'm sorry, Bay. I just can't have…"

"Save it," I snapped. "It's your loss, and I'm going to walk out of here gleefully knowing that's a *stone cold fact!*"

I looked Jefferson dead in the eyes as I took out my badge and credentials, placing them on the conference table. He would not see my pain. I refused to let him see me tremble, though trying to hide it seemed to make it harder to conceal. Jefferson watched me put my whole world on that table, a world that had saved me from what I could have become without it, what I *had* been before it. His eyes dropped, and he took a long look at my C-cups one more time, licking his lips. The image of him with the bloody steak popped into my head again. Without looking back at Porter, I turned and walked out of the office, heading to a nearby storeroom to get an empty box.

The bullpen was dead silent, way quieter than it should have been. I felt the weight of every pair of eyes on me as I made my way to my cubicle. I stood in front of my desk and realized there was nothing here I needed to take. No personal items whatsoever, though I'd worked here for eight years. Just the usual office supplies and a few files. At the top of the pile was the Farah Gordon case. I wouldn't need that anymore. I flipped the empty box onto my desk in annoyance and headed for the door.

From the corner of my eye, I watched Shia through the glass wall of the tank as I made my way out. He started pulling off his gloves and headed for the door closest to where I'd pass. I pretended not to notice him. I didn't want him to feel like he *had* to come say goodbye to me, but at the same time I was glad I'd be able to.

In my hurry to escape, I turned the corner into the hallway too fast and slammed right into another person turning the same corner. Papers went flying, and suddenly a familiar flash of burning pain erupted in the left side of my neck.

"Ah! Shit!" I cried, reflexively grabbing my neck and covering it with my hand as much as humanly possible.

Shit! They never appeared in a place so visible! My neck? Seriously? What the fuck was this one going to look like?

I looked at the person I had run into. His eyes briefly held me captive; they were a clear stunning cognac color that looked more orange than brown. He was about my age and very tall, at least 6'4", and terribly handsome. He had wavy, neatly styled black hair and tan skin. There was no way he worked here because he had on a very expensive, custom-tailored, three-piece suit.

"I'm sorry," I said, hardly able to come to my senses with those stunning eyes on me.

He didn't respond and just stared at me, half in a crouch, with one hand pressed flat against the wall behind him. His body was taut and alert, as if he were ready to make a run for it—or make a grab for me. His eyes seemed to look right through me, and I felt oddly exposed.

Though I truly would like to have stayed and looked at him a bit longer, I had to get out of there *immediately.* "I'm sorry," I said again and ran passed him.

I sprinted down the hall toward the exit, keeping my hand covering my neck. I wasn't about to wait for an elevator so I threw myself into the crash bar to the stairs and ran down three flights. Throwing the exit door open on the street level, I hurried to my car and quickly climbed inside. After taking a few deep breaths, I took my hand from my neck and stared out the windshield.

My neck? Why did it have to appear on my neck? And what the hell was so significant about running into a rich suit I didn't know? Why would that have caused it?

I reached up, clicked the dome light on, and leaned toward the review mirror to see the new tattoo that had appeared. My brows dropped instantly. "The fuck is that?"

I leaned in closer to get a better look, but it didn't alleviate my confusion. It was three strange symbols, each about the size of a half dollar coin, in a vertical line. The tattoo resembled something like the black Hebrew symbols down the middle of my back, only it definitely wasn't Hebrew. I had no idea what language this was.

I sighed and sat back heavily in my seat. Well, at least it wasn't ugly. The symbols were actually kind of pretty and whimsical looking. I glanced up in the mirror again before starting my car. Looked like me and Google had a date tonight while I tried to figure out what these symbols meant. They had to be important if they'd appeared on my damn neck; at least they'd *better* be important! With them being so visible, it looked like I was returning to waitressing—pretty much the only kind of job that actually allowed for visible tattoos, and even that was sometimes touch and go. I might even have to head back to bartending. Good tips, shitty company. Then again, maybe once I figured out what the symbols were, they would tell me what I was supposed to do next.

I sighed again, trying not to think about the fact that I wouldn't be coming back here tomorrow, and headed home.

2

By three in the morning, my chin throbbed from resting heavily on top of my desk while I stared at my laptop with my homepage opened to the empty search engine. Nothing even *remotely* resembled the symbols on my neck, even in the most ancient of recorded languages. I knew ancient languages, too, having minored in them in college.

I stood up, slammed my laptop shut, and gazed around my messy apartment. The kitchen, set in a dark square cove in the wall across from me, was in the worst condition. My sink and counter overflowed with ceramic plates. The moonlight through the windows made the edges shine like eyes accusing me of being a slob. I wasn't, though. I was just busy. Hunting down Banner had been a month-long endeavor and my dishes hadn't been a priority. They rarely were.

My heart sank a little when I realized I couldn't use work anymore as an excuse not to clean. Losing my job hurt more than I could have ever imagined it would, but I couldn't let myself feel the pain because it would blur my focus while I investigated. Taking a deep breath, I hardened my heart against having lost my purpose in life and decided I'd only grieve when I figured out what happened—and got my damn job back. There were kids in the world that still needed me. I would not, I could not, abandon them.

Before going to bed I went to my full-length mirror and looked at the new addition to my body art. They really were very pretty, yet simple, too. They looked like some sort of odd, filigree version of Gallifreyan letters—the fictional language from the TV show *Doctor Who*—but not exactly. I'd never seen this elegant language before.

With a sigh, I turned my focus from my neck and took off my robe. Standing naked in front of the mirror, I admired my entire collection. My tattoos were odd for more than the fact they appeared out of nowhere; they'd been a part of my life since I was born. They appeared randomly, usually during some significant life event, or discovery, or choice I made. Their black ink never faded, each one growing with me as I aged, never becoming dull or distorted. I had about twenty unique pictures on my body, mainly concentrated on my upper arms, torso, hips, and thighs, with a couple small ones on my ankles. They were all well-hidden under my clothes. Decorative lines filled some of the blank spaces of skin between each picture and symbol, all varying in width and design, giving the entire assortment a cohesive and rather attractive look.

I turned around, pulling my thick, long blonde hair in front of my shoulder to allow me an unobstructed view of my back, where my largest and favorite tattoo was. It was a massive, incredibly detailed black outline of a pair of wings. They started at my shoulders, came all the way down each side of my back, and wrapped around so the ends of the feathers stopped at my hips. I still hadn't learned their purpose. I just knew they'd appeared on me the second I'd drawn breath as an infant, and I only knew that, because when I was eleven I happened to get a glance at the file my social worker had on me while he was out of the room. A few pages in, I'd seen the list of my first tattoos in a section titled "miscellaneous notes."

I already had nine tattoos by the time I was eleven, and I remembered most of them appearing. My wings, though, had always just been there. After investigating the convent that had delivered me, I found out from the Mother Superior, who had been a postulant at the time, that those wings had been discovered on my back not long after I'd been born.

With what I'd been through in the foster care system, perhaps the only purpose of my wings had been to get me through my childhood. I severely doubted I would have survived without them. No matter how dark things got, no matter what I was told, I always had my wings wrapped around me as a reminder that I was special; I was not a mistake. When I was little, I often pretended I was being hugged by them. Through four sexually and physically abusive foster fathers, one similarly abusive foster brother, and one bipolar physically abusive foster mother, the wings' presence gave me a tiny bit of self-worth, likely allowing me to survive because, really, what other five-year-old girl had a pair of Angel wings hugging her?

A gentle knock made me jump. I snapped my head to my front door and saw the crack of light under it was obstructed by a shadow. I snatched my robe off the floor, threw it back on, and grabbed my Beretta M9 out of my top dresser drawer. Keeping aim on the door, I slowly moved toward it as the soft knock came again. I pressed the muzzle against the wood and cracked it open. Shia was in the hallway holding up two paper bags from a local 24-hour Chinese restaurant.

"Hungry?"

My cheeks almost hurt from the grin that came to my face. I put my gun casually behind me and opened my door the rest of the way. Leaning against the frame, I gazed at him without an answer. It was so good to see him but I didn't want to seem overeager about it.

His arms dropped to his sides. "I saw your light on and took a shot you'd be up." He gave me a genuinely sad look. "You left so quickly that we didn't get a chance to say goodbye."

I rested my head against the doorframe, looking at him inquisitively. "Isn't this a little inappropriate?" I teased.

He looked up at the ceiling and bobbed his head from side to side as if he was pondering the possibly. "I could see the issue if we were coworkers, but"—he looked at me, his smile sweet but still a little sad— "after the scene at headquarters, I'm going to assume we're not coworkers anymore."

I pressed my lips together in silent acknowledgment. Looking at his clear blue eyes and slightly disheveled black hair, I realized for the first time how attractive he was. At the lab, he was always in a lab coat and scrubs. Now he wore a pair of jeans, dark brown work boots, a snug-fitting green-and-black textured shirt, and an open black leather jacket. He was actually really hot for a nerd.

He peered at me with inquisitive playfulness. "So, are you going to let me in or…?"

I chuckled and opened the door further. "Come on in."

He smiled and stepped through. After a quick glance

around my apartment, he spotted my kitchen to the right and headed toward it. Meanwhile, I discretely put my gun down on a short table behind me.

"I wasn't completely sure what you liked, so I just got all of the basics," he said, setting the bags down on top of my kitchen table.

"Good thing the basics are my favorite," I replied, flicking on the dim yellow light in the kitchen.

Shia glanced back at me and did a double take, his smile fading. "Fuck, Bay," he said, stepping forward. He took my chin in his fingers and turned my face, giving him a clear view of the new tattoo on my neck. "What the hell?"

I pulled away from his hands, a little uncomfortable.

"What did you do?"

I shrugged and casually indicated the tattoo. "My last 'fuck you' to the boss."

Shia looked at me sadly and shoved his hands deep in his pockets. "And where did you find a tattoo artist that works in the middle of the night?"

I gazed at him a little warily. "A friend."

He nodded and looked at the floor, clearly not believing me but catching my hint not to pry.

When he looked up again, his eyes paused near my chest, clearly catching sight of another one of my tattoos peeking out of the collar of my robe. His eyes came up to meet mine, and I suddenly felt the shift in the mood. It became hot, and his eyes lit up with desire.

"Another one?" he asked, taking a step toward me and reaching for my collar. He gently pulled it aside to reveal the entire tattoo.

It was a kind of tribal figure of a mother holding an infant in her arms in the negative space between the lines of black ink. I remembered the exact second this one had appeared on my skin—it was the day the nun had told me that my mother died giving birth to me. That tattoo had quickly been followed by the torn-up dove lying in a pool of black blood on my left thigh, which appeared when she also informed me that I was the product of my mother having been raped.

Shia took another step closer. "How many do you

have?"

I glanced down. "A lot," I said plainly. I couldn't get into this with him. The last thing anyone needed to know about was my magically appearing tattoos.

I felt the heat of his body as he took another step toward me and one of his hands rested on my hip over my robe. "Can I see?"

I brought my eyes up to his, trying to gauge what was happening in case I was reading too much into his actions and he didn't really want me the way it felt like he did. His eyes shamelessly held mine hostage, and my heart started to pound making me feel feverish. I nodded, giving him permission.

He gently pulled the collar of my robe back until it fell off my shoulder, exposing my breast. We seemed to make the decision to give in to the desire at the exact same time because he swept in fast, pressing his lips against mine as I aimed for his. My entire body went limp, my arms dropping to my sides as he wrapped both of his around me and held me tightly. I tried to lift my arms to touch his face, but they wouldn't comply. My brows dropped as I tried to lift them again, but nothing happened.

Then my eyes flew wide with panic! I suddenly realized that my legs were dangling listlessly underneath me and that Shia was actually holding me up. My entire body was numb!

My head fell away from him as my neck went numb, too. When his face appeared in my line of sight, my heart clenched in panic and horror. A disgusting brown liquid was smeared all over his mouth, with more liquid coming from the pores of his lips like beads of brown sweat. He looked down at me and my heart seized; his eyes were darker and more lifeless than those of any predator I'd ever arrested. Cushioned by nothing—not a shred of humanity, nothing of decency—they were just evil.

"Well, that was just way too fuckin' easy," he said with viciousness I'd never heard in his voice before. He casually wiped the cuff of his sleeve over his mouth, and the blue of his eyes turned a deep blood red as his lovely tan skin turned a creepy corpse-like gray.

I screamed, but nothing came out. His eyes stirred a terror so deep I felt like I was drowning in a sea of the worst emotions known to mankind. The depths of darkness in those eyes tore at my heart like no predator's ever had. I furiously fought him in my mind, but my body wouldn't move. I screamed at my paralysis, whatever was causing it, commanding my arms to punch and my legs to kick, but nothing worked. Breathing was my only movement and I couldn't take in breaths as fast as I needed them.

Shia slid his hand under my legs and picked me up. I fought hard, flailing about inside myself and screaming until my temples were throbbing.

"Oh, shh shh shh shh," Shia said with false concern. "You can't fight me, Bay, and if you keep trying, all alone in that little head of yours, you're going to give yourself a stroke."

He walked me over to my bed and laid me down with my legs hanging off the side and started unbuttoning his jeans. He pushed one of my legs to the side with his knee, completely exposing me to him. Fighting and screaming in my head, I kept trying to move. I begged my arms to come up, but they didn't. Shia soon stood naked from the waist down and put himself between my legs. I flailed in my mind, but my body still didn't respond.

Suddenly I heard the sound of wood exploding and Shia snapped his head to my front door. I commanded my neck muscles to turn to see what was happening, but they didn't obey. Another barrage of explosions came which I knew were gunshots, and Shia was thrown backwards out of my view. I demanded my legs to move, to get me up, to run, but I stayed immobile and naked on the bed. Another man entered my line of sight with his gun aimed at where Shia had fallen. It was the rich suit I had run into in the hallway!

He glanced at me briefly, his cognac eyes like two tiny fires in his face, before he looked behind him. "Booth!"

A moment later, a tall, beautiful, muscle-bound black man appeared in my vision. He had smooth clear skin, a thin, well-trimmed goatee, and bald head. His eyes were a stunning and lovely light green. There was something about him that instantly calmed me. He leaned over, quickly wrapped me up in my blanket, then picked me up off the bed and carried me out the busted front door of my apartment. I watched the ceilings change from the dull light tan of hallway and stairwell, to the blood red of the lobby. Finally, I was looking at the night sky.

Booth quickly got into the back seat of a car with me on his lap, and another one of my rescuers came into view as he closed the door behind Booth. He was tall and thin with fluffy, tousled brown hair and smooth, lily white skin. He rushed around the back of the car out of sight, and I heard the three other doors open and close, followed by the squealing of tires as we peeled away.

My frozen eyes were fixed on the back window. Before my apartment building disappeared in the distance, I caught a glimpse of Shia's terrifying, strange face hanging halfway out my bedroom window watching the car pull off. Blood splattered his cheeks, and the front of his shirt was soaked around several bullet holes in his torso. My heart clenched in terror. That many gunshots should have killed him! This just wasn't real. It couldn't be.

"Roy," I heard the handsome businessman say from the passenger seat. "Can you do anything?"

The thin white guy's face appeared above me, his large brown eyes looking into mine. He was quiet a moment. "No," he replied. "It was a pure level five."

"Damn," a female voice said from the driver's seat. "A Queen's venom takes six and a half days to wear off; that's if she makes it through the symptoms of the poison."

"She'll make it," the businessman said confidently. Hearing these people speak and being near them seemed to be easing my nerves. For some ungodly reason, I felt safe with them. "Roy, can you at least clear the venom from around her eyes so she can close them and rest?"

"That I can do."

Roy's face appeared above me again, and suddenly his brown irises turned a shiny, silvery-gray color, his pupils constricting to a small black pinpoint. Instantly I felt my eye muscles unfreeze and my gaze darted wildly around the car. So much for that safe feeling they provided!

"Uh, Gyllian?" Roy said with concern, as his eyes faded back to brown. "Her heart rate just increased."

I moved my eyes to look in the front seat and saw the

businessman turn to look back at me. His brows dropped. "Why is she terrified?" After studying me another moment, his pretty, near-orange-colored eyes turned the same silvery gray.

I felt my heart explode in my head and I started to pant. This wasn't real! I was dreaming! I had to be. None of this was real! People's eyes didn't change color like that! What the hell was this? What was happening?

"She is panicking," Booth's worried deep voice boomed in a thick African accent.

Gyllian's eyes went back to orangish and he looked up at Roy. "Put her to sleep. Something is wrong."

Roy put his warm fingertips on my forehead, and then darkness came.

––––––

My eyes opened slowly only Christ knew how many hours or days later. I was so feverish and sweaty that it felt like someone had poured a bucket of hot water on me. I could move my body, but just barely. I felt heavy all over, as if my bones had gained eighty pounds and swelled to the size of tree trunks. My vision was blurry, but after blinking a couple of times it cleared enough to allow me to see that I was in a big plush bed. It had sturdy looking gold bedposts and thick comforters.

I was surrounded by brick walls, giving the room the feel of a dungeon. No windows or slits allowed natural light in. There was a wooden door to my right leading to parts unknown. Another door, this one round and concrete, called attention to itself in the middle of the wall across from me. I'd never seen round doors before, other than in bank vaults, and this one looked similar. The room was warmly lit with candles and oil lamps, some on stands and some mounted on the walls, giving the place a friendly yellow glow. It was cozy, despite the brick walls and emptiness.

I tried to sit up to investigate, only to fail and fall back down, dizzy. I felt something tug at my arm. Glancing down, I noticed an IV sticking into my flesh. Adrenaline soared through me as my fighting instinct kicked in, invigorating me, giving me enough energy to pump strength into my weak limbs. Were they drugging me? I was woozy enough for it to be true. I ripped the IV needle out, tossing the tube aside, and put pressure on the small wound as I attempted to remember what had happened and how I'd gotten there.

"Bailey."

I snapped my head to my left. Standing next to the bed was the businessman, though no one had been there a moment ago. Wait. His eyes! In a tidal wave of panic, I remembered his irises changing color. So had the other guy's. And so had Shia's!

I scrambled off the opposite side of the bed, putting as much distance between me and him as I could manage. With adrenaline-fueled strength, I grabbed a tall candle stand next to the bed and held it out, keeping my back up against the wall. "What…the fuck are you?"

"It's okay, Bailey," he said calmly, holding a hand up. "No one here is going to hurt you."

My strength was seeping out of me fast, as if I were standing over a drain and some asshole had pulled the plug. My fingers were too weak, and the candle stand threatened to slip from my grip, but for my life, I held as fast as I could.

"My name is Henry Gyllian," he went on. Bringing his other hand out from behind his back, he produced a file that was about three inches thick. "And you're Bailey Kennedy."

"So?" I glanced around the room for a way out. There was nothing but four brick walls and two closed doors. The big round one had to weigh at least 1,000 pounds.

The man opened the file and gazed down at it. "You grew up in foster care?"

"Yeah. So what?" His eyes were the pretty cognac color right now, but I *knew* I'd seen them change.

He closed the file and put his hands behind his back, putting it out of sight. "And your mother died in childbirth, correct?"

I felt my lip twitch in rage at the mention of my mother. "How exactly is that *any* of your goddamn business?"

"Can you show me which tattoo appeared on you when you learned of her death?"

My eyes widened as disbelief slammed into my stomach. I couldn't have heard that right. I had to still be tripping on whatever drug Shia had dosed me with, or whatever was in that IV. "What did you say?"

His face was completely impassive. "Can you tell me which tattoo appeared when you learned of her death?"

How did he know about my tattoos? Without another word, he turned his head to the side and pulled down the white collar of his shirt. I had to blink the blur away a couple time before I understood what he was showing me. He had the exact same tattoos on his neck that had appeared on me when we ran into each other.

The candle stand suddenly became very heavy and slipped from my grip, clattering nosily to the floor. I sunk down beside it, but before my knees could hit the stone, Gyllian was somehow right next to me, catching me. My heart stopped as I looked up into his face. I wasn't above admitting to myself that I was afraid.

But as he looked down at me, I saw a brief softness settle in his eyes, which brought a small measure of comfort. He wasn't going to hurt me. There were a million ways he could have killed me since I'd been passed out, but he hadn't. He was protecting me.

The softness I saw vanished quickly then, as if he hadn't meant for me to see it. One hand slid under my legs, the other went around my back, and he lifted me into his arms and carried me back to the bed. He set me down gently and situated the covers over me before perching himself on the edge of the mattress.

"We all received the exact same tattoo, at the exact same time, in the exact same place on our bodies."

I closed my eyes as a wave of nausea hit me. "What...what do you mean? What is this?"

"You should rest," he said. "You're still not well. The fever should break tonight."

I opened my eyes when I felt him stand, but before I could even see him leave the room, I passed out.

3

When my eyes opened again I was in a much friendlier place, and I was certainly in much better condition. I wasn't burning up and there was no IV in me. As I sat up, I felt almost refreshed, if filthy. I'd been lying in fever sweat for God only knew how long, and I felt gross. I needed a shower.

I found myself in a large, luxurious bedroom that looked like something out of a *Better Homes and Gardens* magazine for the Fortune 500. The walls were a light bluish-gray with white trim, and there was a white carpet. It was tastefully decorated with furniture of the same bluish-gray color. Two picture windows to my left allowed sunshine to pour in through the white sheer curtains. It wasn't a place I was familiar with, but it didn't make me nervous.

Before I even lifted the covers off me, the bedroom door opened. I felt around for my Beretta out of instinct, but when Gyllian came in, I relaxed. If this man wanted to kill me, there would have been no need to rescue me. He wore loose tan khakis and a well-fitting light blue sweater. He had broader shoulders and more shapely and attractive limbs then I first realized; features his suit had hidden well. Those nearly orange eyes were something out of *Ripley's Believe It or Not*. He was an incredibly beautiful man, so beautiful it was almost difficult to look at him, but I made myself do so anyway.

"How are you feeling?" he asked, putting his hands behind his back in military fashion.

I rested heavily against the headboard. "All right, all things considered."

He nodded. "I understand this has been difficult for you, but I promise there are answers and explanations for all of it."

"Really? Even for why the only person I considered a friend tried to rape me?"

"He was a Demon."

I tried not to look at him like he was insane…and failed. "I'm sorry?"

"Your friend was a Demon. Not human."

I just stared at him.

"You don't believe in Demons?"

I started to subtly look around for a quick exit, unsure of how to answer. I didn't want to piss him off by disagreeing with him. He might snap, and I had no weapon to defend myself.

Gyllian exhaled in a sigh of strained patience. "I'm going to take your silence as a 'no' and ask you, why not?"

I flinched, realizing he was annoyed with me. Apparently he wasn't as charming as he looked. I rubbed my forehead with my fingertips, feeling my guard go up, and then swung my legs down from the bed to prepare to leave.

"Look," I said. "Do I believe in evil? Yes. I see it every single day at work." I dared meet his eyes with defiance. "I *know* evil is real. But personified versions of it that have minds of their own? Hell no."

He looked at me straight on. "Why not?"

My eyes narrowed. "Because it's not logical!"

"Any less logical then magically appearing tattoos?"

I stared at him. He had me there. I paused, biting my bottom lip as I took into consideration what he was saying. I wanted to argue, I really did, but I wasn't sure I actually could, not after seeing what Shia had become.

"So…so what? Demons are real? Magic is real?"

Gyllian nodded. "Demons, yes. Magic?" His face twisted a little. "Not quite, but it's the best description for you now."

I glanced down and rubbed my fingertips on my forehead again. I thought about the brown beads of liquid I'd seen seeping out of Shia's lips, the blood-red eyes and gray skin that had appeared instantly. The reality I knew could not explain that. But what did I know about reality anyway? I had tattoos that suddenly, or *magically*, appeared on my skin since birth.

I looked at Gyllian and sighed. "All right," I said with a helpless shrug. "Talk to me."

"This will probably be easier if you were more refreshed. Maybe you'd like to clean up and eat something? You've been bedridden for a week."

My eyes went wide. "A week?"

Gyllian nodded again. "That's why we had the IV in you. You would have dehydrated otherwise."

Looking down at myself, I realized how limp and greasy my hair was and I recalled how grimy I felt. Oh man. After a week in my own fever sweat, I was now standing across from this abnormally beautiful man.

"Uh yeah," I said, eager to get out of his sight. "Actually, that sounds good."

"I'll have lunch made while you shower. The bathroom is behind you. I've put out some clothes that should fit you."

I cleared my throat awkwardly. "Thank you," I said before he disappeared into the hallway.

I stared at the empty doorway for a minute or two. I should hightail it out of there, I knew, but my curiosity was overwhelming. How did he and I have the same tattoos on our neck? How did he even know about my other tattoos?

I'd never gone searching for answers to my mysterious ink. I'd figured no one would have a clue even if I did go looking. So, I'd just kept them a secret, lest I end up strapped to some mad doctor's surgical table. Suddenly Gyllian was offering me answers I hadn't realized I wanted or needed. For only the second time in my life, I wondered, really wondered, what had caused them or where they had come from.

I was six the first time I'd wondered about them—the earliest age at which I remembered one appearing on my skin. I was in a police station with my social worker, Paul, about to press charges against my first foster father. At first, I'd been too afraid and had adamantly told Paul I was going to lie because I didn't want to get in trouble. I knew what punishment would be waiting for me back at the house if I said anything. After hours of Paul gently trying to convince me that I was safe, I agreed to tell the truth. That's when the flash of pain erupted on my left shoulder and my tattoo of a very detailed hand holding a lightning bolt appeared.

Oh, the fit I threw. Paul ended up having to pick me up and carry me out of the police station while I flailed in his arms.

After calming down, I told Paul about the pain I'd felt in my shoulder. He gently rolled up my sleeve to look, and we both stared at the new ink. I asked a lot of questions after that—what was it, what was the matter with me, why was I so wrong? Paul told me very simply, but sincerely, that there was nothing wrong with me. I was just special. I carried those words, those simple kind words, into my adult life. No matter how broken the path I walked was, and it was very broken, he'd made me believe I was special.

Paul convinced me to keep my tattoos a secret, like a superhero keeps her identity secret. And since I liked the idea of being a superhero, I did. Until now, I'd never wondered where they came from again. They were just there, a part of my life. Now the answers seemed to be waiting downstairs.

I blew out a breath and headed into the bathroom. I probably spent more time in there than I needed, but I found it difficult to leave. I'd never showered in such a luxurious bathroom before. The place was huge, with rose-colored marble floors and walls, two sinks that looked like crackled glass bowls set on top of the counter, and a huge clear glass shower where the water came out of the ceiling like a hot downpour. The shampoo and conditioner smelled like they came from a high-end salon, and I didn't even recognize the brand name, something in French.

When I finally stepped out, I dried myself off quickly and got dressed. The clothes Gyllian laid out fit perfectly—a simple pair of jeans, white tank top, and pink button-down shirt that I wore open. I found a blow dryer and combed and fluffed my hair. I looked better and felt more prepared to go face that stunning man downstairs.

On my way out of the bathroom, I stopped in my tracks. The gorgeous thin guy was standing in the bedroom.

"Hi," he said sweetly.

I blinked to try to keep my eyes from growing embarrassingly wide. He wasn't as thin as I'd originally thought. I could see the definition of his abs and chest through the black t-shirt he wore, and his exposed arms looked like they were being strangled by the material. Up and down both his forearms were black ink pictures and different symbols that didn't match any of mine. Only the symbols on the side of his neck were the same. He was very tall, too, like Gyllian. Being so cut and covered in tattoos made him look like a badass, which was a serious turn on. His smile, so boyish and innocent, clashed with the rest of him. He was beautiful, though, in a way that reminded me of Gyllian's odd beauty.

I couldn't explain such attractiveness. It was as if these guys had some sort of inner light that seemed to reach out from inside of them and wrap them up, amplifying their physical beauty to something damn near impossible to process. Both their eyes shared the same odd quality, too, like I was looking into the depths of gemstones. Their surfaces were smooth and clear, but they revealed layers and layers that seemed to go on forever.

"I've been sent to escort you to the living room." He looked at me curiously. "I beg your pardon, but your hair is lovely."

I flinched and then grinned. "Well…thank you."

"I mean," he said quickly, suddenly looking nervous, "that's not to say the rest of you isn't lovely as well. It's just…I mean…because you *are* lovely. All of you is lovely and I…wait. I didn't mean that in an inappropriate way. I just meant…oh crap."

I actually started laughing. It was real laughter, not the fake, polite laughter I'd mastered my whole life. It was genuine, pleased laughter that I could feel in my stomach.

A relieved smile came to his face, and he stepped forward, holding out his hand. "My name is Roy, Roy Sevlov."

I took his hand and smiled. "I'm Bailey, but everyone calls me Bay."

"Bay. Lovely name, too. Reminds me of water. Gentle water."

My grin widened at the strangeness of that statement, and I found myself genuinely pleased. It seemed so…honest.

"Come on," he said, gesturing for me to follow as he headed for the door. "We have a lot to discuss."

My brow cocked up. "Yeah, I'm starting to gather that."

He stopped in the doorway and looked at me sympathetically. "This has been a lot, hasn't it?"

I sighed. "Yeah."

He gave me a small smile. "Well, have no fear. All the answers you seek can be found downstairs." His expression became sad. "Even some answers you'll wish you never went looking for." As if he just realized what he'd said, his eyes went wide and his expression became apologetic. "I'm so sorry. I didn't..." He sighed and deflated a little. "That was probably the last thing you wanted to hear, right?"

Again, his honest charm seemed comforting. I smiled. "It's okay."

"No. It's not," he took a step forward. "I'm so sorry."

I smiled a little more. "Really. It's okay. I figured this wasn't going to be a picnic considering you all had to save me from a...Demon." The word left a bad taste in my mouth. I still wasn't sure how nuts this lot was going to turn out to be, so I had a hard time saying it.

"We're a team," Roy said somberly. "We look out for each other." He sighed through his nose. "We have to now."

I nodded hesitantly, not entirely comfortable with how that sounded.

"Come on," Roy said, and we headed out of the bedroom.

From the hallway I could oversee the large living room downstairs. The house was luxurious! The living room below was bright, wide open, and homey looking. It was mostly white aside from the lovely blue trim and floral pattern of the furniture. Two plush couches faced each other with a glass coffee table between them. A dining area was toward the back with a corner of the kitchen visible to the right before it continued behind a wall.

As I headed down the stairs, I could see Gyllian sitting at a small desk against the wall of the steps, writing something. Booth stood next to the couch that faced the stairs with his arms crossed, and for the first time I saw the woman who belonged to the voice in the car. She got up from the couch Booth was next to and came toward me with a smile as I rounded the banister. Like the men, she was abnormally beautiful.

She looked to be from India, with smooth, flawless, dark olive skin, and stunning dark blue eyes. They shone like the guys', with layers of depth I could drown in. Her straight black hair fell to the middle of her back, and her body belonged on the cover of *Maxim*. When she held her hand out to me, I couldn't help noticing she had a pretty henna patterned tattoo covering the back of her left hand, ending at a point beneath the knuckle of her ring finger.

"Hello, Bailey," she said. I took her hand and shook it. "My name is Trish D'Alia, but everyone calls me Fox."

I nodded. "Bailey Kennedy, but everyone calls me Bay."

She nodded and released my hand. "Bay. Wow. It's truly, *truly* a pleasure to meet you." I thought I saw tears spring up into her eyes, but I wasn't completely sure until she started dabbing at them. "I'm sorry," she said, keeping her smile bright. "I'm just really happy you're here."

I nodded awkwardly, baffled by this stranger's joy at seeing me.

"Bailey," Gyllian said from behind me.

"Bay, please," I said, turning as he rose from the writing desk.

"Bay." He held his hand out, gesturing to the couches.

I nodded and went to the couch Booth was standing next to and sat down. "Booth, is it?" I asked, looking at him.

He dipped his head in a nod. "Marcus Mensah, but everyone calls me Booth."

I nodded as Gyllian and Fox sat on the couch across from me while Roy went to the kitchen.

"How are you holding up?" Gyllian asked, bringing my attention to him.

"I'm okay."

"Good. We're going to try to ease you into this as best we can, but a lot of what you're about to learn will be…difficult, to say the least."

I nodded as Roy came back holding a white platter nearly overflowing with mini-sandwiches. He placed it on the coffee table between the two couches. "Lunch is served." He returned to the kitchen and brought back five tall cups and a pitcher of water.

"Thanks, Roy," Gyllian said, and everyone reached for a sandwich.

It was awkwardly quiet for a moment as we all ate. I wasn't sure where to begin. Was I supposed to start asking questions, or were they just going to start talking? I didn't know anything about them except that they had rescued me from some…thing and they knew about my tattoos. After three sandwiches and a long gulp of water that practically emptied my second glass, I dabbed my mouth with a napkin and looked around the room.

"So, do I just start with some questions?"

Gyllian nodded. "That's fine."

I swallowed heavily as Roy took a sentry position beside the couch across from me with his arms crossed. I felt more nervous than I liked. I wasn't sure which would be worse— if these people were certifiable or if they actually weren't.

"You said Shia wasn't human."

"I did," he replied, resting his clasped hands against his chin.

Oy. This was going to be tougher than I thought. "Was he ever human?"

"We don't think so. There are rare cases where Demons possess humans, but certain circumstances have to be met. Demons can't just possess anyone. They must be summoned and then the one summoning the Demon volunteers as its vessel, its host. Most Demons, however, just disguise themselves as humans, as you witnessed."

"Whoa, whoa!" I said, holding up my hand as I replayed what he'd just said. I was having a hard time thinking Demons were even real, and now he was going on about Demons possessing humans.

"I'm sorry," Gyllian said. "I didn't realize that would be too much."

I sighed and bowed my head. I was going to have to pay close attention. Demons could possess humans, but it was rare. Okay.

I looked up again. "So, Shia was a Demon the entire time I knew him?"

"How long did you know him?"

"Since I started at the Bureau. Eight years."

"Eight years?" Fox gasped and looked at Gyllian, who ran the side of his finger across his bottom lip. Both Roy and Booth also shifted a little uncomfortably. Shit. I didn't like those reactions.

My heart started racing. "What? What is it?"

Fox sighed and shook her head. "Given how Demons

34

work, eight years of one being topside is very damning news."

"How do Demons work?"

"Demons can't just come to Earth willy-nilly," she said, gesturing with her hands. "It takes human souls, and a lot of them, to sustain a Demon up here for a length of time."

"Human souls?"

Fox nodded. "It takes about three human souls to sustain a Demon on Earth for a single day. That's 1,095 damned human souls in order to keep a Demon topside for a full year. It's not an exact science, but that's the gist of it. So, to keep your Demon topside for eight years"—Fox clutched her chest— "that's 8,760 damned human souls." She looked over at Gyllian. "That's a lot."

He stood from the couch, shoving his hands in his pockets, and went to stand behind it. "Yeah."

I resisted the urge to massage my temples. "Okay, why would 8,760 people damn their souls to sustain a single Demon?"

"Humans are oblivious," Gyllian said, shaking his head as he leaned over the back of the couch on his elbows. "This day in age, Hell is a myth to them, a scary story."

"Hell?" I interrupted. Now I needed to believe Hell was real?

"If humans really believed in Hell"—he met my eyes seriously— "if they knew what it was, what happens down there, they'd go mad with fear. Literally, stark raving mad." Gyllian straightened and gripped the back of the couch. "Without a fear of Hell, it's very easy for Demons to get human souls because humans don't think there are any consequences for their actions, least of all eternal ones."

Small question. Small question. I needed a small question.

"I heard you in the car. You called Shia a level five, a Queen. What does that mean?"

Gyllian's and my eyes locked for a moment, and I caught a glimpse into the layers. He seemed calm and controlled on the outside, but in that small moment I saw something different, something he was doing well to hide. In the back layers of his gemstone eyes, he was nervous, maybe even afraid.

"It means," Gyllian said, "your friend was a very powerful Demon. Only one class of Demon is more powerful than Queens, the Kings."

I blinked. "Chess?"

Gyllian nodded. "Demons have six distinct and different appearances and power levels. We've named their levels after chess pieces. Pawns are level ones, the lowest level Demons."

Fox pulled a stack of papers off the end table beside her and placed one on the coffee table between us. It was a color drawing of a terrifying, white-skinned humanoid creature with completely black eyes that bulged so far from their sockets that they nearly popped out. It had faded gray cracked lips and black goo drooling from the corners of its mouth.

I clutched a fistful of my shirt as I looked at the picture. "That's a Pawn?"

"These are Rooks," Fox said and laid down a picture of a creature with grayish purple skin stretched too thin over a humanoid skeleton, one side of its face completely caved in. Parts of its body were red where it looked like it had been burned deeply in a fire. In what was left of its face, a red glowing pupil was set in a bulging white eye.

I swallowed heavily.

"Bishops," Fox said. The next drawing was of a pale-skinned creature with an elongated head. It had burned holes in its face for eyes, no nose, and a mouth wide open that was far too big for its face. It looked like it could swallow a human body whole. The pointed black rotted teeth each had to be three inches long and a half an inch thick.

I clutched my shirt harder, trying to hide the panic the drawings were inducing.

"Knights." The next was another humanoid thing with skin as black as an expensive leather jacket, cloudy blue eyes, and long pointed ears and fangs. The entire surface of its skin had long, spidery bulges on it, as if its network of veins were swelling through the surface, about to burst open. It also had black leathery wings on its back, like fictional dragon wings.

I rubbed my hand over my forehead trying to comprehend that these things were real. How did these people even know this? Did they have a Diane Sawyer moment with Satan or something to get intel on his minions?

Fox's dark blue eyes came up to my face with compassion. "Queens," she said and put down a picture of what Shia had become. I closed my eyes and turned away. It was the most human looking Demon, with gray skin, blood red eyes, and brown venom dripping down its chin.

"And Kings." The last picture was of another humanoid looking Demon. Its eye sockets glowed with a fiery orange and yellow light. Its entire vein system glowed with the same fiery light throughout its skin, as if fire ran through its system like blood ran through a human's. It had dark brown markings, symbols of some sort, on its neck and shoulders. Its small teeth were thin and sharp, like a mouth full of needles.

"These are just the militant figures," Fox said. "Never mind the other mindless, primitive, deformed"—she shuddered— "*things* they also have down there."

I reached out and flipped over the pictures so that I didn't have to see them. As I did, I realized my hands were trembling. It wasn't just the way the creatures looked, as terrifying as that was. It was the whole unsettling feeling they stirred in me. Demons were something nightmares couldn't even get right because nightmares were still based in the human realm of consciousness and perception. These things were something outside of that realm entirely. The fear these Demons provoked was something beyond a human's means to handle. It was a deep, raw and almost tangible fear, like a living thing that could grow and devour the human heart and soul, eating life and hope.

I tried to calm down by rubbing the back of my neck, maybe massage the terror out, but those pictures were burned into my memory now. I needed to move. I stood and walked to the tall windows behind the couch, putting my back to the room in an effort to alleviate my rising anxiety. The others remained quiet. I knew I was refusing to let this fully sink in. I didn't want Demons to be real—evil personified, in living, breathing, intelligent form, with will of their own and the ability to act on that will. But I knew, deep down, that they were telling me the truth. I'd seen it! I *saw* what Shia had become. I pressed my fingertips into my forehead. My core was shivering.

"Hey," I heard gently beside me. I saw Roy gazing at me

sympathetically. "Do you need to take a break?" he asked. "It's a lot, I know."

I wasn't sure. I wanted to walk away and pretend none of this had ever happened, but it was too late for that now. I already had one of these things come after me. Eight years. A Demon had befriended me for *eight years!* Why?

At that thought, I turned to face Gyllian. "Why?"

He glanced around at the others. "You're going to have to be a little more specific than that."

I stared at the three symbols on their necks, identical to mine. Suddenly my fear was replaced by anger. "Why are you here? Why am I here? Why, or how, do you even know *anything* about Demons?"

Gyllian came around the back of the couch and took a few steps toward me. "Are you sure you're ready for this?"

"No, but I think it's too late to escape it now, isn't it?"

Gyllian nodded. "Yes."

"So, come on then. Make this make sense to me."

Gyllian took a breath, never breaking eye contact, and put his hands into his pockets. "The main purpose of a Queen-level Demon is to spread Demon seed."

"Demon seed?" I asked. I really didn't like the sound of that.

"Queens come topside to breed with humans." My eyes went wide. "Which is what your friend was going to do to you."

I blanched. "What for?"

"To breed Drakes. Those are what we call half-Demon, half-humans. Drakes are difficult to deal with, more than Demons in some ways, because they don't need human souls to stay on Earth; they have their own. They can stay topside as long as they like and wreak havoc during their entire lifetimes."

"Why do Demons need to breed Drakes?"

Gyllian pressed his lips together again, seeming to brace himself for his next words. "Because Hell needs to swell its ranks."

My eyes slowly closed. I couldn't hide my shaking, so I pressed my hand into my neck tattoo as a weird measure of comfort and crossed my other arm over my chest. "Why does

Hell need to swell its ranks?"

"It makes it easier for Hell to destroy everything in its path when it rises."

I sighed and bowed my head. I had a feeling he'd say that. "So the world is ending?" I asked.

"Not quite," Gyllian said, surprising me, and I looked back up at him. "Do you know anything at all about Lights of the Fall or Lights of the Fallen?"

My eyes went wide, and the world shifted out of focus for a moment. Nothing was real. When things snapped back, I was nearly in a flurry of rage or mad with panic, I wasn't sure which.

"Those were the first and last words my mother ever said to me." I stared at him allowing myself to get angry. Hearing him say those words, for a moment it was like he'd taken something precious away from me. Those words had been something my mother, *my mother*, had said to me. "How do you know them?"

Gyllian pressed his lips together sympathetically. "Lights of the Fallen is what our neck tattoos say."

I shook my head. "I studied ancient languages in college and I couldn't find anything resembling these symbols."

"It's Sumoch," he said. "No human knows about Sumoch."

My eyes narrowed. "Then how do you know about it?"

"Well," he sighed, "the first logical guess would be that we're not human."

I blinked as that sentence hung in the air. All of them were looking at me, gauging my reaction. I wasn't sure what they were expecting. I could only manage a small shake of my head. "What?" As much as I wanted to deny it, the fact remained that I had magically appearing tattoos and weird abilities no other human being had. "So what the hell are we?"

"We're Angels," Gyllian said. I flinched. "Well, half-Angels. Heaven calls us Nephilims or Nymphs, which is Sumoch for Lights of the Fallen."

I stared at him blankly.

"Sumoch," he went on when the silence dragged, "is the language the Angels speak."

Logic. I needed to argue something a little logical at the

moment. "Enochian is the language Angels supposedly speak. It was barely covered in a single chapter in one of my college texts and written off as a myth or the concoction of a madman."

Fox shook her head and stood from the couch. "Enochian is real, but Sumoch predates it. It is the truly pure language of the Angels because it was never given to humans like Enochian was."

Trying to come to terms with this wasn't going well. My brain wanted to explode or sleep, and I actually thought I might faint or something. "Angels?" I said and Fox nodded. "Soldiers of Heaven, Biblical, feathery winged Angels?" I shook my head. "You've got to be kidding me."

Booth, who had been silent since I came down the stairs, narrowed his eyes at me. "You didn't put up much resistance believing in Demons," he said. "Why do you balk at Angels?"

I met Booth's pale green eyes. They held an inner fire that I knew I probably shouldn't want to mess with, but I couldn't resist. "Because evil is easy to believe in. It's everywhere. You can't miss it. But Angels?" I shook my head again. "If Angels are real, why is there so much wrong with the world? Why don't they do anything about it?"

"They *did* do something about it," Gyllian said. I waited patiently, expecting this to be a crock since evil was very much alive and well in the world, and no one was doing shit about it, certainly not Angels. "They conspired with the Demons of Hell to cleanse the Earth of it."

My eyes went wide and I looked around at them all. "Why would Angels, who are supposedly considered good, want to join forces with evil? And why would evil want to cleanse the world of itself?"

"Because the Angels blame humanity for the evil in the world," Gyllian replied. "And Demons love nothing more than to kill and torture humans. It's the very reason they exist."

I rubbed my neck tattoo again. "So, you're telling me that Angels want to use Demons to wipe out humanity? And Demons are agreeing to this because they get to destroy humanity?"

Gyllian sighed softly. "Yes."

I blinked again and pressed my palm into my neck tattoo so hard that my hand grew hot. I glanced at all of them again, looking for any sign of betrayal or doubt. Part of me was still waiting for one of them to yell, "Gotcha!" and start laughing at how gullible I was, but their faces stayed stoic and somber, and I knew this wasn't a joke.

"A few years ago," Gyllian started to explain, "the majority of Angels decided humanity had run its course. They'd become too corrupt, too violent, and too evil. So they agreed Hell should be released into the world to cleanse them, like in the days of Noah and the flood. Only instead of flood water, you get Demons and Hell fire."

The end of the world. Never thought I'd live to see the day. "Okay," I said. "Do we have a date? How long do we have? I have a few things on my bucket list I need to…"

"Bay," Gyllian said with deliberate patience. "It's not over yet."

My brows dropped. "You're kidding, right? Angels *and* Demons are working together to annihilate us. I'm pretty sure that means game over!"

"No, it doesn't," he replied. "There's us."

Now I was beginning to think he *was* daft. "I'm sorry, us?" I asked confused. "What exactly is 'us' supposed to do about it?"

"You heard me tell you that we were not human, right?" Gyllian said.

"Yeah," I said carefully.

"Well, we're the ones who are supposed to stop it."

That was it. My eyes started shifting everywhere, looking for the front door. It was time to go. If the world really was ending, I had shit to do.

"I know you're dying to bolt," Roy said, stepping forward with his hands up, "but you haven't heard everything yet."

"Oh, I think I've heard enough. I'm not human, and the world is ending. What else could you possibly have to tell me?"

"Perhaps a bit about our efforts to stop Hell from rising," he said.

I shook my head. They were insane. They actually

thought we could stop a Demon apocalypse? "Look, I've already had one of these things come after me, and there was nothing I could do to stop him so—"

"Then stay with us," Roy said.

This conversation was starting to piss me off. "And what the fuck are you going to do about the end of the world?"

"You saw what our bullets did to the Demon that attacked you," Gyllian piped in.

"Yeah, but you didn't kill it," I said, putting my attention back on him. "Shia was looking out my bedroom window as we drove away."

"The ammunition we have can't kill a Queen," he said a little sharply, and I could tell he was losing his patience with me. "It can only stun one. It kills Knight Demons and below."

"What about Angels?" I asked, and he deflated a little. "So you can't kill Angels either." I shrugged. "Then what good is any ambition to try to stop either?"

"We have more than weapons at our disposal," Gyllian said.

"Like what?"

"Like our abilities as Nephilims."

A cold feeling suddenly snaked its way out of my heart and filled my veins with ice water. I began to shiver as the realization hit me again that I wasn't human. "Abilities?"

"You have to have noticed them throughout your life. There's no way you couldn't have," he insisted.

My mind immediately went to the fact that I only slept once a week. It also went to my occasionally enhanced speed and strength. They were amazing advantages in my job, but I wasn't sure how helpful they would be against Demons and Angels.

"What about them?" I asked, my voice shaking a little.

Gyllian took a step toward me. "Where do you think they came from?"

My heart was racing so fast that I felt my blood pounding in my ears. I couldn't even answer him.

"Not all the Angels conspired to raise Hell," he explained. "Five of them did something different, and they weren't just any five Angels, but the five Archangels; Michael, Raphael, Gabriel, Uriel, and Jophiel."

I was panting. "What did they do?" I asked quietly.

"They sent us.

"What do you mean 'They sent us'?"

Gyllian tilted his head from side to side in consideration. "Perhaps 'created' us is a better word."

"Created us? What do you…?"

Suddenly it dawned on me, and my eyes went wide. Before I could stop myself, my entire body liquefied. Roy caught me around my chest and carefully moved me over to sit on the couch. I stared at the floor, unable to look at any of them. I was numb. I took deep, deliberate breaths to keep from passing out.

Roy crouched in front of me, holding my shoulders. "Are you all right?"

"Our…our…they…"

Gyllian was soon crouching down beside Roy and looking up at me. "My father," he said, "was the Archangel Gabriel."

Roy's compassionate eyes met mine. "Raphael was my father."

"Uriel was my mother," Fox added behind them.

"My mother was Jophiel," Booth said to my right.

"Your father"—Gyllian said, drawing my attention back to him— "was the Archangel Michael."

4

A sudden flash of burning pain ripped into my left side. I cried out and clutched my arm against it. Another tattoo had appeared. Based on the size of the pain, it was going to be a large one.

"What is it? What appeared?" Roy asked, looking at me with alarm.

I slowly lifted my shirt. Beginning from the bottom of my breastbone and stretching down around my left side was the tattoo of an incredibly beautiful and elaborate double-edged sword. The tattoo was so long that the point of the sword went under the waist of my jeans. I stood up, making Roy and Gyllian stand as well, and pulled down one side of my jeans until my entire hip was exposed. The sword tip stopped at the side of my rear end. It was the biggest tattoo I had now, aside from my wings.

"Michael's sword," Fox suddenly whispered with reverence.

My head snapped in her direction. This was not happening. My father wasn't…he wasn't…he was a rapist! I pulled my jeans up then shoved past Roy and Gyllian as I headed toward the front door. I had to get out of there.

"Bay, wait!" Gyllian was in front of me instantly. "The Demons out there would love nothing better than to get their hands on a Light, especially Michael's daughter."

My heart clenched at the reference of being someone's daughter. "Michael is not my father!"

"Yes, he is!" Gyllian yelled, cutting off my kneejerk reaction.

I couldn't be referred to as anyone's daughter. My mother was dead and *any* remark about the man that hurt her hit a barrier in my mind. I didn't want to think about him. I didn't want to know about him. I didn't want to have anything to *do* with him!

"My father, that son of a bitch you seem to revere, raped

my mother," I said in a low trembling voice. "Did you know that?"

Gyllian shook his head. "No, he didn't."

My eyes went wide. I strained to rein in my emotions. I couldn't think about him. My...father. I couldn't. The hatred toward the man who'd given me life was too ingrained in my identity for me to release it.

"Listen, I'm just going to go," I said and passed Gyllian, heading for the front door.

"Isn't it better to know?" Gyllian called from behind.

I paused, staring at the front door. I wanted to leave, but something inside me was begging me to stay. What if it were true? My heart ached to hear them out, to have them explain more, but this was a topic I wasn't sure I could deal with. I slowly turned to face Gyllian. He was looking at me over his shoulder, his orange eyes silently begging me to stay, though he seemed to be trying to hide it.

My throat was dry, and I knew my voice would be hoarse, but I had to ask, "How do you know my father didn't rape my mother?"

"Because I saw it." My brows dropped as he turned and came toward me. He stood so close to me that he had to look down at my face. "You're not the only one with special abilities, Bay."

Tears threatened to brim, but I held them back as best I could. "So, if my father is who you say, and he didn't rape my mother, then where was he when I needed him?" Gyllian didn't flinch. "Where was he while I was being abused by my foster parents? Hmm? Why did he just leave me in the system to rot?" I had buried this shit long ago, and if it didn't stay buried, I would fall completely apart. "Tell me what kind of fucking Angel does that to a child. *His own child*, according to you."

It was so quiet I could hear them breathing. Gyllian looked back at the others. "None of us knew our Angelic parents for long." He looked back at me. "They were killed a long time ago."

I looked at him confused. "How can Angels die?"

"By being human when they are attacked." I stared at him with wide eyes. "Our parents," he continued slowly, "the

Archangels, voluntarily cast themselves out of Heaven and became mortal in order to create us." I stopped breathing. "They were eventually murdered once they were located by either Hell's Demons or the Angels who are instigating the apocalypse."

A thousand thoughts went through my mind, so I clung to one, the possibility that my father hadn't, in fact, hurt and abandoned my mother. "What kind of threat did the Archangels pose if they were mortal?"

"They weren't killed because they were a threat. They were killed for revenge because they fought against the Angels and Demons who are trying to raise Hell."

I swallowed heavily. I didn't like how my mind was wildly circling around Michael, the Archangel. "And they 'fell' to create us?" Gyllian nodded. "Why?"

"So we could stop it."

I shook my head. "You actually think we, the five of us, are supposed to stop the entirety of Hell from coming here?"

"Not only are we supposed to," he said. "It's the only reason we were born."

"But we're mortal, too!" I cried.

Gyllian sighed. "Come with me. I want to show you something." He started away.

After a quick glance at the others, I followed him. My curiosity had gotten the better of me.

He led me across the bottom of the stairs I'd descended before, past a luxurious bathroom on the right, and turned the corner. He pushed open a single door on the back wall to reveal a room that looked like a small garage. It was barely large enough to fit one car, but nothing was inside, and there were no other doors. He reached in as if to click a light switch, and suddenly a gentle motorized sound filled the space. I took a step back when the entire floor slowly started rising on visible hydraulic arms, and stopped at the top of the door, revealing a concrete stairway. We followed it down to a round concrete door. Ten feet in diameter, it was the same kind that I'd seen in the dungeon room where I had first awoken.

Gyllian pulled it open and my eyes went wide. It had to weigh 1,000 pounds! He didn't say a word as he looked back at me then went through. A bright friendly light immediately illuminated the doorway.

I stepped through and found myself in a large hallway that ran to the right. It had flawless light-colored bricks on the bottom half of the walls and smooth gray concrete on the top. Five round heavy concrete doors were across from the entry point, making the place look like a strange apartment hallway. A vertical hall was to the left leading to the back of this…building. The provided lights were simple oil lamps, only they didn't burn orange like flames were supposed to burn, they burned white! The lamps were placed high up along the seams of the walls and ceiling.

This place was amazingly large! Bigger than the house above ground. I could hardly believe it.

"This way," Gyllian said and led me to the left. He absently tapped his knuckle on the first apartment labeled with a '1' as we passed. "This is where you woke up the first time after you arrived," he said and then headed up the vertical hallway.

This hallway was pretty bare but long. Four square doors were halfway down, two on each side. They were open, but it was too dark for me to see inside yet.

"What the hell is this place?" I asked looking around.

"It's our apocalypse bunker."

"Apocalypse bunker?"

"If we fail to stop Hell from rising, this is where we will hole up. It's completely warded against every Demon, from the Pawns to Kings. I have some Angel warding up as well, but I can't put too much up or it would affect us, too, since we're half Angels." I blanched. I still hadn't fully accepted that yet. "Angels are incredibly powerful, but so far they haven't found us here."

"What do you mean it's 'warded'?"

"Spells. Lots of spells, some more ancient then creation, are etched into just about every foot of the cement down here—the walls, the floor, the brick, everywhere. Demons can't come in. The magic of the spells wards them off, hides us. Even if they somehow managed to break through the warding, each individual room is warded as well. Demons will not be able to stay in this general vicinity long enough to try to break into our individual rooms. And even if they somehow managed *that*, we have backup rooms hidden down a secret passage."

"Jesus. Paranoid much?"

Gyllian looked at me. "We don't take chances."

"Clearly."

Gyllian looked ahead of him again. "Upstairs is very loosely warded, enough to keep us hidden, but not necessarily enough to protect us. We knew the Demon we rescued you from was going to try to find you, which is why we took you down here right away. Stronger warding."

I shook my head. "How do you even know this stuff?" I asked. "Things like what kills a Queen, what stuns it, or even what the hell a Queen looks like? Or a Pawn, or a Knight? I doubt they teach 'Demon Rank and Anatomy 101' in high school."

For the first time since running into him, Gyllian smiled at me. The sight of it shocked me. It was warm and his eyes smiled with his mouth. He even had a dimple in his left cheek. He cleared his throat uncomfortably and quickly looked away, the expression of cold indifference returning.

"Did I...did I just see a smile?" I half teased him. He only gave me a stern sidelong look. I faced the hall ahead of me. "I guess not."

We reached the large doors halfway down, and I realized the rooms were enormous! They were each at least half the length of a grocery store and even wide enough to fit six aisles. Each was stocked to the brim with shelves of food and supplies and other living necessities. Gyllian didn't stop at them.

As we continued down the hall I noticed small, evenly spaced vents along the edges of the floor. I bent over, holding my hand over one, and felt the soft cool breeze coming up explaining where the breathable air was coming from.

One lonely closed door was to my left before another horizontal hall stretched to the right with four more doors. They were all rectangular wooden ones, not the ridiculous round concrete ones from the first hallway. We passed the first door which was closed. Through the next door I saw a giant empty wash basin, the kind used to hand wash clothes in the 1700s, and clotheslines strung throughout the expanse of the room. There was even a hand water pump fixture. It looked like the backyard of a colonial pilgrim. Five metal scrubbers rested against the sides of the tub. The room had clearly never been used. It was completely clean—like, newly built clean. Gyllian took me into the third door, a fitness center that contained every free weight and non-electronic exercise equipment known to man.

"No electricity?" I asked, looking around.

Gyllian looked at me like I was an idiot. "What post-apocalyptic world do you think has electricity?"

I had to smile at that.

He shook his head and headed to the middle of the fitness center. "I've established this bunker so it can fully sustain us without electricity. There's a narrow cave system with a natural spring right beneath us for water and plumbing, and air which comes up through the vents in the floor."

I shoved my hands into my pockets. I was feeling a little disturbed at how positive he was about the possibility of this Demon apocalypse.

"How did you afford to build this place?"

"We'll discuss that later, along with how I know what I know about Demons." He gave me a warning look not to bring it up again and I held up my hands in surrender. "Now, the reason I brought you here is this." He indicated the bench press. The bar on the bench was full of weights, at least 1,000 pounds...on each side. In front of the bench was a full-length oval mirror with a golden frame.

"And?"

"Lift it."

I gave him an absurd look. "Excuse me?"

"I want you to lift this."

"Um," I glanced at the bar before meeting his eyes again. "There's 2,000 pounds on thing."

"I'm aware."

"I can't lift that!"

"Yes, you can."

I looked at him stunned. He was serious. I understood we had abilities, great. But abilities like *this?* I shook my head. "You're nuts!"

"When you lift it, I want you to look at yourself in the

mirror."

"You don't seem to be grasping the concept of me *not* being able to lift this."

Without even lying down in the proper position, Gyllian grabbed the bar with one hand and lifted it over his head. My eyes went wide as his irises turned that strange, shiny, silvery-gray color I'd seen in the car.

"What the…"

He stared at me with those eyes for a moment before putting the bar back down and they faded back to amber-brown. "Your turn."

"But…I…I…"

"Lift it."

I started chewing my bottom lip nervously. Gazing at the bar for a moment, I contemplated what it would be like to lift it. Then I looked back at Gyllian. "Will my eyes do that?"

He nodded. "When we use our abilities, our eyes go Angelic. A trait from our parents."

I sighed and looked at the bar again like it was a venomous snake I was no less charmed by. Lifting that bar meant a lot of things. And if my eyes did that…

I brushed my fingertips over my forehead before reaching out and taking hold of the bar. I glanced again at Gyllian, who only nodded. Clenching my teeth, I gripped the bar tightly and suddenly I lifted the 2,000 pounds with one hand. My eyes went wide as I stared at it. I might as well have been lifting a bag of bread! A strange warm sensation went down the middle of my back at the same time. I was about to mention it when I looked into the mirror and saw my usual light blue eyes had turned that shiny silvery gray color. It startled me so much that I dropped the weight bar and it slammed into the cement floor with a deafening clang and crack.

"Damn it!" Gyllian cried as he bent down to pick it up and rested it back in its proper place.

"I'm…I'm sorry," I said, looking at my reflection still, watching my eyes fade back to blue.

He sighed, "It's fine."

"I," I cleared my throat to try and compose myself, "I felt something warm on my back when I lifted it."

"It was one of your tattoos." I looked at him. "When our abilities are in use, aside from our eyes going silver, whatever tattoo brings about the magical effect gets warm."

The tattoo that had gotten warm was the string of Hebrew symbols down my back that, loosely translated, read "Weapon of Mass Destruction." As I thought back to my recent encounter with Banner, I realized the same spot had gotten warm when I was running at top speed after him. The Hebrew symbols had to be responsible for my excelled abilities. It was a good thing I kept them hidden then, if my eyes were changing color when I used them.

Gyllian gazed toward the door with his jaw working in what looked like annoyance or impatience, or both. "You don't like me very much, do you?" I asked.

His eyes snapped to me before he shook his head. "It doesn't matter whether I like you. We have a mission, and we have to trust and respect each other and work as a team, or seven billion human beings are going to die."

I narrowed my eyes. "So, you don't like me, but I'm supposed to trust you with my life?"

He rested his elbow on the weights and leaned toward me. "We can't do it without you, so whether I like you or not, I *will* have your back. That you can believe."

"Why should I?"

"Because you're going to help us save the lives of these humans I most definitely *do* like." He shook his head. "I will do anything to protect them. It won't take you long to learn that about me."

It was safe to say that "reality" stopped here. It failed any explanation for any of this—these abilities, my eyes changing color, magically appearing tattoos, Demons, Angels. If all of that was real, then my father...no. I couldn't think about that yet.

I sighed and tucked some loose strands of hair behind my ears. "So, what now?"

"We go back upstairs and you tell me if you are going to stick around so we can get to work trying to stop the Angels and Demons from releasing Hell on Earth," Gyllian said and started out.

"What's your plan to try and stop it?" I asked, catching

up to him in the hallway.

"I've been at this task for over ten years. The main objective is to find when, where, and how Hell is going to rise."

"You mean you don't know? You know everything else."

"I know what I need to know." He was deliberately avoiding eye contact. I wasn't sure whether to be relieved or insulted.

"Yeah? News flash, I don't know any of it. Or did you miss the confusion and horror I've expressed since we started talking?"

"You were raised in foster care. Your mother should have told you everything Michael needed you to know." At the mention of Michael, my heart thumped hard against my chest like a rubber mallet against my ribs. "Her death was obviously not expected." Gyllian finally looked at me, and I even saw some compassion in his eyes. "I'm sorry for your loss."

"Thanks," I replied, unable to break eye contact from him for a moment, until he looked away.

We headed up the stairs back to the main house. Gyllian's sympathy was as surprising as his smile. I'd only spent a few hours with him, but I could already tell he hid his emotions well, never wanting anyone to see them if he could help it. He let a little slip through here and there, but he was not someone I could see myself warming to.

The others were still gathered in the living room when we appeared. "You all right?" Roy asked.

"Yeah," I replied a little uncomfortably.

"Did you see your eyes change?"

I nodded and rubbed the back of my neck.

"Creepy, right?" Roy said with a playful smile.

I actually laughed again, the same kind of genuine laugh Roy had gotten out of me earlier. "Understatement," I said as I passed him to go back and sit on the couch. I grabbed another mini sandwich off the plate and started eating.

Roy sat down on the edge of the coffee table in front of me. "So how are you doing? Really? With all of this?"

I sighed. "I don't know. I'm okay I guess," I affirmed.

My face scrunched and I shook my head. "Maybe I just always knew there was something wrong with me. I mean, obviously these tattoos were weird, but"—I sighed— "getting confirmation is weird. Though at the same time, it's actually a little comforting…knowing, you know? *Knowing* what it is." I took a bite of my sandwich and swallowed. "These Demons though"—I shook my head— "that's a little hard to deal with."

Roy nodded. "I hate to say this, but it doesn't really get any easier." He gave me a helpless shrug. "You just kind of get used to it. Demons are…" he stopped and looked away a moment, shaking his head before looking back at me. "They still scare me, and I've killed quite a few over the past eight years."

My mouth went dry, making swallowing my sandwich suddenly impossible. I picked up a glass of water and drank some to moisten my throat.

Roy leaned closer. "Can I ask you something?" I nodded and put my water down. "What tattoo did you get when you were born? The one on your back."

I looked at him curiously. "How did you know my first tattoo appeared on my back?"

Roy tilted his head, indicating the others. "All of ours did. I just assumed yours did, too."

I smiled and put my half-eaten sandwich down. I loved my wings. I had no qualms with showing them off to anyone who wanted to see. I stood and pulled my hair over one shoulder as I turned to present my back to him. Taking off the pink flannel shirt, I tossed it on the couch and then lifted my white tank top, exposing my back.

"Whoa," Roy said and stood.

Usually standing in my bra with a wide-eyed guy near me meant the next step was the bedroom, but Roy wasn't looking at my undies. He was checking out my ink. Fox and Booth even moved closer to see. Apparently it was impressive. Gyllian took a few steps toward me, too. None of them were shy about wanting to see my tattoos, examining them with scrutiny. I ended up unclipping my bra to clear their view.

"Wings," Roy said as he boldly began to trace his finger

over the lines. "Are you kidding me? *Wings?*"

I wasn't sure how I felt about that reaction. What was wrong with my wings? I felt Roy's hand caressing my right wing and Fox's fingertips dragging lightly down the middle of my back.

"Look at the Hebrew writing," Fox said. "Bay, when did this writing appear between your wings? What happened?"

"It was during my fitness evaluation for the FBI. I had just learned about my abilities—weird speed, strength, agility, endurance. It warmed up, too, when Gyllian had me lift the weights downstairs."

"Gyllian, do you know what that says?" Fox asked.

"It says Weapon of Mass Destruction," I piped in. I looked at Fox over my shoulder with a smile. "I told you I studied languages in college." She returned my smile.

"How can you pay attention to that boring writing?" Roy exclaimed. "Don't you see the two massive wings on her back?"

"What's wrong with my wings?" I finally asked.

"Not a thing," he said, his beautiful, smiling face appearing next to me. "You can just fly, baby."

"What?" I barked.

Without a word, only an impish grin, Roy took a step back and pulled off his shirt.

Gyllian went to him quickly and rested his hand on his shoulder. "It might be too soon for that."

Roy grinned and shook his head. "It's too late, man. I just told her she can fly. She's gotta see sooner or later."

I clipped my bra closed and pulled the tank top down before turning toward the two of them. "What are you talking about?"

Gyllian sighed and gave a reluctant nod before taking his hand off Roy's shoulder and walking behind the couch. Roy, turned putting his back to me. His tattoo was of two downward crossed Katana blades surrounded by fire, which took up most of the space on his back. He reached his arms up, and my eyes went wide when his hands seemed to disappear into his skin at the hilts of the swords. Before I could cry out, he slowly pulled his hands "out," and I watched the two swords materialized in them, complete with the flames around the blades! The tattoo remained on his back even as the flaming swords became real.

"Holy fucking shit!" I cried. What in the name of Christ had I stumbled into with this lot?

Roy turned to face me with boyish glee, holding his burning swords up. "Holy fire. This fire kills any Demon or Angel dead as soon as it touches them."

I was gaping. "Do all our tattoos do that?"

"No," Fox replied beside me. "Some abilities, like our enhanced physical abilities, don't need to materialize, but every tattoo holds some ability."

I looked around at them all. "Let me see yours."

Fox grinned and glanced at Gyllian, who rolled his eyes. Without waiting for a response, Fox began to unbutton her shirt. Booth also started to pull his own shirt off.

Gyllian rubbed a hand over his face. "All right, we'll just share our main abilities right now. It's almost 1:00 pm and we've got to get to sleep."

I looked at him curiously. "What for?"

"We have to work tonight," he said as he pulled off his blue sweater.

"Work?" I asked. "As in jobs?"

Gyllian draped the garment over the arm of the couch. "It has to do with the plan to stop Hell that I mentioned downstairs."

He turned around and pulled his white t-shirt off, and my eyes went wide. His tattoo was a large and very elaborate black hourglass set in an intricately decorated cradle. The bottom bulb was broken though, with black sand spilling out of it.

"Time manipulation," Fox said, standing in a silky gray tank top. She smiled.

I took a few steps toward Gyllian, unable to look away from his back. Staring at it, something unexpected started to stand out that made my eyes go wide. Long light pink scars crisscrossed over the entire surface of his skin, from his neck to down under the waistband of his khakis. The scars vanished under his tattoos like mine did, but this amount of scarring was the worst thing I'd ever seen. Almost in a trance, I brought my hand up and touched a few of the long lashes, wondering what could have caused such extensive damage to him.

Gyllian went stiff immediately. He quickly spun around, grabbing both my wrists, and yanked me against him so fast I didn't even have time to cry out. "Don't," he said through clenched teeth. "I'm showing you my tattoo. That's it."

I stared at him in horror and agony, unable to imagine what could have caused him that amount of pain. Before I realized it, my hand was coming up to his face and rested on his cheek. "What happened to you?"

His eyes went a little wide, and he stared at me silently. After a moment, he gave me a small shove away. "Go to sleep. All of you," he barked before heading toward a door off the main living room. He opened it, momentarily revealing a large bedroom, before slamming it closed behind him.

Roy came up to me as I looked after Gyllian. "None of us know where he got those scars," he said softly.

I glared at the bedroom door. Did he really hate me so much that he would be offended I expressed concern for him? I hadn't done anything to warrant that kind of animosity from him!

I started toward the door to confront him, but Roy jumped in front of me. "Don't! Don't," he said, holding up his hands. "Gyllian is not someone you want to fuck with. Trust me."

I narrowed my eyes. "Look, maybe you got the impression that I'm some sort of delicate damsel with my reaction to all this Demons-and-magic-are-real shit, but trust me when I tell you that *I'm* not someone you want to fuck with."

I pushed past him and grabbed the doorknob but found it locked. I was not in the mood for this shit. I stepped back and kicked the door open classic FBI style. It exploded inward and Gyllian spun around, still shirtless, aiming a Glock at me.

"You listen to me, you arrogant dick!" I walked up to him until the barrel of the gun was pressed firmly between my breasts. "I don't give a fuck who your daddy is or who you think you are. You don't get to talk to me like that! Fuck you and your precious humanity. The Demons can have them!" I turned and left the bedroom, heading for the front door.

"Bay, wait!" Roy cried, grabbing my shoulder.

"Get off!" I yelled and shoved him away from me.

I snatched the pink flannel shirt off the couch and put it on as I continued out. My purse was hanging on a hook next to the front door, and I grabbed it before throwing open the door and slamming it shut.

Even though the sun was bright, I shivered a little without a jacket. It was a typical cool, windy Chicago summer day. I needed a coat but I wasn't about to go back and ask them for one. I gazed around, trying to get my bearings. It looked like I was in the suburb of Beverly. The next street sign I came to said South Winchester Avenue. Yes, Beverly. There were no cabs to be had in this area, not without a phone call, but a main road was about three blocks away.

I had to think anyway.

I'd seen the worst of humanity since I was born. Every good virtue, kindness, honor, nobility, were long-forgotten myths as far as I was concerned. Maybe Demons were real. Maybe Heaven and Hell wanted to wipe out humanity. Whether it was true or not, it seemed like we had it coming. I certainly wasn't going to argue otherwise. In fact, as far as I was concerned, it seemed a little overdue.

5

Once I reached the main road, I hailed a cab and had him take me back to my apartment. My mind raced the entire ride home. The cabbie probably thought I was nuts given how often I shook my head and sighed, trying to process what I had learned.

My mind seemed to hit a wall whenever I tried to think about the Archangel Michael. It was like my brain, on a whim of its own, refused to process anything having to do with him. Every time I tried to focus on that, my mind instantly switched to some other part of the conversation, or to what Shia had done, or to a case I'd left open before leaving the Bureau. My mind went anywhere else it could go.

The cabbie pulled up to my apartment building and I stepped out. As the car pulled off, I found myself staring up at the window from which Shia had been hanging out, the front of his shirt covered with blood, his eyes the same ugly red color as they watched the car speed off. Eventually I had to force my eyes down to the curb in an attempt to not think about it. Shia was not going to take my life away from me. I'd had people in my childhood take more than Shia had. He wouldn't win because I hadn't let the others win. With resolve, I walked into my building with my head held high— though I definitely wished I had my gun.

I walked into the lobby and paused as a weird sense of vertigo came over me. I felt almost offended by how unchanged the place looked. It was the same red walls and worn brown carpet with the frayed tear at the foot of the steps to the left. Same rows of neon lights were above, with the corpses of insects from last fall still making them look spotted. I glared around the lobby. How dare it look exactly the same, as if my whole world hadn't just been turned inside out by Demons and Angels and magic!

I shook my head and went to the stairs. Normally I wouldn't have to explain my week-long disappearance since

I had no job, no friends, and no family, but uniforms would likely be investigating the gunshots. That would lead them to my busted front door and empty apartment. Just in case, I came up with a vacation excuse. I'd tell them I wasn't even here when it occurred.

I was still working on how I was going to explain things when my door came into view. I expected to see a chaotic mess of crime scene tape and evidence markers, but there was nothing, and my door was completely intact. I blinked as I slowly stepped up onto the top step. I knew for a fact Gyllian and his crew had kicked it in. I stood outside a moment before I tentatively reached for the knob and turned it, wishing again I had my gun with me.

I pushed the door open with my fingertips. It swung wide and hit the wall behind, so I knew no one was hiding there. I squinted suspiciously at my apartment. It was immaculate. Everything was clean and organized and put away. My curtains were even open and the windows had been washed, allowing the bright early afternoon sunlight to pour in. I quickly and quietly went to my dresser and was surprised to find my Beretta in the top drawer where I always kept it. After making sure it was loaded, I went through the rest of my room, clearing every corner to assure myself I was alone.

When it turned out to be empty, I looked around, confused. My place should have been a wreck since that's how I'd left it. The smell of rotted Chinese food Shia brought should be stinking up the joint. My door should be in splinters on the floor. Instead, I'd found everything in perfect condition. My bed was even made, and I *never* bothered with that, not even on cleaning days. All my clothes were folded in my dresser and hung neatly in my closet. I wondered for a moment if my landlady had done all this. Maybe she was planning on renting it out, fully furnished.

"I'm sorry," a voice suddenly said.

I spun around with my gun out, but fear slammed into my chest when I saw Shia standing there. He looked normal. He looked like my friend again, which made me hesitate on the trigger. As we stared at each other, he slowly brought his hands up in surrender.

My heart was pounding in my ears and my mind was

racing. He was a fucking Demon! But was he? Why couldn't I pull the trigger?

Shia gazed at me with compassion, which shocked me further. He could be standing in the lab right now, like all those times I'd seen him through the glass walls of the tank, only without his scrubs. He had on a black V-neck sweater and tan khakis. Normal. His black hair was stylishly disheveled, and his eyes were crystal clear blue. Normal. My hand aiming the gun started to tremble. Despite everything, he had been my friend.

"I think we both know that won't hurt me, Bay," he said gently.

My teeth clenched and unclenched as I tried to tell myself to pull the trigger. But I *knew* him!

"You're a Demon?" I asked, at a loss.

Shia nodded and continued looking at me sympathetically. "Yeah, I am."

I cocked my gun. I couldn't get my head on straight. This guy was supposed to be a Demon. He'd almost raped me! He'd poisoned me! But I knew him. I'd known him for eight years. We'd sometimes meet for coffee or lunch if I wasn't in the field.

"If I wanted you dead, Bay," he said, "don't you think you would be by now?" He nodded toward my gun. "I know those bullets won't hurt me. But I haven't moved yet, have I?"

The way he was looking at me froze me where I stood. I honestly wasn't sure I'd be able to do it. What would be the point anyway, though? My bullets were harmless.

"Come on, Bay," he said with a small playful smile. "I cleaned your apartment and everything. I even wiped your neighbors' memories so there wouldn't be an investigation."

I swallowed heavily. I shouldn't trust him. I knew I shouldn't. "What do you want?" I asked without lowering my gun.

"I wanted to apologize and hoped you would talk to me."

"About what? You almost raping me?"

He sighed softly. "If it makes you feel any better, my boss gave me a whipping that lasted a week straight. A week in Hell is like a year here." His eyes narrowed slightly. "Do you know what it feels like to be mutilated for an entire year? I paid for it, and I barely touched you."

"Your boss?"

"Will you please put that down?"

I debated it. He could have me again easily if he really wanted to, but he remained unthreatening. I found myself curious as to what a Demon could possibly have to say to me anyway, so I slowly lowered my gun. I also couldn't deny a part of me missed him.

Shia smiled and put his hands in his pockets. "I don't suppose you'd let me buy you a coffee?"

I swallowed down the screams that wanted to rise in my throat. "As long as it's expensive."

Shia grinned widely. "Starbucks it is then."

I resisted the urge to smile and watched carefully as Shia headed for the door. I fell into step behind him as we left my apartment. The closest Starbucks was only two blocks away. As we started in that direction, I thought it was going to stay quiet, but it didn't.

"I miss you," Shia suddenly said with genuine sincerity, making me look at him. He was staring down at the sidewalk. "Work's not the same without you."

I looked at him absurdly. "You're still with the Bureau?"

He smiled. "What can I say? I grew fond of it."

I stared at him. "That's…weird, Shia."

He chuckled, "Yeah. I know." Then we fell silent the rest of the way to the café.

The Starbucks was packed with at least thirty people sitting at the tables and booths. There was a low rumble of conversation that joined the hiss of the milk steamers and the grinding of the ice blender. We ordered our usual coffees and found the only empty booth in the back right corner.

"Do Demons actually drink coffee?" I asked as we sat down.

"No," he replied and took a sip. "But I figured this would put you more at ease."

I looked at him over the top of my cup. "And why would you care if I'm at ease?"

"Okay. You caught me. I don't." His eyes narrowed, and suddenly it got very dangerous in that booth. "But I was latched to a pole for a fucking year when I'd barely touched you, and I want to know why."

I reigned in the panic that was now stirring in my chest like a whirlwind. But then Shia looked at me with more intrigue than danger, and that eased my nerves a little.

"How up to speed are you?"

"On?"

He rolled his eyes. "Everything you didn't know existed before the night you left."

I set my cup down deliberately on the table. "Oh, that."

"What have your Nephilim pals told you?"

My eyes narrowed on him. "You know what I am?"

"Of course I do," he said plainly. "I've always known." I opened my mouth to say something, but a distinct tightness around my throat cut off my words, and Shia was glaring at me again. "Look, this will be a lot easier on you if you just tell me how much you know. What have the others told you?"

The tightness left and I glared at him, trying to hide the terror pounding in my head. Shit. I'd made a mistake. "Not much, considering your venom had me sick out of my mind all week."

His gaze narrowed suspiciously. I ran my fingers through my hair, scratching my head a little, as a distraction to myself more than anything. *He hasn't hurt me yet. He hasn't hurt me yet,* was the mantra I chanted in my mind to keep myself calm. Thinking fast, I thought about trying to turn the tables on him and get some information that could help the others. It was worth a try if I made it out of here.

"You said your boss was upset with you," I finally managed, meeting his eyes.

"Yeah. To say the least."

"Why?"

Shia sat back crossing his arms and shook his head. "I don't know. That's why I wanted to see you. Granted, my actions were impulsive, but it wasn't anything unusual enough to earn me the year I got on the post."

I narrowed my eyes a little. "You know what I am. Your boss knows what I am. Why would you get in trouble for doing something evil to me? Demons are evil, right?"

"No worse than humans," he scoffed.

I brought my cup to my lips again. "That I can agree with."

Shia's jaw dropped, and he looked at me with wide eyes. "Holy shit," he said before a menacing grin came to his face.

My brows dropped. "What?"

"You hate humans," he said, as if he couldn't believe it. "You hate them as much as the Demons and Angels do!"

"So?" I shrugged and took a sip of my coffee, more out of discomfort than from actually needing one.

Shia barked a short laugh, and a primitive light of excitement came to his eyes. "You couldn't care less if we wipe out the Earth, could you? That's why you're not with the other Nephilims right now. You want nothing to do with Gabriel's Son's crusade."

Something was wrong. Deeply wrong.

"No wonder my boss got pissed that I almost raped you. You're an ally, a really powerful one!" He was still chuckling. "Wait until the Angels find out a fucking Nephilim has no bleeding heart for the humans!" He threw his head back and laughed.

I blinked.

Suddenly I was on my feet leaning over the table, and the entire café was full of running and screaming people. I looked around, confused, for a second until I looked down and saw Shia choking on a sword tip stuck in his throat. Blood bubbled up around the blade, dribbling down the front of his sweater and his eyes were wide. I followed the sword up to its hilt and I was surprised to find it in my hand.

No. I shouldn't be surprised. I'd done this. I'd reached into the sword tattoo that appeared at Gyllian's house and stabbed Shia. But…it was like it happened too fast for me to know it was happening. But I remembered.

I looked back at Shia and leaned down so our noses nearly touched. "I may have no love for humans," I told him in a low voice, "but I *definitely* have no love for Demons." I thrust the sword deeper until the tip was stopped by the back of the booth and Shia's entire body went limp. He wasn't coming back to life from this one. I oddly knew that much.

I pulled out the blade and gazed at it. The entire thing, from tip to hilt, was made of glass so clear I could see the floor through it. The hilt was round with a teardrop-shaped bulb at the pommel and two matching teardrop bulbs on each end of the cross-guard. Two thin pieces of glass twisted up the grip and cupped the bulb on the end like a pair of loving hands. Its beauty was unparalleled to anything I'd ever seen.

Suddenly the sirens and the screeching of cop cars snapped me back to reality. My eyes went wide as I realized what I'd just done. I was a murderer! I couldn't explain this away! My heart squeezed so hard I lost my breath. My life was over. I stared in panic as four uniform cars surrounded the front entrance and two more appeared at the back of the cafe.

Shit. Shit, shit, shit!

I was looking around for an escape route when suddenly everything went still outside. It was incredibly quiet, too, like the world desperately needed to take a breath but couldn't. I didn't hear car engines or horns blaring or the low rumble of city life. It was just profoundly silent.

"Bay!" someone called. I spun around to see Roy standing at the front entrance holding the door open. "21 seconds!" he yelled. "Move!"

I ran to him, and both of us flew out the door, Roy pulling me in front of him down the street that ran alongside the café. From what I could make out in our hurried escape, the uniforms looked frozen in mid-run while reaching for the guns at their belts. Cars were frozen, bystanders frozen. The whole world had become a 3-D painting through which I was running.

Roy pulled me across the street and down an alley between two buildings. Stopping there, I spun to face the frozen scene again, resting my hand on my forehead. My head was pounding with adrenaline. First, I'd thought my life was over, now suddenly, I was safe with Roy.

A few seconds passed and the world breathed again. The cops were all running into the Starbucks with guns drawn while I watched them from across the street. What the hell was happening to me?

"Roy," I said, turning to face him. "What the fuck?" That's when I saw Gyllian standing there. His eyes faded from that shiny silver Angelic color back to orange-brown. "Time manipulation," I said breathlessly.

Gyllian nodded. "With limits."

"You…" I breathed. "You just stopped time?"

"Only for thirty-five seconds," he said taking a step toward me. "That's my limit. I can do anything I need to do with time, but only for thirty-five seconds. Anything longer and I get into God's territory. That's not for anyone, even half-Angels, to be messing with."

"You…you just stopped time." My brain hadn't caught up with the events yet.

"And you just killed a Queen Demon," Gyllian said, "with an ability you had no idea how to use."

I suddenly realized the sword was still in my hand. "How?"

"You're your father's daughter," Gyllian said and smiled. "Angelic instincts come with the territory of being an Angel's offspring."

I tried to ignore the thump against my chest whenever my parentage was brought up. "How do I put it back?"

Roy smiled. "Touch it to the area your tattoo is in. No, no," he said when I started to lift my shirt. "It doesn't have to touch your skin. It's magic," he said with a mischievous smile. "Just bring your sword up to the general area of the tattoo. The magic will take care of the rest."

I touched the hilt to my breastbone and an incredibly queer sensation came over my skin, like a piece of it just disappeared, giving way to a gentle wind tunnel. "Ugh!" I cried. Before I realized it, the sword wasn't in my hand anymore. I quickly lifted my shirt, exposing the tattoo and making sure it was still there, before I looked back up at Roy and Gyllian. "That was weird."

Roy laughed. "I can't wait for those wings of yours to come out and you have to put *them* back. That will be interesting."

My eyes went wide. "You think my wings can manifest?"

Roy nodded. "No doubt."

"Can I do it now?"

"NO!" both of them cried, making me jump.

"Not right now," Gyllian said more softly. "Wings

would not go over very well with the humans. You should wait for a more private opportunity."

I nodded reluctantly as they started down the alley. After a small sigh, I followed. There was still too much I didn't understand, and these people had the answers, so I needed to follow them for now. Out the other side of the alley a black SUV was waiting with Fox in the driver's seat and Booth in the back. All of us climbed in, and Fox pulled away.

I sat there looking out my window thinking about Shia. I'd never killed anything before. Why wasn't I upset? I should be feeling something, shouldn't I? I wanted to ask the others, but I wasn't one for asking advice. I didn't know them anyway, so I let the silence linger. It quickly became more uncomfortable than I was willing to admit, though.

"How come Fox drives?" I blurted out. "I mean, Gyllian seems to be the team leader here. Why doesn't he?"

I glanced at the review mirror and saw Fox's eyes crinkled at the corners, so I assumed she was smiling. "I drive because of my main ability."

"What's that?"

"To protect all of you."

My brows dropped. "Protect us? We can't protect ourselves?"

"In battle, certainly. I help protect you between battles."

"Battles," I scoffed in disbelief. This conversation sounded like something out of *The Lord of the Rings*. "How do you protect us between battles?" That seemed like a useless ability, but I didn't know anything about *my own* abilities, never mind any of theirs.

She shrugged a shoulder. "Lots of things."

"Gee, thanks for clearing that up."

She chuckled. "I'm not being difficult, Bay. My ability activates as a situation calls, and it often changes."

"Well what has it manifested into so far?"

"We've kept our activities discreet, so I really haven't had to push my ability too hard. But so far, I've been able to wipe memories in order to protect Gyllian on a few difficult occasions. I've also been able to slow our descent out of a fifteen-story window so we landed unharmed." My eyes went wide. "I've also been able to accelerate a car past its labeled speed limit to escape a difficult situation while maintaining control and order of the car's mechanical mechanisms without letting up on the gas or leaving the driver's seat."

"Like she did the night we got you," Roy said beside me.

Fox nodded. "It depends on what kind of protection is required at each given time, but my ability can only manifest in direct protection of all of you, or one of you."

"Speaking of the night you got me," I said, leaning forward a little, "how in the name of Christ did you know where I lived and that I was being attacked by a Demon that exact moment?"

Gyllian looked at me over his shoulder. "When we ran into each other in the hall I knew who you were because of the way our tattoos appeared. I have connections in the FBI and acquired your personnel file to get your address." He shook his head. "We didn't know you were under attack. We just came prepared."

I nodded and sat back in my seat, crossing my arms. "So, what's the big plan to deal with Hell?"

"It's elaborate," Gyllian replied looking out the windshield again.

"Okay. Let's get back to the house and you can fill me in."

"We're not going back to the house." I looked at him quizzically. "We're only ten minutes away from work, so we might as well head in early so you can get acquainted with the place."

"Work? Wait. You were serious when you said you had jobs?"

"Bay," he said looking back at me again. "How are your bartending skills?"

6

Fox pulled up to a nightclub in the center of the city called Placids. "Oh shit," I muttered to myself, knowing the place well. "What in the holy hell are we doing here?"

Fox parked the car and Gyllian got out, then ducked down and looked at me in the back seat. "I own it." He closed the door.

"Wait. What?" I quickly got out of the car and went around it toward him while everyone else climbed out. "What are you talking about? I *know* who owns this club, and it's not you."

"How do you know it's not me?" he asked with an over exaggerated look of curiosity. I could have sworn I saw a glint of charm and playfulness in the very deepest layers of his eyes. He was enjoying this a bit.

"Because I've observed a few interrogations involving the owner of this club. His name is Dimitri Dinahe, and he's a scumbag. The man traffics in just about every illegal substance known to humanity through here, including some shit humanity has never even heard of, like biochemical agents that a few terrorists were interested in last year. He also does some money laundering on the side and runs six of Chicago's major prostitution rings."

I sighed, thinking about Ming and Kalonownski, who were the heads of the anti-terrorist and white-collar crime units. Both had dealt with Dinahe more than a few times.

"The guy was too good at covering his tracks, so the FBI couldn't pin anything on him," I added, crossing my arms.

"Short guy, right?" Gyllian asked.

I looked at him, confused. "Yeah, about 5'5."

"Bald? Black?"

My eyes narrowed. "Yeah."

Gyllian crooked his finger, directing me to one of the large windows of the building next to the club. All five of us lined up in front of it, and my eyes went wide when I saw my reflection…because it wasn't mine. None of our reflections were right. I was now 5'4" with short, pixie-cut black hair, very tan skin, and brown eyes. Plus, all my tattoos were gone. When I looked down at my real body though, everything still looked the same. I looked up again and my heart raced as the reflection mimicked my movement.

"What the fuck?"

"That's my doing," Fox said. I looked at her and saw her eyes were Angelic silvery gray. She was smiling. "This is one of the ways I protect you. I only use these disguises for club related events."

I looked back at their reflections in the window. They all looked different. Fox was now 5'5", with shoulder-length, curly red hair and very white skin. Her reflection had green eyes and lovely freckled cheeks. Roy was 5'7 with spiky blonde hair, blue eyes, a very slight build, and one earring in his right ear. Booth was a 6'0" beefy bald white man with a brown goatee and brown eyes. And Gyllian was Dimitri Dinahe, the same man I'd seen being questioned by Ming and Kalonownski through the two-way mirrors at headquarters on several occasions.

I slowly and carefully turned to face Gyllian and the others as I reached for my Beretta as subtly as I could. "You're a crime boss?" I asked. My FBI training in overdrive, I started looking around for possible escape routes. I was taking a risk by facing them and putting a building behind me, but it was the only way I was going to get a clean shot off if I needed to.

Gyllian's hands came up. "Before you get skittish again, let me ask you something."

"Okay," I said carefully.

He leaned down a little, bringing himself to my eye level. "Do you think we'd hear anything about Demon activity in white collar, suburban circles?"

I blinked and focused on him for a moment instead of my escape options.

"I doubt an overworked, single soccer mom would have much information about Demons rising from Hell. Between a job or two, and ballet or karate lessons for her kids, there really isn't much time to focus on the seedy underground of

Demonic life."

Regrettably, that made sense. I pressed my lips together and felt myself uncoil slightly.

He shrugged. "Think of it as undercover work."

I hated undercover work, but my chest relaxed and I felt my attitude shift slightly. I tried for a moment not to see things through the eyes of the law, but through the eyes of a bunch of half-Angels trying to save the world.

"To learn about Demonic life," Gyllian went on, "you have to stay close to Demonic life."

I chewed my bottom lip as I took my hand off my gun, though my skin started to crawl at the thought of working with criminals. A huge part of me wanted to cuff Gyllian right now and take him straight to Ming and Kalonownski. I remembered how some of his interrogations went. He was an arrogant, snide S.O.B. and it had been Gyllian the *whole* time. I think I even recalled seeing Roy and Booth in the interrogation room in their disguises. Fox probably was, too.

Gyllian let out a short sigh. "This is going to be an issue, isn't it?"

I nodded once. "It might be."

Gyllian's eyes took on an air of annoyance and respect, as paradoxical as seemed. My guess was he respected me for my ideals but was annoyed that I was staying true to them, as if my whole reality hadn't seismically shifted in the last twelve hours.

"How about this," he said, shoving his hands into his pockets. "You need a job and I'm offering you one." He indicated the others with a tilt of his head. "They all work here. Booth is a bouncer, Fox is a dancer, and Roy is a bartender. I have a long bar though, and Roy needs help. Interested?"

I sighed and looked around uncomfortably. I wasn't going to be able to completely ignore the crime I knew happened here, even though I did understand the reasoning for it. "Let me just make something really clear right off the bat," I said.

"All right."

"If any kind of sexual crime happens here, I will lose my shit." I held up my finger. "I swear to *God*, Gyllian, I will tear your entire fucking club down to its studs with zero consideration for you or your cover. Do you understand me?"

"Will you make an exception for my prostitution rings?" I narrowed my eyes briefly and then crossed my arms, sighing heavily. "Those bring in a lot of intel," Gyllian said. "Get a man drunk and pillow talking, and he often spills his guts in ways he's not even aware of in the morning."

I swiped my fingertips over my forehead before crossing my arms again in consideration. I really wasn't sure if I could deal with that, but some part of me, however small, kind of egged me on to do so.

"Okay," I said, nodding and meeting Gyllian's eyes, "as long as the prostitutes are not forced, or beaten, or abused in *any* way by their pimps or johns."

Gyllian nodded. "I can accept that. So," he said and started for the doors of the club, "can you bartend?"

I thinned out my lips as I fell into step beside him. "Yeah, I've done my share. It's how I paid my way through college."

"Welcome aboard then. Your shift will be the same as Roy's starting at 6:00 pm. The club closes at 3:00 am Friday, Saturday and Sunday, and cleanup is about an hour."

I glanced at Roy, who was already smiling at me. "Partners, baby!"

His enthusiasm made me chuckle. Roy and Booth opened the glass double doors of the club, and Gyllian swept into the building like a boss. His entire demeanor and mannerisms shifted as he clearly got into character. His stride became smooth and long, with what the street folks called "swag." His eyes were empty and calm and detached, like he was the king of the world and everyone else only existed to serve or entertain him. I was so fascinated that Fox had to softly clear her throat a couple times to get my attention. When I looked over, I saw her latched onto Gyllian's arm.

He held his other arm up to me. "Smile," he said, looking down at me with a smooth, cool turn of his head. "Look like you think you're the luckiest girl on the planet to be with me."

I interlaced my arm with his and put on a fake toothy grin. "You mean act like a flake?" I said in a high-pitched voice.

He genuinely smiled and looked out ahead of him. "Exactly."

His demeanor made me smile a little more genuinely. The transformation was amusing to watch. Even seeing as little of Gyllian as I had so far, this easy swagger was something I didn't think he was capable of. He seemed too uptight to come off so smooth, but he was actually marvelous at it.

The club was barely recognizable empty. I'd never actually partied here when I was young, but I'd done plenty of stakeouts at this place. There were always whispers of crazy criminal activity taking place. Being on the sex crimes unit though, I'd only been concerned about places like this when whispers of human trafficking reached my ears. Gyllian had better not be involved in that shit. If I found out he was... Well, I'd already warned him about what would happen.

The club was luxurious. Front and center was the giant dance floor. Ringing the perimeter of that were lots of high round tables with tall stools. In left corner close to the entrance was the elaborate DJ booth. On the right, almost taking up the entire wall, was the long 'S' shaped bar that could seat a hundred people easy—definitely a two-person job. Past the dance floor was a large cluster of more round tables where people could eat or drink. To the left of those was a staircase that led up to the private balcony for the owner, Gyllian, and high rolling customers. On the back wall was an elaborate stage area with several small S-shaped stages branching out from a larger main stage in the center. Several poles for the dancers decorated that area from floor to ceiling. A plush-looking VIP area in the back left corner next to the stages contained magnificent white couches and chairs and marble tables. To the right of the stages were a couple of doors that had to lead to restrooms, kitchens, and backstage areas.

Gyllian suddenly kissed my cheek, which stunned me stupid for a second until I saw him lean over to kiss Fox's cheek as well. I realized he was just playing his character. Fox elegantly unlaced her arm from Gyllian's and halted. I took the hint and let him go, though less gracefully. Gyllian didn't miss a step as he headed over to Johnson Baser, the assistant manager, who was holding a portfolio of business reports, no doubt. I knew that douchebag well enough. He was always in the interrogation room for questioning, and he always got away. We could never make a charge stick.

"Come on," Fox said, lacing her arm with mine. "I need to get ready and you need to change."

I looked at her, confused. "Why?"

Her silvery gray eyes met mine. "You can't bartend in flannel. Come on," she said, cuddling closer to my side. "I have plenty of low-cut shirts and tank tops you can choose from." She gently but swiftly pulled me alongside her. "Now Booth is going to be with Gyllian all night because it would look strange if the owner of such a prestigious club didn't have his own entourage," Fox explained as she swept through the doors to the backstage area.

My eyes went wide instantly at the ridiculousness of this dressing room. To both sides of me were overstuffed racks, and more racks, and then more racks, of costumes made of more materials and color combinations than I could name or even have imagined. It looked like an overstocked thrift store for clowns and fairies.

"Gyllian usually spends all night on the private balcony, where he either conducts business with his most promising clients—"

"You mean the worst criminals," I said, ducking under a gold, feathered skirt sticking out on the right.

She smiled at me over her shoulder. "That too." She faced forward. "But also, to have a bird's-eye view of the activity in the club. If something looks promising, which in our case means suspicious, he'll have me or Roy investigate." We came out of the back side of the racks, and Fox went to the right and sat down in the very last chair of the row of mirrors that took up the entire right wall. "Roy will be with you behind the bar otherwise. Your job is to eavesdrop on bar conversation to see if anything promising—"

"Suspicious," I corrected.

She smiled and picked up a small jar of something shiny. "If anything suspicious is discussed." She gestured me into the chair across from her. I hesitated a moment before sitting down, and then she got to work putting some makeup on me. "If you hear anything about 'masters' or 'leaders,' keep your ears tuned toward that conversation. Demons love titles like that and relish in forcing humans to address them as such. The arrogance," she said in disgust. She dabbed at some other makeup at her station before leaning toward me again and rubbing it on my cheeks. "Listen for anything indicating bosses of shady and mysterious origin or powers. They're likely Demons. Also take notice if any of the creeps in the club seem overly afraid of their bosses and don't want to discuss them much, or if they discuss them in a fearful or reverential whisper." She switched brushes and dabbed something else on me.

"What do I do if I hear anything like that?"

"Let Roy know for now."

"For now?"

Fox dipped a thin brush into yet another kind of makeup before leaning toward me again with it and poking around my eyes. "When we get back to the house, Gyllian is going to share what we already have with you and better coach you on how to gather intel here. After that, you'll be better equipped to make the proper call on what action to take when you hear that kind of stuff. Depending on the situation, you either run up and tell Gyllian, have someone fetch Booth to come to you, or just take your own mental notes."

An odd sense of relief came over me. "So, I guess my FBI training doesn't need to be totally wasted, huh?" I instantly felt stupid as soon as the words left my lips. I shouldn't have allowed her to see how much my job at the Bureau had meant to me. She gave me a gentle sympathetic smile as I cleared my throat uncomfortably.

"No darling," she said sweetly. "It's not wasted." Then she dabbed a little bit more at my face before sitting back. "There."

I looked in the mirror, which showed my real reflection, and my face went slack with surprise. I'd never worn such glamorous makeup before. I usually just threw on the basics, eyeliner and mascara, to go to work. I couldn't even name the stuff Fox had put on me, but I actually looked stunning.

"You like?" she asked.

"Whoa," I said, touching my face.

"I'll take that as a yes," she said and stood. "Come on.

We need to find you a better top." I stood up and followed her.

"How could I see my own reflection while you were still using your abilities?"

She looked at me over her shoulder. "I still have to protect the others in the club. But I shifted my ability so you could see yourself."

"Wasn't that kind of pointless? No one will even see my real reflection, right?"

Fox looked back at me. "Oh, don't worry. The facade I have you in will look just as glamorous as you do. I choose what your projected face looks like, makeup and all. This is just for you."

We smiled at each other before Fox faced forward again. She seemed to know right where she was going in this daunting plethora of chiffon and silk. She stopped at one rack and started sifting through it with a sense of purpose. "The bartenders have to wear black to keep the joint classy, but it doesn't mean you can't wear sexy black," she said, rummaging. "Ah ha. Here." She pulled out a tiny vest-like black top. It had a very low-cut V-neck and was covered in shiny black sequins. I looked at her like she was nuts, but I took it. I'd never worn anything so tight and revealing in my life. "And then…" She started rummaging through another part of the rack, which held a good number of pants. She pulled out a pair of black satin skinny ones and handed them to me. Oh man. "And finally…" She went to the very back wall covered in small cubbies, where at least a thousand pairs of shoes rested. There was even a ladder parked to the far left so that the cubbies at the top could be reached. Fox bent over and then spun to face me with a wide, proud grin. In her hands was pair of black stilettos with five-inch heels made of shining chrome.

I shook my head immediately. "My feet will be killing me in two minutes flat with those on. I won't survive the whole night behind a bar."

Her posture drooped a little and she gave me an exaggerated sad puppy-dog face. "So, no?"

I chuckled. "No."

She twisted her mouth to the side like a pouting child,

which was actually adorable, before she faced the cubbies again. Pulling out another pair of shoes, she turned to me, this time holding a cute, comfortable looking pair of black flats.

I nodded once. "Perfect."

Fox brightened. "Now let me curl that beautiful blonde hair of yours, and you'll be ready to stun them all!"

I chuckled as we headed back to the makeup stands. "I'm just serving them drinks."

"Goodness no," Fox said as she reached between two mirrors to plug in a curling iron. She faced me and flourished her hands. "You're serving them a fantasy."

I shook my head, still grinning, and sat down. "That's the dancers' job."

"No, no, no. It's everyone's job here."

I shook my head again. "If you say so."

"I do say so." She stepped up behind me. "Now hush. I'm making you glamorous."

I laughed as Fox got to work curling my hair.

7

I slipped back into the routine of a bartender disturbingly easily. But my FBI ideals didn't mesh well with what was going on all around me. Shoddy business deals went down everywhere I looked. Cases and cases of drugs were being exchanged, mostly in the VIP area. Someone in Gyllian's private balcony even pulled out an M-4 carbine assault rifle from a large case to show it off, loading and unloading it while talking a mile a minute. This dude even brought all the good toys, like a PAQ-4 infrared site and an M-203 40 millimeter grenade launcher, as accessories.

Most disheartening, though, was how many law officials I recognized— cops, agents, lawyers, district attorneys, and judges. I had worked with these people, or at least had interacted with them on the job. No wonder this club never got raided. "Losing" evidence and covering up crimes would be easy for these folks. Based on what I was seeing, there was zero hope for the justice system. It disturbed me on a level I hadn't known was possible. For eight years I'd worked for the justice system. In my wreck of a life, it had given me purpose and direction when I'd desperately needed it. I'd believed in that system. I'd believed in the law. Until tonight.

I felt betrayed.

All I could do now was try to gather intel for these half-Angels. But I was finding it really difficult to even give a rat's ass, especially now. Let the Demons come and clean up this fucking mess. Hell, the *Angels* had initiated this cleansing of humanity! How could you argue when *Angels* had lost hope?

One dynamic duo perusing the tables kept catching my eye, two young attractive guys who looked like they could get any dancer they wanted on the stage. Yet as I watched, they were hitting on the least attractive girls in the whole joint. They looked affluent and, based on my experience, could not have a genuine interest in these girls. Luckily, the girls they attempted to pick up were with a group and just wanted to party with their friends, so the boys moved on. At about 1:00 am though, one of the boys managed to take a seat next to a decently attractive, fuller figured girl sitting at a table with a friend. She seemed sweet, reacting to the boy's attention with shyness and a lot of giggles while boy number two got her friend onto the dance floor. I watched them for about a half an hour. Roy had to get on me a couple times to pay attention to the bar, but something felt wrong. I'd been an agent long enough to know when to trust a feeling like that.

As the night wore on, the full-figured girl became more and more fall-over drunk. I'd been watching her drinks though. She'd only had one in the entire hour I'd been keeping an eye on her. She shouldn't be that drunk at this point. At 2:00 the attractive boy got her to her feet. She was stumbling, half asleep, as he led her toward the back door. My eyes narrowed at the tight, ungentlemanly grip he had on her wrist as he practically dragged her to the exit that led to the alleyway.

Rohypnol.

I threw my bar cloth down, ran to the far end of the bar that opened up to the tables, and grabbed the first waitress within arm's reach. "Take over the bar for me."

The waitress yanked her arm from my grip. "Get off me, bitch!"

I was not in the mood for this shit! Clenching my teeth, I gripped the back of her hair in a tight fist, then grabbed her upper arm, and forced her behind the bar. "I will slit your fucking throat if you don't take over the bar right now!" I gave her a little shove behind the counter. "You can have my tips!"

Before she could respond, I was running toward the back door from which they'd left. I smashed the crash bar and it flew wide open, hitting the brick wall behind it. Across from me, against the adjacent building, the boy had the girl up against the wall. Her skirt was pulled up around her waist, and her panties were dangling off one ankle. She was lucid enough to be trying to fight him off, but he was already reaching for his zipper.

"Hey!" I yelled and started for him.

He looked over his shoulder just in time for me grab the back of his hair and pull him away from her. She fell to the

78

asphalt with a cry and weakly started crawling away. Spinning the boy to face me, I punched him square in the jaw, sending him flying backwards. He hit the wall hard and slid down it. I was shaking so badly with rage that I couldn't even see straight. I gripped the top of his hair and yanked his head down. In the same instant, I brought my leg up so his nose connected with my kneecap. Blood splattered the brick wall behind him and he was down for the count.

Panting, I looked for the girl, who had paused in her desperate retreat. "Hey, hey," I said, crouching in front of her. She looked ready to panic. "It's okay. You're okay. Hey. Look at me." Her eyes met mine. "I'm going to take you home, okay? Where do you live?"

I heard the door to the club open again. "Nicki!" someone cried. I looked over and saw the friend come sprinting out. "What's going on? What happened?"

"He...he..." Nicki tried to say, pointing to the boy.

"He roofied your friend," I explained.

"Fuck! I knew we shouldn't have tried this sleazy club," her friend said as she started to pick the other girl up.

"Are you both all right? Do you need a ride home?"

"No, no. Thanks." She got her friend to her feet and I straightened up. "We only live a block away. I'm going to get her home. Can you"—she nodded her chin toward the unconscious scumbag. "Can you call the cops for us?"

I nodded. "Sure." Like the cops would give a shit about an attempted rape. They were too busy getting their booze on in the club.

I watched the two girls start down the street and then slowly faced the boy, who was just coming to. I wrestled with two sides of myself as I stared at him. There was the FBI agent in me that really should call the cops and have them do a formal report etc., and then there was the sexually abused child in me that realized I wasn't a fucking FBI agent anymore. I was the offspring of the most powerful Archangel in all of history, lore, and myth.

As the boy's eyes opened, I lifted my foot and shoved it into his throat, pinning him hard against the brick wall. I watched with unbelievable satisfaction as his eyes bulged and he desperately clawed at my ankle to try to free himself. He was the second person I would kill today, and, oddly, I wasn't disturbed by that fact. I was more disturbed that I seemed to have accepted the idea that Michael was my father.

Suddenly a pair of arms wrapped around me and pulled me away before I was done crushing his windpipe. I managed to grab the person's arm and flung him out in front of me, slamming him into the wall across from me. It was Roy.

He slowly put his hands up before smiling. "You know, you look pretty terrifying with those eyes."

I flinched. Suddenly, I realized the Hebrew tattoos down the middle of my back had heated up. I hadn't even meant to activate a tattoo. I calmed myself down and felt my back cool off.

I glared down at the boy. "That pig just tried to rape a girl," I explained.

Roy nodded and carefully took a step toward me with his hands still up. "I'm sure he did. But you stopped him."

"And now I'm going to kill him."

Roy shook his head. "No, you're not."

"Excuse me?" I said, peering at him.

Roy took another step toward me. "You're not going to kill him."

"And why not?"

"Because I'm not going to let you. You're not a murderer."

I crossed my arms. "I seriously doubt it could be considered murder for killing an attempted rapist. What is one measly little sex offender, really?"

"He's a human being."

I scoffed. "You give him way too much credit."

"I'm not letting you kill him," Roy said matter-of-factly. His brown eyes were confident and steady. "And is one measly little sex offender worth fighting me over, really?"

I sighed and looked down at the boy, who was unconscious again. I shook my head and started back toward the club. "Fine. Let the apocalypse get him."

"Whoa! Hey." Roy took my arm stopping me. I looked back at him over my shoulder. "We're trying to *stop* the apocalypse, remember?"

I jerked out of his grip. "Yeah," then started toward the

club again.

"Bay." He took my arm again. I went still. "Talk to me."

I bowed my head, keeping my back to him. "Who's watching the bar?" I asked. I didn't really care. I just needed to buy myself a moment to decide if I wanted to talk to him about this.

"I got another waitress to help."

I nodded. This was something I felt completely unprepared to share with him, but at the same time, felt completely safe letting him know.

"Look, I'll be perfectly honest with you," I turned to face him. "I hate human beings," I said. "I hate the state the world is in. At the moment, I really couldn't care less if Hell rises and kills everything and everyone. There is no hope for the world." I shook my head. "Not anymore. People are evil."

I expected him to get angry, to hate me, but the compassion that came over his face completely took my breath away. I'd never had anyone look at me with such tenderness, tenderness I definitely didn't deserve.

"Listen," I said, trying to do damage control. "I understand innocent people, like children, will be killed when Hell rises, but some of them might actually be better off dead than in the situations they are in. I lost count of how many times I wished one of my foster parents would go too far and kill me." I froze. Clearing my throat uncomfortably, I glanced away to avoid his eyes. I'd just shared way too much vulnerability with him, *and* I was talking about my childhood. I never talked about my childhood, not with anyone. I had to force myself to meet his gaze again. "I just don't see people the way you do."

He shook his head. "You like humanity more than you think you do," he said gently.

"How's that?" I asked, my voice shaking.

He reached up and, without breaking eye contact with me, rested his hand on the side of my neck and took a step forward. "You don't become an FBI agent because you hate humanity. You become one to save people."

A storm erupted inside of me, but I pretended that his words didn't strike a strange cord in me. "I became an FBI agent to save myself."

"Did you?" he asked, looking unconvinced.

"It was either find something to live for, or die in a downward spiral of drugs, alcohol and men. I chose the former."

"You could have chosen to do anything," he continued, shoving his hands in his pockets. "Yet you chose a profession that allowed you to help people, to help the humanity you claim to hate so much."

I felt holes being punched in my defenses, defenses I built over a lifetime of abuse, but something about these Nephilims made me feel safe. Something about them made my reservations waver. But I couldn't allow myself to give in. Trust was fragile, and I still didn't know them. So, I did my best to dam up those holes.

"I became an FBI agent to exact revenge on sexual predators who ruin childhoods and lives, like mine was. Every perp I arrested was a surrogate for the foster families that abused me, nothing more. Foster families that had me at their mercy when I was just a child who couldn't defend herself. Since I had no one to defend me, I decided to be the defender I never had."

Roy surprised me by smiling gently. "That's a pretty passionate speech about defending children who, moments ago, you said would be better off dead."

I flinched. "Some of them would be!"

Roy shook his head and took another step toward me so he was looking down at my face. "If you truly believed that, you would never have chosen a profession that allowed you to help them."

I stared at him. I hated how much sense that made. Once I was no longer a ward of the state, and after I went mad, unconsciously trying to kill myself every day for three years, I could have done anything. Why an FBI agent? To put away perps. To legally be able to kick their asses if they crossed me. That was why. But I couldn't deny the passion I had for the children and the sex-crime victims I'd saved throughout my career. They were the reason I kept my nose so firmly fixed to the grindstone, to get them the hell out of the situations they were in. The bottom line, the absolute bottom line, was saving them. The mission that ardently defined me was sparing as many victims as I possibly could from my childhood trauma.

"But the world is so evil, Roy."

He nodded. "It is."

"Have you even looked around? Have you *ever* really looked around? Did you *see* every single level of our supposed 'justice system' hanging out in that club with open crime going on in front of their faces?"

Roy nodded. "I have, and I've seen a lot worse." His eyes narrowed a little. "You think you're the only one familiar with evil, Bay? You have no idea the kind of Hell I've seen."

I crossed my arms and shrugged. "So tell me."

He sighed softly and walked past me to the alley wall and leaned a shoulder against it. "My father, Raphael, fell to Earth in Russia. He was killed when I was six." Roy's large brown eyes shifted to the brick wall. "After that I went through a few abusive fosters homes, mostly physically abusive, before I ran away at fourteen." He looked at me again. "I wanted to disappear and found some seedy folks to help me do it." He shrugged. "Turned out those seedy folks didn't want me found either."

I leaned my shoulder up against the wall facing him.

"I was tall and strong. Gifted in a lot of physical areas, like we all are, even without using our abilities. So, I was put in the underground fighting rings." He shook his head. "The kind of dark, deep hole you never find your way out of, where money is God and you are as disposable as the paper your owners wipe their ass with."

My hand went to my mouth as Roy took a deep breath. He was struggling a little to get this out, I could tell.

"I was kept in a single cell with a dirt floor and nothing but a filthy mattress and a wooden bucket to piss in. For years, I had to fight for my life every single Friday, Saturday, and Sunday night. Every. Single. Week," he said slowly to drive the point home. "No time to heal. No medical care. Nothing. I went into the ring with broken fingers, arms, ribs, head, face, it didn't matter. I was good though, and my owners made a lot of money off me. But being that good was also a mistake." He pressed his lips together, and I could almost see the horrific memories pass through his eyes. "Because it got to the point that if I didn't fight well, or I lost a fight, punishment was involved. They would beat the shit out of me themselves and then handcuff me in the corner of the cell so I couldn't even make it to my bucket. They wouldn't feed me either for the entire week before I had to go fight again."

Roy took the bottom of his black t-shirt and lifted it up, exposing his defined abs and chest, and pointed to a tattoo over his heart. It looked like a bold black figure of a hand with a swirl in the palm.

"I got my healing ability when I was twenty, after a head injury put me in a coma for three days. So, for four years, before Gyllian found me, I could at least heal myself after a fight, which put me in top-notch shape to fight the next weekend." He pulled his shirt back down. "That meant no more punishments because I didn't lose a fight again." He glanced at the ground and remained quiet a moment. "I killed a lot of people in that ring, Bay." When he looked up at me again his eyes were bloodshot and glistening. "A lot."

I couldn't help but marvel that, through all of that, he'd still somehow kept a trace of boyish innocence. I saw it whenever he smiled at me. How such a loving and truly beautiful person could come out of such tragedy was impossible for me to understand.

After a few silent moments, Roy cleared his throat. "Come on," he said, pushing himself off the wall. "We still have an hour left of our shift." He headed back toward the club.

I hesitated, trying to imagine what he'd been through. What that had been like. Oddly enough, I also wondered what it was like for him to know his Angelic father. Was that where the boyish innocence I saw came from?

"Hey, listen," Roy said, making me turn around. He was peeking around the corner of the door. "You've never seen the Lights fall, have you?"

I felt stunned. "You mean our parents' fall?" Roy nodded. "Um, no. I haven't."

Roy smiled, that boyish charm shocking me for the first time now that I knew what he'd been through. "Gyllian's got the news footage from the classified archives of NASA if you want to watch it. That shit was classified *above* top secret."

"It made the news?"

"Sure did."

My heart and head were pounding with my pulse. "How come I've never heard of it?"

"You underestimate the power of the government and its influence over the media. It was all explained away as an elaborate hoax."

"Oh really?" I said flatly. "So it was classified above top secret because it never happened?"

Roy gave me a playful wink. "Exactly."

I chuckled. "How did Gyllian get a classified tape from *NASA?*"

He smirked. "In case it escaped your notice, Gyllian is not hurting for cash. You saw the bunker, right?"

I started laughing. "Well, yeah."

"He funded that entire thing *and* paid off every single contractor to keep quiet about it ever being built. Gyllian can buy a little classified video tape from NASA."

I looked at him skeptically. "You stole it, didn't you?"

Roy's smile spread wide across his face and he chuckled, "All right, guilty." I laughed. "So do you want to watch it? You should know, though"—his face turned a little sympathetic— "that your dad fell last, so news crews couldn't capture his fall."

My heart gave a hard thump against my ribcage at the mention of Michael...my dad. I still couldn't wrap my head around that. I gave Roy a curious look. "If Michael fell last, how did the news crews miss him?"

Roy gave a tilt of his head. "You'll understand when you watch the tape. So would you like to?"

"I would actually really love to."

He grinned. "Okay. We'll watch it when we get home."

"Home?" I asked. Roy looked at me, confused. "That's Gyllian's home, not mine."

His brows dropped. "You're not staying?"

I flinched at the unexpected request. "Well, I mean, I don't know. No one actually asked me if I wanted to, or told me I could."

Roy grinned again. "It's implied, Bay. It's the only place we're all safe."

"Well, what about all my stuff?"

"We can pick it up tomorrow."

"But, uh," I began a little nervously. "I'm not sure that's a step I actually want to take yet."

Roy's smile brightened. "You will."

I smiled and gave him a little playful shove though the door. "You don't know that!" I said, and we both laughed as we made our way back into the club.

We got behind the bar again, and the waitress I had grabbed came straight at me. "Handle me like again, ho, and we gonna have a problem. You feel me?"

This bitch. Roy actually managed to get me in a good mood, and she had to go and ruin it. I placed one hand deliberately on top of the bar, and the other on the back counter, completely blocking her path, and then slowly leaned forward, making her cower back. "We've got a problem now."

The girl stared at me for a long moment. I could see the struggle in her eyes, the desire to restore her respect, and the curiosity over whether she could actually win in a fight against me. I just waited without flinching or blinking.

She wisely decided not to fight me. "You a special sorta crazy, ain't you?"

I tilted my head menacingly. "Don't cross me again and we won't have a problem. You feel me?"

She nodded, trying to keep the fear from her expression. "I feel you."

"Good." I lifted my hand off the bar and turned to the side, allowing her to pass and get back on the floor. She glanced back at least eight times before she felt she was safely away from me.

Roy was smiling broadly at me as he ran a bar rag around an empty mug and shook his head.

"What?" I asked lightly. "I'm not going to be stomped on just because I'm the new girl. Respect!" I said and threw up a gang sign that was popular in Chicago.

Roy threw his head back and laughed, and I continued to the other end of the bar, smiling.

———

By the time 4:00 am rolled around, cleanup was done, but Gyllian still had a few people up on the balcony he was meeting with. Booth stayed with him like a silent sentry. I was at one of the tables in the middle of the club with a few of Gyllian's prostitutes, who were ready to call it a night. A tall bottle of Jack sat on the table, but only the prostitutes drank it. I noticed that Fox and Roy, who were up at the bar, each had a bottle of water like I did. I absently wondered if they had learned the hard way about alcohol like I had.

I barely paid attention to the company at the table because my eyes were on Gyllian in the balcony. I wondered what kind of seedy business he was conducting up there. His company looked of Asian descent, Japanese it seemed. Japan was a force to be reckoned with, and I couldn't recall if we'd pissed them off recently or not. I hoped this was a drug deal going down rather than a weapons deal.

"If you stuck in the life," one girl said and sighed, "there are worse pimps to be stuck wit." She was a dark-skinned pretty black girl in her early twenties with a mane of smooth, spiral curls framing her face. She had a distinctive red streak on the left side and long red fingernails to match.

"So…Dimitri treats you well?" I interrupted.

The girl looked at me and shrugged. "He don't abuse us, but there's nothing rosy about the streets."

I nodded and let the conversation fade into the background again as I looked up at Gyllian. A few minutes passed before my attention was jarred back to the prostitutes, when the girl I'd spoken to said something conversationally about one of her johns tonight.

"He talk like he scared to death of the woman," the girl, Robyn, said. "Always lookin' around the room, jumpin' at shadows like his boss is listenin' through the walls."

"Who's this?" I asked.

Robyn gave me an annoyed look for butting in again, but answered anyway. "José SanSosa. He a regular of mine. Decent enough du'. Don't ask for weird shit like bondage or worse. He just wants to drink, talk, and fuck."

My interest was piqued as I leaned over the table, giving her my full attention. "How often do you see him?"

She looked offended. "I don' know. Once a week?"

"What does he do?" I asked.

Her head swiveled. "Why you askin'?"

I lightly bounced my water bottle off the table twice and looked over at Fox and Roy, who were just coming toward the table from the bar. José SanSosa. "No reason." I'd talk to them about this later. It seemed like exactly the kind of thing they were looking for.

Finally, Gyllian shook the hand of his guest before he departed. After bidding my company goodnight, the five of us left the club in the same fashion in which we'd entered, with Fox and me on Gyllian's arms and Booth and Roy holding the doors for him. We all piled into the SUV as gracefully as possible, Booth sliding into the driver's seat, Roy in the passenger seat.

"Gyllian," Roy said as we pulled off, "Bay wants to watch the video."

Gyllian nodded and looked at me. "Thanks for being so subtle about stopping that attempted rape."

I looked at him, not sure if he was being sarcastic. My eyes narrowed when I saw he was. I scoffed in disgust before looking back out the window. "You're not going to make me feel guilty about stopping a rape, Gyllian."

"I'm not trying to make you feel guilty. I'm just going to ask you to be quieter about it if you have to do that again."

I looked at him. "If I *have* to do that again?"

"We have a mission we have to protect!" he argued. His bright and fierce eyes reminded me of a tiger's, powerful and fearless. Unflinching. Unwavering. Uncompromising. "Its success hinges on its secrecy."

"For Christ's sake," I said and fully faced him with a glare. "You are a soulless dick, you know that? I will never, *ever* feel guilty for saving anyone from sexual assault or sexual abuse by any means, especially not at the risk of your stupid precious secrets. Ever."

That softness surfaced in his eyes for a moment before the wall of indifference slammed back into place. "I'm glad you saved her. I am. If you can," he said carefully, "all I ask is that you try to do it more subtly next time. An example would be *not* assaulting one of my waitresses to cover your position behind the bar, especially the biggest gossip on my entire staff."

"*If* I can," I said firmly. I kept to myself that I would do exactly what I did tonight if exigent circumstances called for it. If I needed to act quickly to stop a sexual predator, I would raise whatever hell was necessary.

Gyllian nodded and looked out ahead of him while I looked back out my window and Booth continued toward the house, all of us silent.

8

It was a little past five in the morning, and the sun was just starting to come up when we all walked through the front door. Without a word, we gathered on the two couches in the living room and faced the big-screen TV on the wall. Gyllian opened a small safe behind one of the paintings and pulled out a video cassette tape and VCR. I hadn't seen one of those since I was a kid. He did some wiring behind the television and then popped in the tape.

He picked up the remote and looked at me. "Roy told you that you won't see Michael's fall, right?"

I nodded, my insides feeling like they had turned to lead. I was genuinely nervous to watch this. "I understand."

Gyllian nodded and turned on the TV. My palms were sweating, and I found myself wringing my hands. Every time I caught myself doing it, I tried to stop, only to start up again a second later. Before the video started, a hand rested on top of mine stilling my nervous fidgeting. I looked over and saw Roy smiling at me. I smiled in return, grateful for the support.

The video started, and the perplexed face of an old-school news anchor filled the screen. "If you're just joining us, we are following our top story tonight of strange lights in the skies above various parts of the world. These mysterious lights have appeared so far over Australia, Russia, and Africa, and now yet another light has developed over India."

I considered the anchor's big moustache and tweed-style suit. "What year was this?"

"1979," Gyllian answered as he sat down beside me.

"What?" I asked, drawing Gyllian's attention. "I was born in 1980. If these are the Archangels, then Michael must have conceived me right after he fell."

Gyllian nodded. "That's our consensus. All of us were born in 1980, less than a year after the fall happened."

I brought one hand up to my mouth as my body began to tremble. Fear started creeping up that maybe the nun had been right all along. Archangel or not, my father could still be a rapist.

The news coverage cut to a four-way split screen of all four of the lights in the skies. They were stunning. They looked like oval moons with rays of golden white light stretching out around the edges. They were bright enough to be distinct during the day in Australia, and even the clouds over Russia couldn't obscure it. Most magnificent was the depths of them. They reminded me of the eyes of my new companions. Whether or not the world believed in Heaven, at that moment, it had to have felt it existed on the other side of those lights.

Then each of the four lights started to get brighter. The news anchor and some clueless NASA official's voice faded as I slowly stood from the couch, staring at the screen. It started to sink in that I was watching an Angel fall to Earth, an *Angel* fall to Earth.

Gyllian soon stood beside me with his eyes glued to the television. "My dad, Gabriel, was the first one to fall."

I looked at the light over Australia as a ball of white fire, the size of a city block, jettisoned from the sky and smashed into the ground making the screen go white. That was an Angel, *an Angel*, in that ball of fire. Exactly thirty seconds later, Raphael, Roy's father, fell in the same manner over Russia. Then the light over Africa fell.

"That was my mother, Jophiel," Booth said.

Thirty seconds later the light over India fell. "My mother, Uriel," Fox said.

Thirty seconds after Uriel fell, I suddenly felt like I had been physically punched in the chest. I realized my dad had fallen the exact same way in that moment, somewhere in the world. Maybe New York City which was the city listed on my birth certificate.

The news anchor was giving meaningless insight about emergency vehicles heading to the crash sites and for all citizens to stay indoors for their safety. The video snowed out after that. Gyllian went to the VCR, took the tape out, and put both back in the safe.

I didn't move. My hands were on my cheeks. This was real. My father…*my father* was an Archangel. Not even any

Archangel, as if that wasn't ridiculous enough, but *Michael*, the most powerful Angel in all of Heaven—the soldier who had cast Lucifer down according to Biblical lore—and he had fallen to Earth just like that.

"Wh…wh…"

I had questions. I had a lot of them. Most of them concerned my dad, and that was awkward. I'd hated the man my whole life, first thinking he'd abandoned me and my mom and then hearing he'd raped her. But Michael, the Archangel, wouldn't have raped my mother, would he?

Not sure where to settle my eyes, I allowed them to rest on Gyllian, who was already looking at me with gentle compassion. He could manipulate time. "Could you…" How could I even phrase this? "Would you mind…showing me…" My voice failed me.

"The interaction between your mother and father?" he finished.

I felt my face get hot under my hands and my tongue became too heavy to speak, so I just nodded.

Gyllian gestured me closer with both his hands. I hesitated a moment before finally taking a step toward him. When he put his arms around me, I felt myself burn hotter.

"Hold on to me," he said with surprising tenderness.

I took my hands off my face and awkwardly embraced him.

A moment later my surroundings faded to black except for a dim spotlight above that seemed to be on both of us. I felt the sensation of a whipping wind pulling at my hair and my clothes, but not one hair on my head moved. I eventually looked up at Gyllian's face just as he looked down at me, and my gaze became uncomfortably locked on his silvery gray Angelic eyes. I had to force myself out of the trance when light faded back into view.

Clearing my throat uncomfortably, I looked around at my new surroundings. We were in the living room of an old, horribly decorated one-bedroom apartment. The floor was made of wooden panels, warped and bumpy with age and use. Everything was ragged and clearly used, from the furniture to the wallpaper. The lamps were the old-style tabletop lamps with yellow bulbs and shades. Even the telephone, which was ringing now, was one of those ancient rotary dial types.

I took a few steps to explore the apartment, but Gyllian pulled me back to his side. He slid his hand around my back to rest on my opposite hip. "Stay with me."

My eyes went a little wide. Why did that statement make my heart race? "Okay."

He looked at me with his eyes still silvery gray. "You have to stay in physical contact with me or you'll appear back at the house in real time."

I swallowed heavily and nodded before looking back into the apartment.

"Coming! Coming!" I heard a woman's voice say.

When my mother came into view from behind a wall to the kitchen, my eyes went so wide that I felt the muscles pull. I'd never seen her before, not even a picture. "Lights Fall" was all I'd had of her my whole life. Now she was standing in front of me.

"Mom." I found myself whispering as intense, wild emotions bubbled up from my chest. I felt like a child. Tears welled up, and it took everything I had to stay at Gyllian's side and not run to embrace her. I found myself clutching Gyllian's shirt with a trembling fist in an effort to stay put.

To anyone else, my mother was probably not an impressively beautiful woman, but she was stunning to me. She had a round, childlike face with big dimples, fair skin, and light hazel eyes. She was incredibly skinny, but she didn't look unhealthy. She was just tiny, standing only about 5'3." She had sandy blonde hair that fell just past her shoulders and was styled in the 1970s Farrah Fawcett feathered flip. She was barefoot and wore a pair of high-waist, light purple bellbottoms and a gray silk top with buttoned cuffs and a wide, turned-down collar. Green nurse's scrubs were draped over her arm as she crossed the kitchen, placing a single dish in the sink, and then came into the living room to answer the phone.

"Hello?"

"Turn on the news!"

I jumped a little when the voice, obviously on the other end of the phone, came to my ears. I looked up at Gyllian. His Angelic eyes turned to me again and he nodded without giving me an explanation as to how he'd done that. It didn't matter. I turned my focus back on my mom.

"Come again?" she asked.

"Turn it on!" the female voice on the other end said.

"I can't now. I have to be at work at 10:00 tonight."

"Now, Megan!"

The hysteria in the other woman's voice made my mom freeze at first. Then she raced around her couch, stretching the coil of the cord to the point the phone nearly fell off the table, and turned the television on.

My mom's eyes went wide when she looked at the screen. "What the hell?" came out of her mouth as she slowly sat down. Gyllian guided me closer so I could see the television screen.

"Isn't it beautiful?" the other woman said.

My mom tilted her head to the side curiously. "Beautiful? What the hell is it?"

"No one knows. NASA is stumped. They made an official statement saying this was an unexplained and unforeseen event."

"Fucking *NASA* doesn't know what this is?"

"No! It's wild, right?"

"The same NASA that put men on the moon a decade ago?"

"Yeah! Unreal."

The news went back and forth between coverage of the four countries I had just watched back at Gyllian's house. It was the exact same coverage—same news station, anchor, everything. My heart melted a little as I realized that my mother and I had watched the exact same thing, even thirty-three years apart. In a small way, I had connected with her.

"Have they moved?" my mom asked.

"No. They've just been there, steady, which gave news crews plenty of time to arrive on the scene. Riots are already starting, and people are claiming it's the end of the world."

"They may be right," my mom half muttered to herself.

"What?" the other woman cried. "What do you mean? Do you...what do you think? Is that what you really think?"

My mom rolled her eyes. "Pam, I just..."

Suddenly there was an enormous ripping sound, so loud

that my mother dropped the phone and pressed her hands to her ears. It sounded like the sky itself had ripped in two pieces! Not a second later, the apartment building started shaking so violently my mother was thrown to the floor.

"Mom!" I cried uselessly and tried to run to her, but Gyllian had a firm hold of me and kept me tight to his side.

"You can't do anything!" he hollered. "This already happened thirty-three years ago. You're just an observer."

I settled, but my mind was going wild, watching what my mother had experienced. I felt my fist clench around the material of Gyllian's shirt again. I had to stay calm. I had to, or I would lose this.

The shaking lasted only about fifteen seconds before it abruptly stopped. My mom took her hands off her ears and sat up, gazing around in confusion. Suddenly the sounds of people screaming came from outside the two cracked-open windows of the apartment, and I pulled Gyllian over to look. My mom obviously heard it, too, since her attention was drawn there.

The woman on the other end of the phone was screaming over the receiver. "Megan! Megan! I'm calling the police! Pick up the phone! Megan!"

My mom looked like she was about to grab the phone back when a bright white light suddenly appeared in the sky. My eyes went wide and my heart started racing when I realized what I was about to see—my dad's fall. I clapped my hand over my mouth and looked up at Gyllian, astonished, only to find him already looking down at me with a gentle smile and deep tenderness in his eyes. He was letting me see my father's fall since it wasn't on the video tape.

I tried to find the right words but came up empty except for a whispered, "Thank you."

"You're welcome."

Behind me, I heard my mom pick up the receiver. "I have to call you back," she said before she appeared beside me and Gyllian. An enormous spot of golden white shimmering light hovered right over Central Park. It *was* New York City.

"Dad," I whispered.

The light stayed steady and calm, giving people ample

time to start to gather in the streets and gawk. Folks stopped their cars in the middle of the road, many stepping out to look. Some rational part of my brain hoped first responders were clearing Central Park right now. People were idiots, though, too busy rubbernecking to get the hell out of the way.

Suddenly the light started getting brighter. My dad was falling. Right now, right this moment, he was falling from Heaven. People below gasped and cringed against the person closest to them as if it would somehow keep them safer. My mom glanced behind her at the television, which drew my attention as well. The other four lights all over the world were also getting brighter. I put my attention back on my dad's light spectacle and watched, wondering what could have been going through his mind as he was falling. Was he in pain? Was he afraid? Did Angels feel any of that at all? The city below was heavily silent and incredibly still, as if it were holding its collective breath, waiting.

Suddenly someone screamed, and in a flash of light that seemed to fill the entire world, a massive ball of white fire came down from the sky and slammed into the park with unbelievable force.

The wave of the aftershock distorted the air, which rippled like a pond when a stone is thrown in. My heart seized in fear for my mother as they approached, but I only had enough time to take in one breath before glass exploded all around me. I ducked on reflex, though nothing touched me, and watched, half in panic and half in horror, as my mom was thrown fifteen feet away from the windows.

"Mom!" I screamed and tried to run to her again, but Gyllian yanked me back.

"Bay, stop! She's okay."

My mom landed hard on her back behind the couch with her eyes closed. I was shaking so badly I thought I would shake completely apart. But her eyes opened and she sat up, looking around, trying to figure out what had just happened. When she stood, pieces of glass tinkled to the floor from her hair and clothes. Her arms were a little cut up, but overall, she was all right. She half-walked, half-stumbled back to her now-busted windows and looked out. Up and down the street, every window of every building was blown out. Car windows were blown out, too, and some cars were even flipped over on their sides. People were either picking themselves up off the ground or already running. I shifted my gaze to Central Park and saw the orange glow of a fire at the impact site. Sirens and horns of emergency vehicles were already blaring.

"Shit," both my mom and I said when people started to stampede in all directions, including into her apartment building.

My mom ran to her front door and quickly locked the chain and two deadbolts. She even went so far as to push a large oak wood desk in front of it. Then she reached into the top drawer and grabbed out a revolver, aiming it at the front door. I found myself wondering why my mother, a nurse, had a gun in the first place. A moment later, banging began on her door, becoming so hard that it bowed inward. Her gun went up, and her stance went stiff and still. I smiled. My mom was a little bit of a badass.

Suddenly I felt the sensation of wind pulling at me again. "Gyllian wait!" I cried. He couldn't be taking me back now! "What are you doing?"

"Nothing else happens tonight," he replied as I looked up into his Angelic eyes and the dim spotlight appeared above us again. "I'm just moving forward to the morning."

I looked back at my mom as natural light returned. She had sunk to the floor and fallen asleep against a wall facing the door. A soft knock jolted her awake. Her eyes went wide, and she clumsily scrambled to her feet aiming her gun again, though she was clearly still drowsy. The street was surprisingly quiet. The soft knock came again.

I knew who was at the door and my heart was racing. My hand found its way into Gyllian's. I interlaced my fingers with his, and then pulled him toward the door to get a better view.

My mom slid the desk out of the way and put her gun behind the wood as she slowly cracked it open with the chain still on. She was so short that when it opened I could see over her shoulder, and my eyes went wide. There he was. My father.

He was the most unnaturally beautiful man I'd ever seen. He was at least 6'6" with shiny tousled blonde curls, an elegant but strong square jaw, and eyes that looked like Apollo blue diamonds. The only thing marring his perfection was the fact that he was filthy and sweaty.

"Dad," I nearly choked as I looked at him.

"Hello," he panted in a voice that was deep but soothing. "I'm so sorry to bother you, but…" He looked down, and only then did I realize he was clutching his stomach. I dragged Gyllian closer to the door to look over my mother's shoulder, and saw a pool of blood where my dad had been gouged by what looked like rock debris. "I was wondering if you could help me."

My mom slammed the door closed and took the chain off before quickly opening it again and helping him inside. I watched them pass me with wide eyes. These were my parents. My mother and my father. And my dad was an Angel, a real live Angel.

"Thank you. Thank you so much," he panted as my mom silently guided him to the couch. With a few grunts and heavy breaths, he lay down in obvious pain.

"Stay here," my mom said.

He smiled a smile that seemed to physically stab me in the stomach from its beauty. "I'm not going anywhere."

My hand came up to my mouth as I stared at him while my mom left the room. There was an incredible warmth and softness about him, like the whisper of an innocent child that made your heart melt no matter what they said. I stood there for a moment and just stared at him, my father. *My father.*

My mom eventually returned with a heavy-duty first-aid kit. She knelt on the floor in front of the couch and started to cut off his white t-shirt with a pair of scissors. Every part of her was trembling except her hands. She had a surgeon's hands, steady.

"What is your name?" my dad asked in a gentle voice.

It took my mom a moment to answer. "Megan. You?"

"Michael."

My hands came up to my cheeks as tears filled my eyes while I watched my parents interacting with each other. It was a good thing Gyllian still had an arm wrapped around me, or I would have lost this.

My mom peeled my dad's shirt away and I focused my

attention on his wound. It wasn't as bad as I'd initially thought. She took a few minutes to clean it and examine it closely. "There's no debris left I can see, but only an x-ray will determine that for sure," my mom said professionally. "The hospitals are certain to be overwhelmed right now, though, and this is a wound I can fix well enough on my own if you're okay with that."

My dad nodded once. "That's fine."

My mom grabbed a suture needle and thread from the first aid kit. "I don't have a numbing agent. This will hurt," she warned.

"It's okay," he replied.

My mom nodded and got to work. I watched in awe and curiosity as she mended him. I'd sewn a leather jacket once, badly, and that jacket complained more than my father did. He didn't even flinch when my mom started sewing him up with no antiseptic to numb him.

A long heavy silence passed before my dad spoke again. "You don't talk very much."

My mom glanced up into his smiling eyes, and I saw her blush a little before she went back to her work. "Not when I'm concentrating."

My dad stayed quiet the rest of the time she worked on him.

"That should do it," she said about ten minutes later. "But you still need to go to a hospital. You might need surgery if there is any debris left inside the cut."

"Thank you," he said as he sat up.

He then gently took a hold of her arm and their gaze met. My hands came up to cover my mouth as I watched desire erupt in both of their eyes, and my mom leaned in to kiss him.

He didn't rape her. My father did *not* rape my mother!

At that moment, everything faded to black except for the dim spotlight above me and Gyllian. I bowed my head into my hands and started sobbing. If there was a higher being in the world, I thanked him or her for that little bit of mercy, the knowledge that I had not been conceived by the violent act of rape. I was not a product of the same vile sexual crimes that had defined my childhood.

9

Gyllian gave me a little squeeze around my ribs and a rub up and down my sides, which prodded me to look up again. We were back in his house. It took me a moment to compose myself. I wiped my cheeks and looked around at the other four people in the room. I saw them, for the first time, in their true light. They were the children of *Angels*. Finally, it seemed to sink in that *I* was the child of an Angel, too.

I looked up at Gyllian. "Can I…I mean, is there some place I can go to…learn. To find out…about…more?"

Gyllian nodded. "Follow me," he said, and started out of the living room.

I gave a weak nod to the other three as they all looked after me with compassion and deep affection. Gyllian crossed the bottom of the stairs, and a strange thought popped into my head. "Hey Gyllian, I thought your time abilities were only good for a few seconds."

"I was granted more time for that," he replied without looking back at me.

"By who?"

He paused outside of a closed door and faced me. "By the person who granted us these abilities, and allows us to use them."

"You have a boss? Who?"

He gave me a small smile. "It's way too soon for you to know that."

I narrowed my eyes and was close to arguing with him, but I didn't want to sully what he'd just done for me. I was too grateful to him for that, so I kept quiet.

He opened the door and reached in to throw a switch. The lights came on to reveal a magnificent library with tall, shiny, dark brown bookshelves on three walls. On the far right was a small alcove of four windows that went from floor to ceiling with luxurious tan and gold curtains. The curtains were all open, allowing a split view of the trees and lawn on

100

the side of the house. Inside the alcove was a decorative heavy wooden table with legs carved into griffons and two chairs. A light wood floor peeked out from between two brown-and-cream, expensive looking area carpets. In the center, a plush couch and loveseat faced each other, both cream colored with dark brown trim, with the back of the couch facing the door. A shiny dark wooden coffee table that matched the shelves sat between them.

Gyllian walked to the shelves on the left. "Everything Angel and Demon related is here." He faced me and nodded. "I'll leave you to it," he said a little dismissively and left.

Staring at the book spines, I wasn't even certain what I was looking for. What did I really want to know about in this unbelievable situation? I had too many questions, but I needed to start with one. What did I want to know the most? I wanted to know about my dad. I looked at the books at eye level for anything mentioning Michael or Angels. All of them looked ancient, which was good. I doubted I would trust any modern sources claiming to know anything about Angels. Most of the books lacked an author's name, and any author who was identified was obscure. Without authors, how the hell did Gyllian even know these books existed, never mind where to find them?

A rolling ladder went all around the library. After positioning it, I finally found a few topics on Angels on the top shelf and grabbed them. I brought them to the coffee table between the couch and love seat and then went back for more. Running my finger down one line, I saw an incredibly old looking book simply titled *The Archangels. Volume I: Michael*. I snatched it from the shelf and started reading it as I made my way down the ladder.

Time was soon lost to me as I read about the ancient Heavenly battles my father had commanded and led—from the formation of creation, to casting out of Lucifer, to the battles for humanity. Many that I was familiar with in the Bible, like the battle at Jericho, were all written in epic detail. More so, they were written from an Angel's perspective, as if my father had written the book himself. Maybe he had. I was prepared to believe anything at this point. One thing was certain—my father was an incredible warrior.

I found the books on the other Archangels, too—Gabriel, Raphael, Uriel, and Jophiel. They all had their own separate volumes. All of them had unique roles in Heaven, gifts, accomplishments, responsibilities, and interactions with humanity. My dad seemed to have the least interaction with humanity of all five of the Archangels. He was too busy commanding Heaven. His social skills must have sucked when he fell to Earth. I couldn't help wondering how long my father had stayed with my mother after I was conceived. I got a small chuckle when I pictured them trying to date. There was no way to tell if that had even happened, though. My father could have left the same day he met her. He could have been *killed* the same day he met her for all I knew. From what I'd read about him, though, I probably would have cut off my own arm to get to know him, to talk to him, to spend time with him.

Days passed. I wasn't certain how many, as I was too absorbed in everything I was reading. At one point, I was curled up on the couch with a book on the Archangel Gabriel, Gyllian's father, when I heard the library door open. Looking behind me, I saw Gyllian come walking in. His hair was disheveled, and he was in a pair of dark pajama pants with a gray t-shirt, looking like he'd just woken up. Only then did I realize it was night—and it certainly wasn't the same night I'd first come into the library.

"You've been in here for three days."

"Oh. I'm sorry," I said.

The moonlight reflected off his skin as he passed in front of the large windows to sit on the loveseat across from me.

"You don't have to apologize to me," he said with a shrug. "The others were worried about you."

I looked back at my book. "And I suppose you weren't."

"I knew you were fine." I glanced at him over the top of the book. He wasn't even looking at me, but instead gazing out the windows. "Have you slept at all?"

I shook my head, looking back at the pages. "I rarely sleep. Only once a week, and I'm hardly ever tired." I couldn't help glancing up at him again.

"It's probably your endurance ability."

I shrugged. "Maybe," I said, looking back at my book.

It got quiet. I let it stretch a bit, hoping he would break the silence, until I couldn't stand it anymore. I looked up at him once more, only to find him already staring at me. "Are you staying?" he asked.

"Staying?"

"Here. Are you moving in? With us?"

I rested the book against my chest and sat up. "I don't know," I replied. "This is your house."

"You're safe here, and if we get any leads on where Hell might rise, we can respond quickly as a team."

I felt my mouth start working nervously, my abuse at the hands of humanity never far from my mind. I shook my head as I sat back and looked at my book. "I'm not quite ready to commit to this mission of yours yet."

I glanced up in time to see his brows drop. "Why not?"

I shook my head and avoided eye contact with him by looking at the pages. I didn't want to say anything because I knew it would piss him off, but at the same time, he needed to know where I stood. "Maybe it's time the world ended."

When I glanced up at him, he was glaring at me. I could see his temper boiling behind his eyes, but he carefully reigned it in. "If that were the case," he said, thin-lipped, "then we never would have been born."

I looked back at my book, hoping that would be the end of it. I wasn't in the mood to have him try to convince me otherwise, but then I heard him take a deep breath.

"Let me tell you something about these Angels and Demons you seem keen on siding with," he said. I rested the book against my chest and sighed. "*They* could be responsible for the abuse in our lives."

My eyes narrowed in confusion and I shook my head. "Why?"

"Because we are the only ones who can stop them." His eyes were hard. "If they found us when we were young, maybe when our parents were killed, why *wouldn't* they try to break, hurt, and destroy us? Why *wouldn't* they try to turn us against the humans by having us suffer at the hands of humanity?"

My mouth went dry as I realized the possibility actually held some merit.

"Why do you think our Angelic parents were killed?" he went on. "Why do you think the Demons and Angels were hunting them down? Why do you think we lost them so young? So our parents, the ones who sacrificed everything to save humanity, wouldn't get the chance to teach us to love humanity. So they could never raise us to be kind, and gracious, and forgiving of humanity. You never even *knew* your father because he was priority number *one* on everyone's hit list!" Seeming to realize he was yelling, Gyllian lowered his voice a little. "The Angels and Demons wanted to make sure that he never got a chance to teach you, the most powerful one of us, to love people."

I was trying to keep it together, but this was one hell of a grand design he was pitching. I didn't like to be singled out anywhere, and now he was telling me that Angels and Demons had orchestrated my entire childhood to bend me to their purposes? That I was not only central to the Earth, but Heaven and Hell, too? It was insane!

"The Angels and Demons needed to make sure you never even *wanted* to save humanity, so they turned you over to the worst of it," he said in a low voice. "*All* of us were subject to the worst of humanity, to insure our hatred of people, to insure our lack of conviction in trying to save them. That way, the Angels and Demons could raise Hell and wipe them out without any opposition."

I found myself in a staring contest with him as I absorbed what he'd just said.

He eventually stood from the loveseat, his eyes never leaving my face. "Think about it." Then he left the library without another word.

My gaze shifted to the windows, and my fingers drummed against the back cover of the book. Even though I desperately wanted to dismiss the possibly, I found myself mulling it over. It made too much sense to deny, and an odd sense of betrayal came over me. Putting a child through the trauma I'd been through made sense for Demons. But Angels? They really had gone dark. I shook my head and eventually went back to my book to continue reading about Gabriel, a good Angel.

My studies eventually turned to Demons, a far vaster

topic it turned out, than Angels. Again, I wasn't sure how many days passed, but my guess was another three or four because I started to get tired. It had been a week since the last time my head hit a pillow, and that had been after Shia drugged me. I finally reached the point at which I couldn't stay awake and curled up right on the couch in the library and fell asleep.

When I awoke, I was covered with a blanket, and a tray of food was sitting on the coffee table. Only then did I realize I hadn't eaten. Weird. I wasn't starving. I sat up, wrapped the blanket around my shoulders, and ate the soup and sandwich anyway. The soup was still lukewarm, so someone had dropped it off within the hour.

As soon as I finished, I picked up the book on Demon possession I'd been reading and curled up again to continue.

"All right!" I suddenly heard from the doorway.

I looked over my shoulder and saw Roy coming in. He was dressed in his bartender best, with his shaggy brown hair freshly clean and a bright smile on his face. He came around and sat on top of the coffee table, delicately pinched the book out of my hands, and set it aside.

"It's been eight days," he said. "I'm officially ordering you to take a study break."

I smiled as he took my hands and pulled me to my feet. Not letting go, he started walking backwards out of the library, towing me along, and I started laughing.

"You're taking a shower and coming to work tonight. I'm not doing another shift without you because we got slammed yesterday. Plus, you need to get out of the house, like, now!" I giggled as he towed me into the luxurious master bathroom across the way and gave me a little push into the door. "Fox is picking out some clothes for you, so let's go." He clapped his hands twice. "Chop, chop!"

I was still chuckling as I showered up. Heading to the club tonight would be better, now that I was more prepared about what they were dealing with. Plus, I really did need to get out of the house.

10

"You seriously know your way around a bar, huh?" Roy said over the noise of the music and crowd as he passed behind me with a tray full of empty mugs he was taking to the tap.

"Yeah well, I had to pay for college somehow," I responded as I lifted a tray of a dozen full shot glasses, plus one shot glass of water, up onto my shoulder and headed down to the opposite side of the bar. Six ritzy pretty boys sat down that way. I set the tray down and passed out the glasses, making sure to lean over more than necessary, allowing them a nice glimpse down the front of the black halter top Fox let me borrow.

"You know," one of the boys said, looking at me lopsided.

Here we go, I thought to myself with a mental sigh.

"If I get wasted tonight, I'm blaming you."

Luckily, I had years of practice reigning in my patience with these entitled little shits. "Oh yeah?" I responded, leaning heavily over the bar, giving him another nice long look down my shirt. "How are you gonna blame me? You're the one that can't hold your liquor." The group erupted in loud "Ohhhhh's!" and dissing sounds toward their friend. I smiled at the boy and threw back my water shot before heading to the middle of the bar.

Two shady-looking businessmen sat there together, talking in hushed voices. Both of them had expensive suits and haircuts. Roy and I had stuck relatively close to them without being invasive, keeping their drinks flowing and eavesdropping when we could. I'd caught a few sound bites that, to my ears, seemed like a serious nuclear weapon exchange being orchestrated.

I took a bar rag from under the counter and began to wipe down the empty place beside them. As I did, I glanced up at Gyllian, who stood on the private balcony looking out over the activity of the club. He seemed as intently focused on the two men at the bar as Roy and I had been. He was also keeping his eye on a large group of about twenty-five high-level street gang types sitting in the VIP area. Some of them I knew from a few interrogations I'd conducted on possible sex trafficking circles. Four of them I had arrested numerous times. One of them I'd put in the hospital with a broken eye socket when he'd made a grab for me in the elevator after we were forced to release him. Gyllian also had his eye on a woman in a long black evening gown sitting by herself at a table next to the main stage. She was staring up at him with unwavering and unblinking eyes. I didn't like the way she was looking at him. I liked even less the way Gyllian slightly fidgeted when his gazed passed over her. It was subtle to the untrained eye, but I could see it; he was nervous.

"Hey sweetheart," I heard next to me. I looked and saw one of the two businessmen addressing me with a smirk. He glanced at the bar rag in my hand. "If you want to polish something so badly, how about I take you out back to shine my cock?"

Memories of my past flooded my brain. That, coupled with feeling helpless that I couldn't arrest this motherfucker because I wasn't an agent anymore, made something snap. My fist shot forward, and I cracked him so hard in the jaw he flew ten feet backward from the bar.

Simultaneously, a flash of burning pain erupted in the middle of my chest and I screamed in pain! New tattoos never felt like this! It was usually a brief flash of heat and then nothing. This burning lingered like I was being branded! I wanted to clutch my chest but was afraid my hand would catch fire. Instead, I gripped the edge of the counter so hard my arms trembled and my knuckles turned white.

Roy was suddenly by my side, grabbing at me and asking what was wrong. I barely heard him over my own screams.

When the burn finally subsided, I felt the same stillness of the entire world that I'd felt at the coffee shop when Gyllian stopped time. Opening my eyes, I realized time hadn't stopped, though, and the sight made me gasp and stupidly cower against Roy. The club was silent, but everyone and everything was a slight blur as they moved backwards before my eyes! Waitresses walked in creepy, jerky, backwards movements from table to table. Liquid from glasses seemed to float up like it was being sucked back into their respective containers. I clutched Roy's shirt in a trembling fist as I watched.

"It's okay. It's okay," Roy said, holding me protectively against him. "Gyllian is just rewinding time."

"Wh... Why?"

I looked up at his face and found he had a playful smirk on his lips, though his eyes betrayed his concern. "We can't have you knocking out our biggest customers, Bay. We need their intel."

I looked back at the bar and saw the business man I had punched suddenly float upwards from the floor and then forward. His bar stool straightened on its own, and he was magically placed back on top of it...but he didn't look the same!

I gasped and stumbled away from Roy hitting the back counter.

"Whoa! Hey, hey!" Roy said. "What's wrong?"

I was trembling so violently I had to grip the counter behind me to try to hold myself still. The business man had no eyes, just fiery orange light where his eyeballs should be. All his veins were lit up with the same kind of orange light, like he had fire for blood, and I knew exactly what I was looking at. It was a King Demon!

"Bay!" Roy cried. "Why are your eyes silver? What's wrong?"

I couldn't look away from the blurry crowd, and I stopped breathing, because the entire club was riddled with Demons! I could see them! I could see all of them through their human disguises!

"Bay!" Roy cried, taking my face in his hands. "Gyllian's almost done! You have to get it together!"

I shook my head and ran to the stockroom. Standing inside, I was shaking so badly I held on to a supply rack to keep still. A low hissing sound, like a gentle wind tunnel, came from inside the club, and suddenly the racket of music and voices filled my ears again as everything went back to normal. I couldn't turn around to look. I couldn't even move.

Realizing my chest was still warm, I looked down and saw the new tattoo right in the middle of it, just above my breasts. From upside down, it looked like a large eye with detailed flames surrounding it and a teardrop about to fall from the corner of the bottom lid. A new ability. A new ability that let me see Demons through their human disguises.

I stumbled to an empty section of the wall and pressed my back against it, then slid down to the floor, tucking my knees under my chin. Shaking, I stared at the wall across from me, afraid that if I moved my eyes I would see the fiery-veined Demon sitting at the bar.

Fox suddenly turned the corner of the stockroom. She was dressed in a purple and white satin two-piece costume and a white robe she hadn't bothered to fully close. "Bay! Bay what's wrong?" She asked, dropping to her knees in front of me.

I couldn't answer her. I was paralyzed, completely afraid that thing would hear me, as if its fiery eyes were watching me, demanding my silence from a place I couldn't see.

Fox got to her feet quickly and went to the fridge. She grabbed something out and rushed back to me, pressing a cold bottle of water against my cheek. "What is it, sweetheart? What's wrong?"

I snatched her wrists, making her jump and gasp in surprise. I needed to feel her in my grip, an Angel, something that claimed to be able to fight Demons, and forced the words past the fear of my sealed lips. "I can see the Demons that are disguised as humans."

Fox's eyes went wide. "What?"

I released her and pointed to my new tattoo. "Every level of Demon is in that club right now, mostly Queens, and there are over a hundred of them."

Fox's jaw dropped just as Roy came rushing in. "Bay, I need you out here. I'm dying!" Fox looked over at him. One look at her and Roy's expression melted into horror as he quickly came to crouch beside us. "What is it?"

"She has a new ability," Fox said, "and we have a big problem."

"What? What do you mean?" Roy rested his hand on my shoulder, looking between us both.

Fox gently pulled the edge of my shirt aside, revealing my eye tattoo, and told him. Roy's usually confident, unwavering expression gave way to alarm, which was enough to send a spike of fear shooting through my gut again.

"Shit," he said.

We were frozen a moment, just looking at each other, and I felt truly and properly afraid for the first time in a long time. If they looked scared, that was bad news, and I knew it.

"Hey kid! Where's my damn scotch!" someone yelled from the bar.

Roy glanced over his shoulder. "All right, listen to me. This ability is probably like most of the others—you can turn it off. Do it, and let's get through the rest of the night. We'll figure it out at home when we can talk to Gyllian."

"We have inventory tonight," Fox said.

Roy wiped his forehead with his fingertips. "Shit, that's right. Gyllian has to leave first." He gently took my shoulders in his hands and met my eyes. "We should be out of here by dawn. We can talk to him as soon as we get home." He stunned me by leaning in and firmly kissing my forehead. "It will be okay." With a sweet, reassuring smile, he left the stockroom to get back to work.

Fox gathered my hands into hers, brought them up to her lips, and kissed them before helping me to my feet. "He's right. It's going to be okay, sweetie." She gently moved a piece of hair away from my face and tucked it behind my ear. "We're all here, and we've got your back."

I nodded, though I wasn't fully convinced of that. I'd only known them for two weeks. For nearly half that time I'd been unconscious from Shia's venom, and during the other half I'd been alone in a library. How could I know they had my back?

Fox squeezed my hands before she left the stockroom.

I took a few deep breaths and then slowly made my way out to the bar again. Pausing in the doorway, I caught a terrifying glimpse of a Pawn Demon at the end of the bar beside me. Black, bulging eyes and black drool dripping down its gray cracked lips and white chin. My eyes went to the floor instantly and I turned the ability off. My heart sank down into my toes from relief when my chest cooled. I looked back at the Pawn and saw it was an attractive blonde man with blue eyes, wearing jeans and a beige sweater.

"Hey honey, how about another Jack and Coke? Only"—he glanced down at my chest and leaned heavily over his elbows on top of the bar— "why don't you join me for this round?"

I walked away without a response. Oh man, I was not going to be able to get my flirt on after what I just saw. I doubted I would have any interpersonal prowess whatsoever for the rest of the night. My tips were going to suck.

11

Gyllian stood facing the wall next to the windows with his head bowed so low, the top of his head rested against the plaster. "How could there be a hundred Demons in the club?"

"Really?" I asked. "You're actually surprised this many Demons have gotten so many human souls to stay topside? The world is evil, Gyllian. People are evil."

"We get it, Bay!" Gyllian yelled, spinning on me. "You hate humanity! We hear you! It's not like you haven't made that crystal fucking clear enough since you got here!"

My eyes went wide. Emotion from Gyllian. It was oddly good to see because, for once, he was being real with me. He wasn't hiding behind that stuck-up wall of indifference.

"Don't be pissed at me because I was right!" I cried. "Have you even considered that those are just the Demons in the club? Never mind the rest of the world!"

"You don't get it, Bay!" He cried. "You don't get anything, not yet. That many Demons on Earth *shouldn't* be happening so soon. Not without us knowing!"

I crossed my arms. "I thought you didn't know when Hell was going to rise."

"We don't."

"Then how do you know it's 'too soon' for this many Demons to be topside?"

"For a lot of reasons, one of them being because of the research we've done over the past ten years, and continue to do." We glared at each other briefly before he turned and addressed the rest of the group. He sighed and rested his back against the wall with his hands in his pockets. "Hell has apparently gotten a bigger jump on inflating their ranks than we thought. But why wasn't I warned?"

I felt my eyebrow cock up. Warned? By who? I hated their reactions to what I'd seen last night. Something unexpected had occurred, and they weren't doing well with it.

After a quiet moment, Booth shrugged. "Look at who

your source is."

Gyllian looked at him, surprised, before shooting me a nervous glance that made my eyes narrow. I glanced at Roy who looked confused. As did Fox.

Secrets? Oh, hell no!

"You need to cut this shit out right *now*, Gyllian." He shifted his eyes coldly to me. "You want me to trust you? You want me to go into battle with you? Don't keep secrets from me." My eyes became slits as I silently dared him to challenge me on that. "What 'source' is Booth talking about?"

"Bay, it's not –"

"If you don't tell me, I walk." His eyes softened slightly, and I shook my head. "I don't extend trust easily as it is, but I certainly don't extend it to people who deliberately keep secrets from me." We stared at each other for a moment. I could see he was wrestling with this. "What source?" I asked in two short bursts.

"It's a Demon," he said finally. "A Knight, if you really want to know."

My eyes went wide. "Yeah. Because getting help from a lying, conniving piece of shit Demon makes *perfect* sense."

"Believe me, if I had any other choice, I would take it."

"An Angel, maybe?" I suggested with a jerky shrug.

"Why? Because Angels are *so* much more trustworthy?"

"So trust a *Demon?* Are you kidding me?"

"Angels are about *a thousand* times more powerful than Demons. Hell yes, I'd rather deal with a Demon!"

"But if you can find a Demon willing to help you, there's got to be an Angel. No side of war is free of spies."

Something dawned on me then, and my heart felt like it might burst out of my chest. "Your scars," I breathed, and Gyllian's eyes went wide. "Your scars," I said again, searching his eyes. "You're letting that Demon torture you in exchange for the information she has, aren't you?"

Gyllian stared at me, astonished. "How do you know that?"

I realized the outside of my left arm was warm, and I searched his eyes, suddenly able to see the depths of them. I took his face in my hands as images flooded my brain that I could only voice in fast, almost incoherent whispers; "With fire whips, and spiked bats, and razors, and…for years." Some sort of image of time passing flashed through my mind. "Ten years. You've been…with this Demon. Ten years. Hurting you. Burning you. Cutting you. Bleeding you. Suffering."

Gyllian gripped my wrists and pulled his face out of my hands. He stared at me with wide eyes.

"Are you crazy?" I whispered. All I could see was what that Demon had done to him. It ran like a vial video loop in my mind, things I couldn't believe, things the worst of human imagination hadn't conjured in any horror movie, show, or book.

"What did you just do?" he asked, still holding my wrists.

I shook my head a little, not sure myself. The images had just come, unbidden, and *certainly* unwanted. My soul felt sick. I felt like I could throw up blood forever and never get rid of the stain those images left me with.

Fox came next to me, gazing at the spot on my shoulder that had gotten warm. "It's a truth ability," she said and looked at Gyllian angrily. "It extracts the truth from its target in the form of images in Bay's mind."

Looking down, I realized it was my tattoo of a very detailed hand holding a lightning bolt with wings. It was the tattoo that had appeared when I was six and was getting ready to report my first foster father for sexually assaulting me.

"Bay didn't activate it," Fox said in a tight voice. "So clearly she needed to know about this."

"I think we all did," Roy said, his voice shaking. All of us looked at him as he glared at Gyllian. "Why didn't you tell us?" he asked, taking a step forward. "Why is Booth the only one who knows?" Everyone looked at Booth, who stood there impassively, waiting for Gyllian to explain.

Gyllian sighed. "He bandages my wounds." Roy looked enraged. "There are special herbs he knows about, which are the only thing that help the pain."

Roy took another step, looking ready to explode. "I could have healed you!"

"They were Hell wounds, Roy," Gyllian fired back, "inflicted by an undiluted Demon." He shook his head. "You can't heal wounds that pure."

"You went to *Hell* to be tortured?"

Gyllian sighed again. "It's where she takes me when we meet."

Roy was staring at him with a murderous look. Suddenly, standing before me, was the Russian underground fighter. "You found me *first* Gyllian!" he yelled. "And you didn't have the sack to tell me you were dealing with a *Demon?*" Roy's eyes went Angelic, then his fist shot out, striking Gyllian so hard in the face blood splashed the wall behind him before his head nearly went through it. "I've been with you eight years!" Roy screamed. "Eight years!"

Gyllian looked back at him, blood pouring from his mouth onto the floor. "What do you want me to say?"

Roy eyes faded back to brown and he shook his head, "Nothing." He turned and left the living room. A moment later I heard the motorized lift of the floor opening to the bunker, but it didn't close.

After a last glance at Gyllian, I followed Roy.

I headed down the stairs and into the hallway with the apartments. I noticed the round door labeled with a "3" was open and went to it.

"Sorry about that," Roy said as soon as I stepped into his room.

I looked around, stunned. This room was very different from mine! There was wall-to-wall light green carpet. The left wall was the same color green, but it had gorgeous light-colored wood that formed a bunch of small, short shelves up the whole wall. Each shelf held abstract pieces of metal artwork, or a picture frame, or an empty decorative vase. The other three walls were smooth steel gray with some decorative oil lamps lighting it up. The king-size bed had a rich red wood frame and matching headboard that spanned wider than the sides of the bed, each end serving as a night stand. This room was actually homey and inviting, not a brick wall dungeon like mine.

"I'm not able to lie," Roy said as I made my way slowly toward him. "I probably would have handled that better if I could." He was sitting on the floor against the decorative shelves with his knees up and his elbows resting on top of them.

115

I sat down next to him, still looking around his lovely room. "Nothing wrong with a little honesty."

"No, I mean it's one of my abilities," Roy said. "One I can't turn off, like you can't turn off your endurance."

I looked at him. "Oh. Sorry to hear that." My brows dropped. "Wait. How do you covertly hunt Angels and Demons if you can't lie?"

He smiled gently. "I'm a master evader. Or I just stay silent. Or I set up circumstances, even fake ones, in a way that makes them true to me."

I grinned and looked around his room again. I let the envy surface playfully in hopes of lightening the mood a little. "How come I get a dungeon for a room, and you have this?"

Roy chuckled, "Because you haven't decorated yours yet."

My face lit up, "Can I do that?"

"Of course you can. Just tell Gyllian what you want and he'll make it happen."

I hummed thoughtfully and found myself thinking about colors and how I might want to decorate my room. I wasn't sure if I should be upset thinking about decorating a room that was only supposed to be used if the apocalypse happened. Plus, I still wasn't sure I was staying. I shook off my Martha Stuart mentality and put my focus back on the issue.

"Roy, do you think there are any Angels that can help us? At all? I mean, if Gyllian can find a damn Demon, there's got to be at least one Angel."

Roy shook his head. "Gyllian tried. I know for a fact he did, just because I know Gyllian. He would never turn to a Demon for help unless he absolutely had to, or…" Roy paused and sighed before looking away from me.

"What?"

He looked back reluctantly. "Or he was told to."

I squinted. "Told to? By who?"

He ran a hand through his hair and sighed. "Look, I'm not sure I should be telling you this."

"Roy," I said in warning tone. "Don't be Gyllian and keep secrets."

He shook his head. "It's not that at all. I'm just not sure it's time for you to know. I think it's too soon."

I chewed the inside of my bottom lip as I stared at the opposite wall. "Fine," I said. "Same offer stands. You either tell me who you're getting your orders from, or I walk." I looked back at him as he pressed his lips together, looking worried. "This intel you all think is too soon for me to understand, I want to know, now. Like how Gyllian knows it's 'too early' for so many Demons to be topside. Or what 'granted' him the ability to use his time manipulation longer than the designated thirty-five seconds. Or whoever might have sent him behind enemy lines to be tortured for intel."

"I don't know if Gyllian was sent to that Demon or if he went on his own. I just—"

"I don't care," I snapped. "Who do you answer to? Tell me, or I'm out of here, Roy."

Roy pressed his lips together again and sighed. "God."

I stared at him, and for a split second I thought he was joking. But his eyes clearly told me he wasn't. I pinched the corners of my eyes as my world was suddenly set ablaze with such rage that I wasn't sure I was going to be able to contain it. I'd never believed God was real. Never wanted to, never had a reason to. Now, Roy was telling me he was. A complete and utter sense of abandonment came over me because the question now had to be asked: If God was real, then what the fuck had I done to earn such loathing from him that he would subject me to the abuse and pain I grew up with?

I sniffed and stared down at his carpet. "Are you trying to tell me God is real?"

"I'm not *trying* to tell you anything," he said gently.

I didn't answer him. I didn't dare because I feared I would start screaming.

"Come on, Bay," he said after a moment. "You're going to believe in Angels and Demons and Lucifer, but not God?"

I quickly got to my feet and walked a few paces away.

"Every war effort has a General," Roy went on. "God is ours. He gave us our abilities. He also determines how we use them. If you didn't activate your truth ability upstairs to see"—Roy's voice broke, and he had to clear his throat— "to see what Gyllian had been through, then God did. He let Gyllian keep his time manipulation activated long past when it was supposed to expire. If an ability of ours doesn't activate, then God is stopping it. He is in charge. Not us."

That was a huge fucking pill to swallow. I crossed my arms over my chest. Hearing this, it was almost like I could feel God's eyes on me suddenly, like I was being physically touched by them. Amid my distain toward such a being, I felt dirty. If God was real, then he knew what I had done in my life, and what had been done to me. What the fuck was he looking at when he saw me?

It also begged the question, if God was real, then what was he doing letting his Angels team up with Demons to kill off humanity? And if God wanted to kill off humanity, why let his Archangels fall to Earth and create the five of us to stop it? It didn't make sense, so neither did God. He couldn't be real.

"Don't try to figure out God, Bay," Roy said behind me. "No one can. We're just supposed to trust him."

"Bullshit," I barked and faced him. "If he's real, he'll get my trust when he fucking earns it."

I expected Roy to argue or give me the useless, "but God really does love you if you believe" speech. Most Bible thumpers did. But he just looked at me with gentle sympathy and compassion and nodded his head. I put my back to him once more and shook off the burden of God. If he was real, that was Gyllian's bag to deal with, not mine. God was none of my business, and I was none of his. I had enough shit on my plate.

I ran my fingers through my hair, pulling it over my shoulder, and faced Roy again. "I think we need to try to find an Angel. They may be dicks, but they're not known for getting their jollies by torturing humans like Demons are. Maybe we can at least get some information you need."

Roy came to stand in front of me. "I think it's worth a try."

I nodded. "Do you think Gyllian had any leads when he first went looking for an Angel to help? You know, before he settled for a Demon."

"He might have. Let's go talk to him."

My brow cocked up. "You okay to talk to him? You sort of just cleaned his clock."

Roy smiled brightly. "Guys get over things quick.

118

Besides, punching each other is how we show love." I chuckled. "Gyllian can take a hit anyway. He'll be fine."

I nodded. "All right."

Roy and I went back upstairs and headed for the living room to find Booth and Fox alone and looking pained. "Where's Gyllian?" I asked with some caution. Their expressions told me I wouldn't like the answer.

"We think he went to see the Demon," Booth said.

My eyes went wide. "He what?" Roy and I said at the same time.

"We couldn't stop him," Fox said with tears in her eyes.

My heart started racing and I had to resist the urge to punch the wall. "What the fuck happened?"

"We don't know," Fox whispered.

"What do you mean? He didn't just disappear!"

"Actually, that is exactly what he did," Booth said. "He told us he was going into the bathroom to clean up. When he took a bit longer than expected, we went to check on him and he was gone."

My worry for Gyllian went through the roof. I couldn't panic. I needed to think. Think! I needed to get him back. I couldn't, I *wouldn't* allow him to suffer *one more time* at the hands of that Demon! Not after the images I'd seen in my head. I forced down my fear for him, like I'd done a thousand times in my career when I knew I was close to rescuing a victim. Gyllian was the victim now and I needed to focus. *He* needed me to focus.

My memory began pouring over what I'd studied in the library. Like a set of flash cards, the information flicked through my mind's eye, but I saw each one as clearly as the pages of the books I'd read. Realization dawned on me when I recalled something about Demon summoning, and I looked at the others.

"What bathroom did he go into?"

"The one right around the corner."

I quickly went to the master bathroom across from the library, everyone piling in behind me. My eyes went right to the medicine cabinet mirror. I knew it would be there. I yanked it open and, sure enough, on the back were the remains of a summoning sigil drawn in blood.

"Shit!" Roy cried.

"Oh no," Fox said, covering her mouth.

Gyllian had smudged the sigil well enough that I couldn't copy it and summon the Demon here myself.

I closed the medicine cabinet and shouldered my way past the others. Facing them again, I tried to stay calm, but I was still too new to this world. I had no training in it, and my FBI training was useless. Being unable to rely on that was keeping the door to my emotions open a crack and I couldn't focus properly. Procedure and protocol always helped keep my emotions in check, but not this time. There was no training for this, no procedure. I was helpless, useless, and I couldn't save him. I kept trying, thinking, and running scenarios of possibilities through my mind, but they all stopped at "Gyllian is in Hell."

Booth leaned against the wall across from me. "He will be back," he said somberly. "Gyllian has been through this numerous times before."

"So that makes it *okay?*" Roy cried.

"No," Booth said staying calm, "but it allows the hope of his return."

I ran my hand through my hair, gripping it a little too tightly in a fist. "Okay," I said, trying to find a solution. "Let's start here. He's in Hell. So how do we get to Hell?"

Fox's eyes grew large. "You want to go into Hell?"

Booth shook his head. "Right now, we would be powerless down there."

"Fucking Christ!" I cried, as the door to my emotions opened a little more. "Our weapons won't work?"

"Our weapons work, but our magic will not. Not yet," Booth explained.

"Well," I said with exaggerated calm, "I was saving people long before you lot found me. So, show me where your weapons are and a door to Hell, and we can get him back."

"Bay, you don't understand," Fox stepped forward. "These are not people. They're Demons! Some are very powerful, and Hell is incredibly vast. We'll be caught long before we find Gyllian."

I looked at them each in turn. "So we do nothing?"

"No," Fox said softly. "We wait for him to return."

I rubbed my hands over my face. I couldn't believe this. They weren't going to help me find *their* friend, and I couldn't do it without them.

I had to get out of there.

I went to the front door and snatched my coat off the hook, pausing a moment when I saw my car keys hanging there. My car was here! I snatched them up and headed out, slamming the door behind me. I quickly got into my black SUV, which was parked along the street at the edge of the lawn, and pulled away with a squeal of the tires.

Propping my elbow on the door, I rested my mouth against my knuckles, and my mind went wild. How helpful could a Demon be? Like it wouldn't lie through its teeth just for the fun of it. If humans could lie as easily as they often did in the interrogation room, the lying of a Demon had to be on a whole other epic level. Gyllian was stupid for going to a Demon for help! What was he thinking? If he was dumbass enough to volunteer for a torture session with a Demon, why should it bother me? Why *did it* bother me?

I lightly chewed on my knuckles, thinking about him. I might have been okay if I hadn't *just seen* what the Demon put him through. I might have been okay if I couldn't see the scars on his back as clear as a full moon at night. I shook my head and bowed it before looking back up at the road. I could throw blame at Gyllian all I wanted, but that didn't take away from what I'd seen being done to him. I cringed violently as the video loop went through my mind again. No one deserved that and I wanted to get him out! But I was stuck here, useless.

I passed the entrance to the Chicago Riverwalk and parked my car in the first empty space I could find. After buttoning my coat and shoving my hands deep into the pockets, I got out and headed for the stairs. I needed to walk this off, or I was going the crash my car out of pure frustration.

12

It was cool and windy, like Chicago always was, but people still milled about the walk like it was eighty-five degrees. I paused along the railing near an outdoor café. My brooding over Gyllian and worry for him had left me feeling incredibly defeated. Crossing my arms on top of the rail, I rested my chin on top of them, and looked out over the water. A few boats lazily passed across my line of sight and my mind drifted.

I'd obviously never been to Hell, and I'd barely even encountered a Demon, but I knew the Sunday school horror stories. One of my foster moms had been a religious nut. She would call me a "devil's spawn" because of my unexplainable tattoos. She'd "cleansed" me once a week, every fuckin' Sunday in a scalding hot bath, scrubbing me down with a Brillo pad trying to clean off my tattoos. Despite the many scars as I had from that and other abuse, my tattoos were never harmed. They'd never even faded. My scars just kind of disappeared under them. She eventually got so distressed that she tried to cleanse them using straight bleach right out of the bottle. When the chemical burn started showing, she took the red, burning, blistering and peeling of my skin as a sign that God was burning off my devil tattoos. After I hadn't shown up for school for three days, one of my teachers had the rare mindset to call the police. The cops turned up, and so did my social worker, to take me to the hospital.

I sighed as a First 22 Daysailer slowly drifted across my line of sight. I hadn't thought about my social worker in a long time. Paul was the only kind adult I'd ever known, but he was also someone I hated with a passion because he was the one who always put me in those horrible foster homes. At the same time, though, he was also the one who always came to rescue me when the abuse came to light. I seriously doubted it was a job requirement of his, but he used to stay with me at police stations and hospitals whenever I was admitted. He even stayed overnight when the occasion called for me to remain for observation.

As soon I was out of the system at eighteen, I went so far off the rails, I made Lindsay Lohan look like Elizabeth Walton. After two years of killing myself with alcohol, drugs, and men, Paul found me again by chance. I was lying in an alleyway that was flooded with garbage and smelled like piss, nearly dead from a heroin overdose. Paul got me to Mercy Medical and stayed with me for my very last hospital visit. He took me in himself for a little over a year after that, during which I got sober and got my head on straight. He was also the one who put the possibility in my mind of becoming a cop and hunting down the sick sons of bitches that took advantage of children like I had been. He made me believe I could actually do it, too. When I finally made the decision that I did want to go to college, Paul paid for my first year at the University of Illinois at Chicago. He probably would have paid for the whole thing, but I refused his help quickly and left the minute I was able, in the middle of the night, without a goodbye or an explanation. I didn't have any reason to trust an adult or accept their help back then, and I certainly wasn't capable of appreciating such compassion. I ended up finishing school with a bachelor's degree in three years, paid for by my bartending tips, and joined the FBI straight out of college at twenty-four.

As my thoughts drifted, I suddenly became very aware of the quiet behind me. I looked over my shoulder to find every single person at the café and on the Riverwalk standing and staring at me. My eyes went wide as I fully turned around, putting the river at my back, and instinctively yanked out the glass sword from my tattoo. No one moved. I wasn't even sure anyone was breathing.

A tall guy at the front of the crowd took a step forward. He was incredibly stunning, with lily white skin and black shaggy hair that nearly fell into his serene blue eyes. He was at least six and a half feet tall with a long narrow V-shaped torso.

"Hello Michael's Daughter," he said with a smile.

Shit.

"Peace," he said, raising his hands in a gesture of surrender. "We just want to talk."

I took in a slow breath and tried to remain calm. "Who the hell is 'we'?"

"Well, me really."

"Who the hell are you?"

"My name is Kye. If you access the magic of your fire eye tattoo, you will see who I am."

My heart started racing. I hated the magic of that tattoo. The terror of seeing those Demons in their true form last night was still with me. But I couldn't let this guy know I was afraid. I pressed my lips together and sighed as I accessed the magic, and my eyes immediately went wide. I took a step back, the railing of the Riverwalk now pressing into my spine. Behind Kye was a whole score of Demons, but Kye was an Angel!

His white wings were folded up behind him, and each feather was at least as tall as I was. They were so big that the ends rested on the ground behind him like the train of a wedding gown. He wore a white silk sleeveless top and pants that sparkled in the sunlight, his feet were bare, and there were decorative glass braces around each of his well-defined upper arms. A soft halo of white light surrounded him, looking like it was coming straight out of his skin to embrace the whole world. I'd never seen anything so beautiful in my life. With a genuine, kind smile, he looked over his shoulder and began to slowly lift and spread his wings. I gasped like an idiot. They expanded at least fifteen feet to either side, giving him a stunning thirty-foot wing span.

My amazement drained out of me, though, when I glanced at the Demons standing dutifully by. I turned the power of my tattoo off, putting them all back in their human forms and hiding the Angel's wings and light from my sight.

"You're one of the Angels trying to raise Hell."

"I am," he responded, taking a careful step closer to me. "And from what I understand, Bay, you are not completely against us on that matter."

I swallowed back my surprise and tried to put myself into professional mode. Roy and I wanted to find an Angel, and here one was. Interrogation strategies and different angles I could try to exploit flew through my mind in a flash, but nothing stood out that I could use. I had to buy time, which meant letting him talk.

"From what you understand, huh?"

Kye nodded and took another step forward. "You were very open with your friend Shia about your feelings toward humanity, how they were no different than Demons." He slowly shook his head. "And I don't blame you." His eyes grew sad, "Especially after what you've been through at the hands of humanity."

My eyes narrowed, though I felt much less defiant then I was letting on. "Don't stand there pretending you know me."

"But I do know you," he said, taking another step. His crystal clear blue eyes peered at me with such compassion through the black locks of his hair that I felt my resolve start to crumble. "I know everything about you."

I began to tremble. I wanted to melt, but stayed solid by sheer force of will. I couldn't fall apart, never fall apart; but just looking at this creature made my insides started to feel as fragile as a house of cards. I had to hold it together. One crack in my composure, one flaw, and the defenses I'd built over a lifetime of abuse would burst. The longer he gazed at me, though, the more my resolve weakened. Kye took one more step, and suddenly my knees collapsed. They hit the concrete hard, and my house of cards came tumbling down. I suddenly cried. I cried so hard I couldn't even breathe.

Kye slowly got to his knees in front of me and embraced me, while I shook so violently I felt him shaking with me. "I know, sweetheart," he said gently. "I know what these humans did to you."

As exposed as I felt, in a place of vulnerability I hadn't experienced since I was young, I also felt safe, like I could fuse into this Angel and stay content and protected forever. He wouldn't hurt me. With my defenses obliterated and all these mushy, weak parts unguarded for the first time in decades, I was still safe with him.

Then came the gunshot.

I jumped when Kye threw his head back and screamed. He slapped a hand over a fresh wound on his upper arm, but silvery gray blood was already oozing between his fingers and dripping down his arm.

"No!" I screamed.

In desperation, I moved to add pressure to the wound, but Kye was gone before I even touched him. I clutched my chest as the emptiness of his absence threatened to draw me in a sea of madness. I couldn't breathe. I wanted him back *right now!*

Suddenly I felt a familiar heaviness surround me. When I looked up, everything on the Riverwalk was frozen, even the air was still. Gyllian. He was near, and he was stopping time. I searched frantically and caught sight of him not far off. He was on his knees with his shirt off and aiming his Glock in my direction. *He'd* shot Kye!

I was about to scream at him when I saw the condition he was in. Blood was splattered across his neck and arms and he was so sweaty he looked like he'd just gotten out of the shower. His arm dropped limply like it was too heavy to hold up and his gun clattered noisily to the pavement.

"Twenty-seven seconds!" he yelled and then collapsed to his side with his back to me.

My trembling hand came up to my mouth. From his neck down to his tailbone, his back was torn to shreds. The entire surface of it was black with blood, and I could barely see any skin left.

"Gyllian!" I heard Roy yell. Roy, Fox, and Booth were all running up the Riverwalk toward us. "Booth," he called. "Grab Gyllian!"

Booth's eyes went Angelic as he snatched Gyllian from the ground and, with enhanced strength and speed, turned and ran in the same direction from which they'd come.

Roy came to me with his eyes Angelic as well. "Bay, listen to me." He crouched down near me. "I need you to put your sword away." He gently took my hand holding the weapon and guided it up to my chest. "Put it away and hang on to me, okay?"

As soon as the wind tunnel sensation came over my skin and my sword vanished, Roy snatched me up from the ground. The breeze from the speed he was running at stung my cheeks and nearly forced my eyes closed. Something felt wrong though. They'd told me we were supposed to take on the entirety of Hell's armies. So why were they scrambling and running from these Demons? Something was wrong! I started to squirm in Roy's arms.

"Bay! Wait…hang on!"

Roy eventually slowed down near a black sedan. "Put me down," I panted as Roy struggled to keep hold of me.

"Bay!"

"Put me down!" I screamed.

Roy gently set me on my feet near the driver's side. I was panting as I held my hands up, warding them away as I backed up. "Get away from me," I said, glancing at all of them. I saw Booth gingerly loading Gyllian in the back seat, being careful that his back didn't touch the leather.

"Bay, we have to leave!" Roy said.

I didn't move. I didn't let Roy near me. Why were they running?

"Eighteen seconds," Gyllian groaned.

Roy's eyes faded to brown again as he looked at me. "Bay, listen. We have to go. What's the matter?"

"An Angel was here," Gyllian replied from the car.

Roy's eyes went wide. "Oh shit."

I just wanted Kye back. I wanted him holding onto me. I didn't want to be alone anymore, and I didn't feel alone near an Angel. I felt safe.

"Bay," Roy said gently, holding his hands up and taking a step toward me. "What you're feeling right now is very real. It's the result of being near the powerful presence of an Angel. They are holy beings. They are supposed to ooze comfort and peace and all those wonderful things you felt when it was close to you."

My insides shook, longing for the comfort Kye provided. "Couldn't he come back? I wanted him to stay but Gyllian shot him!"

"I know," Roy said, taking another step toward me. "I know you wanted him to stay, believe me. I know how powerful an Angel's presence can be. But listen, I'm half Angel." My racing heart slowed down a bit as I looked into his large, pleading eyes. "Come close to me and see if you can feel the same thing."

"Really?" I asked, more desperately than suspiciously.

Roy nodded. "You won't feel it as potently, but you'll feel it."

I was usually more skeptical of claims like that, but I wanted the peace and comfort and safety back so badly that I swept into Roy's arms without a second thought. I felt it as soon as his arms closed around me. It was there, the calm, the safety. It wasn't as strong, but it was there, and my body nearly went limp from relief. I was safe. Roy could hold onto me, and I would be safe.

"Come on, Bay." Roy kissed the top of my head. "We have to hurry."

"Don't go," I said, clutching him tighter.

Roy squeezed me. "I'm not going anywhere," he said softly. "I promise."

Roy and I separated long enough to get into the car, but I was immediately snuggled up against him again before he'd even closed the door. He put his arm around my shoulders, and I buried myself into his side. I knew this wasn't normal. It was certainly unlike me to give in to such vulnerability, but the safe feeling these Angels provided wasn't like anything I even knew existed, not in this evil, greedy, hateful world.

Fox took off at a speed that made the world outside the windows blur. Catching a glimpse of her eyes in the rearview, I saw they were shining silver. Then I looked over at Gyllian. He was leaning heavily forward with his forehead pressed against the back of the passenger seat and his eyes closed. Beautiful, self-assured Gyllian suddenly looked so small and broken. He had to be in a state of agony I could scarcely imagine. Pieces of his skin were so torn up that they curled back, revealing layers of sinewy muscle underneath. My heart writhed at the sight of him and at the fact that no one was able to comfort him.

Well, if Angels were supposed to ooze comfort and peace, then I could, too.

I pulled away from Roy and rested my forehead tenderly against Gyllian's shoulder where there was no damage. I expected some protest, but instead his eyes opened into slits and he looked over at me. Then he sat up a little, leaning heavily against the car door, and stiffly lifted his arm to drape it around my neck. I lowered my cheek to his chest to ease his strain. Gyllian's peace and calm washed over me just as I hoped mine was washing over him. He closed his eyes again, and we drove in silence for a moment.

"How did you find me?" I asked.

Gyllian swallowed heavily and licked his lips. "The Knight told me where you were."

"How did she know? And why would she tell you?" I asked curiously.

Gyllian sighed softly, keeping his eyes closed. I felt bad for interrogating him, but I needed to know. "Demons are powerful creatures. They hear whispers in shadows, and word travels fast in any supernatural realm." I grinned when I realized he was quoting from one of the books on Demons I'd read. "She heard what was happening on the Riverwalk, and just to torture me mentally, she told me an Angel was working on you." His eyes opened into slits again and shifted over to me. "She thought it was hilarious the way he was playing on your hatred for humanity to shake any conviction in saving them." His eyes closed, and he readjusted his head against the window more comfortably. "I knew it would work, too, if I didn't get him away from you."

"How did you get to the Riverwalk?"

"I have abilities you're not aware of, Bay."

I supposed that was good enough. I rested my head more comfortably on his chest and, though I wasn't due for another five days, I felt myself become tired. The encounter with the Angel had drained me in a way I was not well acquainted with. Even as my eyes dropped closed, I knew the sleep I needed now had nothing to do with a physical need, but an emotional one.

13

Rubbing the fog from my eyes sometime later, I realized I felt very calm and relaxed in a way I'd never known. I felt downright lethargic. What the hell had that Angel done to me? I wanted to just lie in bed for the entire day and not move. I'd never felt like that. Usually I was always on the go, or wound so tight I had to *stay* on the go. For some reason, right now, I just wanted to stay asleep.

When things came into focus, I realized I was in Roy's section of the bunker. I wondered what I was doing there and tried to sit up, but stopped when I felt a small weight on my side. Looking down, I saw an arm draped over me. Carefully looking over my shoulder, I saw Roy behind me in the bed sound asleep. I sighed and went limp on the mattress with my back to him again. That's why I felt so weird. His Angelic presence had been washing over me for however many hours I'd been asleep beside him, deepening my sleep with the calmness that came from being near an Angel.

I closed my eyes and was about to go back to sleep when I remembered Gyllian's injuries. My eyes flew wide open. I carefully lifted Roy's arm off me and placed it by his side. Then I quietly got out of the bed and tiptoed to his concrete door. Pulling it open with a little Angelic strength, I stepped into the hallway.

Roy was room number three. I was room one. I wasn't sure what room was Gyllian's, so I tried room two first. Slowly opening the door, I was met with a dungeon-like room that looked a lot like mine. There were no decorations or colors, just four brick walls, brass candle stands and oil lamps. A plain wooden box spring sat in the middle of the room with Gyllian lying on his stomach looking asleep. I hurried to his side and gazed down at him. His wounds were, thankfully, covered with some sort of greenish salve or ointment. Strips of green organic looking cloth crisscrossed over his back, hiding the damage.

"It's not as bad as it looks," Gyllian mumbled.

I jumped and looked down at his face as he shifted his eyes up to mine. I was so unbelievably relieved to hear his voice that I sunk down into the chair beside the bed. As my eyes scanned over his injuries, I remembered this was not the first time he'd endured this kind of torture, and that he did so voluntarily.

I shook my head. "What could have possibly been worth this?" I asked. "Why would you do this to yourself? What were you *thinking* asking a Demon for help!"

Gyllian's eyes closed. "Bay, is lecturing me really necessary right now?"

"No. I'm just"—I paused and sighed— "I'm just worried about you."

He opened his eyes into slits again. "I know." We stared at each other. "Thanks for coming, Bay."

I swallowed heavily and nodded. "Of course."

His eyes closed again, and he seemed to fall asleep instantly.

I was not the sentimental type. I never had been. But looking at Gyllian's sleeping face, I felt a strange warmth for him burst to life in my chest. He and the others had somehow come to mean something to me. I still didn't see eye to eye with them about what they were fighting for, what Gyllian had endured *this* for, but they mattered to me in a way I'd never really let anyone matter to me before.

"It is a side effect of the medicine," I heard from the doorway. I looked over as Booth came in the room. "Deep sleep." He paused at the foot of the box spring and crossed his arms. "I am surprised he awoke for you."

I turned my gaze back to Gyllian and his injuries, and I felt incredibly protective of him all the sudden. "Booth, we have to get him away from that Demon."

"I agree."

I looked up at him. "Why did he leave in such a hurry to go see it? Did he tell you anything?"

Booth grabbed a nearby chair and pulled it up next to Gyllian's pallet. He sat down, leaning heavily over his knees with his elbows resting on his thighs. "It was the number of Demons you saw at the club. It has made us all nervous.

Leaving the way he did was a desperate effort to see if he could get any answers for it."

"Let me guess, the Demon wasn't very helpful."

Booth shook his head. "The Knight didn't give Gyllian much, no."

"Of course it didn't because working with a Demon is useless." I turned my eyes back to Gyllian.

"Not completely useless," Booth replied. "The Knight does give us the substance for our bullets."

I recalled reading about special substances that affected Angels and Demons. "What's so special about it?"

"The only substances that can harm supernatural beings, like Angels and Demons, have to come from a supernatural place." He held his thumb and index finger together so close that they almost touched. "Our bullets are made with small glass tips that are filled with particles of dust from Hell. The dust contains rock, ash, dirt, and bone from the ground of Hell itself. The glass tip breaks on impact and releases the dust into the creature's supernatural system, poisoning it. Results vary." He nodded his chin toward Gyllian. "When Gyllian goes to see that Demon, he brings back enough dust to supply our whole arsenal for a month."

"No one questioned where the supply came from?" I asked, recalling how surprised Roy and Fox had been at the fact Gyllian was dealing with a Demon.

Booth smiled bitterly. "Gyllian told them he had a spell to get him into Hell to gather it, one that required a few days rest after casting."

"So he could heal," I said flatly. Booth nodded.

I sighed and shook my head. I hated the idea that the Demon was actually useful. That dust alone would almost be worth Gyllian's injuries since it was all they had against the creatures. But it still didn't kill Queens and Kings or Angels.

"What about a substance from Heaven?"

Booth's brows dropped. "Heaven?"

I nodded a little confused. "Yes, Heaven. What kind of substance would Heaven be able to provide for the bullets? I bet it's far more effective than Hell Dust."

He raised an eyebrow. "I actually don't know. We've never had an Angel to deal with on the matter." He shrugged his hulking shoulders and sat back in the chair. "The only Angels we know of that were against the rising of Hell were our parents."

I looked back at Gyllian and thought about Kye. I doubted he would help us, but maybe I could get the name of another Angel that might. Interrogation tactics started flying through my mind again as I wondered how I might manipulate a name out of him. On the other hand, Kye could turn me into the trembling, sobbing, pathetic mess I'd become on the Riverwalk.

"There has to be an Angel that will help us."

Booth affectionately looked at Gyllian. "I would certainly feel more comfortable if he was seeing an Angel for information and supplies rather than a Demon."

I nodded. "I would, too."

"It will be difficult to find any Angel willing to betray their cause, though, and Angels are difficult to find in general."

I nodded and stood. "I'll pray to one."

Booth stood as I started for the door. "You are aware that you need an Angel's name for your prayer to be heard? Our parents were the only Angels known by name."

I paused and looked at him over my shoulder. "I have a name."

"You do?" He started toward me as I stepped into the hall. "Who? The Angel from the Riverwalk?"

I faced him. "I need to raid your armory." They had to have one. I also needed to get as far away from the house as I could before I called Kye down for a chat.

"Wait," I heard Roy call. Looking, I saw him coming out of his room. "I'm coming with you."

I debated it briefly as he made his way toward me. I didn't want to put him in danger, but backup was always a better plan. If there was one thing they'd drilled into us at the academy, it was that "two is one, and one is none." The FBI buddy system basically told us not to do anything alone. Besides, he'd known Gyllian the longest, certainly longer than me, so who was I to tell him to stay put?

"All right," I said. "Where's the armory?" We both had our swords, his Holy Fire blades and my father's, but I didn't want to take any chances. It was better to be overly prepared unnecessarily than underprepared ever.

"Come on," he said and led the way.

We went up the vertical hall, and Roy opened the first of the four doors in the back hallway. Inside was a large organized armory with blue walls and steel gray racks, cages, cabinets, and counters throughout. Every cabinet and drawer was filled with knives, swords, guns, and ammo—every kind of weapon I'd ever even heard of. There were automatics, semi-automatics, assault rifles, sniper rifles, regular side arms, and everything in between.

Roy pulled a bag off a hook next to the doorway and tossed it to me before continuing to some nearby cages mounted on the wall. Holding it up, I saw it contained a handful of black weapon holsters. The largest was big enough for a 58 assault rifle, yet sleek enough to keep it secured tightly to my back. Two smaller holsters allowed four more guns, two on each of my thighs. There was one holster for my chest, granting another two guns on each side of my torso. Then there was a belt holster, allowing two more guns on my lower back and one on each hip. Along the length of the belt were two rows of slots to hold extra magazines. All together these holsters brought my personal arsenal to a total of one rifle, twelve handguns, and sixteen extra magazines.

"Jesus Christ."

"Here," Roy said, tossing me two more things. "Put these on."

Catching them one after the other, I found they were a pair of black leggings and a black tank top made of polyester and spandex blended material that was popular workout attire if you could afford it. Next, he tossed me a pair of mid-calf black combat boots with five dagger holsters on the outside of each one. I stared at him.

He just smiled and pulled off his shirt to put on his own black sleeveless top. "This material is flexible, stays cooler, and absorbs sweat faster if we get into a battle."

With a shake of my head, I placed everything on a nearby counter and both of us changed into the black clothes. After strapping on the extra holsters, except for the rifle holsters we wouldn't use right now, Roy walked me down the aisles created by the long gray steel counter tops. We both grabbed some handguns—Roy a couple of .45 millimeters and .22 millimeters, while I stuck with the familiar weight and feel of the .9 millimeters and .45s. He opened a couple cabinet drawers, revealing rows of extra magazines laid out for each gun. A second drawer held matching ammo organized the same way. We both got to work loading our magazines.

I took a moment to look closely at one bullet. Turning it over in my fingers, I saw the shifting of the dust in the glass tip. "Impressive."

Roy smiled.

I watched him for a moment. There was something oddly calming about how comfortable he seemed to be in this environment. The way he so casually loaded and handled the guns, holstering them with barely a glance before he was tending to the next task to arm himself.

"How long have you been doing this?" I asked, focusing on my own arms.

"Since I met Gyllian eight years ago."

"How many"—I paused a moment because the word still seemed weird to me— "*battles* have you been in since then?"

"Not many. A couple dozen. We're pretty covert with our activities since we're trying to gather intel. The last thing we need are Angels on our ass. Demons we can deal with well enough in small numbers. Angels"—he shook his head— "not so much."

That still bothered me. Why were they running from Demons? We were supposed to be able to take on Angels, too, since they were instigating the whole apocalypse. But another question sparked in my mind.

"How come the Angels *haven't* come down on your heads?"

Roy shoved a full mag into his .22 and tucked it away in a holster behind him. "We have a few theories about that. The warding around the house and the bunker help, but also"—he shrugged— "they think we're insignificant anyway. They are so certain there's no way we could stop them that they don't bother with us. Either that or we're being hidden and protected from them."

"By who?" Roy just glanced at me, and I understood. "Ah," I said, going back to loading my magazine. "God, right?" I paused, waiting for an argument, but none came. "What about Demons? How come there's not an army waiting on the front lawn day and night?"

"Same reasons, we assume. On top of that, Demons are too busy gathering souls and making Drakes to pay attention to us. Plus, we don't think the vast majority of Demons even know what we look like or that we even exist. If they did, we'd likely be dead by now. The encounters we've had with them so far were accidental run-ins, not direct assaults on us." He tucked a .9 millimeter into a holster next to his chest. "It's got us a little nervous, though, that an Angel and a pack of Demons cornered you on the Riverwalk." He shook his head. "Now we're not sure what they know about us."

"But Shia was a Demon, and he said he knew the whole time what I was."

Roy shook his head without taking his eyes off his work. "Demons lie. If he knew you were a Nephilim, he would have killed you rather than"—he stopped abruptly and looked at me, then took a measured breath— "rather than try to breed with you."

I looked back down at my work and thought about that encounter. It had been only after I met back up with Shia that he said anything about knowing what I was. Now it made sense why he didn't come after us that night. He hadn't been prepared to face the children of the Archangels.

I was a little hesitant to ask the next question, but I felt like I needed to know before I went looking for the same Angel. "Why did they corner me on the Riverwalk? What was the point?"

Roy shot me a wary side glance. "Gyllian said the Angel was trying to dissuade you from helping us stop Hell from rising."

It dawned on me then exactly what Kye had done. He'd taken my abuse, and twisted it into a reason for him to comfort me, all in an effort to reinforce my hatred for humanity so I wouldn't want to save it. It was masterfully done. I'd been so wrapped up by the power of an Angel that I couldn't see the manipulation.

"Yeah," I said. "It seemed like it."

"Truth is," Roy said after a moment, "we're no real threat to Angels or Demons, or to their overall plan." He gave me another sidelong look and a mischievous smile that lightened my heart. "Yet."

I smiled gratefully, though it felt a little forced as we put a few more magazines in our belts filling the extra slots. There seemed to be a significant amount of gravitas behind that "yet." We were supposed to stop Hell from rising, but we weren't ready "yet." I didn't dare to ask why because I was afraid it had to do with me. I was the rookie here, and there was still so much I didn't know. I must be the one holding us back, and I didn't like how that felt.

When all my holsters were full, I put my hair back in a ponytail as we both headed for the hall. Before leaving, Roy reached behind the door, pulled out a long black trench coat, and handed it to me. I hesitated before taking it because it reminded me way too much of *The Matrix*.

"It will hide your weapons in public. Plus," he said with a toothy grin, "it's Chicago. It's windy and cold."

I couldn't help the smile that came to my face as I put the coat on. It fell to my ankles, hiding my weapons easily. "You guys really are prepared for war, aren't you?"

"We have to be," he said, putting on his own long, black coat.

We left the armory and headed back toward the bedroom hallway. As we turned the corner we were met by Booth and Fox. "We want to come," Fox said, clearly having been informed by Booth of our plans.

I shook my head and walked past her. "Not this time."

"Why not?"

I pulled open the round concrete door that led up to the house and faced her. "I'm going to meet with an enemy of ours. If all four of us go, no Angel is going to show up." I pressed the button on the wall that raised the floor. "I don't even want Roy to come, but I'm not going without backup." The hydraulics went quiet and the floor went still. "Stay here and look after Gyllian."

Roy and I made our way up the stairs. "Now that you know what being in the presence of an Angel feels like," he said, hitting the button to lower the floor again, "you should be able to withstand it a little better if one shows up."

"I hope so."

Roy took a set of keys off the hook next to the front door, and we left the house. As we got into his black SUV, he looked at me. "So where are we heading?"

I sighed, gazing out the windshield. "Somewhere that's big, open, and private."

I looked at him as he scowled. "It would probably be better if we went somewhere that was small, defendable, and public."

I shook my head. "Two reasons. First, I don't want this Angel to think we're going into battle. Picking an open, private place extends a measure of trust to him, indicating a desire for a peaceful meeting."

Roy's eyebrows went up. "You realize the risk?"

I nodded. "I do."

"And the second reason?"

I smiled at him. "I have to learn to use these wings at some point."

A huge grin spread across his face. "Well then, I know just the place."

14

The sun was down by the time Roy turned off a main street and onto a remote access road running parallel to it. To the left was an enormous abandoned dirt plot the size of a baseball field. The head and taillights of the traffic on the closest road twinkled in the distance like the stars themselves. This was perfect. Roy put the car in park and reached for his door handle.

"Wait, Roy," I said, resting my hand on his thigh. He looked at me. "I need you to keep your distance."

"What?" His face scrunched. "I'm not leaving you alone out there."

"I won't be alone. You're here. But I need you to be my backup, not my accomplice." He sighed heavily and looked out the windshield, seeming to debate it. "Please."

He looked over at me. "I'll keep my distance, but my swords will be out, and if things go sideways, even an inch, I'll kill whoever shows up. If you're not okay with that then we're leaving."

I gave a soft resigned sigh and nodded. "I'm okay with that."

He nodded once. "Good." We both got out of the car. I rounded the hood as Roy reached behind him and pulled out his Holy Fire swords. He crossed his arms and leaned back against the car door, the orange fire flickering off his face and silvery angelic eyes.

I walked into the empty dirt clearing, trying to get out of earshot of him and feeling a little nervous about it. I had to control this conversation, and that might require me saying some things Roy wouldn't like to hear.

"Bay!" Roy hollered so sharply that I actually jumped a little. "That's far enough."

I stopped immediately. I thought it was far enough away anyway. Praying wasn't my forte in the slightest, so for a while I just stared up at the night sky wondering how to begin.

Well, I needed an Angel's name so, "Kye?" I called. "Um, if you're…"

"I'm here," I heard behind me.

I spun around to see his pretty white face lighting up in the night like he was reflecting the moonbeams, and lost my breath for a moment. I tried to gather my wits to speak, but my eyes wandered all over him, trying to settle in one place. I had to control this! I couldn't lose it again. My gaze finally settled on his upper arm, which had no sign whatsoever that he'd been injured.

"Your arm is okay."

Kye glanced at it before looking at me with a slightly amused smile. "Angels heal quickly."

I nodded. "Good. That's…that's good."

It fell uncomfortably quiet a moment before Kye gently chuckled. "Walk with me. We'll chat." I looked past him at Roy, still leaning up against the car. "Don't worry," he said following my gaze. "He will still see you." I smiled appreciatively as we began to walk. "What is it that's on your mind?"

I needed to figure out where his head was at and see if he'd give me any freebies without my trying very hard. I decided that the P.E.A.C.E. method of interrogation was probably my best bet in this situation. Be his friend, gain empathy, get him to talk. "Listen, I don't know how much you really know about me, but…"

"I know everything about you."

"So you know I'm fairly new to this whole Angels and Demons thing, right?"

"Fairly new? You're not even a month into it."

I nodded. "Yeah."

"And you're wondering what's going on?"

"Not necessarily that, I just…" I stopped walking and faced him, casting a glance at Roy. "The only point of view I have on the whole issue is from those four." I shook my head. "I'm an FBI agent. Everything in my training tells me that having one biased point of view on a subject, especially something as big as the apocalypse, is never a good thing. I need a second opinion, but I'm not about to try to talk to a Demon. I know you're buddies with them and all, but I have no—"

"I am no friend of the Demons," Kye interrupted.

I looked at him, confused. "But I thought—"

"Bailey—"

"Bay."

Kye smiled, "Bay. There is a difference between being friends with those vile things and using them as a means to an end."

"Using them to wipe out the humans, you mean."

Kye looked at me meaningfully. "I know you have suffered terribly at the hands of humanity. I know all about what you went though as a child, the innocent, special little child you were." He reached out and tenderly touched my jaw. His blue eyes became intense and angry, but he still spoke softly. "I know all about the creatures that took away your innocence so young." I wasn't sure if it was my imagination, but Kye's eyes looked like they filled with tears before he dropped his hand and quickly looked away from me. "I apologize. I seem to be getting emotional."

I stared at him, unable to decide if he was being genuine in his concern for me or if this was more manipulation. He seemed sincere, and I couldn't deny that my heart was aching to be cared for the way he was expressing.

I shook my head. "You don't have to apologize. Do you know how long it's been since someone cared enough to get emotional for me?"

Kye nodded. "Since the night you found your social worker hunched over your Department of Child Services file and weeping."

My eyes went wide. "How do you know about that?"

Kye took a step toward me and took my face into both his hands. He was so close that he had to look down at me. "I told you, I know everything about you. Angels can look at a person and see their entire life. All of their memories and feelings are revealed to us in the blink of an eye."

I felt a powerful longing to sink into Kye's arms again and stay there forever. It was like a physical pull I couldn't resist. He was so beautiful, not even just physically with his blue eyes and black hair. He made me feel safe and truly cared for. Almost beyond my own will, my head came down to rest on his chest.

He encircled me in his arms. "It's okay," he said softly. "I know."

"I'm sorry," I whispered. "I don't mean to be so pitiful."

He chuckled, which sent goosebumps tingling up my legs. "You never have to apologize to me for this." He sighed. "This is what I miss the most about humanity, when they used to come to us and God for love and comfort. They don't do that anymore," he said with heavy sadness.

I waited for him to tell me more, but he didn't. I didn't press the matter and just let Kye hold me for a good span of a few minutes. I could feel my resolve breaking down again. He was an Angel. He was a holy being. He couldn't be evil. He couldn't be! It felt too good to be near him. If he was evil, why hadn't he killed me yet? He wasn't short on opportunities. I could not synchronize the picture Gyllian and the others had painted of these Angels and the kindness and compassion Kye offered me right now.

Gyllian. It was the thought of Gyllian, back home and severely injured, that allowed me to focus again. A Demon had done that to him, and this Angel was helping those fucking things come to the surface. No. I would not crumble in this Angel's arms again. They were evil.

"Listen," I said, lifting my head and pretending to wipe my eyes, "I still don't have my head on completely straight with the whole Angels and Demons apocalypse, but I would like to talk to you more about it if I can. Just"—I glanced in Roy's direction— "not at this moment. I don't want him to get suspicious."

Kye nodded. "I understand."

"I also want to talk to you about possibly doing me a favor."

"I can try."

I pressed my lips together. "Are you aware a Demon has been meeting with Gabriel's Son and supplying him with the Hell Dust that caused your injury?"

Kye's eyes went wide and his blue irises faded to the same silvery gray color as mine when my abilities were in use. "I wondered where you were getting your ammunition."

I nearly flinched. It wasn't just his sudden harsh tone

that startled me, but I'd finally caught a glimpse of his true nature. The way he distanced himself from me by saying, "I wondered where *you* were getting *your* ammunition" told me that he *was* manipulating me. Damn, I was good at my job. Be his friend, gain empathy, get him to talk. Now it was time to get what I wanted.

"I was wondering if you would be willing to kill her for me?"

Kye tilted his head with intrigue, and his eyes faded back to blue. "But then you won't have dust for your ammunition."

"I don't care," I replied without a shred of regret. "I care more about Gyllian than I do about our supplies and intel from Hell."

Kye smiled a little. "You realize Gabriel's Son is going to be displeased with you for revealing his source to me?"

I thinned out my lips. "Gyllian's life is more important to me than what he thinks of me."

Kye tilted his head again, seeming amused. "I see you are telling the truth, but I also see you have something you want in return for revealing a traitor to me. Something *more* than the creature's demise."

I nodded. "I was hoping you would be willing to teach me how to use my wings."

A corner of Kye's mouth went up in a sweet half smile. "Your wings," he said affectionately, likely having seen in my memories what that tattoo meant to me.

"They're supposed to manifest," I said, "but I don't know anything about flying."

Kye nodded. "I will grant that request, simply because I enjoy your company."

Asshole. "Thank you." I glanced back at Roy and shifted uncomfortably before looking up at Kye again. Now it was time to get out of here unscathed. "Listen, I hate to ask, but I'm going to need your understanding for the time being."

"Understanding?"

I nodded. "I'm going to stay with Roy, Gyllian, Fox and Booth and learn from them about how they plan to stop Hell from rising because I don't want to betray them, not until you give me a good reason too."

"Your childhood torture isn't enough?" he asked,

sounding almost offended.

Careful here, Bay, I told myself.

"You'd think it would be but"—I glanced at Roy again, his orange Holy Fire blades flickering in the distance— "I like spending time with them." I took a deep breath and sighed before looking back at Kye. "They care about me. They care about me in ways I'm not sure I deserve because I definitely don't reciprocate it. So if I kill a Demon or two or ten with them"—I pressed my lips together— "I need your understanding that it's because I'm still on the fence about this Angel and Demons thing until I hear your side."

Kye was still a moment before he nodded once. "I can extend that grace to you. I believe, however, it will only take one more meeting to teach you to fly and to share my point of view with you. Just come alone."

I nodded. "Definitely."

"When would you like to meet again?"

I glanced at Roy again. "I'm not sure when I'll be able to slip away from the others. When I can, I'll come here and pray for you. Is that all right?"

Kye nodded. "That will be fine." He smiled. "I look forward to our next meeting."

"I do, too." Then he was gone, and I headed back to Roy and the SUV.

"Took you long enough," he said as I approached. "How did it go?"

I rounded the front of the car as he put his Holy Fire blades away. "That depends."

Roy's eyes narrowed suspiciously as they faded back to brown. "On?"

I crossed my arms and rested them on top of the hood. "On how you look at it."

"Bay?" he said in a warning tone.

I pressed my lips together and met Roy's eyes defiantly. I refused to be ashamed of protecting Gyllian. "Kye is going to find out who Gyllian's been dealing with and kill her."

"Bay!" Roy cried.

I held up a finger at him. "Don't start!"

He threw his arms out to his sides. "That Demon was the only source we had to get the dust for our bullets!"

144

"I don't care!" I retorted. "I'm not going to let Gyllian subject himself to torture for some stupid dust that doesn't even kill Kings, Queens, or Angels!"

"That's not your call!"

"I just made it mine!"

Roy sighed heavily and crossed arms on the hood, sagging until his forehead rested on them. He was quiet for a moment before he looked back up at me. "Don't get me wrong, I'm glad Gyllian is safe from that damn Demon, but I'm thinking long term here. We don't know when Hell is going to rise, and what if we run out of bullets by then? Is this Angel going to give us the substance from Heaven?"

I sighed. "It wasn't the right circumstances to ask."

"Bay!"

"I'm still working on gaining rapport with him!" I said in my defense. Roy let out another frustrated sigh and bowed his head. "I'll deal with the Angel. Right now, we'd better start narrowing down when Hell is going to rise."

Roy looked away to the side. After a moment, he huffed a sound that was almost like a laugh and shook his head. "Yeah," then reached for the car door.

"Hey," I said, feeling the need to do some damage control. I rounded the SUV and stood in front of him with a smile. "Want to see something?"

Roy surprised me by smiling, too. "You know it."

Still grinning, I took a few steps back. I couldn't believe how fast my heart was racing. I blew out a few nervous breaths. I had stared at my wings so often in the mirror when I was little. I knew every curve of the ink in the design and where every feather was placed. My back suddenly got really warm. I gasped a little when I felt the gentle wind tunnel effect come, as if all my skin just vanished. With a gentle whoosh my wings appeared and expanded wide to my sides.

"Holy fucking shit," Roy choked out.

I was trembling so hard I could barely keep myself standing as my hand came up to my mouth. They were magnificent! They were the same size as Kye's, but my feathers weren't white, they were *black* like the ink on my skin! I looked at Roy, my heart pounding so hard I felt it in my temples.

He smiled. "They are beautiful."

I nodded, my emotions literally choking me from speaking. They were real. My wings were real.

A gust of wind suddenly blew, and I was instantly lifted off my feet. I squealed in surprise and grasped for something to keep my feet on the ground. Roy's hands were the first things there as he reached for me. Both of us were laughing as he pulled me back down onto my feet. I kept a tight hold of him so the currents wouldn't lift me again.

"My wings probably saved my life when I was a little girl," I blurted out of nowhere.

Roy's expression softened. "Yeah?"

I nodded. Oh God I didn't want to go here, but I couldn't seem to stop myself. "Sometimes," I began, "when I knew my foster fathers were gone for the night or passed out, I wrapped myself in only a sheet and sat on the floor with my back to a mirror and just stared at them, for hours." I was genuinely surprised at myself. That Angel must have done more of a number on me than I'd thought. Why was I telling Roy this? Why was I allowing him into this precious part of my life? I never let anyone near this part of me, ever. "Sometimes I would close my eyes," I closed my eyes. "And reach over my shoulder." I let go of one of his hands and rested it on my own shoulder. "And pretend I could feel the feathers in my fingers." I swallowed heavily as my eyes opened. "It would give me strength to hold on for one more day."

Roy reached up and tucked a loose strand of hair behind my ear and smiled. "You don't have to pretend anymore."

I smiled. Looking over my shoulder, I attempted to bring my right wing around in front of me. I gasped when it actually moved, and I *felt* it move! Different muscles in my back and shoulders flexed to shift it, and the thin hollow bones beneath the several layers of feathers moved on command. The breeze on my wings felt like a breeze on my skin, only my feathers seemed supersensitive to it. I felt the smallest micro air current, even the temperature differences in each one, which would likely go toward helping me fly when I got around to it. In a place where I should have no feeling, I felt my wings as much as I could feel my face. I lifted my hand and reached for my beautiful black feathers. When my fingertips touched them, I gasped a little again because they were softer than the down feathers of a goose. Even weirder, I could feel my fingertip touching my wing.

"May I?" Roy asked.

I looked at him and laughed. "Of course you can."

Roy gingerly reached to touch my feathers. I let out a small shout of surprise when I felt him touch this new extension of myself, and both of us started laughing.

"I can't wait until I learn how to use them," I said, running my hand over the top curve of my right wing.

"Did the Angel say he would help you?"

I nodded. "He did."

I expected an argument since Angels were our enemies, but Roy smiled instead. "Good."

I sighed as I folded both of my wings behind me. I giggled a little, feeling the ends of my feathers brush over the ground behind me. That wind-tunnel feeling filled my back again, and suddenly they were gone. Though I'd only had them out for a short time, I already felt like a huge part of me was missing.

"Listen," Roy said as he gently dropped his hands to his sides. "Have you ever had fun?"

I chuckled. "What?"

"Have you ever had fun?"

I shrugged a shoulder, feeling a pang of shame for my wild past. "I'd venture to say I've probably had too much fun in my life. I really went off the edge as soon as I was out of the system. I mean *way* off the edge; partying, clubbing, drinking, drugs, anything and everything in between above and beyond, and it almost killed me."

Roy shook his head. "I don't mean the kind of stoned-out-of-your-head fun you're talking about; I went there too when I was a teenager. I mean really good, *clean* fun."

I had to think really hard about it. All I could remember was being a recluse as a child, in and out of hospitals and police stations. Then there was the stoned-out-of-my-head fun he mentioned. After that, nothing but school and homework once I got into UIC. Finally, there was just work once I got into the FBI.

"No," I said. "I don't think I have."

Roy smiled broadly. "Well, you are tonight."

"Oh really?" I replied playfully as he made his way to the driver's side door.

"Yup! And I know just where to go."

Grinning like an idiot, I headed for the passenger side in a hurry and climbed in.

Since Kye had gotten near me, something was different. For better or worse I wasn't sure yet, but it didn't feel bad at the moment. It was like he'd lifted some sort of burden off me that I wasn't aware I'd been carrying. Now that it was gone, I didn't know what to do with myself. I felt so free. So, I was off to have some good, *clean* fun with Roy.

15

When Roy pulled up to the place forty-five minutes later, I threw my head back and laughed! It was a country western club called the Bullhorn Ranch.

"Really?" I said, looking over at him.

He was grinning like a buffoon as he parked the car. "You better believe it, baby!"

Grinning, we both started to take off our guns, holsters and knives. I was never comfortable without an easily accessible gun though, so I kept the small Rugar .38 special stuffed behind the waistband of my pants. The rest we put on the floor in the back seat, and Roy covered them with our trench coats. That left us in our matching black tank tops, black pants, and heavy black combat boots. We looked weird enough as it was, but a lot of our tattoos were exposed, too. We probably looked really out of place here. What if there was a dress code? Roy didn't seem to be giving any thought to that, though, as he smiled and opened his door, which made me grin as I got out.

We were greeted right away by the wafting sounds of Vince Gill's "What the Cowgirls Do," and the heavy boot stomping of synchronized line dancing. Accompanying that were the hoots and hollers of wannabe cowboys and girls in Chicago, Illinois.

After paying the twenty-dollar cover charge, Roy beelined to the bar, which had me laughing. "I thought we were supposed to be having 'good clean' fun?"

He smiled. "That's why we're only getting beer."

I chuckled. While we waited for our drinks, I watched the people on the dance floor. They all looked like they were having the time of their lives. Funny thing was there were no fancy laser lights or bass that made the floor and walls shake. It was just a large group of smiling, happy people, having a good time. This was new.

Roy grabbed our beers from the bar and we walked over

to an empty table. The center dance floor was a square pit, a mite shorter than the rest of the bar. Roy and I sat at a table against the back wall just next to the lively trench of dancing people. Watching so many folks having such a good time made it hard to stop smiling. Roy and I had only taken about three sips of our beers before a song came on I didn't recognize, and Roy's face lit up like the Christmas tree in Rockefeller Center. His reaction was accompanied by loud hoots and hollers and a mass surge of people onto the dance floor.

"It's the 'Watermelon Crawl!'" Roy said, standing.

"The what?"

Roy didn't answer me as he grabbed my hand and towed me onto the dance floor. I was laughing as he got behind me. "You know I have no idea how to do this right?" I shouted to him over my shoulder.

"You'll learn quick! Just don't stop moving."

I stumbled like an imbecile trying to follow the moves of the dance, but it wasn't as embarrassing as I feared because each time I screwed up, I would look at Roy and we would both just laugh hysterically. It wasn't a shameful kind of laughter either, like he was making fun of me for stumbling around, but a joyful "Who cares if you stumble?" kind. I was used to the other type that made you feel like an idiot. With Roy, it wasn't that at all. He took hold of my hips a couple times to direct me, but eventually the pattern started to emerge: Toe to heel, triple step. Toe to heel, triple step. Hip wiggle right. Hip wiggle left. Turn and turn. Stomp. Stomp. By the second verse I had my thumbs hooked into the front of my pants and I was stepping and stomping like a pro with the rest of them. With one song, I was already having the time of my life. I suddenly knew what Roy meant about good clean fun. This was it, and it was marvelous. I wasn't drunk or high, and the music didn't give me a headache; I was just dancing and being silly and having a good time doing it. Silly was something I never thought I'd get to do. When the song ended, everyone including Roy and me erupted into claps and cheers, and then we headed back to the table.

"Not bad for clean fun, huh?" he asked as we sat down.

"I've been missing out!" I said then took a sip of my

beer. Roy chuckled and took a sip of his as well. I listened to the next song for a few moments before addressing Roy. "You were born in Russia, right?" He nodded. "So what in the world sparked a love for country music? Do they even *have* country music there?"

Roy chuckled. "Country music was rare in Russia for sure, but I think that's why I loved it so much. I enjoy special and unique things," he said with a grin. His eyes seemed to smile whenever he did, crinkling in the corners. "So when Gyllian brought me to the states, I completely delved into the culture." His eyes slowly panned over the crowd. "People in the country music world are just so"—he scrunched up his face a little in thought— "happy. It's not like the angry, entitled, oversexed sounds of the mainstream rap and R&B scene, and it's not the fake, electronic sounds of the lame pop scene. It's just light and happy and makes you feel good." He took another sip from his bottle. "It reminds me of when I was happy."

I wanted to ask him another question, but I didn't want to pry into something that was none of my business. Since Roy had to be honest, I didn't want him to feel obligated to tell me.

He caught me staring at him, though, as I debated whether to ask. "What?"

I gave in to curiosity. "Did you know your Angelic dad?"

A smile slowly spread across his face. "Yeah," he said with a nod.

"What was that like?"

He sat forward with his arms crossed on the table. "I remember he loved to cook." That made my heart swell. "There was something about the hundreds of combinations available to him when creating sustenance for his dependent offspring that he took incredible joy in. Food was a new and unusual concept for him, and he loved it."

I smiled. "What about your mom?"

Roy shook his head. "The Angels, or Demons, got her when I was still a toddler. My dad couldn't save her."

I rested my chin on top of my beer bottle. "I'm sorry." Roy smiled in gratitude.

I found myself wondering what it would have been like to have my dad around. What kind of dad would he have been? Would he have loved to cook, too?

A thoughtful look passed over Roy's face. "I also remember he would lie in bed and talk to me before I went to sleep, every night. He would explain who and what he was, why he was there, why I was born. Though I was too little to really grasp what he was saying, never mind understand the magnitude the importance of what he was saying, I still remember him talking to me about it even back then." He smiled. "He would always tell me how great I was going to be someday. Always."

"He sounds wonderful," I said honestly.

Roy nodded. "He was. I loved my dad." He sighed heavily before taking another sip of his beer. "I was six when he was killed by an Angel."

"How do you know it was an Angel?"

Roy shrugged. "It's a toss-up, I suppose. Since our parents were mortal after they fell, it could have been either. But I'd put my money on an Angel."

"Why?"

"Because our parents' fall, to create us, was a direct move against the Angels trying to raise Hell. The Angels would have wanted revenge and likely stopped the Demons from interfering."

I stayed quiet in thought. The four of them kept suggesting that we were stronger than Angels, but that didn't make sense. Gyllian had been tortured nearly to death by a damn Demon. We'd run from those Demons on the Riverwalk, too. If we couldn't even take a stand against Demons, beings a thousand times weaker than Angels, how were we expected to take a stand against Angels?

A rude sounding clunk broke my train of thought, which pissed me off. Both Roy and I looked up and saw a tall, barrel-chested guy standing over our table. He had an oily helmet of greasy black hair that was slicked back like a shady used car salesman's. His slimy, arrogant smirk made something deep inside me twitch uncomfortably. The clunk sound was him loudly placing a beer bottle down on top of our table.

"Well," he said in a low gurgled voice. "If it isn't

Raphael's Son and Michael's Daughter."

My eyes went wide. Then, as if by silent command, Roy and I were on our feet so fast our chairs were knocked to the floor, and we pulled the guns from our belts. Hysteria instantly filled the club, and a stampede out of the building began. No one came near us, rushing instead to the back exit.

"Really?" the slimy salesman said with a tone of overconfidence I didn't like. "As if we weren't prepared."

As the building emptied, I realized at least a dozen people remained. All of them were lucid and calm and were staring at me and Roy with deadly intent. I warmed up the Hebrew tattoo down the middle of my back, enhancing my physical abilities, and nearly smiled when Roy's eyes turned silvery gray at the same time. I activated the magic of my flaming eye tattoo next so I could see what we were dealing with. Roy would need to know. When the salesman's human disguise lifted, the putrid appearance of a Pawn took form. Casting a quick glance around the club, I saw a mix of Pawns, Rooks, and Bishops. Luckily nothing of higher rank was here, or our bullets would be useless.

"Well," I said, glaring at the Pawn down the barrel of my gun, burying the terror this creature evoked in me under the confidence I felt with Roy by my side. "What a lovely bunch of bottom feeding underachievers." The Pawn's face melted in surprise. I gave a deep exaggerated shrug. "Nothing higher than a Bishop wanted to bother with your mission to try to take out two of the Lights of the Fallen, huh?" I cocked my revolver. "Probably because they knew you'd fail."

Roy suddenly flipped the bar table up, knocking the Pawn to the floor with the table landing on top of him. He grabbed my hand and yanked me to the closest exit. "Get out of here!" he yelled, shoving me out the door ahead of him. I spun around in time to see the Demon's pale arm come up over Roy's shoulder and yank him back inside before the door slammed.

"No!"

I started pounding uselessly on it. Flashes of Gyllian's injuries went through my mind. I refused, I *refused* to let Roy become subject to that. Not on my fucking life! So, I took a deep breath, shoved my panic deep down into my core, and buried it with anger, a response that was second nature to me.

With my teeth clenched and my breath coming in pants through the corners of my mouth, I took a step back and kicked the door in with my Angelic strength. It splintered into a thousand pieces before my eyes, but the pieces didn't crumble to the floor. They floated weightlessly before me. As I stepped through, my shoulders pushed some floating splinters away like I was in an airless vacuum. Everything was moving too slowly to be possible. The Demons in the club stood almost frozen. Their hungry, animalistic eyes were on Roy as he was being dragged back in. Even Roy was frozen, bent over backwards in mid-struggle with the Demon.

It wasn't Gyllian slowing time down because he was home. It was me moving too fast! It was almost the same as when I'd killed Shia, only I was experiencing my speed this time.

I raised my gun and fired one shot, putting a bullet between the eyes of the Pawn that was dragging Roy. Roy floated a moment, and then slowly, centimeter by centimeter, began to fall as the Demon behind him fell backwards just as slowly.

In four steps, I reached Roy and grabbed his wrist. Yanking him up, I shoved him behind me toward the door while keeping my gun aimed at the other Demons. The dreamlike slowness ebbed when he was safely behind me, and everything went back to normal speed.

"Move!" I yelled, and we both ran toward the parking lot. The SUV was thankfully not far.

"Shit!" Roy yelled, pulling out his keys. "This is why we don't go anywhere alone! Gyllian could have stopped time, or Fox could have jettisoned us off!"

I looked at him, surprised. "Are you blaming me?"

The car beeped, and Roy and I yanked our doors open. "Really?" he said as we piled inside and he put the key in the ignition. "You're going to get defensive?" The engine roared to life. "Now?"

I couldn't believe it. "You're the one wanted to go dancing!"

"I did!" he cried as he threw the car in reverse and slammed on the gas. Dust erupted all around the car. "And I don't regret it for one second!"

"Then why are you angry at me?"

"What?" He swung the car around, facing it in the right direction in a single smooth motion. "I'm not angry at you!" He slammed it into drive and hit the gas again.

"You're yelling at me!"

"I'm not! I..." He paused and met my eyes a moment, seeming to settle a little. "I just don't want anything to happen to you," he said more softly. He looked in the review mirror. "Shit!"

"What?" I looked out the rear window in time to see three SUVs peel out of the parking lot after us. "Shit."

Roy sighed and shook his head. "We have to lose them or we're dead."

I looked at him, feeling the familiar frustrating and annoying ping in my chest that we were running from a few Demons. Something was wrong among my newfound friends, and that sinking feeling came again that it was my fault somehow.

"All right," I said, "let me drive."

Roy glanced at me. "Why?"

"Because I'm a trained FBI agent," I said and slid into the middle of the seat right next to him. "I know how to lose a tail."

"All right," he said, putting his arm around my shoulders and arching his back so I could get a little bit behind him. I put my feet down under his and took over the pedals. Then Roy pushed himself up, lifting his rear end off the seat so I could get more behind and under him. I reached around and took the wheel as he started to go to the side.

"You got it?" he asked.

"Yup. Go."

Roy released the wheel and pulled his feet over to the passenger side of the SUV. "All right G-woman, get us the hell out of here."

I reached over my shoulder to buckle my seatbelt. Roy did the same. Then I slammed on the gas.

I started off by dodging and weaving through the traffic on the highway, going up onto the shoulder and cutting in front of heavier traffic to try to lose the Demons. They managed to stay close to us, though, repeatedly. I quickly realized I was going to have to do this the harder way and started looking at highway signs. The next exit led to an inner-city area. Perfect. There would be lots of people and traffic lights. I accelerated and headed over to the shoulder again to get off at the exit.

"Um, Bay," Roy said, "shouldn't we *avoid* heavily populated areas?"

"I know what I'm doing."

"I'm sure you do"—he paused— "when dealing with humans."

I looked at him. "What?"

He sighed softly. "Human tails can be lost in heavily populated areas because human beings are hardwired for self-preservation. They stay out of harm's way, avoiding other people, places, and things because their survival instincts demand it. But Demons don't give a fuck." My heart sank. "They will mow down anything and anyone in their way, even at harm to themselves. They don't care." He sighed again. "You go into a heavily populated area, people are going to die."

Shit. The basic strategy of losing a tail was to get them lost behind heavy traffic and people. But Roy was right. Demons would mow down a stroller in the middle of the street if there was one in their way. Shit! It seemed the only way out of this was to try to shoot our way out.

"Roy, get our guns ready."

"No."

I glanced at him. "What?"

He shook his head. "We can't waste our bullets, Bay."

My eyes went wide. "You're kidding me, right?"

"Listen, if that Angel actually kills Gyllian's Knight, and we can't find an Angel to deal with, the dust we have in here and the little bit back at the bunker is all that's left."

I rubbed my forehead vigorously with my fingertips. There went my last strategy. I couldn't pull off into a heavily populated area, I couldn't shoot at them, and trying to lose them on the highway wasn't working.

I glanced in the rearview mirror again at the three tails. "How did they even know where to find us?" I asked, trying to buy some time to think.

"Good question," Roy replied. "My money would be on that Angel you met dropping the dime."

Shit. He was probably right.

Suddenly an idea came to me about how to get away from these Demons. It wasn't even really an idea but a leap of faith, an enormous one. My concern wasn't for myself though, it was for Roy. I was okay with dying. I was not okay with him dying.

"Roy." He looked at me. "Do you have anything in your tattoos will let you get out of the car safely and leave me to deal with them?"

Roy's eyes became intense. "Even if I did, I'm not leaving you."

"Roy –"

"I'm *not* leaving." He shook his head. "We don't leave each other behind."

I couldn't believe he was going gallant knight on me right now. "I don't need you to save me, Roy!"

"Who said anything about saving you?" he said without even blinking. "I said I'm not leaving you."

I couldn't deny how good it felt to hear him say that, but my worry for him kept me from being thrilled about it. "You're an idiot, you know that?"

He smiled brightly. "I've been called worse."

I grinned and shook my head as I raced through the traffic with the three SUVs close on our bumper. I sighed softly and allowed myself a moment to think. Angels were real. Demons were real. Roy and the others had said so, and I'd seen it for myself. They also said God was real. I glanced at Roy as he gazed out the windshield. He believed God was real. He'd told me God was real. I didn't want to believe him, but right now I *had* to.

Bracing myself to push the limits of my belief because I had no other option, I glared up at the night sky. "Let's dance."

"What?" Roy asked.

I ignored him and pushed the gas harder. If God allowed us Nephilims to exist, then he had better pull a massive miracle out of his ass to save us.

157

"Show me you're real, you son of a bitch," I muttered.

When we started to cross the overpass of Salt Creek, I pressed the gas petal until I was pushing it into the floor. With a final glance in the rearview mirror, making sure those bastards were right behind us, I cut the wheel hard to the left and yanked the emergency brake, spinning the car so the driver's side door faced the oncoming traffic.

I instantly felt the heaviness of everything around me as the world slowed down. This time it was a lot like the heaviness that I'd felt when Gyllian had manipulated time, but much bigger. I could barely breathe from the pressure surrounding me. When Gyllian screwed with time, it usually happened around me. This time it was happening *to* me. My mind worked just as fast, but everything I saw, and everything I was doing, was slow. Lifting and turning my head to look out the window was like moving through mud. I watched the three SUVs slowly approach inch by inch. I waited for the dip of their front bumpers, or the smoke from the tires as they slammed on the brakes, but none of that happened. They wanted to kill us and they were about to succeed.

I waited, but no miracle was happening. We were still in the car.

Shit. I knew God wasn't fucking real. Or if he was, he didn't give a shit about us. Maybe my dad had made a mistake by creating me. Had the Archangels rebelled against God by creating us to fight Hell? A Hell that God himself wanted to rise? I supposed if that was the case, we'd be doing God a favor by dying here.

As I watched the beginning of the impact of the first SUV into my door, I blinked. When my eyes opened again, time was working normally and I was suddenly looking down at my feet. The SUV was far below being impaled by the three SUVs before it erupted into flames that exploded all over the highway.

I blinked again and suddenly found myself rolling on the ground. I bumped and jerked before finally coming to a harmless stop on my side in some short grass. I waited a moment, partly in disbelief, partly trying to allow my brain to catch up and understand what just happened. I did a quick self-diagnosis; nothing was broken, sprained or twisted.

Sitting up, I didn't see anything strange, except for the fact I was on the edge of Salt Creek beside a thicket of trees. It was quiet, too. Too quiet.

"Roy?" I called.

"I'm here."

I got to my feet and stumbled toward the sound of his voice. He was on the ground nearby. I knelt beside him as he groaned and rolled onto his back. "Are you okay?" I asked, helping him sit up.

"Yeah." After running his hand through his hair, he looked up at me. "What the hell were you thinking?"

"I wasn't. I just…"

"She acted on faith," a new voice said.

I reflexively reached for a weapon, but instead of reaching for my gun, I found the hilt of my father's sword in my hand. My fiery eye tattoo warmed up as I spun around and saw an Angel behind me.

She was skittish looking, waiting in a low crouch with one leg out to her side and her hands resting on the ground in front of her. She looked ready to bolt. She was in all white like when I'd first seen Kye, with pale blonde hair fanned out against her shoulders and sapphire blue eyes. Her white wings were slightly out to her sides, not extended enough to take flight, but not fully relaxed either. She glared at me suspiciously, slowly shifting her body weight from one leg to the other, waiting for a reason to take off.

"Did you pull us out of car?" Roy asked.

The Angel gazed at him. "You gave God no choice."

My eyes went wide. Fuck. So not only was God real, but he wanted us to exist! That meant he *didn't* want Hell to rise. I felt an incredible weight drop onto my shoulders. It was hard to fathom. God *himself* had a mission for us. I didn't know whether to be honored or pissed. My default wiring caused me to lean more toward pissed. No one asked us if we wanted this burden. God sure as hell didn't! He'd just *decided* to saddle us with it. And where the fuck had he been while all of us were going through our various Earthly versions of Hell?

Roy slowly came around me, staying in a low, unthreatening crouch as he addressed the Angel. "God told you to rescue us?"

"Yes. Now I have to go."

"Wait!" Roy cried.

"I *must* go," she said more firmly. "The others will kill me if they find me."

Suddenly Kye was standing behind the new Angel. He didn't materialize, he didn't appear; he was just there! My eyes went wide when I saw him holding a dagger in his hand.

"No!" I cried.

Before I even realized what I was doing, I swept the female Angel up in one arm, putting her in front of me and Kye behind me, and then pain exploded in my back. I gasped sharply, unable to even scream from the burning sensation that spread through my entire system as if my blood had caught fire!

The female Angel vanished from my arms, and I dropped to my knees. My whole body throbbed. Trying to focus, I looked around and saw something that looked like Roy crouching in front of me. I blinked. It *was* Roy. His eyes were Angelic, his teeth bared, and his Holy Fire swords flashed in his hands. He suddenly brought them both together in a scissor-like motion above my head. Through the pulsating fog of my vision, I saw Kye's head land on the ground beside me with the severed end of his neck on fire. His detached body landed beside it, also burning. The Holy Fire consumed the two parts in a split second until there was nothing left, not even a pile of ash.

A single amazing thought ran through my head; we *were* stronger than Angels!

I collapsed fully to the ground. I thought I heard Roy saying something, but it was soft. Straining to hear as he gathered me in his arms, I realized he was praying.

"God please help me. Please help me! Save her. Please save her!"

16

Everything was still foggy when my eyes opened. I looked around and wasn't sure if I was in a hospital or in the bunker. The wall to my right had a large glass window with a sliding glass door like in an Intensive Care Unit. I also heard a heart monitor beeping. If I was in the bunker, there shouldn't be electricity—unless the lack of electricity only would happen after the apocalypse hit. But the other walls of the room looked very much like the bunker walls, with the smooth brick along the bottom and gray concrete on the top.

I blinked a couple times to focus better and realized the hospital room seemed to be in the corner of a much larger room beyond the window. I couldn't make out much, but there were maps on the walls and a couple of white boards with notes drawn all over them. I saw a whole lot of pictures and papers and stacks of files covering a few tables. The place looked like a mix between an Air Traffic Control Center and FBI Headquarters.

A sullen-looking Roy suddenly approached the sliding glass door and opened it. He stepped inside with his head down and closed it behind him.

"What's the verdict?" I asked. Roy's head snapped up, and I smiled. "Am I going to make it?"

He quickly closed the distance between us and got down beside my bed, holding my hand. "I can't believe it. You're awake."

My brows dropped. "It was that bad, huh?"

"Yeah it was that bad!" he said passionately. "How do you feel?"

"Weak. Tired. Very tired, and I never get tired."

"Well you were stabbed with an Angelic weapon. We're still trying to identify which one so we can treat you better, but those things are no fucking joke."

"You can't heal me?" I asked curiously.

He shook his head. "I can't heal such pure injures. Not

161

from Heaven or Hell. Give me any human, Nephilim, or Drake injury any day of the week and I can heal it, but a wound from a pure Angel with a pure Heavenly weapon? No way. Same with a pure Demon and pure Hell weapon."

"Well, sheesh," I teased. "Then what good are you in a war against Angels and Demons?"

Roy smiled broadly, but it was brief and quickly melted. "Hey listen," he said, seeming terribly sad, "I sort of like you." He smiled slightly. "Like, a lot. So could you do me a favor and not die? Please?"

I grinned at him. "I'll do my best."

He smiled a little more genuinely and then kissed the hand he was holding. "I'd appreciate that."

"How long have I been out?"

"A couple days."

I groaned at that, but then a thought occurred to me. "That Angel, the female Angel, is she all right?"

Roy nodded. "Thanks to you."

"And Kye?"

"Dead."

"You killed him?"

Roy nodded. "Holy Fire kills everything; Angels, Demons and everything in between. So does your dad's sword."

"My dad's sword!" I said in almost panic. "Where is it? It was in my hand when I was stabbed!"

"Shh shh!" Roy said as he stood up and leaned over me, resting his hand on my cheek. "I got it for you. I was able to put it back in your tattoo."

I sighed and relaxed, placing my hand protectively over my tattoo. "Thank you." I would have been devastated if I'd lost it. It was my father's and it was all I had of him.

With a smile, Roy leaned down and kissed my lips unexpectedly. I stared up at him in shock when he pulled away. Luckily the sliding door opened, saving me from trying to think of what to do next.

"It was a tack dagger." The blonde female Angel came sweeping in the room. She was still dressed in all white, but her wings and the ethereal white glow were gone since my eye tattoo wasn't activated. "Very poisonous to Angels, but blessedly"—she came to the opposite side of the bed and held out a small rose-colored clay cup— "you're only half Angel." I glanced at the cup suspiciously. "Drink this. It will flush the poison."

"What is it?" I asked, taking it.

"Does it matter? It will help you feel better."

"Says you."

Her expression dropped in confusion. "Of course says me. I just said so."

I almost grinned. She clearly lacked understanding of sarcasm. That was fine. I could be rude without sarcasm. "Tell me again why I should trust you?"

"Do. Don't. It's up to you. You saved my life. I am simply returning the favor. I can't make you want to live though."

This time I did grin. She was way too foolishly honest to be attempting to kill me right now. I drank the liquid in the cup. It felt like swallowing silk and tasted like a delicious rum cake. It coated my throat so thickly that I could feel it slide all the way down into my stomach.

"There." The Angel took the cup. "My debt is repaid. I thank you and goodbye."

"Wait," I said before she took off. "Have you been here the entire time I've been out?"

She nodded once. "I have."

"She flew us back here from Salt Creek," Roy said.

I looked at him, confused. "I thought there was warding or spells or something around the bunker that kept Demons and Angels out."

"God wants me here," the Angel said abruptly. "Mortal spells do not hold sway over him. He is protecting me. I needed to help Gabriel's Son identify the weapon used to stab you so you could be saved."

I felt my lip twitch at the mention of God. "Well, thank you." I said. "What's your name?"

"Sari. Is that all?"

"No. I have some questions, and I need your help."

She looked at me confused. "I brought you and Raphael's Son back here. I helped identify the weapon that stabbed you. I got the antidote. I believe I've gone above and beyond my required debt to you, Michael's Daughter."

What a strange and fascinating creature. "Why are you helping us?"

"Because God commanded it."

I narrowed my eyes at her curiously. She was different somehow. She seemed oddly sincerer than Kye. A whirlwind was going through my mind about how to approach this being and question her, but I didn't really think I needed any special tactic. She, for some reason, was not my enemy.

"I need more help from you."

"But I don't owe you anything else."

I couldn't help but smile at that. "You owe me an explanation."

"Do I?"

"Yes, you do. I got stabbed by Kye. You owe me an explanation as to why I took a blade in the back for you."

"I believe that's only something you can answer," she said with a small shake of her head. "Why would I need to explain *your* motives?"

"Why was Kye going to stab you? You owe me that much."

"Why does it matter?"

"Because Kye was my friend."

Sari's eyes got dangerously narrow. "You were friends with traitorous diabolical abomination of –"

"Whoa whoa!" I said, holding up my hands, shocked at her feral reaction. "Easy. Maybe friend is too strong a word." I searched her face carefully to make sure she visibly settled before I tried talking again. "What I mean is, we interacted with each other on a couple of occasions, and he never hurt me." Sari seemed to calm down. "He and I had an arrangement that he can't complete now, so you need the see the tasks through."

Sari crossed her arms. "Why exactly is that?"

"Because if I hadn't gotten between you and Kye, Kye never would have stabbed me, and in turn Roy wouldn't have killed him. Thus, what I asked of him would have been completed. So you owe me their completion before our debt is squared." I wasn't sure if that was entirely true, but it sounded good.

Sari sighed heavily and rolled her eyes. "What were the tasks?"

"There was a Knight Demon hurting Gyllian—Gabriel's Son. She was giving Gyllian information and supplies to help our cause, but it required he subject himself to torture at her hand." I looked at her evenly. "I want her dead."

Sari nodded. "If God allows it, it will be my pleasure to oblige."

I tried not to blink much. I didn't dare take my eyes off the Angel, lest she vanish by the time I looked back at her. I hadn't brought this matter up with Kye yet, but she didn't know that. "Here is the problem; that Demon was giving us the Hell Dust we need for our bullets. If you kill her, we won't have a supernatural substance supplier anymore. I need whatever substance Heaven has that kills Demons." I sighed. "And Angels."

Sari nodded once. "I know the substance. If God allows it, I will bring some to you. Anything else?"

"One last thing." I started to sit up in the bed. With Roy's help, I was able to get my knees under me and I summoned my wings out. With a whoosh, they spread wide to my sides, the tips of my black feathers touching both sides of the room. Sari's eyes got so wide I actually worried they might roll out of her head.

I resisted the urge to glance at my wings, keeping my gaze fixed on her. "He was going to teach me to fly."

I heard the sliding glass door open, and Fox, Booth, and Gyllian all came in, gawking with wide eyes. Fox was saying a string of something in Hindi that sounded like a prayer and resting her hands on her cheeks. I noticed Gyllian walked stiffly, not yet healed from his torture session, but it was good to see him on his feet.

"Bay," Fox said in a whisper, "they are magnificent."

I smiled at her before looking back at Sari. "I was given these wings for a reason. If God really wants us to fight this war, I need to know how to use them."

Sari didn't speak. I smirked a little, realizing I'd have to put them away in order to get anything done. Folding them behind me, I felt the queer sensation of a wind tunnel on my back before they vanished. With Roy's help again, I was able to lie back down in the hospital bed.

Sari looked like she could barely catch her breath. "Bailey, I must go."

My brows dropped. "What? Wait. We need…"

"I will return," she interrupted quickly, but gently. "At least I'm pretty certain I will return. I just need to confer with other parties in the war." Before I could argue, she was gone.

I sighed, settling back down on the pillows.

"Bay," Fox gasped and came to the side of the bed, gathering my hand into hers. "Those wings! They are superb! Glorious!"

Her excitement had me grinning. "Thank you."

Gyllian approached the foot of my bed with his hands in his pockets. "How are you feeling?"

He looked terribly pale and very tired. "I'm all right. Whatever antidote Sari gave me seems to be working. How are you feeling?"

"I'll live," he said with a shrug and glanced away. "Listen, I hate to push the matter, but we need to know if you're with us or not." He looked at me intently. "If you are, it's all in. You move in here. You train here. We share our intelligence, the whole nine. We fight Demons and Angels and try to keep Hell from rising. If not, then—"

"I'm in, Gyllian," I interrupted.

He paused. "You are?"

I gave a shrug. "I've already got my first battle wound. I can't turn back now even if I want to." I smiled at him, but he looked at me suspiciously. I sighed. "Look Gyllian, I'm still not sure how I feel about your mission but"—I paused— "for better or worse, I belong here with you guys."

Roy stood over me with a smile. "I told you, you would."

I grinned. "Don't look so smug. You've got to help me move in."

Roy sneered playfully. "Moving furniture? Please. Piece of cake. I'm half Angel."

"Or," Gyllian said, drawing me and Roy's attention, "you can pick out new furniture from scratch if you like."

Roy smiled at me again. "What do you think?"

"I think I need some HomeGoods catalogs."

Roy and I laughed before he leaned down and kissed my

forehead, "Sounds good to me."

I looked at Gyllian. "Listen guys," I said, glancing at the others. "Could you excuse us for a bit? Gyllian and I need to talk."

"Sure," Fox said lightly. "Come on you two." She started to usher Roy and Booth out of the room.

"I'll see you later," Roy said, and all three of them left through the sliding glass door.

I looked back at Gyllian, examining him briefly. "You look like shit."

Gyllian rolled his eyes and went over to the corner of the room where a plush white leather armchair sat. He grabbed the back of it and, making his eyes go Angelic, moved it with ease over to the left side of my bed. "Forgive me. I missed the YouTube tutorial on how to look sexy after a Demon torture session."

I stared at him. "Did you...just make a joke?"

Gyllian smiled, stepping in front of the chair. "Tried. Tried to make a joke."

"Since *when?*"

His grin widened little, and then, pressing down into the arms of the chair, he slowly and stiffly lowered himself into the seat. When he was settled, he sighed softly and relaxed. "So," he said. "Ask."

With some effort, I pushed myself up so I was sitting straighter in the bed. "All right, why did we run away from the Demons on the Riverwalk?" Gyllian's expression changed to confusion. "Why did Roy and I have to run from the Demons at the club? I'm assuming he filled you in on what happened. I don't understand how we're expected to fight the entirety of Hell when we have to run from a few small packs of Demons."

"Okay," Gyllian said. "That's not where I thought you would start."

"Where did you think I would start?"

"Maybe with questions about God?"

I sneered. God was the last thing I wanted to talk about, and I felt offended he would even think I cared. God was obviously real, which just made me hate him all the more. "God?" I barked. "Okay, you want a question about God?

167

Here's one: Why is he such a dick?"

Gyllian's face got so red I thought he was going to explode, and I felt a small flash of satisfaction for getting him that upset. But the dangerous, wide-eyed stare he gave me, paired with his red face, made my insides shrink. My fresh hatred for God wouldn't let me back down, though, and I braced myself for a fight with him.

Gyllian slowly shook his head. "How can you talk about something you don't understand with such certainty?"

"Oh, I understand," I replied. "I understand God didn't save me from any *one* of my foster parents."

I was losing control. I could feel myself start to unravel. It was like when Kye got near me. I had to stay calm, or I would be lost to the memories of my past. I could feel them rising over the dam that had taken me sixteen years to build and a single encounter with an Angel to penetrate. I could not crumble! If I lost control, I feared where the flood would take me.

"If God is supposed to be this benevolent, almighty, all-powerful being, then where the *fuck* was he when I was getting beaten and starved and raped by my foster families?"

"Bay, you—"

And the dam broke.

"I was four years old, Gyllian!" I screamed. "And a forty-two-year-old decided it would feel really good to have sex with me because I was so fucking small." Gyllian's face went pale. I was panting as the floodgate of raw wounds and emotions opened up. "Where the fuck was God while that pig was behind me moaning about how good it felt because of how tight my little pussy was? Where was God when my 'tight little pussy' wasn't tight enough anymore and he decided to sodomize me? Where the fuck was God while I was screaming and bleeding from the pain?"

Gyllian moved so fast I didn't even see him budge until he was already sitting on the bed hugging me. I sobbed and beat his shoulders with my fists as memories—horrible, horrible memories—threatened to rip me apart inside. I couldn't breathe! I was loudly gasping for air over his shoulder as things I had long shoved away began to surface. Gyllian didn't let me go, though, he didn't even back off. So

I clutched his sweater in my fists and held on to him as I rode the waves of my horrific past and felt the dam crumble into oblivion.

I could feel the pain again of being raped so young. I felt his hands on me and the tearing of my flesh as the blood ran down my thighs. I remembered the fear as I watched it slide down and land on the sheets. I recalled the fear of knowing the punishment that was in store for me because of the stains it would leave.

I remembered my second foster father and my fourteen-year-old foster brother taking turns having sex with me on several occasions, sometimes at the same time. One night, when I was eight, my brother was sodomizing me while my foster father held my head on his lap, forcing himself so deep down my throat that I threw up. When it happened, he only forced my head down harder onto his lap, using my vomit as a hot lubricant that made him scream in ecstasy. I eventually couldn't breathe and mercifully passed out.

I felt the stabbing of the hunger pains, like my body was eating itself, muscle and bone, to stay alive. I felt the cigarette burns on my arms, neck, chest, and butt. I felt my bones break and my head swell as I was flung down stairs or into walls or doors.

I relived the darkness of the closets I was shut in for days. I could smell and feel my own human waste all over me while I sat in those closets waiting to be freed. I remembered the scalding hot baths afterwards. I felt the beatings with the belts, and the cuts from the coat hangers as I cleaned up my own waste inside them.

I clung to Gyllian and trembled in the flood of these memories. He was the only anchor that was keeping me from being swept away by the torrential waters. He was the only reason I was able to remember that I was safe now. I'd won. I'd beaten my abusers because I'd survived, I'd lived, and I'd done something amazing with my life.

As the flood waters began to ebb, I inhaled Gyllian deep into my lungs. He smelled like clean laundry and a summer breeze. I let his smell ground me in the present, and pushed the past away. The fear left me trembling in his arms, but the memories faded.

"Where was God, Gyllian?" I moaned. "Why didn't he save me then?"

Gyllian remained quiet for a moment, and I realized he was petting my hair. He was so gentle with me, holding me the way he was. I was safe with him.

"Are you up for a trip?" he asked in a husky whisper.

"Where?" I asked.

He slightly pulled away and I found myself lost in his cognac eyes. "God has something to show you."

I blinked. I wasn't sure how I felt about that.

Gyllian caressed the side of my head, and his sunset eyes roamed over my face like he was looking for the meaning of life itself. "Will you come with me?"

I swallowed and barely managed a small nod.

"Can you stand?"

I nodded again, and with Gyllian's help stood from the bed. He stood directly in front of me, resting his hands on my hips, and suddenly his eyes went Angelic.

The room began to blur and fade like a watered-down painting. When things started to come back into focus, we were on the docking platform of the Riverwalk. It was completely empty save for one man in a gray business suit standing not far away. The day was overcast and windy, but I had on a pair of thick sweatpants, a long-sleeved jersey, and a hooded sweatshirt, so I wasn't too chilly. The fresh air was welcome and helped clear my head of the remaining fog from the poisonous dagger.

I smiled a little at him. "You can teleport."

Gyllian nodded, but his focus was on something in the distance behind me. Following his gaze, I realized he was looking at the man in the business suit. My eyes narrowed slightly before they went wide. I knew him. He'd aged a lot since I last saw him. His golden blonde hair had gone completely gray, and his mouth and crystal blue eyes had some wrinkles in the corners, but he was still tall and broad shouldered and beautiful.

"Paul," I said softly, turning. It was my social worker. The only kind adult I'd ever known.

"His name is not Paul," Gyllian said gently.

I looked back at him. "What?"

take a step. Even as I approached, I wasn't sure if I was going to hit him or hug him. He waited, his faced pained, as if he was expecting the former. I still wasn't sure what I was going to do, until he was in front of me. I knew his face well, very well, and like a ton of bricks I realized I was looking at my father's face, *my father's face*! And I burst into tears and pressed my forehead into his chest.

The way he eagerly gathered me in his arms made breathing impossible, and I sobbed like the ground could swallow me whole at any second. This cry was different though, deeper. It wasn't the result of some magical whammy an Angel could put on me by being near me; this was the cry of a girl who had missed her father.

"I know, baby," he whispered. "I know."

Hearing him call me "baby" sent a jolt of shock through me that manifested into more violent trembling and sobbing. I pressed my face more firmly into his chest to try to muffle it.

"It's okay, honey. I'm here. I'm so, so sorry."

His voice wrapped around me like a cozy blanket. I knew his voice. I'd heard it many times, but I'd never heard it with the knowledge that it was my father speaking to me. With each gentle, comforting word he said, I trembled a little more and had to hold him tighter. Twenty minutes must have gone by before I was breathing relatively normal again. Even after calming down, I was afraid to let him go. I clutched at the back of his jacket, holding it in my trembling fists like he would disappear if I didn't.

Slowly I was able to lift my face. "Dad," I choked out, which only sent me sobbing again. I'd never said that to anyone before.

He pulled me into an embrace again and kissed the top of my head. "It's okay, sweetheart. It's okay."

Another few minutes passed while I pulled myself together and tried to think of something to say. I was overwhelmed by the fear that I'd say something wrong. Humor. Maybe humor would work. It was likely my safest option.

I sniffed, choking down my sobs as I looked up into his face again. "So you're the Archangel Michael, huh?" I asked with a nervous chuckle.

He smiled, which sent a wave of relief through me. "I used to be, but"—he swallowed hard— "humanity is a hell of a thing to happen to an Angel."

My eyes traveled over his features, absorbing every curve and wrinkle, every twinkle in his aquamarine blue eyes. "You're completely human?"

He nodded and wiped the tears from my cheek with his thumb. "Yeah."

"I don't…" I tried to begin, but stopped. Too negative. I didn't want to scare him off. I swallowed heavily. "I need your help."

Michael nodded. "That's why God told Henry to bring you here, so we could talk."

"Henry?" Gyllian!

I turned to look for him over my shoulder and saw him a few yards away. He stood with his back against a banister and his hands in his pockets as he gazed out over the water. The breeze lifted the hair off his forehead, and my heart swelled before it melted into a puddle, settling in my stomach in a sweet churning mess of emotions. This was the second time he had brought my father to me.

"I can't stay long, Bay," my dad said, drawing my attention. His eyes were sad but serious. "The Angels and Demons think I'm long dead, and it needs to stay that way." He tilted his head toward a nearby bench. "Come on."

I warily released the death grip I had on his clothes and we went over to it. "How long do we have?" I asked as we sat down beside each other. The words burned in my throat, as I knew he was going to leave after this and I might never see him again.

"Long enough for you to get the important questions out," he said, leaning forward and kissing my temple.

When he pulled back I just stared at him. His eyes were so kind and gentle, his smile soft and tender, but he was so strong. I knew he was strong because of the way I'd grown up with him, because of the way he'd carried himself and the way he'd dealt with me and my situation. I remembered a shouting match that erupted between him and the cop taking my abuse report against my foster mother when I was sixteen. She was an upstanding citizen, a churchgoer, and I was her troublemaking white trash foster kid. The cop, Officer Evany, was glib about my report, even snide as he subtly called me a liar and clearly didn't believe a word I said. But my dad did. He almost got arrested that day, but the Captain came in and defused the situation.

"How are you alive?" I asked him, my voice shaking. "All the other Archangels were killed. Why not you? And why didn't you ever tell me who you were?"

My dad gave a short sigh, and I panicked for a second, thinking I'd upset him, but then he gave me a small smile. "I've been protected so I could be with you through your difficult upbringing." He glanced down at his hands, which were holding mine. "I couldn't tell you who I was because my anonymity helped protect us both." He looked up at me. "You *had* to be kept safe."

I shook my head. "I wasn't exactly safe, Dad."

He nodded, though his eyes stayed sad and glittered with some unshed tears. "From the Angels and Demons you were." I swallowed. "That's why we needed to stay apart as much as possible. The Angels and Demons were always looking for us, all of us. They found the others. They would have found us, too."

My mouth went dry as I tried to form the next question, terrified of upsetting him and driving him off before his due time. "I don't understand. If..." I resisted the urge to clench my teeth. "If God could protect you so thoroughly, letting you live up to now, why couldn't he have kept us safe together?"

"Oh honey," he said and brought my hand up to kiss it, "because it wasn't in his plan."

The words, "His plan?" settled in my chest, threatening to rise out of my mouth unbidden in a loud shriek. I couldn't argue with him, though. I wanted to get the most out of my time with him. This line of conversation would get me nowhere and could end in an argument. I wasn't about to risk that. Not for anything.

I swallowed heavily. A change of subject was in order. "You fell from Heaven and became mortal, completely human. Why?"

He smiled a little playfully. "Well, Angels can't

conceive children."

I couldn't help but smile. "That's not what I meant, but..." My voice trailed off, and I looked at him, confused. "Wait. If you were completely human, then how am I half Angel?"

"Because when we fell we weren't completely human. None of us were. Our true Angelic form is not something that could go unnoticed by the humans of Earth, so we had to be disguised. We each had a human shell if you will, a vessel specially created by God so we could temporarily pass as humans while maintaining our Angelic power, which was to be passed on to our progeny. As soon as I was intimate with a human—with your mother—everything I was poured into her, creating you, and I became truly human."

I swallowed heavily again. "You didn't rape my mother, did you?"

Pain and regret darkened his eyes. "In a way I did."

I felt my heartbeat in my cheeks and ears. "In what way?" I asked my voice cracking.

"I didn't hurt her or force myself on her," he said and swallowed, "but I did use my power to alter her will to make her think she wanted to be intimate with me."

I was shaking. "Why?"

He swallowed heavily. "I only had twenty-four hours to conceive you, Bay. Or everything would have been for nothing. There would be no chance for the world to survive if I didn't conceive you in time." He met my eyes pleadingly. "I hope you can forgive me," he whispered. "I'm not offering this as an excuse, but a reason. If it helps a little," he went on, "I explained everything to your mother after. She forgave me and bravely, *bravely* took on the burden I'd put on her." He clutched my hand in both of his, "and that was to give you life, and then give you up."

I felt like I should hate him for that, but I just couldn't bring myself to. I knew hatred, I knew people who deserved it, but my dad wasn't one of them. What he was saying was going to take some time to process, but I didn't want to waste whatever time I had left with him on the fence.

I leaned toward him and rested my head on his shoulder. He put his arm around me. "You always made sure I

176

remembered the last thing she ever said to me." I swallowed. "Thank you for that."

He kissed my head. "You're welcome, honey. I'm so sorry you lost her as early as you did."

I nodded and sat up again, wiping my cheeks of any remaining tears. "Me too." I took a deep breath and tried to compose myself before meeting his eyes. "So as the former General of Heaven's armies," I said as we both smiled, "what can you tell me that can help me? I don't know what to do with this enormous threat I was put here to face."

He sighed gently. "You have to ask smaller questions than that, baby. We'd be here for ten years if I were to get into everything."

"I'm okay with that," I blurted out.

His face brightened a little before he leaned forward and gently touched his forehead to mine before kissing it. "I'd give anything to stay."

I swallowed the urge to moan "Then why don't you?" I wanted my dad. It was pathetic, but I didn't care. I wanted my dad. But I couldn't waste my time begging him to stay when I knew it was impossible. What did I need most? I wasn't sure, but allies seemed like a good place to start. Sari popped into my head.

"Are all the Angels with the Demons? Because I met one today that made me unsure."

"You mean the Angel you took a tack dagger for?"

I looked at him curiously. "How do you know about that?"

He smiled warmly. "God keeps me updated on you. I ask him often enough."

That made me grin, and my dad's smile widened, which prompted me to rest my head on his shoulder again. He gathered me tightly against him for a moment before I sat up. "How many Angels are there like Sari? Ones that don't have it out for us?"

"Maybe a dozen," he replied. "All of them are in hiding though. Their numbers are so few already, and the other Angels will kill them if they are spotted."

I sighed and cast a glance at Gyllian, who was still gazing silently over the river. This was his fight, a fight he was passionate about, even if I wasn't. Any information I could get to help his cause would mean something to him, and that meant something to me.

I looked back at my dad. "Would those dozen fight with us?"

"If God lets them."

My brows dropped at the unexpected response. "Why wouldn't he?"

"He might not want to risk them, but I'm not sure. I can't speak for him."

I sighed in frustration and glanced away over the river with my anger toward God still burning bright.

"Bay," my dad said gently. "Don't think that the five of you can't handle this. It's why you were created. It's why I fell, why all five of us fell. You are equipped; you just have to believe it."

I shook my head. "It's not that."

"Then what?"

I didn't want to get into negative territory, but I needed to ask. "Why is God letting any of this happen?" My dad pressed his lips together sadly. "If he loves humanity as much as all the books on him claim, why doesn't he just smite the Angels trying to raise Hell? Then none of this would be happening at all. You'd still be running Heaven, I could have been born to a loving family, and the world would keep spinning." I shrugged. "Why let *any* of this occur?"

His expression became sympathetic. "God has his reasons."

I grinned mirthlessly as anger started to burn in my throat. "That's it? That's all there is to it?"

My dad shook his head. "It's never been in me to question him. I won't start now."

My jaw was working as I looked over the river. I could not take out my anger on my father. I could *not*.

"I think I may know his motives though," he said.

Returning my attention to him, I noticed the hesitation in his eyes. "But you're not going to tell me, are you?"

He shook his head, "I'm sorry. I'm not him."

I looked over the river again. Another change of subject was in order.

"Broad strokes, Bay," my dad said suddenly. "Everything God allows to happen, even this, is because he is good, he loves humanity, and he wants them to come home to him."

I needed to get off the subject of God, and fast. "So you fell from Heaven," I said a little shortly. "You willingly subjected yourself to mortality and suffered in the muck and mire of humanity, all of in order to create me so I could help save them?"

"Yes."

"Why?"

He pressed his lips together and sighed. "Because God loves them."

I licked my lips and chuckled mirthlessly as I looked over the water once more. It always came back to God. From what I understood, God loved everyone, including Satan, so anything on the subject was useless to me.

"Since you've seen what it's like down here, do you regret falling?"

My dad sighed and rubbed my back affectionately. "I'm not going to lie to you, Bay. I've seen things that have made me wonder."

An enormous wave of relief hit me upon hearing that, far more than I expected. He bowed his head and brushed his fingertips across his forehead. I smiled a little, realizing I'd gotten that tic from him.

"You see horrible things as a social worker, my own *daughter's* case being the worst I've come across." He shook his head as if he were seeing my injuries all over again. "Such unbelievable evil I thought only existed in Hell." He sighed, his countenance softening a little as he looked back at me. "But I have seen goodness too, goodness even the Angels were not capable of."

I was surprised by that. My dad had seen it all. He still believed they were worth saving, that they were worth his fall, that they were worth his suffering, worth his daughter suffering. I couldn't deny that it pissed me off.

"You *willingly* sacrificed being an Angel for humanity's sake," I said, realizing I was bordering on having an argument with him, and I was terrified about it. But he had the same kind of single-mindedness that Gyllian and the others had about saving them, something I just didn't get. "All of the Nephilims have suffered horribly at the hands of humanity. You've seen *firsthand* the evil it's capable of in *my* case file. Yet you still think it deserves to be saved?"

My dad shifted to face me more fully and gathered my hands into his. "Here is the thing you and many humans don't understand about suffering and why God allows it."

My brows dropped at that. "Okay."

"Without suffering and pain, there would be no compassion." My brow cocked up. "There would be no way to even cultivate compassion without pain and suffering." He kissed my hands without breaking eye contact. "The Garden of Eden is a perfect example. Adam and Eve never had to suffer or want for anything, so they had no humility, no compassion, no love, no understanding, no sympathy of what bringing evil into the world could mean. In a world where everything is wonderful, nothing is, because there is no ugliness to show people the wonderful." He tucked a finger under my chin. "Pain and suffering call for compassion, but compassion itself can't exist without the suffering."

I couldn't believe this was actually making sense to me. "So that's how God dealt with a broken world? By using its brokenness to cultivate love and compassion?"

He smiled. "Something only God is capable of pulling off."

I shook my head. "What about the people who don't feel compassion?" I asked, trying not to sound like I was arguing. "My abusers didn't."

"That is on them, honey, not God."

That felt like a stab to my heart. It was as if he, my father, was saying it was okay that my foster parents abused me because they couldn't help it!

"God gave all humans free will and choice," my dad went on. "Their choices are not his fault, though they certainly love to blame him for them."

My anger toward God manifested into a glare at my father. "So what about me and other innocent kids who fall victim to the compassionless? God left us, *me*, to suffer so we could become more *compassionate?*"

"He *let* you suffer," my dad stressed before he shook his head. "But he never left you."

I sneered. "I felt pretty alone, Dad," I shot back.

"I know. I'm not saying it was fair, I'm just saying there was a reason."

"What reason could there *possibly* be for that?"

I was shouting, but I was past caring. My own father was telling me that my suffering, my abuse, had an easy explanation and that my abusers had been "just broken." I wanted to scream!

He placed a hand on my cheek, and it shocked me how comforting that was. Here I was, yelling at him, arguing, and he wasn't even defending himself; he was comforting me. When I yelled at people, it was to keep them at a distance, a distance my father surprisingly refused to allow, and that felt unexpectedly good.

"For one thing," he said holding my eyes hostage with his, "it produced the best damn FBI agent in the nation." I stared at him in disbelief. "I know exactly how many children you saved and how many predators you arrested. I know exactly how many victims from sex trafficking rings you broke up, who are safe and sound, some of them happily married and starting young families of their own. I know exactly how many rape victims sleep better at night because Agent Bay Kennedy was working their cases, and put their rapists behind bars. All because you knew what it was like to be the victim of sexual predators. You wouldn't, you *couldn't*, give up on any of those victims because of that."

The overwhelming praise was making me nearly dizzy. Someone of my flesh and blood, my *father,* was proud of me. I was a damn good agent. I knew it, everyone at headquarters knew it, and my passion for the job definitely stemmed from the black roots of my childhood. As I thought about what my dad was saying, and saw the light in his eyes as he praised my work, something clicked into place. It didn't make my trauma easy to accept or remember—nothing about that would likely ever be easy—but that there had been a good purpose for it? *That* I might be able to come to terms with someday.

Michael.

I heard the gentle ethereal call in my ears and jumped.

My father's face scrunched in agony as he kept his eyes locked on mine. "Please Lord," he whispered. "Give me more time."

My eyes went wide when I realized that it was God talking.

I would if I could. But she and the other children have work to do.

Spikes of fear went through my chest. My dad was leaving. God was taking my father!

He pulled me into an embrace, and I could feel him shaking. "Bay," he choked out. "I've got to go."

"No," I moaned as I held him tight and tears started to burn my eyes.

"I'm sorry, honey." He rested his hand behind my head and kissed my cheek. "I've got to."

"No, Dad. Please stay." I didn't care how childish I looked or sounded. I just wanted my father.

He kissed the side of my hair over and over again. "I love you, sweetheart."

"I love you too, Dad," I sobbed.

Suddenly the solidness of him faded, and my arms were empty. He was gone. Just like that, I was left shaking and trembling alone on the bench.

I wasn't sure what I felt. Hatred? For who? Why would I feel hatred when I'd just seen and spoken to my father? Anger? I shouldn't feel anything negative, should I? But I did. It was all mixed up with the unbelievable joy at seeing him. I was shocked, happy, hurt, alone and a million other things mixed up in between. What the hell?

Gyllian was suddenly crouching in front of me, looking up at me with softness and compassion. "Are you all right?"

I shook my head. "No," I said, my voice cracking. Then I sniffed. "And yes."

I wiped my cheeks, not really sure how to answer that question yet. I needed my father. I couldn't have him. So I needed…I needed something to do.

I looked at Gyllian as a few last tears fell. "Take me home," I said more pleadingly than I intended. "I need something to do."

Gyllian stood and held his hand out to me. "Good thing

I've got plenty for you to do."

I took it and he helped me to me feet. I was so emotionally, and still a little physically, drained that I closed my eyes and rested my cheek on his chest. I didn't expect a response from him, so I was surprised when he embraced me tightly with his jaw against the side of my head. I sighed in a mix of contentment and frustration as Gyllian took us home.

18

As soon as we were back in the hospital-like room we'd left from, I immediately headed for the sliding glass door that led into the bigger room beyond.

"Whoa, hey," Gyllian said, taking my arm. "You still need to rest."

I shook my head. "My mind needs to be occupied." I shrugged. "So fill me in." The look he gave me said he was about to argue, so I forced a smile. "You're up and about just two days after being tortured by a Demon." Gyllian pressed his lips together. "So I have no excuse to do anything less, do I?"

He sighed. "All right." He passed me and pulled open the sliding glass door.

I still needed answers, like why we were running from Demons, but right now my emotions were in tatters and I just had to do something normal for a minute. My hopes were dashed when I stepped into the large room and over a dozen Fox clones were making the room hop like a fully staffed military command center. My eyes went wide. Each copy was concentrated on a different task; a few were flipping through files, one was shredding something, another was crossing something off a white board, another was writing something and sticking the note on another board. Booth and Roy both sat at a cluster of six computers in the middle of the room with the real Fox between them.

"Check Malaysia again," Roy said.

"The activity there is still promising," Fox replied.

"What about South Sudan?" Booth asked as he got up from his computer and went to one of the whiteboards that was covered with a list of countries and cities, many of them crossed off. He picked up a marker and crossed off Sri Lanka.

"Cross it off," one of the Fox copies called. I looked to my left and saw her gazing up from a clipboard. "Sulfuric levels in the White Nile returned to normal and have held

184

steady for over two months."

"Haiti?" Roy asked.

"Still not sure," the real Fox said. "Activity is still in the normal range, but it hasn't ceased for an abnormal length of time."

"What the hell?" I whispered, stunned.

All the Fox clones looked at me at once and smiled at the exact same time, in the exact same manner, which was unnerving. "Welcome back, Bay," the real Fox said before looking at her computer screen again. The clones all returned to their duties as well.

"Hey," Roy said, coming out from behind his computer. "How are you feeling?"

"I'm…" I looked around at all the busy Fox clones. "I'm confused."

Roy grinned. "I'd say that's fairly normal since you've never been in here before." He beckoned me to follow as he headed back to his computer. "Welcome to our day job," he said, spinning to face me with his arms out.

"Day job?" I asked, still taking in the activity and trying to make sense of it.

"Gyllian can explain better, but first things first." Roy picked up a small unremarkable cell phone from beside his keyboard and handed it to me. "Burner phone. All our numbers are programmed into it already, and we dispose of them once a week. This is day one of this phone. Just see Fox in seven days for a new one so she can program all of our new numbers for that week into it."

"Once a week?" I asked, appalled. "That's an awful lot of phones to go through."

"Gyllian owns the majority of stock at Trac Mobile." He smiled. "We get them for free." I looked back at Gyllian, who had a slightly smug smile on his face. "We were thinking Chinese for lunch," Roy said, addressing him. "That okay?"

Gyllian nodded. "Sounds good."

"Bay?" he asked. I nodded absently, still taking in the room. "I'll order," Roy looked at me with a playful smirk. "Enjoy the info download," he said, sitting down and going back to work.

I gave Gyllian a small shake of my head. "What?" I

185

asked, utterly beside myself.

My reaction made him smile as he came around to stand behind Roy. "The simple version of what you're seeing is us trying to figure out where Hell is going to rise. The complication comes when you realize what that search entails."

I spun my finger around, indicating the room. "And the clones?"

"One of her abilities."

"I've got more dazzle than this, too," Fox said winking up at me. I couldn't help but grin.

"Nothing would get done here without her." Gyllian looked around the room. "*All* of her."

The dozen Foxes all paused in their activity and looked at Gyllian with a charming smile. It was sweet, but the way they all moved in sync was incredibly creepy.

"Okay, so how exactly are you trying to figure out where Hell will rise?"

"Mainly earthquakes these days," Gyllian said, pointing to the computer monitors that Fox, Booth and Roy sat behind.

I leaned over Roy's shoulder to get a closer look at his screen. The type was incredibly small, but I could see it was a list of locations worldwide in alphabetical order. Panning my gaze over to the other screens I saw the same thing, only different locations. The scroll tabs were miniscule, which meant these lists were incredibly long. It looked like they had every single city in the world up on those six screens. Beside each location was a continuous stream of current seismograph readings.

"Ho-ly shit," I said, amazed.

Gyllian leaned back against the edge of a table behind him and crossed his arms. "The activity of the Earth is a constant thing, as we all learned in fifth grade. What we look for is increased earthquake activity, or abnormally prolonged activity, in every city of every country in the world."

I looked at him over my shoulder. "What would that tell you?"

"Increased earthquake activity could mean they are drilling or even just gathering in large numbers, which could indicate the place they will emerge."

I stood up straight. "The Demons have to *drill* to get to the surface? They can't just materialize?"

Gyllian shrugged. "We don't know."

"What do you mean? That's how they get here now."

"In small numbers. There are always little cracks in the dimensional wall of Hell that allow the passage of a few Demons at a time, but they are hardly big enough to let Hell's entire army up here. We don't know how they plan to pull that off, so we're covering all of our bases."

"Meaning?"

Gyllian nodded to the left and I turned to look. Taking up just about all the available space on that wall were much larger computer screens with significantly different readings on them. The largest screen, about the size of a home theater screen, had an animated map of the whole world aglow. Abstract moving colors brought the map to life and had numerous small readings I couldn't make out. Some of the smaller screens beneath had categories listed like Doppler radar, temperature, solar radiation, and a whole slew of satellite labels. Each monitor was numbered one through twelve.

"That's the meteorology station where we monitor weather patterns all over the world. Any increase in storms or strange weather, like a heat wave in Siberia or a snow storm in Cuba, we monitor. That kind of activity could also indicate Demon activity."

"Satellites?" I asked, pointing limply in the direction of the screens. "You have your own *satellites?*" Gyllian just smiled, and my eyebrows dropped. "Seriously?"

"Twelve of them. Bought, built, and put into orbit."

I scoffed, though my laugh didn't hold as much scorn as it did disbelief. "Jesus," I muttered.

"Over there," Gyllian said, dipping his head forward. To the right of the hospital room we'd come out of, was a very well-lit area that looked a lot like a small version of the lab back at FBI Headquarters. "That's our biology station, where we run samples from all over the world—things like water, sand, plants and any other organisms necessary to find abnormalities."

"Like what?"

He shrugged. "Anything. Increased acidity in water or soil, for example. High amounts of sulfuric acid could indicate increased volcanic, or underground activity, which is another possible indication the Demons could rise there. We also look for any marginal abnormalities of organic life, mass deaths for instance, which could also be an indicator."

"So wait," I said rubbing my forehead. "Underground activity? You mean Hell is actually underneath the planet?"

"Eh," Gyllian said his face scrunching. "Yes and no. Hell isn't actually sitting there in the physical core of the Earth. It's down there, but through a supernatural wall which is, in fact, Satan's prison from when he was cast down."

"So it's there but not there?"

"Look at it this way," Gyllian said, straightening. "Pretend this room is all you knew of the entire world. This was it. This was the physical Earth." He pointed to the door on the right. "Now pretend that door was invisible, but *you* had the ability to see it. You could walk through it and enter an entirely different place, an entire different section of the bunker that no one else could see or even know about. That's what Hell is."

"Hell is in a different dimension," I stated.

Gyllian's brows dropped. "Yes. But I thought you wouldn't understand me if I simply said that."

I gave him a flat stare. "I spent eight days and eight nights in your library, Gyllian. I learned a thing or two about the supernatural and other dimensions. But to get here, on Earth, the Demons would actually have to come up from underground?"

"We think so, since the core of the Earth encapsulates Hell's dimension, and Demons can't go through the door itself. The walls of Hell, the Earth's core, are our best lead, so we monitor unusual underground activity."

"Why can't the Demons go through the door?"

"Because God sealed it himself," he stated in a tone that ended the discussion. "Over there." He nodded to the right wall where another large but dark screen was mounted on the wall next to the exit door. There were a few smaller monitors mounted beneath it and a clean organized table under those with only a few thin piles of papers neatly stacked. "That's our astronomy station. The big screen lets us toggle through live feed of every single major telescope in the world."

"What do you think you're going to find in space if Hell is underground?"

"Anything. Satan is as much a supernatural intelligent being as God is, and both of them can manipulate heavenly bodies. We look for any strange movement or alignments of known stars and planets, unscheduled comets, increased radiation from the sun. All of which might be a sign or a warning for us."

"This," he said, jerking his thumb over his shoulder behind him, "is where we profile highly influential people that may be Drakes, Demons, people working for Demons, or possessed by Demons—basically anyone we could speak to who may have information about where Hell might rise."

I gave him a small half smile. "You mean interrogate."

Gyllian responded with a playful and slightly mischievous grin. A full smile spread across my face as I stepped up beside him and stared at the wall. It consisted of corkboards and whiteboards covered with pictures, articles, Post-its, scrap paper, and notes. On the tables beneath the boards were piles and piles of files, with boxes of more files underneath the tables—personal files, criminal files, everything.

Suddenly I felt right at home.

I saw pictures of people I recognized from all over the world—politicians and military personnel from every country, known terrorists and criminals, mobsters and military heroes, high profile bankers and CEOs, and a few celebrities. They were mostly people of significant wealth and power. Each cluster of photos was arranged in a pyramid scheme, or a tree of power, indicating who was believed to be at what level in the organization with which they were likely connected. Some of these people I'd seen across the evidence boards during my time as an agent. I'd even arrested a decent handful of them.

"I don't know about all that other stuff," I said, taking off my sweatshirt and tossing over the back of a chair, "but I can definitely help with this."

"We figured as much," Gyllian said.

I looked over at him. He had a broad and confident smile. "What do you mean?"

He tilted his head toward Fox. "She has a knack for seismology and majored in it in college." He nodded to Roy. "Biology." He tilted his head to Booth. "Astronomy." He pointed to himself. "Meteorology." His smile softened and he nodded toward me. "Profiling."

I shook my head. "So?"

He seemed to find my question humorous as he stood up from leaning against the table. "There are five scientific and intellectual areas of study that could help us locate where Hell is going to rise, and the only five Nephilims to exist in history just happen to specialize in each discipline?" His smile became a smug smirk, and he looked at me pointedly with those amber eyes of his burning into my retinas. "That's not a coincidence."

I pressed my lips together. I knew what he was trying to say, that there was a purpose, a reason, even a designer behind that. I knew which designer he wanted to indicate, but I just didn't want to hear it. I needed to concentrate on something normal for a while, so looked back at the boards on the wall without a response. My silence seemed to amuse him further as I watched him from the corner of my eye.

"Roy," he said, disappearing from my side, "call Hung's and order lunch. Tell them I'll be by to pick it up."

"Whoa hey," I said facing him. "Do you think that's a good idea?"

"You don't like Chinese?" he asked with a grin.

I flinched. "What? No. I mean Roy and I were cornered in public not two days ago. I was cornered on the Riverwalk before that. And none of you were thrilled at hearing about the Demons in your club. I don't think we should go anywhere alone."

"Don't worry, Bay" Fox said without taking her eyes of her computer screen. "I have him disguised."

I shifted uncomfortably as Gyllian stared at me. What was with him? This playful side he was suddenly displaying was odd for him. "Just…be careful."

With a nod, he headed for the door.

"Bay," Roy said, pulling out his cell phone, "what would

you like?"

I put my focus back on the wall. "Um, just some chicken fingers and rice. And beef teriyaki sounds good." My stomach suddenly growled loudly, and I placed my hand over it as if that would silence it. "Maybe some spare ribs, too."

I realized I hadn't eaten in a while. The last meal I remembered was the soup someone had brought me during my library binge. I never usually ate much, likely because I was half Angel and didn't need to, but I certainly hadn't gone this long with so little food. Hopefully Gyllian would be back soon.

I pulled out the chair my sweatshirt was draped over and sat down. I was frustrated to find thoughts of my dad trying to encroach on my concentration. I had to force them away. I didn't have time to think about that. As much as I wanted to, it really just brought pain because he wasn't there with me. I needed to occupy myself somehow, and those boards were the best way to do that. This was what I was good at. This was where I belonged. This was what made sense to me, investigating, profiling, solving. I couldn't do anything about my dad, wherever he might be now, but I could do this.

I picked up a dry erase marker and absently pressed the back of it to my bottom lip as I focused on the faces on the boards. I had only one question I needed to answer: "Who would be the most useful in finding out where Hell might rise?" I started with the people I was already personally familiar with. With my newfound knowledge of the supernatural, I delved into their files with a brand new fervor.

It didn't take long to realize these files were way more detailed than anything the FBI had. How in the hell had Gyllian gotten a hold of these? This kind of intelligence was uncensored CIA level! I pored over them for at least an hour in amazement. If there was a Heaven, this was it for me. There weren't enough hours in the day I could spend with my nose in this paper. These files held information about past crimes, including some juvie crimes the FBI knew nothing about. Some had high-level international contacts, and associates that were in the black for the FBI, including some black ops and deals classified as Top Secret, were before my eyes in print. I couldn't believe this!

As I went through the files and considered my own career with the Bureau, some pieces started to fall into place. A web of connections, contacts, facts and events started to take shape in my mind, and a couple of frontrunners we could talk to came to center stage.

"What's in your head?"

Yanked out of my concentration, I jumped at the unexpected sound. Roy was sitting beside me with his back to my table, smiling. I looked up at the boards. "I'm thinking we want to talk to Justine Nuwart."

"Who?" he said, looking over his shoulder at the wall. "She's not on the board."

"No," I conceded, sitting back and crossing my arms, "but she's the Associate Deputy Director of FBI Headquarters in Quantico."

One of his brows went up. "Why is that important?"

I sighed. I was used to dealing with people who already knew the inner workings of the Bureau. "Because she heads up two major departments in Quantico that contain eleven sub-departments. Among these"—I eyed him pointedly— "is the Training Division." He didn't flinch. "The Training Division assesses, trains, and *selects* FBI undercover agents." His face brightened as he caught my drift. "She also oversees the *placement* of undercover agents."

"Holy shit."

I nodded. "Need to get Demons or Drakes topside with new identities and influential jobs? She's the woman to see. There is virtually *no* red tape for her, especially if she's a Demon. She could put any Demon or Drake just about anywhere she'd like, and no one would be the wiser to question her."

"But the Demons she places would have to pass as agents first, wouldn't they?"

"One of the other sub-departments she oversees is the Records Management Division." His eyes widened. "For someone at Justine's level of authority, it's not impossible to doctor some paperwork even without being a Demon. It's basically a signature and then, ta-da, new undercover agent. Also, the Finance Division is another sub-department she heads."

"Lord, have mercy," he said, his eyes still wide.

I nodded. "That means all these 'undercover agents' she places, who should be getting regular paychecks, can vanish from the payroll without a trace. The Resource Planning Office, another sub-department of hers, is none the wiser to their existence, and the Demons can get on without question."

"Fuck," he said. "How did someone with that level of authority not make it onto our boards?"

I shook my head. "She wouldn't have. Compared to the people you already have up here, she's a nobody. She's not rich, and she's got people above her, the Director, Deputy Director, Chief of Staff, and all the public officials. You wouldn't have seen it." It was quiet a moment as I stared up at the wall. "All these people," I said, indicating them with a swing of my marker, "if they're Demons or Drakes who needed identities, they likely crossed her path. If we get her to talk, she might be able to tell us who the Demons are that we should be interviewing to find out about Hell rising."

"All right," Roy said with a nod. "We'll let Gyllian know when he gets back."

I nodded and leaned over my table and started sifting through files again as Roy scooted back to his computer. Who would be the second most beneficial person to interrogate? I looked up at the boards again, pressing the bottom of the marker to my lip thoughtfully. One person came to mind, but then Gyllian returned, and the smell of Chinese food dominated my senses.

"Ugh," I half moaned as he came in with three large paper bags. "That smells so good."

He smiled and headed over to an empty metal table near the hospital room, placing the bags on top of it. "Take a break everyone. It's lunch time."

Everyone left their work stations, stretching their backs and rubbing their eyes. The dozen Fox clones disappeared as she Booth and Roy headed to the table to eat. I dropped my marker on top of my files and headed in the same direction, my stomach growling at me the whole way.

19

Gyllian sat at the head of the table to my left. Booth sat on the opposite side nearest him. Fox was next to Booth, and Roy was next to her. I went to a chair on the empty side of the table and tried to ignore the fact that I was by myself on one whole side. I picked out my food and chopsticks and dug in heartily.

Only two bites in, Roy spoke. "Bay's got an idea," he blurted out.

Gyllian nodded. "I figured as much. What is it?"

I swallowed the bite in my mouth and dug in for another. "We need to interrogate Justine Nuwart."

"Nuwart?" Gyllian said. "*Agent* Nuwart?" I looked at him, a little surprised that he knew who she was. "She's not on the wall," he said, picking at his rice.

"I know," I said and explained it the same way I had to Roy.

Gyllian nodded. "Okay. Let's do it."

"That's it?"

He looked up at me blankly. "That's what?"

I sat back heavily in my chair. "Since I got here you have been an insufferable emotional shut-in. Now suddenly you're joking and smiling and agreeing with me with no argument. What's with you?"

"You're upset because I'm being agreeable?"

"Yeah," I said matter-of-factly. "I wouldn't mind if it wasn't so damn sudden."

Gyllian dropped his food container on top of the table and sat back heavily in his chair. "Well, maybe it's because of what you shared with me in the hospital room." I stared at him. "Maybe it's the fact that you summoned an Angel, a powerful enemy of ours, to protect me from a Knight Demon. Maybe it's the fact that you almost died by the same Angel. *Maybe*," he said with emphasis and sat forward, "I realized I was being an asshole and I'm trying to correct it. Pick one, and we'll go with that," he concluded, snatching up his container again.

The silence lingered for a moment. "I'm sorry," I said picking at my rice again. "I guess I still just don't know you all that well."

"My favorite color is green," Roy said out of nowhere. Surprised, I looked up at him and saw him smiling. He shrugged. "What else do you need to know?" I grinned, and everyone else started chortling.

"Orange here," Fox said, holding up a chopstick like an actioner making a bid. Our laughter gained some volume.

"White," Booth added with a brilliant smile to match.

I looked at Gyllian. He was shaking his head at the others but had a smile on his face. "Gray," he said, looking back at me.

"Purple," I said, and we all laughed.

I looked at Roy with as much gratitude as I could muster for defusing an awkward moment and found him already looking at me. He gave me a quick wink before we both focused on our food again.

"Seriously though," Fox said suddenly. "Let's get to know each other." She placed her container of rice on the table and flipped her smooth black hair off her shoulder. "Roy shared his Hell on Earth with you. It seems you shared yours with Gyllian, so I'm going to share mine."

I gazed across at her, not completely sure I was ready for this. "Okay."

"I was a sex slave in India."

My heart clenched immediately along with my fists, and I unintentionally crushed the food container in my hand. I hated sex crimes more than anything in the world. I placed the container on the table top and sat back in my chair with my arms crossed, bracing myself.

Oddly enough, Fox was smiling. "I knew a spectacular sex crime agent like you would have issues of her own in this area. No wonder we get along so well."

That coaxed a small smile out of me. "Yeah. That must be why."

Fox interlaced her fingers before daintily placing them on top of the table. "My Angelic mom, Uriel, was killed when I was four, and my human dad was actually able to keep us both hidden and safe until I was ten. He was former military, so he knew a thing or two about survival, and knew of *more* than a few holes we could hide in. We moved around a lot. After he was killed, I was found on the streets by a low-life drug lord and quickly sold into slavery."

Rage pounded at my temples. "You were ten?"

She nodded somberly. "I doubt I need to go into detail with you about what kind of hell that was."

My teeth clenched. "Not really."

She smiled, though it was a little forced. "After my ring was broken up when I was eighteen, I had nothing, no one, and I was hooked on crystal meth, my ringleader's drug of choice to enslave us." She shrugged. "I had to pay for my habit somehow, so," she sighed, "I became a prostitute in the slums of Delhi."

My heart was racing so fast my pulse seemed to take over my entire body. I could feel it in my ears all the way down my legs. I blew out a short breath like I was blowing out a candle and tried to keep calm.

"That's what I had become, until Gyllian and Roy found me in a brothel when I was twenty-six." She looked at Roy and smiled. "Roy's healing ability got me clean with no withdrawal symptoms, and I've been tracking and fighting Demons with them ever since." She smiled at Gyllian. "And thanks to him, I graduated two years ago with a degree in Earth science and seismology."

I rubbed my forehead with my fingertips. It had ended up well, but I *knew* what it was like to be a sex crime victim. It was something you lived with and dealt with every single day. "I know this is completely useless to say but"—I shook my head— "I'm so sorry."

Fox smiled. "My faith got me through it. God completely restored me and, believe it or not," she said, meeting my eyes, "he can restore you, too, if you let him."

My heart sank down into the pit of my gut. I didn't know what to say. Why was this entity such a focus with these people? So God was real, okay. But I didn't get why they seemed to think so highly of him. He was the one letting all the shit happen in the world.

Fox shrugged. "It's just a thought. Things change when

you let him in. From the inside out, things"—she sighed and picked up her food container— "things just get better." She smiled. "It's hard to explain."

I looked down at my food without a word, and everyone started eating quietly. I was glad because it gave me a second to think. Both Roy and Fox were victims of abuses no one should have to experience. I'd seen victims of tragedies like theirs, and those people were never really okay again, mentally or emotionally. What confused me the most, and fascinated me at the same time, was that not only did all four of them seem relatively happy and well adjusted, but they were also doing their damnedest to save humanity, the same species that had tortured them so terribly. I'd already seen how far these Nephilims were willing to go, what Gyllian was willing to suffer, to save them.

Their dedication to the human race, after what they had been through, made me question for the first time my own hatred for humanity. I thought back to the smiling faces of the people on the dance floor at the country western club. What had those people done to me? Really? Was my childhood their fault? Did they deserve the Demons of Hell torturing and killing them?

"Gyllian," Roy said suddenly. "What about Nuwart?"

Gyllian nodded. "We'll set it up. Probably start recon tomorrow."

"Set what up?" I asked.

"An interrogation."

My eyebrows went up as I silently wondered how they planned to accomplish that. "If we're going after Nuwart," I said, "we'd better take a gander at Corwin Killiner as well."

"How come?" Gyllian asked, taking another bite of his lo mein.

"If Nuwart is the muscle behind this kind of Demon activity, Killiner will be the bank, and those two are good friends."

"That's not in our records."

I shook my head. "It wouldn't be. They're very secretive about it because of Killiner's unsavory background. It wouldn't reflect well on the Associate Deputy Director of the FBI if she and Corwin were found in the same social circle."

"Makes sense," Gyllian said with a shrug.

"We need to get them together if we can," I continued. "If they are working together, interviewing them at the same time makes it easier to try to get one of them to flip on the other. Plus, we don't want to allow either of them ample time to raise the alarms in Hell that we're sniffing around."

"You realize that to keep our involvement quiet we're going to have to kill the two of them after we question them, right?"

"If they're Demons."

"Even if they're not."

I pressed my lips together until I felt the heat of my blood leave them. For some reason, Gyllian saying that bothered me, though I wasn't sure why. He stared at me with a detached, ready-to-argue look. Staring back, it dawned on me that he *would* kill these people. Human or not, he would kill them, and perhaps that's what bothered me. Gyllian didn't strike me as a murderer, but as I'd noted before, we still didn't know each other very well.

"Okay," I finally said.

Gyllian looked surprised, and then a spark of gratitude shot through is eyes. "Fox, Booth," he said, "you two start recon tomorrow." They nodded, and Gyllian looked back at me. "Did you get anything else from the files?"

I shook my head. "Let's see what we can get from these two first."

"We figured Killiner might be heavily involved," Gyllian said.

I nodded. "If the Demons are making plans to bust through to the surface, they'll need money for equipment and supplies—drills or explosives or something. They'll also need funds to move that equipment, so they'll likely be acting like a terrorist cell." I gazed across the room to the photographs on the boards. "To find terrorists, you don't look at the terrorists themselves because they're impotent without funds." I took a bite of my rice. "Find out where their money is coming from, and you'll have your head-honcho Demons. I guarantee you that." I gazed at the photo of Corwin Killiner and gestured in that direction. "With his background, and the fact he's probably the richest man in the world, we'll want to interrogate him thoroughly. If he's not involved somehow, which I highly doubt, he'll know a fellow one-percenter who is."

"Okay," Gyllian said.

Something dawned on me then. "Hey, what about Angels?"

Gyllian's expression became confused. "What about them?"

"Well, you guys have a CSI lab on steroids down here, all geared toward tracking Demons. What about Angels? Aren't they the muscle and brains behind letting the Demons rise?"

Gyllian shook his head. "Angels are impossible to track."

"How come?"

He shook his head. "There's just nothing of them to track. They're too powerful. They don't even rustle the leaves when they fly by trees. Demons are less powerful and far more substantial. They leave tracks and trails and evidence behind we can monitor and trace. Angels don't."

"But we're supposed to be more powerful than Angels, aren't we?"

Gyllian glanced down at his food, looking suddenly uncomfortable. "We're supposed to be."

Something in his tone made my shoulders tighten. "So we're not?"

He looked back up at me. "In a lot of ways we are, otherwise Roy never could have killed one. But, in some important ways, we're not powerful enough yet."

"Yet?" I asked. That word seemed to hang heavily among my new found companions. "What do you mean? There's room for improvement?"

Gyllian put his food container on top of the table, and the way he looked at me made it abundantly clear that I was not going to like what he had to say. "Yes. That's why we had to run from the Demons on the Riverwalk, and why you and Roy had to run from them at the club. We are very limited in our abilities at the moment."

"Well," I huffed in annoyance. "What if Hell rises tomorrow? Are you telling me we couldn't fight it?"

"Not right now, no."

"What? What do we have to do?"

Gyllian sighed and glanced uncomfortably at the other three. I suddenly realized all of them were looking at me. "*We*," Gyllian said loosely, indicated the others, "don't have to do anything."

I was frozen for a moment, staring at them in disbelief, and then I dropped my container on top of the table. "Something is wrong with me," I stated. Everyone was silent. I leaned back in my chair crossing my arms. "Well, what is it?"

Gyllian shook his head. "You have to figure it out on your own."

"Excuse me?" I said in disbelief, narrowing my eyes.

Gyllian shook his head again. "It's something you have to come to terms with on your own. We can't force it on you."

"Can you give me a nudge in the right direction?"

"Sorry. No."

I glanced at all four of them as they looked at me, seeming almost ashamed. My teeth clenched, and I pushed away from the table and headed for the door. No one stopped me. This was unbelievable. If Hell rose before I could be "fixed," the end of the world would be on *my* head personally. Great.

———

I stayed in the library that night, except for the trip I made to the intelligence room to grab some files while everyone was asleep, and then some clothes from the dresser in my dungeon. I found myself staring into the night, obsessively pondering our situation.

The number of Demons topside didn't sit well with me. Neither did our little team's lack of preparedness. The Demons were already here in vast numbers, and the five of us were still running from small packs of them trying to figure shit out. I couldn't help thinking that the Demons had already placed themselves in high-level positions to do whatever they were going to do. For all I knew, a hidden Demon at headquarters was responsible for me getting fired. How were we supposed to fight Hell when Hell was already here?

"Hey," a gentle voice said.

I looked over my shoulder and saw Roy enter the library in only pajama bottoms. "Hey," I replied before turning back to the windows.

The silvery moonlight reflected off his skin as he came around and sat on the coffee table across from me. "Are you okay?"

"I'm fine," I replied without looking at him.

"You're lying."

I shifted my eyes over to him and saw him smiling at me. It drew a smile out of me. "Okay, I'm lying," I replied, then lifted the file to study it more.

Roy gently pinched it out of my hands and set it on the couch beside me. "What's wrong?"

I sighed. I didn't think I wanted to say anything, but my heart ached to get it out at the same time. What was it about Roy that allowed me to trust him with the mushiest, most vulnerable parts of me? I'd never trusted anyone like this.

I glanced down. "It's complicated."

"I've got all night."

I met his eyes again and saw complete acceptance in them. There was no judgment, no condemnation, just genuine concern and eagerness for me to tell him what was bothering me. He'd proven time and time again that he genuinely cared about me, so why was this still hard?

"It's weird. I…" I paused. Was I really about to expose myself like this to him? Yeah. I was. "I don't want to let you guys down."

His brows dropped curiously. "How are you letting us down?"

I sighed heavily. I was sure I was about to sound like an idiot. "I may not care if Hell rises, but"—I sighed again—"but I don't want the end of the world to be *my* fault. I don't…" The words felt stuck on my tongue. As much as I wanted to hold them back, they needed to be voiced. They needed to be shared with Roy, who I trusted with this part of me. "I care about each of you like I've never really cared about anyone and I just,"—I shook my head and looked down at my lap— "I want you all to be proud of me."

God, that sucked to say. I felt a wave of embarrassing

heat rush to my cheeks. It sounded so stupid. I half expected Roy to burst out laughing.

Instead he leaned forward and rested his hands on the outside of my thighs, his eyes holding mine captive. "Hell isn't going to rise tomorrow, Bay."

"Really?" I asked. "You're so certain of that you'd bet the fate of the world?"

He nodded without diverting his eyes from mine. "Yes, I would."

"How can you tell me honestly that you know Hell isn't going to rise tomorrow?"

Roy moved his hands up to take hold of my hips, which brought his face closer to mine. His eyes burned into me with a confidence and gentleness that made my heart race. "Because at one time, all of us felt the same way you do." I looked at him curiously. "You think it was easy, or quick, to overcome what we had been through?" He shook his head. "All of us at some point wanted to see the entire human race burn."

I shook my head. "What changed?"

He smiled. "God allowed us a healing period as we emerged from our traumas and joined together as a team. He's going to grant you the same thing." I wanted to shut him up because I didn't want to discuss their God, but his eyes were so intense that I couldn't get the words out. "He knows exactly what it's going to take, and how long it's going to take, for you to heal and join the team fully. He's not going to let Hell rise until that happens."

I shook my head and sat forward a little. "So, if God can stop Hell from rising to give me time to heal," my eyes narrowed, "why doesn't he stop Hell from rising indefinitely?"

Roy sighed. "I don't know."

I picked up on some weariness in his tone and looked at him suddenly intrigued. "You have doubts."

A corner of his mouth tilted up in a smile. "Of course I have doubts. I'm not a robot."

"But," I tried to wrap my head around that. "You all have this daunting ambition and confidence in your mission to stop Hell from rising. How can you have doubts?"

"That confidence you've been seeing is our faith."

My brows dropped. "But you just said you had doubts."

"I do."

I sighed heavy in annoyance. "Do you have doubts or faith, Roy?"

He gave a small chuckle that was a mix of sympathy and playfulness. "You can't have faith without doubts."

I stared at him. "What?"

For some reason, that made him chuckle more. "Faith is the bridge over the canyon of doubts." I continued to stare. "The doubts are there," he went on, "but faith is what gets you through them."

I shook my head. "That's ridiculous."

He smiled more brightly. "You'll get it eventually. Right now, you just have to accept the time you've been given and allow yourself to heal, allow us to help you heal as a team member and a friend." He shook his head. "We can't do this without you."

I sighed and sat back looking out the windows. "Yeah," I said with zero conviction.

He squeezed my hips gently. "Have faith."

I peered at him and shook my head. "Not a real strong suit of mine."

He stood and leaned forward to kiss my forehead. "You'll get it eventually," he said again.

He started around the couch heading for the door. "Hey Roy," I called after him, kneeling on the couch to face him. He half turned in my direction, and the moonlight caught his profile in such a way that a lump formed in my throat. His body glowed silver, and his eyes glittered like diamonds. This was an Archangel's son. I allowed myself a moment to admire his beauty, and then asked, "How can you guys help me?"

He smiled. "Just be with us. Learn from us and trust us."

I nodded and he continued out of the library.

Trust wasn't a real strong suit of mine either.

20

Dawn was breaking and I was still in the library. I couldn't hide forever though. Fox and Booth were starting recon on Justine and Corwin today, and I needed to know what the plan was.

"Fuck it," I muttered and stood. I ran my fingers through my hair, pulled it over my shoulder, and started braiding it as I made my way to the door.

I wasn't even halfway there when Sari was in front of me.

I jumped and stumbled backward before realizing I wasn't in danger. "Jesus!" I cried. How did Angels do that? They didn't appear or materialize, they were just…there. Like Kye the night I was stabbed. It was as if they were standing in front of you the whole time, but you just weren't aware of seeing them until suddenly you were. Or you nearly ran into them. It was bizarre.

"Where have you been?" I asked.

Her eyes rested on me, and a tingle of warning started to slide up my spine. Something felt…off.

"In hiding," she replied. "As are all the Angels still loyal to God."

She came forward, and I involuntarily took a step back, keeping her at a distance. I expected her to be offended, but she didn't even flinch. In fact, her eyes were far less engaging and animated than they'd been when we first met. They seemed emptier, like she wasn't completely here or was listening to something far away.

"I wanted to tell you that I was not authorized to kill the Demon that Gabriel's Son had been working with."

"What?" I barked. "I want that bitch dead!"

She shrugged. "I'm sorry. God wouldn't allow it."

I sighed and crossed my arms. I had some choice, blasphemous words on the tip of my tongue for God, but decided not to share them with one of his few remaining loyal

Angels.

"But he did allow me to bring you this," she said and produced a small decorative jar that rested in the palm of her hand. It was made of milky white marble with shinning silver swirls that flashed in the dawn light. Its outer edges had sharp points so, from the top, it took the shape of an octagon with a crystal glass stopper.

"What is it?" I asked as she placed it on an end table beside the couch.

"It is the Heavenly substance you requested for your bullets, water from Flumine Aeternum which means Eter—"

"Eternal River," I interrupted, still gazing at the lovely little container.

"Yes," she said. "It's from the river in Heaven that runs directly behind God's throne."

"I hate to sound ungrateful," I said looking back at her, "but that amount of water will only give us about ten magazines of bullets." Sari's expression didn't change. "That's just two mags each." She continued staring at me blankly, and I resisted the urge to roll my eyes. "That's only 150 bullets. We need a lot more than that to fight Hell."

"God knows exactly how much you need, and he sent that much."

I pointed to the jar, which could only hold about a cup of water. "He thinks that will be enough?"

"Yes."

I did roll my eyes this time. Whatever. I wasn't about to argue with an all-knowing God, even if I thought he was useless.

"I'm still waiting for word about whether I'm allowed to teach you to fly, but I will let you know as soon as I do."

I nodded. "Thank you."

"Before I go," she said and took a step toward me. I resisted the impulse to step back. "I have a rather bold request."

"Okay."

"Would you allow me to touch your body?"

I looked down at my dark blue jeans and a black tank top then looked at her curiously. "Why would you want to touch my body?"

"Because it is art."

I was both flattered and confused. "Um, thank you?"

Sari smiled slightly. "You're misunderstanding me."

"Clearly."

She grinned broadly, which was creepy since her eyes remained utterly lifeless. "I'm not saying you are attractive, though by human standards I'm sure that you are. I'm saying your body is art. Hand-crafted, knitted, molded, painted, and fused together by God himself." Her hands came up in front of her, palms out. "God's hands created this," she said and took another step toward me. "The crowning jewel of his creation." She looked at me hungrily, like Jefferson used to, and the image of Sari eating a raw, bloody steak popped into my head. "Please feel free to reject my request," she said, not taking her eyes off my chest. "But you are the first human with whom I've had the opportunity of interacting with, and I couldn't stand before such a magnificent creation without asking."

I likely could grant the request. She had already saved my life and helped our cause by bringing the water, but something felt wrong about this. Sari felt wrong. I didn't know how or why, but I'd been an agent long enough to trust my gut on these kinds of things.

"Maybe another time," I said, taking a step back.

Sari paused in her advance and tensed up in rage or fear, I couldn't tell which. Suddenly she was in front of me with her hands on my cheeks. "I'm sorry," was barely out of her mouth before my throat collapsed. My eyes went wide. I couldn't breathe! "They found me," she said, trembling as she took a step back. "I had to."

I clutched my throat and desperately pulled my chest muscles to try and suck in any air I could. None went in! I dropped to my knees, clawing at my throat. My nails ripped off my own skin as I tried to make a hole for some air, but my vision was already darkening.

Gyllian, went through my mind as my head started sinking to the floor. The backs of my hands were blue and my fingertips were covered in blood. *Gyllian, I'm sorry,* came as a last desperate thought before my forehead touched the floor. My hip went down next and I started to sink into oblivion.

But nothing went dark.

Somehow, I could still see.

Suddenly, my body was moving involuntarily. I was on my knees again. Then my forehead came up. Then I was standing. In a really creepy and uncomfortable manner, the moves I was making were the exact same ones I had made when I started choking, but in reverse order.

Gyllian was rewinding time!

When Sari stood five feet away from me again, time returned to normal. I was staring at her, disoriented from the time manipulation, when suddenly the library door burst open. Gyllian, wearing all black, rushed in like a panther, his Angelic eyes fierce. Sari didn't even have time to turn around before Gyllian was slicing up her back so fast I couldn't even see what kind of weapon he was using. I didn't miss the thick silvery gray liquid spraying all over the furniture and floor, though, nor did I miss Sari's scream. In three seconds flat, she was face down with her back completely shredded, like she'd been gnawed on by a pride of lions. Her blood was splattered across Gyllian's face and neck and all over his black clothes.

"Are you all right?" he asked roughly.

I was lost for words, staring at him. His body language, coiled muscles like a venomous snake about to strike, screamed danger. His eyes were hard and merciless. This person, someone I'd had the audacity to think I knew on some level, was far darker than I'd thought—or perhaps had wanted to believe.

"Bay!" he said sharply, making me jump. "Are you all right?"

His eyes faded back to the sunset orange I'd grown accustomed to, which brought me a measure of relief. But when I looked down at the body of the fallen Angel, my contentment evaporated. "No," I growled. I slowly looked back up at him as my temper exploded. "No, I'm not okay! I'm really fucking annoyed actually!"

"Bay –"

"I thought the house was warded?" I yelled. "Protected, right? From Demons and Angels?"

"It is."

"So your God had to have let her in, right?"

"Yes."

"And your God knows everything, right?" My voice was cracking and high-pitched.

"Yes."

"So he knew Sari was coming to assassinate me and let her in anyway?" I screamed.

Gyllian just looked helplessly at me. "He has his reasons."

"Oh," I shook my head and started for the door. "That's it. I'm done." I passed him. "Fuck you and your God."

He grabbed my elbow. "Bay!"

I spun and slammed my palm so hard into his chest he flew backwards into a bookshelf, nearly toppling it. I had no compassion left to even check on him and continued toward the door. Their God clearly didn't think I was worth protecting. He'd just let that Angel into the house, past the warding, knowing she was going to try to kill me. Hell no. No.

I went to the front door, stuffed my feet into a pair of black flats, and snatched up my jacket and keys. I didn't know where I was going, and I really didn't care. I wanted to scream and lash out at God and ask him what his fucking problem was, but I wouldn't give him the satisfaction of hearing from me.

As I drove away, my hands grasped the steering wheel hard. I tried to slow my breathing. I fought to calm myself down. But it wasn't happening.

I slammed on the brakes so hard that my tires squealed and I could smell rubber burning. I stopped dead in the center of the road and threw my car into park. "How the fuck can you justify that!" I screamed at the sky. "Are you a schizophrenic or something? One second you're pulling a miracle out of your ass to get me and Roy off the highway, the next you let an Angel into the house to kill me! Which one is it?" I screamed so forcefully that my body shook. "Do you want me dead or alive? Make up your fucking *mind!*"

I waited. But my questions were met with silence.

"No?" I asked, searching the sky like he might appear and answer me. "I didn't think so," I spat. "And in case I haven't told you myself, I fucking hate you."

A blaring horn suddenly came from behind me. My shoulders jumped up under my ears like I was hearing fingernails raking across a chalkboard. Glancing in my rearview, I saw the driver behind me repeatedly hitting his horn and throwing his hands up.

This guy had to be the unluckiest son of a bitch on the planet.

I opened my door. "Here's what I think of your precious humanity," I growled as I stormed toward the driver's side.

The driver continued yelling as I brought my foot up and put it straight through his window, sending glass exploding all over him. His angry voice filled my ears as I grabbed his shirt in both my fists and dragged him out of the car. I threw him behind me and brought my fist back and punched him once, twice, three times putting him on the ground with dark red blood covering one side of his face and dripping onto the pavement. I glared down at him hoping God saw, maybe even somehow *felt* every punch.

"Daddy!"

My heart squeezed with panic and I spun around. A beautiful little girl with shoulder-length wispy blonde hair was looking out the backseat window and crying. She couldn't be more than four years old and still in a booster seat. My first instinct was to go and hold her, to comfort her like I had done with so many children during my career. But I knew, without taking a step, that she wouldn't want comfort from me. Something heavy suddenly settled on my shoulders. I didn't want to think it was guilt. I didn't want to think it was regret. But it was. I took a breath looking at that gorgeous little girl and wondered what I was doing. I'd scared her. I'd hurt her father. I shook my head. What *was* I doing?

I went back to her car, which had rolled forward and bumped into the back of my SUV, and leaned in the busted window so I could put it in park. I tried to ignore the small girl's terrified screams as I did, and tried to pretend my heart wasn't breaking at the sound of them.

I headed back to my car, pulled out the burner phone Roy had given me, and dialed 911. "I need an ambulance at South Seeley Ave near West 102 Street. A four-year-old girl is trapped in a car." I hung up and, tapping into my enhanced strength, crushed the phone like a cracker and sprinkled the shards into the wind. That would guarantee priority on this call. The little girl and her father would get the attention they needed.

I had to get away from the scene before they arrived, but as I climbed into my SUV, the little girl's face came into focus in my rearview mirror. Her cheeks were shining wet in the morning light. Gripping the steering wheel in both fists, I began to wrestle with whether I had it in me to drive off. I thought I did, but as I looked at her shaking and crying, I bowed my head. No, I didn't. Even if it meant getting arrested, I couldn't leave a child like this.

I gripped the door handle and prepared to go back to her when people came running out of the house closest to us and headed directly toward the little girl's car. It looked like a young mother with two small children of her own. I bit my bottom lip, turned my eyes out my windshield, and then shifted into drive and slammed on the gas. The smoke from my tires and exhaust would obscure my license plate. They would be all right.

As I drove, I gnawed on the side of my index finger, trying to think. My thoughts turned to my little crew and what Gyllian had said about it being my fault that we were limited in our abilities. We couldn't track Angels and had to run from Demons. Something about me was keeping us from fighting Hell properly. But what? What made me so different from them?

Well, they had confidence in themselves and their mission, confidence I knew I lacked. And doubts plagued my every waking moment, despite what I had already seen and been through. But Roy said he had doubts, too. So what was *my* problem? Why were his doubts okay, but mine weren't? He'd also said, "You can't have any faith without doubts… Faith is the bridge over the canyon of doubts."

Faith.

My eyes narrowed as I played with that thought for a minute. Was that the missing denominator? Seriously? Was *that* the reason for their unflinching confidence? It couldn't be! How could something as flimsy as faith cause such drive? Gyllian had been at this for ten years. On top of that, they all, especially Gyllian, had suffered immensely for this mission to find out where Hell was going to rise. It couldn't be faith compelling them. The apocalypse was too big and their sacrifice too extensive to be compelled by something as inadequate as faith!

I finally couldn't drive anymore and pulled into a parking lot. Resting my elbow on top of the door, I gazed out the driver's side window and sighed. I knew something had to change, and it had to change with me. Not Gyllian, not the others. Something had to give, and I was ready for it to give, whatever that meant for me. I'd meant what I'd said to Roy. I didn't want to let them down.

At that moment, I focused on what was outside the windshield. When I saw the sign on the building across the street, my eyes went so wide and my heart clenched so tight that I missed a breath. "Get the fuck out," I said in an astonished whisper. The sign read "Guardian Angel Orphanage" with an outline of blue Angel wings lovingly wrapped around the black lettering.

I jumped out of my car, swung around my door, and stared at that sign in disbelief. This was not a coincidence. There was no way! An intense yearning to see the children came over me, and I knew I needed to go in there. I closed my door and quickly jogged across the street.

Pushing open the glass front doors, I stepped into a small, humble reception area. A little waiting room was to my right with a couple of plants and two comfortable-looking white chairs facing each other at an angle. A rich dark brown coffee table was between them with a few magazines fanned out on top. The reception desk was at the back wall of the waiting room and a short hallway was in front of the doors I entered.

A slender black woman was behind the desk. She had elegant narrow features and looked up at me as I entered. "May I help you?" she asked kindly with a thick African accent.

I glanced around trying to think of something to say. "I'm supposed to be here," came out of my mouth, unbidden, making me sound stoned out of my mind.

The woman looked down at something on her desk, and

her face lit up when she looked back up at me. "You must be Miss Kennedy." My eyes went wide. "Bay Kennedy?"

"Um, how did you know that?"

The woman smiled brightly and stood, coming around her desk toward me with her hand out. "My name is Neesa Lamere. We have been eagerly awaiting your visit."

"Excuse me?" I said and halfheartedly shook it.

She elegantly folded her hands in front of her. "Marcus called a couple of weeks ago and said you would be here today at 8:50 am. It is on my calendar."

My brows dropped. "Marcus?" The woman looked at me, confused. Then it dawned on me. "Oh, Booth!" How had Booth known I would accidently wind up here at this time and this date? "Uh, sorry. I've just known him as Booth."

Neesa smiled. "The children are excited to see you."

I was confused and slightly suspicious. "Can I ask why?"

"They know all the other Lights." My eyes went wide. "You are the only one they have not met."

"Wait, wait," I said, holding my hand up and closing my eyes as I tried to process what I was hearing. "You know…about us?"

Her smile softened. "I see Marcus has failed to enlighten you."

I squirmed a little uncomfortably and stuffed my hands into the back pockets of my jeans. "It's been a little hectic since I joined the crew."

She nodded. "I understand. All the Lights come here when things become too much for them. Spending time with the children helps them recharge and reminds them, after the evil they tend to encounter, what they are fighting for."

I smiled, feeling a little more relaxed but still confused as to how Booth had known I would be here. Perhaps one of his abilities? Premonition? That seemed more like Gyllian's area of expertise, future viewing, but what did I know?

"Come," she said with a smile and started down the hall.

"Uh," I began as I followed. "Do the children know… about…?"

"They do," Neesa said with a nod. "The other Lights often demonstrate their abilities as a way of interacting and playing with the children."

I nodded. I needed to see the kids. I needed them to look at me without fear after the incident this morning. I needed to make them laugh and smile.

Neesa took me through the door at the end of the hall and turned left. Halfway, she pushed open another door on the left that opened to a flight of stairs leading down. When we reached the bottom, a double set of doors stood wide open, and I could hear the gentle murmuring of children. My heart swelled with anticipation and excitement. We went through, and on the left, was a massive playroom. It was colorful, well lit, and very well furnished and supplied. At least a hundred kids under the age of ten were at some sort of table activity— drawing, making bracelets, doing puzzles. A small handful of teachers were scattered throughout the room helping them with their activities.

The smile that came to my face hurt my cheeks. All the children looked clean and happy and healthy, which was very unlike the average orphanage situation. Most orphaned children were downtrodden with understandable, but serious behavioral issues. Not this lot, it seemed.

Neesa didn't even have to announce my presence. As I turned the corner, every eye came up almost all at once, and then gleeful squeals of joy erupted from their little mouths. The next thing I knew, they came rushing toward me and I was surrounded by a sea of tiny people. I started giggling as I crouched down to greet them all with hugs, handshakes, and high fives. Three little boys even took my hand and kissed the back of it. I relished in the joy of their bright faces. Children were so gorgeous and innocent and clean. Uncorrupted by the world, damaged perhaps, but uncorrupted. A few of the kids handed me drawings they had been working on just for me while they'd awaited my arrival. I felt a few squishy wet kisses on my cheeks and a lot of pets and gentle tugs on my hair.

Neesa let the children lavish their attention on me for a few minutes, for which I was grateful. I wanted to make sure I could greet all of them. When she called for them to take their seats, they quickly obeyed.

"Can you show us your abilities now?" one sweet boy

called from his seat.

"Foxy can multiply herself!" a little girl called. "We played jump rope with her, and she was on each end of the rope *and* jumping in the middle!"

I laughed picturing that.

"But Roy has the flaming swords!" an older boy called, giving an elaborate flourish of his hands in a demonstration of a sword fight with an invisible sword.

"Children, children," Neesa called, gently gesturing with her hands for them to settle. "I'm sure Bay has wonderful abilities she would like to share with you. If it's all right, Bay," she said and stepped aside, giving me the floor.

I stepped forward and addressed the kids. "Well, you know all of the Lights have pretty cool abilities, but I *really* think mine is the coolest," I said with a little mischief.

"What is it?" a small boy called, getting on his knees in his chair and leaning heavily over his elbows.

I hesitated only a moment, wondering if my eyes turning silvery gray would scare them. But since they had to be used to it from the time they spent with the others, I let them. "Well, see for yourself." With a whoosh of air, my wings spouted from my back, spreading wide to my sides.

The children screamed at the top of their lungs with excitement. Some of them started jumping up and down. Others climbed on top of the tables, bending over with tiny fists clenched, yelling with joy. I was laughing so hard that my sides hurt!

"Well," Neesa said a little breathlessly, drawing my attention to her. She had her hand over her heart and her eyes lit up. "That is impressive!"

I heard a chorus of pleas to touch them slowly rise up.

"Can you fly?" some asked.

"Fly around the room like an eagle!" someone begged.

"They're black!" came a voice from the back. "Angels have white wings!"

"She's not an Angel, dummy!" a little girl said in my defense. "She's half Angel."

"Now Jasmine," Neesa said in a gentle warning tone. "We don't call each other names. Apologize to Nathan."

With a scowl Jasmine looked back at the boy. "Sorry."

All of their voices eventually congealed into a unified plea of, "Can we touch them? Please can we touch them?"

Neesa leaned close to me. "Is it okay if they touch them?" she asked softly.

I nodded. "As long as they're a little careful. I haven't really tested their durability yet."

"All right children," Neesa said. "If you want to touch Bay's wings, form a line against the wall, and each of you will take a turn." The kids instantly stampeded to the wall on my right. "Be very careful!" Neesa called over the noise. "Her wings are delicate."

So the children got to touch my wings. I made sure to make eye contact with every single one of them as they approached, just in case I missed acknowledging some upon my arrival. I didn't want a single one of them to feel left out because they each deserved my attention, even if just briefly. There was a lot of squealing and giggling and a few sharp screams of surprise when they touched my soft feathers, and every reaction made me laugh.

After the line dwindled, Neesa had them resume their activities. I joined them at the tables, spending a little time at each one so I could play with them all and talk to them. I went to lunch with them when noon rolled around. At four in the afternoon, I finally felt content enough to leave, but even then I didn't want to.

Sudden squeals from the children turned my attention to the door. They were rushing to greet Booth, who came in with a bright, infectious smile. Those who stayed with me waved excitedly and called his name. Booth knelt and gave out high fives and hugs of his own. I found myself giggling. Booth's big imposing form, even on his knees, was like a buoy in the ocean of little people. When he stood, he went over to Neesa, put an arm around her back, and gave her a quick kiss on the lips. I couldn't help being surprised. Feeling like I was encroaching on their privacy, though, I averted my gaze and looked down at the coloring book I was working on.

A few minutes passed before Booth crouched down across the table from me with a gentle smile. "Feeling better?"

I smiled. "Yeah. But how did you know I was going to be here? I didn't even know this place existed before today, and I sort of just stumbled upon it."

"We will talk about it elsewhere. Are you ready to go?"

I sighed. "No, but I guess we have to."

His smile became sympathetic. "Yes," he said. "I'm sorry children," he said a little more loudly, "but Bay and I need to go now."

A chorus of pitiful moans and drawn out "Noooooo"'s filled the room. The children closest latched onto me tightly, refusing to let me go. Booth and I were both chuckling as I kissed the tops of their heads.

Suddenly, it hit me. My smile melted and my heart sank down to the pit of my stomach. Hell was threatening to rise.

I involuntarily clutched the children holding on to me and looked at Booth. He dipped his head in a stiff nod. "You understand," he said softly.

Fuck yes, I understood.

"Kids," I said, kissing their heads once more, "Booth and I have to go." Another chorus of whines erupted, and I forced a smile onto my face. "I'll visit again."

"When?" Jasmine asked, looking up at me as I stood.

I affectionately took her chin in my fingers. "Soon." I locked my eyes on her pretty brown ones as a reminder of what I was doing and why I was doing it. Hell would not get their hands on these children. I would die before I let that happen!

Purpose renewed, Booth and I headed toward the door. We took a few last-minute drawings from kids who ran up to us and then started up the stairs.

"Are you up for a chat?" Booth asked.

"You bet I am."

21

Booth drove us to the Chicago Riverwalk. After a brief and quiet walk along the river, we found ourselves at the docks. A beautiful brown triple cockpit Runabout was the only boat tethered there. It bobbed lazily in the water, its impeccable shine twinkling under the waning sunlight. A few people were milling about, their collars turned up while at the same time holding frozen drinks in gloved hands. Typical Chicago folk, fearless of any kind of chill.

Booth and I sat down on one of the long benches, and I couldn't help thinking about my dad. I glanced at where I'd first seen him when Gyllian had brought me here. I knew he wouldn't be there, but I couldn't deny wishing he were.

"How are you doing?" Booth asked.

I sighed. "Honestly? I'm a damn mess. But," I added, "playing with the kids brought some clarity."

"And determination, too, I think."

I nodded as I gazed over the river. "Definitely some determination." My fingertips brushed my forehead and I sat back, crossing my arms. "I assume you spoke to Gyllian?" I glanced at Booth and he nodded. "Sari just saved my life. Why would she try to kill me?"

Booth tilted his head in consideration. "We think she may have been captured by the Angels and turned over to the Demons to be tortured."

I sighed. "That makes sense. She said, 'They found me. I had to,' while she was suffocating me."

Booth shook his head. "Angels do not have any kind of capacity for pain. God protected them before they became wayward, so they have never experienced such a thing. They will agree to anything if they get a paper cut. It would have been all too easy for the Demons to compel her to assassinate you."

I rested my elbows heavily on my thighs and leaned over them as the God talk began, and with it came the shame of my encounter with that father and daughter this morning. "God isn't protecting the Angels anymore?"

Booth shook his head. "He's protecting us."

I bowed my head and pinched the bridge of my nose. Protecting us? "Then why did God let her in?" I asked, looking up at him.

"She let herself in." My eyes narrowed. "The warding on the main house keeps it unseen by supernatural beings. But since she had been inside when she rescued you and Roy, she already knew where it was."

"But why did God *let* her in?" I asked more forcefully. He knew what I meant, and the look of regret that came over his face, told me he didn't have the answer.

"He will tell you in time why he allowed it to happen."

I scoffed. A change of subject was in order. "Why doesn't God just smite the Angels and Demons and avoid this whole war? I'm certain he could stop Hell from rising himself." I hated this. We'd been created to go to war with Hell and had never been given a choice in the matter.

Booth pressed his lips together in a sympathetic smile. "It is not for us to question his methods; it is for us to obey his commands." I sighed and bowed my head low between my shoulders. "I believe, however," he said, drawing my attention back, "that you will have the answer to those questions, too, before Hell rises." He looked at me with gentle sincerity. "And you will know what to do with the information when it is revealed to you."

I smiled ruefully and looked over the water. A foghorn sounded in the distance, and a breeze blew my hair back before I looked at Booth again. "How did you know to put my name on the guest list?"

He smiled. "I put your name on the guest list because God told me to." My expression went slack. God *told* him to? "He wanted to make sure the children weren't preoccupied with something else so you could visit with them." He dipped his head in a small nod. "He knew you would need to."

I stared at him. "God *talks* to you?"

"He speaks to each of us on occasion, in different ways."

Something dawned on me out of the blue then, an old Bible passage my foster mother had drilled into me with a coat hanger across my back if I recited it wrong. "Now faith is the confidence in what we hope for and assurance of what we do not see."

My eyes went wide, and I looked at Booth.

His expression remained gentle, but intuitive. "You understand."

It *was* faith! The thing the others had that I lacked. The reason we couldn't track Angels and had to run from Demons. "That's why I'm not like you all?" I asked in a breath. "Because I have no faith?"

Booth's compassionate light green eyes locked on mine. "You wander in the canyon of doubts, Bay, and that is a confusing and ominous place to roam. Without faith, there is no way for you to cross over it with the rest of us."

I looked out over the water in utter disbelief. This was unreal. "Because I don't have faith in God, I've handicapped us?"

Booth sighed softly when I looked at him, his eyes filling with regret. "Yes."

I stood and walked over to one of the railings leading down the steps. Resting my hip against it, I crossed my arms and shook my head as I gazed out over the water. Faith. Of all the things in the whole wide world it could have been, it had to be faith.

Booth appeared next to me. He leaned against the opposite side of the rail with his arms crossed and gazed at me expectantly.

"I'm sorry, but I don't think I can change that." I shook my head. "I don't like him."

"Because you blame him for your childhood trauma," he said, examining the ground at his feet.

"Yes," I replied matter-of-factly.

He looked at me. "Did you ever think to blame Satan for that abuse?"

I shrugged and looked out over the water. "Satan, or evil, may have caused it, but God didn't do shit to stop it."

He leaned against me, putting some comforting pressure against my shoulder with his own. "Because he was preparing you to save other children." My heart stopped. "Other children," he said meaningfully, "who are not the daughter of

219

an Archangel and capable of surviving such abuse as you did."

I chewed my bottom lip. That was exactly what my dad had said.

"God created everything about you," Booth went on. "He allowed everything to happen to you as it did because"—his voice became filled with quiet passion — "when other agents gave up on cases, you would not. You could not allow another child to suffer the way you did." My heart started pounding against my ribs. "That is exactly what, and who, God needed you to become to protect his children in the future. Every victim you saved was assigned to you for that very reason. Because you, Bay Kennedy, came out the other side of an atrocious childhood so you could do what you needed to do for all the victims over your career."

Something clicked. I couldn't really explain what, but something clicked.

I thought about my eight-year career as an agent and, for the first time, thought about how things would have been different if I'd had a normal, apple-pie childhood. More than likely, I would have been a typical jaded and burned out agent after five years. I couldn't picture myself with any fight left after the kind of strain the job put you through. But I never burned out. In fact, the exact opposite had happened. As each year had passed and I'd gotten more comfortable in my profession, the more my fire had been stoked. My passion had run deeper, my fight harder. The more victims I saved, the more perps I put behind bars, the more I had wanted. I could directly attribute all of that to my wretched childhood. There was no doubt. As an agent, I was who I was supposed to be. I was doing what I was supposed to do—

"As designed by God," Booth said out loud, which, unbelievably, ended my train of thought perfectly.

My nose burned and I felt a lump form in my throat. It choked me so badly that it took several swallows to get it down. That's what my father had been trying to tell me. I hadn't wanted to hear it, or had been too emotional to hear it, but I heard it now.

In some place deep inside of me, the tumblers fell into place. God made sense. I didn't like it, but he made sense.

The thing about knowing me… an ethereal voice said suddenly. My chest tightened with fear, or perhaps excitement, I wasn't sure which. *Is that you need to look past your own pain and realize there is a purpose for what I allow to happen. A purpose that always directly concerns the wellbeing of others.* I was trembling. *The pain of my children is not wasted*, he concluded.

I placed my hand over my chest. That unexplainable deep place inside me seemed to bloom to life with something new and alive, something I couldn't understand or describe. Something was *there* now, an energy, a stirring, something. It wasn't just a confusing void of darkness and turmoil. It was calm and steady and strong.

Booth put his arm around me. When I looked up at him, he was smiling. "Don't fret too much about what just happened," he said. "I've known God my whole life, and I still don't understand the process of what occurs inside of me when I interact with him."

"What…do I do?" I stammered. His smiled widened so much that his eyes were nearly closed. "He…he just *spoke* to me."

Booth patted my shoulder. "Welcome to this side of God's army."

My hand over my chest went up to my mouth as I looked over the water. I couldn't really process what just happened. I couldn't think of words.

Booth chuckled gently and drew me close until my cheek was on his chest and he was embracing me. "It is all right, Bay. You don't have to figure it out. God will guide you, just as he guides each of us."

I blew out a soft breath and allowed myself to relax against him. We just stared out over the water silently for a few minutes. My brain suddenly seemed off, if that even made sense, and I just concentrated on this new… *thing* blooming to life in my chest.

I eventually lifted my head and looked up at him curiously. "What was your Hell, Booth?"

"Ah," he said, with a small squeeze of his arms. "Well, I was born in a third world country, Bay—severe poverty, disease, civil war. You name it, and I have been through it."

He rubbed my back affectionately. "I lost my Angelic mother, Jophiel, when I was eight. The Demons and Angels did not even need to kill my father since he was long dead from illness." His eyes became sad and I instantly regretted having asked. "After I lost my mother, I was forced into a rebel army as a child soldier." He sighed through his nose, and his throat bobbed in a heavy swallow. "Killed my first man before my ninth birthday."

I shook my head. "I'm so sorry. I didn't mean…"

"Ah," he said with another quick, comforting squeeze and a smile. "We all have demons to put under our feet." He nodded. "You will put yours there, too." I rested my cheek on his chest again, gazing over the water. "I escaped with a small group of refugees when I was sixteen. We fled to a missionary camp from the United States. They took me in, straightened me out, and gave me a job." I felt his chin rest on top of my head. "Gyllian found me there twelve years later."

It was quiet again for a while. The sun was heading down and the wind was picking up, but Booth was like my own personal furnace. A more upbeat change of subject came to mind, and I smiled at him. "So what's up with you and that little beauty back there?"

Booth laughed. "Ah, Neesa. She is quite lovely, isn't she?"

"Come on. Spill!" I urged, giving him a few playful shakes.

He chuckled. "Ah well," he took my hand and we headed back to the bench. "Neesa and I were to be wed."

"What?"

He looked at me with furrowed brows and a smile. "You are surprised?"

"Well, I don't know," I said as we sat down. "I guess I thought we weren't allowed to fall in love or something."

Booth looked confused. "Where did you get that notion?"

I shrugged. "I don't know. The world is ending. I thought love would be something trivial we couldn't waste our time with."

Booth tilted his head in consideration. "I suppose that makes sense. Hell rising is why I decided not to marry Neesa.

When Gyllian found me, and told me about all of it, I tried to leave Neesa behind." He smiled. "But she refused to go." I chuckled. "She would not leave no matter what argument I offered, and we fought. Oh, mercy we fought, but she would not yield. So Gyllian brought her to America with us."

I laughed and threaded my arm through his. "She's a very understanding woman."

Booth nodded. "And stubborn."

I grinned. "For sure. She seemed to really love those kids, too." Booth hummed an affirmation. "Do you have any kids with her?"

Booth's expression dropped into sadness, and I wondered what I'd said wrong. He sighed heavily. "Unfortunately, it is not possible for Nephilims to have children." Reading my confusion, he gave me a sympathetic smile. "The five of us were born sterile because of what we are." He shook his head. "Our lineage, our species, is not meant to continue."

"Oh," I said, trying to ignore the sting of that information. "I'm…I'm sorry. I didn't know."

Booth squeezed my hand. "And I am sorry to be the one to tell you this."

I rested my head on his shoulder. I'd always wondered what it would be like to be a mom, but I'd been afraid I would suck at it. The possibly would have been nice, even if I never took advantage of it. I guess being unable to have kids made sense, though, given our species and our purpose.

We gazed over the river quietly until all that was left of the sun was a thin golden line resting on the horizon. It was a comfortable silence. Noise and business seemed to dominate the lives of the others. Booth was the most serene of them all. Fox was the sweet one. Roy was the excitable one. Gyllian was the busy leader. I wondered what that made me. The rebellious one I supposed, the black sheep.

My thoughts drifted to Gyllian. I still needed to talk to him about the interrogation they were setting up. I hadn't been briefed on it yet. I also needed to tell him about the little jar of liquid that Sari brought for our bullets. For all I knew, though, maybe it didn't contain what she'd said it did.

My eyes went wide. For all I knew, that little jar could

be spewing poisonous vapor throughout the entire house.
I grabbed Booth's arm. "We need to get back."

22

I pushed open the front door and Booth and I poured inside. "Gyllian?" I called into the house.

Silence.

I sniffed the air but didn't smell anything suspicious, not that all poisonous gas gave off an odor. Even if poison were spewing into the air, Booth assured me we would be protected from it. But I wanted to find Gyllian anyway, just to be sure.

"Check the bunker. I will search the house," Booth said.

I nodded and headed for the room leading down to the bunker. "Stay away from the library just in case," I called to him as I pulled open the closet door. The floor was already raised, exposing the stairs, so I quickly headed down and pulled open the large round cement door.

"Gyllian?" I called as soon as I entered the hallway.

No answer, though I doubted he would hear me if he was in the back hallway or the intelligence room. His bedroom was practically in front of me so I decided to check there first.

"Gyllian," I said as I pushed open his door. I sagged in relief when I saw him.

He sat in a plain wooden chair in only a pair of khakis, no shoes or shirt. His feet were crossed on top of an empty table with the chair tilted back on two legs. His arms were up behind his head as his sunset eyes nonchalantly shifted over to me when I entered. For the first time, I got a good look at the tattoos on his torso. He had a few that were concentrated on his right side, over his arm, shoulder, and chest. His filler tattoos between the main pictures and symbols were sexy-looking, jagged, black streaks, like the claw marks of a giant cat.

"So you came back," he declared flatly, shifting his eyes away.

I closed the door behind me and bowed my head, recalling our encounter in the library. "Thank you," I said. His eyes shifted to me again. "For saving me this morning."

The front legs of the chair dropped loudly to the floor, and he came toward me. "This is getting old, Bay. You need to decide. Are you staying or going? Because if you're not going to fight with us, there's no point in fighting at all."

My mouth went dry as I looked into his fierce amber-brown eyes. "I'm sorry."

"Stop apologizing and make a decision!" he yelled and slammed his palm into the concrete door. He stared at me with such ferocity I couldn't breathe, but I couldn't look away.

I nodded once. "I'm with you."

His eyes narrowed into slits of suspicion.

I swallowed heavily. "I went to…" I choked on my words and had to clear my throat. "I went to the Guardian Angel Orphanage today." His expression softened immediately. "I spent the whole day there. They helped me make a decision." I shook my head. "I'll die before I let harm come to those children. I can promise you that. If nothing else, I can promise you that."

A look of deep affection came over his face. "You're not going to die because I won't let you." My heart fluttered so quickly I felt faint. His eyes searched mine with a softness I barely recognized. "I can promise *you* that. If nothing else, I can promise you that."

I tried to breathe, to *think*, but the tenderness in his orange eyes was stirring things up in my heart that surprised me. Suddenly, the desire to touch him overwhelmed my mind and every sense I had and, as if with a will of its own, my palm came up and rested on his cheek.

He went incredibly still, and his eyes widened a little. "Don't," he said, though he made no move to back away from me.

My heart dissolved into a warm puddle and sent little explosions through my whole system. I waited moment, watching his eyes to see what he would do, but he just stared at me. So I drew his face toward mine. I expected him to pull away any second, I was waiting for it, but he didn't, and his lips eventually touched mine. His resolve crumbled into oblivion. He urgently pressed his mouth against mine and swept me up in his arms, pinning me hard between him and the wall behind me.

Kissing him was wildly passionate, but at the same time, a deep tenderness for him that I felt in the core of my soul overwhelmed me. It felt like I was taking a real breath of air for the first time in my life. I inhaled him and clutched his shoulders, anything to get him closer to me. Something about him, about this, felt so incredibly right I could hardly comprehend it.

He unexpectedly put me back on my feet. His hands came up to my cheeks and, holding my head in place, he jerked away. "Don't," he said breathlessly.

I was stunned.

He gently caressed my cheeks with his thumbs. "Don't," he said again, and then slowly and deliberately backed away from me with his hands up as if in surrender.

I felt my cheeks turned a deep, terrible red. "What the hell, Gyllian?" I asked, unable to process the rejection properly with my adrenaline still pumping and the ghostly feel of his hands still on me.

He closed his eyes and turned his face away, keeping his hands up. "I said 'don't' before you kissed me."

"So it's my fault?" I asked breathlessly. He didn't respond. He just kept his eyes closed, his face turned away, and his hands up. My anger kicked in, but I had no right to be angry. Instead, I tried to think of a way to save face. "If you didn't want me, Gyllian, you could have been a little clearer about it."

"Believe me," he said with surprising firmness, "not wanting you is not the problem."

The confession slammed hard into my chest, replacing my embarrassment with concern. "Then what is it?"

He looked at me and shook his head. "It doesn't matter."

"Yes, it does." I approached him. "What's wrong?" He just stared at me. "Gyllian," I said without breaking eye contact with him. "Tell me."

I could see the struggle on his face. "I made a promise," he finally said.

"A promise?"

He was quiet before finally taking a deep breath. "My Hell," he began slowly, "was being a prisoner of war."

My heart clenched. "What?"

Gyllian's wall crumbled. In his eyes I saw fear, I saw vulnerability, and I saw pain…a lot of pain. "I was a POW in Afghanistan for six years." My eyes went wide. "From practically the day I joined the army at eighteen, until I was twenty-four."

My heart was pounding. I knew what those Afghani cells looked like. I knew what the prisoners were fed and how they were treated. I knew because the Counterterrorism Unit was very generous with the information they had on terrorists' prison situations. Gyllian had lived in a cell no grown man could stand in. He had to have lain on a filthy dirt floor in a seven-by-two-foot cage, maybe four feet high, barely bigger than a coffin. He had to have been tortured regularly. He had to have been raped often, likely gang-raped on occasion. He had to have been starved for long stretches, or fed rotten food with maggots growing in sour meat, and forced to sit in his own filth for weeks or months on end. An array of sores and skin rot often occurred in POW cells. Illness and infection ran rampant—lung diseases, blood diseases, fevers, and just about everything in between.

I looked at Gyllian's beautiful clear face and fought with all my might not to picture him in that kind of a situation. I failed. The dark images came, and it was enough to suck the life out of me. A hollowness of grief for him formed in my chest, ready to suffocate me.

"My hell taught me about torture," he said. "So I would fight that much harder to keep Hell from coming up here. I cannot, I *will not*, let Hell come to the surface, Bay," he said with breathless passion.

I stepped forward and embraced him. I couldn't help it. He was in pain, and I wanted to fix it. I expected him to pull away quickly, but he didn't. Instead, he wrapped his arms tightly around me, and I could feel him shaking.

"Everything hinges on you," he said softly into my hair. "If you're not willing to fight, we can't win, and all of our past pain will mean nothing." He pulled away to look down at my face, his eyes locked on mine. "What we went through, all of us, made us strong so we could fight Hell and, more so, so we would *want* to fight it."

I nodded. "Everything happens for a reason."

He looked at me curiously. "It does, but since when do you know that?"

"Booth and I talked after I visited the kids and…" I paused, trying to put it into words, but gave up. "I can't really explain it, but something clicked into place. Something…happened inside of me that made things make sense."

I shook my head, deciding I sounded daft, but a brilliant smile spread across Gyllian's face that lit up his eyes. "Don't even try to explain that," he said. "No one can."

I grinned, grateful to be let off the hook, and looked at him curiously. "You said something about a promise, though." I immediately wanted to bite my tongue in half when my question darkened the light in his eyes. "Shit. I'm sorry. You don't have to…"

He surprised me by resting his hands on my cheeks. "It's okay." He was struggling again. I waited in silence. Clearly this was not an easy topic for him.

"I tried to kill myself in prison," he said.

My blood went cold. The agony on his face made the hollowness in my chest flutter and pulse, like it was a living thing.

"They had cuffed my hands behind my back for several weeks." I felt him start to tremble. "I could only eat what I could lap off my tray. I could only sleep on my stomach, which put my nose right on the foul-smelling dirt floor. My arms hurt. My shoulders hurt. My back hurt. Everything hurt. And I was still being dragged into the white room for…" He choked on the words and didn't finish them; he didn't need to. "They left me alone for a minute when a scuffle broke out among the guards, and I was able to unscrew one of the light bulbs near me." He let out a soft breath. "With my hands still cuffed behind me, I stuck my fingers into the live socket."

I clutched his sides and started to pant with rage and fear for him. But he, oddly enough, seemed to relax a little and even smiled. "That's when God showed up." I couldn't even be surprised. "It was brief, and I didn't see anything. He just seemed to surround me. Then I heard him say, 'My grace is sufficient for you.' When I opened my eyes, I was on the floor. But everything looked different. I didn't see a hopeless hole anymore. I saw a waiting room, a stepping stone, and started my work that night. That spark, that same spark you felt today, came alive in me. I felt whole, at peace, and safe." Gyllian sighed. "In that room I made a promise, that if God got me out of there, I would pay whatever price he asked, without even knowing the price because I didn't care. I wanted to get to work, but there was only so much I could do from my cell." He shook his head. "I leaned heavily on God for two years, covertly making low level connections and networking, until out of nowhere the guard who had been the most brutal to me, unlocked my cell. He didn't say a single word. He just took me out of there as his prisoner and drove me straight to the American Embassy in Kabul. He dropped me off and drove away."

My eyes were wide. I recalled reading a story like that during my week in the library, a prison rescue of that same nature for one of the famous Biblical Apostles. In fact, I recalled reading about it in the tome of the Archangel Gabriel, Gyllian's dad.

Gyllian caressed my hips. "After arriving at the hospital, I got on my knees and prayed, and"—he sighed heavily— "the price God asked of me for my rescue was to stay sexually pure until I was married." He looked at me with his eyes alight with smothered desire, like embers of a fire trying to burst back to life. "But I knew when I first saw you, even without knowing who you were, that you were going to be a problem for me."

I couldn't help the sting that came with that. I'd never meant to be a problem for him.

He took my hands off his waist and tenderly gathered them in both of his without breaking eye contact. "When we ran into each other, and I found out you were one of us, I had to close myself off. I knew if you got near me"—he slowly pushed my hands back toward my chest and removed his own, deliberately separating us— "I would break my promise."

My heart pounded and my mouth was dry. I tried to swallow, but I might as well have been trying to swallow sand. "I'm sorry," I managed to choke out. "I didn't mean…"

He gave a short, airy chuckle. "It's not your fault you're gorgeous." His eyes became sad and he shook his head. "I'm sorry." He leaned forward and unexpectedly kissed me firmly on the lips one more time. I breathed him in like I was taking my last breath before he pulled away and met my eyes. "But I *have* to keep my promise."

I nodded, trying to accept that without pain. I couldn't have him, and I wanted him in a way I didn't even understand. "Just answer me one thing," I said. He nodded, though he looked nervous at what I might ask. I forced a look of playful skepticism on my face. "You're not a *virgin,* are you?"

Gyllian looked stunned for a moment, and then he laughed. It was the first genuine laugh I'd heard from him since we met. "No," he chuckled. "I had plenty of romps when I was a teenager."

"Oh good," I said, feigning relief. "I'd have a hard time respecting you if you'd never had sex."

He shook his head while looking at me with a new softness and warmth that made my heart race. I needed to hide the pain I was in. He didn't need to see it. What I felt for Gyllian all the sudden wasn't his problem. It was mine.

"So," I said, shoving my trembling hands into my pockets and shrugging deeply, "are we going to put our boots in the ass of this war or what?"

He smiled broadly before going to his closet. He pulled out a gray t-shirt and threw it on. "First," he said, holding up a finger as he passed me. I followed. He headed for the door to the main house and went straight to the library. "What is that?" he asked pointing to the white and silver jar Sari had left.

I sighed. "Sari brought it. Supposedly that's the substance from Heaven for our bullets."

"What's the substance?"

"Water from Flumine Aeternum. The river that—"

"Flows behind the throne of God," Gyllian finished, his eyes going wide as he looked back at the jar.

"Yeah," I said confused. "But you realize the Angel who gave it to me tried to kill me a minute later, right?" He nodded and started toward the jar. "Whoa, hey!" I grabbed his arm, stopping him. "I'm not sure you should trust that stuff."

"It's safe."

"How do you know?"

He smiled. "God just told me he provided it."

My eyes went wide and I let him go. A flash of anger returned over God having allowed an Angel to bring me a substance that could help us, while knowing she was planning to assassinate me. I glared up at the ceiling, silently pondering it.

It was the correct alignment of circumstances that got you to the Guardian Angel Orphanage, the voice told me.

My whole body went stiff and my eyes went wide. God had just talked to me again. I lowered my eyes and crossed my arms tightly. I still wasn't comfortable with that, but unfortunately, his reasoning made sense. It was still a large concept to accept, that everything happened for a reason, but damn if it hadn't proven true at every turn so far.

How I long for the day when you trust me, Bay, the voice said, sounding sad.

I cleared my throat and tried to dismiss it. "So it's the real deal?" I asked Gyllian, sparing myself some discomfort. "We can kill Kings and Queens and Angels with that?"

He nodded, picking up the little jar and heading back out the door. "I need to get this to Booth so he can start making bullets."

I followed quickly behind. "He should be around the house somewhere. I was worried it contained some poisonous vapors or something, so we went searching for you and the others when we got back."

"I thought I felt my ears burning," we heard above. Gyllian and I stopped to see Booth coming down the stairs from the second floor. He looked at Gyllian and held out his hand, which Gyllian shook. "All right then?"

Gyllian nodded before handing Booth the small jar. "Think you can work your magic with this?"

Booth examined it. "We can kill Kings and Angels with this?"

"Yeah, but clearly not many," I said.

The three of us continued toward the bunker. "Is that all she gave you?" Gyllian asked.

I nodded. "It's only enough water for about ten mags or so. We need more than that to fight a war, and I doubt any more Angels will be at our disposal to get more."

We started down the stairs. "We have enough," Gyllian said.

"You're kidding," I said flatly. Gyllian pulled open the round concrete door, and we started down the hallway toward the back. "We're supposed to take on the entirety of Hell with just 150 bullets? There are about two million Demons in Hell and about a hundred thousand Angels to deal with. Do the math, Gyllian."

"We only have to take on Hell if it rises."

I threw my hands out to my sides. "Well, great! If it doesn't, then we just have a hundred thousand pissed off Angels to deal with."

Both of them smiled at me. "Have faith, Bay," Gyllian said.

I sighed and crossed my arms. "I'm working on it."

For the first time, I considered the possibly of Hell *not* rising to the surface. What if we could actually stop it and the world could go on as normal? Yet the idea of the world remaining the same still severely bothered me. It was on its way to Hell even if Hell wasn't already threatening to come up here. But the bottom line was that I wasn't going to let Jasmine and Eric and all the other kids suffer at the hands of Demons. I just wasn't.

A thought suddenly occurred to me. "Hey," I said looking at Gyllian. "How did you know to come when Sari attacked me?"

He and Booth glanced at each other before fixing their eyes down the hallway. "I heard you."

"You heard me?"

"When you thought my name."

"When I thought your—" my voice cut off, and my eyes went wide. "You heard me *think* your name?"

He looked down at me with a slightly playful smirk. "You'll get used to it."

"I doubt *that.*" He just kept smiling before looking ahead of him again. "Can you hear what everyone thinks?"

"No, no," he said. "Just you four, and only when you reach out to me first. That automatically activates my ability." He vaguely indicated the right side of his chest. One of his tattoos in the cat-claw cluster must have activated it.

"Why were you already dressed and armed though?"

"I was in Virginia with Fox and Booth, starting recon on Nuwart and Killiner. As soon as I heard you, I teleported back here."

"Speaking of which," I said getting off the topic of him reading my mind because it was weird, "when is that going down?"

"In a week. Next Friday night."

"So we'd better talk. I need a briefing."

He nodded and looked down at me with warm smile. "Let's get to work."

23

Normally I could handle a stakeout, but I was having a hard time tonight in a backless, skintight, white evening gown. I was convinced, too, that my matching five-inch stiletto heels had grown teeth and were enjoying the free samples of my feet. They apparently found the sides of my baby toes delicious.

Gyllian had teleported us to Orange County, Virginia on the shore of Lake of the Woods, where Corwin Killiner was holding a formal party at one of his humbler abodes; a four-story little number that would give Edinburgh Castle a run for its money. The only real difference was the square footage. Killiner's manor was about the size of the National War Museum, and looked a lot like it, too. It had a rustic stone exterior and old wooden windows, though the house looked much less aged than the ancient European castle. It sat in a wide clearing of a perfectly manicured lawn with dense trees ringing it. Glancing to my left, I could see the lake glistening under the waning moonlight. It was mostly hidden by the narrow cluster of trees, but peeking between the trunks, I managed to see the water. Beyond that was another dark tree line on the far shore. This section of the lake was less than a mile across, but it stretched far to the left and right until both sides were out of view.

The party was still in full swing even though it was a little before dawn. The five of us were standing in the side yard of the manor with one of Fox's protection abilities activated that altered perceptions, keeping us hidden from any stray glances while we waited to catch sight of our targets.

"You look gorgeous," Roy whispered.

"Quiet," Gyllian ordered firmly without taking his eyes off the first-floor window we were all staring into.

I smiled my appreciation to Roy, trying to hide the awkwardness I'd felt toward him since Gyllian and I kissed. Seeing Roy in a full tuxedo, though, dampened the awkwardness tremendously. He looked unbelievably hot in it. His brown hair was styled with some special oil Fox had that tamed his mane without making it look like a shiny hard helmet. Having his hair styled like that opened his features up, making his big, gentle, brown eyes even more striking against his white skin.

"There," Gyllian said suddenly. "Bay?"

I activated the flaming eye tattoo in the middle of my chest as Justine passed in front of the window with Corwin. My eyes narrowed. "Well, Killiner is definitely a Bishop Demon, or a Drake."

"Which?" Gyllian asked.

"I don't know," I replied, not taking my eyes off them. "I haven't had a lot of practice with this ability. Justine…" I stared at her, confused. "Something's weird."

"What?"

"She's not a Demon or a Drake, but she's not human either."

"What are you talking about?" Gyllian asked.

I studied Justine for another moment. "I can't really explain it."

"Try!" he demanded.

"Take it easy," Roy growled.

I was tempted to see the look Gyllian was giving Roy, but I couldn't distract myself. We had to know what we were dealing with.

I should have done this during the initial recon, but Gyllian hadn't wanted to risk me or Roy getting close to either Justine or Corwin, since Roy and I were kind of the bait for this trap. Demons have heightened senses, and Gyllian feared they would recognize our scent tonight. He, Booth, Fox had kept a close watch, though, digging into every facet of their lives, digitally and personally, to set things in motion for tonight. There was enough evidence to tell us they were not human, but only my ability to see through their human disguises could tell us exactly what kind of supernatural beings they were, which was vital for the trap.

"The only way I can really describe it is she's got some weird phantom-looking haze inside of her. When she moves, it's like I can see a mixed glimpse of Justine as herself and something else."

"Focus on the something else. What does it look like?" Gyllian said.

My brows dropped as I concentrated on what was inside of her. Its form was indistinct and faint, though. Finally, I thought I caught glimpses of purplish, burned-out sections of skin.

I snapped my head to Gyllian. "A Rook Demon."

Gyllian looked at Booth over his shoulder. "Possessed human," Booth said. "That is why it looks strange." Gyllian nodded and returned his attention to the window.

I remembered reading about that. Possession was when only the spirit of a Demon was inside a human; nothing of flesh was present. That's why it looked phantom-like. It was good news for Justine because a Demon spirit could be exorcised.

I shook my head, though, because I knew this woman. I'd never spent much time with her since she was in Virginia and I was in Illinois and she was so high-ranking. But if you worked at any branch of the FBI you knew who Justine Nuwart was. It would be interesting to find out how a Demon had gotten into her in the first place, since a Demon could only possess a human if the human willingly allowed it. I also wondered if she'd ever had suspicions about who I was. Could she somehow have been responsible for me getting fired? My rage spiked as I realized she had approved the partners that Porter had tried to shove down my throat. Could they have been Demons assigned by her to keep an eye on me? For that matter, was Porter a Demon?

My mind started running wild, and I bowed my head, pinching the bridge of my nose as if it were an off switch that could keep the questions from rattling around in my brain. These kinds of questions depended on how aggressive the Demon infestation was, and none of us had the answer to that yet. But if the hundred or so at the club were any indication, and the fact that Killiner *was* one, it might be too late to even try to stop Hell from rising.

"Bay, are you all right?" Roy asked.

I nodded and looked at him. "I'm okay." My distress had caught the attention of the others as well, and they all looked at me with concern. I shook my head and looked back at the window. "It's just…hard. I know her and she's…" I sighed. "I don't know. It's just hard."

They all nodded their understanding. Gyllian then focused on Roy and me. "Are you two ready?"

Roy and I nodded as I pushed the maddening questions away. I needed to focus. I was nervous enough as it was, and that could spell disaster. Even though I was trained as an undercover agent, I'd never actually done any undercover work. I just hadn't had it in me to wait and put on a show for three to six months in order to arrest one perp, no matter *how* high level. In three to six months I averaged two dozen cases solved at minimum. My efforts paid off in the field, so other agents had done the undercover work in a lot of my cases to find the big fish I'd wanted.

"All right," Gyllian said, his eyes going Angelic. "Let's go."

Gyllian, Fox, and Booth all ran quietly toward the house and, in a magnificent display of supernatural acrobatics, the three of them made their way up the side of the manor to Killiner's office window on the fourth floor. They looked like a mix of mountain lions and chimpanzees in their natural habitat. Fox would swing, or leap, from one window shelf to another before turning to catch Gyllian as he leapt. Then she'd swing him past, or above, her position onto another window ledge or fixture. She did the same with Booth, and they alternated turns catching and swinging each other up, and easing their way over to the left corner. They were fast and silent as they did this. I didn't even hear them scrape the stone siding with their boots. It was amazing and beautiful to watch.

Roy suddenly started chuckling, "Your face."

I glanced over and saw him in quiet hysterical laughter. Smiling, I elbowed him in the ribs. "Shut up." Looking back at the other three, I saw them already crowded around the office window, working on it.

During recon, they'd decided that the best time to get in would be during the party. A few problems occurred with that, though. Corwin's house was powerfully warded against magical intrusion, and the party was admittance by invitation only. No active magic could make it from the outside to the inside of his house without detection. It was smart. That meant we couldn't teleport into the building with Gyllian's ability or we'd be detected. We also couldn't magically fabricate an invitation and walk through the front door, or it would be detected. Our best and, pretty much only option was an old-fashioned break in. The electronic system would already be deactivated because of the party, so it was just a matter of getting through some windows. Luckily, they were an easily accessible 1920s design.

It wasn't long before the office window lifted and Fox gave Roy and me a thumbs-up as her eyes faded back to normal.

"Let's go," Roy said.

We headed for the first floor window at the back corner, where Roy pulled out a pocketknife and worked it into the wooden frame. He quickly managed to slide the half-moon lock into an open position and lifted it. Both of us stepped over the ledge and into a lounge library, closed the window, and waited in the dark, silently counting down. We had forty-five seconds from Fox's thumbs-up to get into the house before she magically changed our appearance. It had to be done while we were already inside; otherwise the warding would detect her magic trying to make it through the walls.

When the countdown ended, Roy and I crept to the door that led to the house. Because we were half-Angels, all our senses were heightened even without magic. So, we waited, smelling and listening for anyone out in the hall.

"Quiet?" Roy whispered to me.

"Quiet," I responded.

"You ready for this?"

I nodded. "I'm ready."

I felt him take my hand. "You can do this," he declared firmly. Then he leaned in and kissed my forehead. "I'll take care of you if things go sideways. I promise."

I smiled and nodded. "I know you will." He would, too. He was the first partner I'd had that I actually trusted to have my back.

He kissed my forehead again, lingering a moment before pulling away. "Let's go."

He pulled the door open and we staggered into the

hallway, laughing and straightening our clothes, pretending we'd just finished an athletic romp in the lounge. We passed an elaborate mirror in the hall, and I paused in front of it to pretend to fix my hair and makeup. Fox's disguise had me with long, fine, orange-colored hair falling to the middle of my back, very white skin, and pretty green eyes. Roy had short, spiky, black hair, tan skin, and eyes so dark that they looked black. After "straightening" myself out, Roy offered me his arm. I took it with a smile, and we both headed into the main ballroom.

Killiner had a full orchestra playing the lifeless crap you usually hear in movies involving rich people's parties. I resisted the urge to roll my eyes at how cliché it was. So was the ballroom. Decorative and ridiculously high arched windows were on the right and back walls, shamelessly showing off the immense landscape on which the manor sat. At the back were round, cloth-covered tables with elaborate floral centerpieces that were probably as tall as I was. Six white columns, three on each side, supported the forty-foot-high balcony. At my feet was a vast black-and-white tile floor where flowing gowns and tuxedos whirled around, spinning and dancing in a form that looked like it belonged in the late 18th century.

"Come on," Roy coaxed, and we stepped out onto the dance floor.

I expected we would go straight across to see Killiner and Justine, who were chatting with a small group of people at the tables, but suddenly Roy spun me around and took me up in full ballroom frame. One hand was on my waist and the other held my hand up. My eyes went wide in terror.

"Easy," Roy said, smiling. "Relax."

I forced a smile, but I didn't even have to see my reflection to know how false it looked. "Roy," I whispered. "I don't know how to dance."

He smiled. "Yes, you do."

"I really don't, though," I said as he began to sway. "Seriously, I don't!" I insisted quietly as my heart started to pound. He just kept smiling as his swaying started to evolve into steps. I sucked in a breath of air through clenched teeth and clutched him a little too hard. "Roy," I said, trying to be firm while still attempting to think about what my feet were doing. "Killiner and Justine are right over there. We have a mission."

"And Gyllian, Booth, and Fox still have to set up upstairs." I stared at him and tried to dance without falling on my ass. "Hey," he said, his expression softening. "I told you I would take care of you, so let me." He paused. "Trust me."

I swallowed heavily and blew out a breath, trying to relax. Almost instantly, my feet fell into sync with his and my eyes went wide.

Roy grinned broadly. "See?"

I blinked a couple of times in disbelief as Roy began to turn me around the dance floor and my feet and body flowed with his more easily.

"You're a control freak," he said a little playfully. "That's why dancing is hard for you. You don't like anyone else taking the lead."

I smiled at the truth of that as he spun me so gracefully that my hair flew out behind me. A thrill went up my spine as he pulled me against him again and I didn't fall.

"It would have looked really suspicious if we just came from the hallway and went straight to Killiner," Roy said. "That's why we had to dance. People needed to forget they saw us come out of the hallway. So, we enjoy the party like we've been here the whole time."

I sighed softly. He was right. But trust was still a leap of faith for me, and faith was shaky ground. Being here, however, in this odd situation with half Angels trying to save the world, I realized how badly I needed to let go of some control. Because I wasn't in control; God was. I didn't like the idea, but it was a fact, whether I cared for it or not.

The song ended and everyone on the dance floor turned to the orchestra and clapped politely before Roy offered me his arm. "Ready?"

I smiled and took it, feeling a little more confident. "Yes."

Both of us made our way to the tables. Killiner had moved to speak to another group, leaving Justine with only one other person. I ran my speech over and over again in my head and let my undercover training kick in a little. It was an act. It was all an act. I had to take the lead because Roy couldn't lie. He could affirm the lies I established to make the conversation believable, but he couldn't initiate a lie of any kind.

"Miss Nuwart?" I said as we approached.

Justine faced me, and I nearly flinched at seeing her. God Almighty, I knew this woman! She still had shoulder-length mousy brown hair styled in a plain bob with a few strands of silver. She was short, just coming up to my shoulder, and had a lumpy figure that really didn't belong in the sausage suit of a black gown she was wearing.

"Yes?" she asked, taking me in with her calculating swamp green eyes.

A pit formed in my stomach. I was talking to a fucking Demon. But I had to get it together.

"I'm Donna Newsham," I said, holding out my hand, which she took hesitantly. "This is my partner, Dax Gordon." She looked at me blankly. "I believe our associate, Barl Hencore, spoke to you about us."

Finally, her face brightened. "Oh, yes. Barl did come to see me about you."

"Barl" had actually been Booth, disguised by Fox, who'd met with Justine to arrange jobs for Roy and me out here in Virginia. Our cover was that Roy and I were Demons needing a transfer from the Chicago FBI to the Quantico Headquarters. It was a little risky because Demon activity was obviously heavy in Chicago, so Justine could wonder why we were being transferred to a place with less activity; that is, if there really *was* less activity here. We had no real way of knowing.

"I trust you received payment accordingly," I said.

"Indeed I did. It was a handsome sum for such a menial service."

"We just wanted to insure your cooperation," Roy added with a false tight smile.

Justine nodded. "Of course. You can't be too careful these days."

By the way she hungrily leered at Roy, I could tell an awkward silence was about to occur. "Do you have the paperwork and accommodations we require?" I asked abruptly, bringing the woman's focus back to me.

She looked annoyed. "I do," she replied, putting down her glass of champagne. "This way," she said and started walking toward Killiner.

"Don't be jealous, baby," Roy said, then slapped my ass and grabbed a large portion of it aggressively.

I narrowed my eyes at him. "She looks at you like that again, I'll rip her tongue out and feed it to my pets."

Roy scrunched his nose playfully before lightly pinching mine. "You're adorable when you get like this."

We spoke loud enough for Justine, but not anyone else, to hear. She needed to know her boundaries, and Roy and I needed to convince her we were Demons. While it was normal for Justine to covet Roy, it was also normal for me to threaten her if she tried to impose on my territory. Thus, the chaos of evil.

Justine gestured toward Killiner with an open palm as he faced us. "Allow me to introduce my associate, Corwin Killiner."

Killiner was a short, thin, unimpressive man with a thin crown of white hair around the back of his head that left the top shiny and bald, and unremarkable blue eyes. The disguise was pretty smart. It was best to keep a low profile as one of the richest men in the world.

"Donna and Dax, I presume," he said with a jerky nod. The word "Demon" screamed in my head loudly, as if I needed a reminder of what I was dealing with. "I assume you're here to collect your documentation and deeds for the transfer?"

"We are," I replied. "I hope our house is to our specifications," I said with an edge of warning.

Booth had told them we needed a large basement for major supply runs of all sorts of criminal contraband, about which he'd gone into vast detail. It made us seem like semi-important Demons since we had some responsibility, but not important enough to make the two of them wonder why they didn't know us. We needed to be influential yet anonymous, and it was working.

"You haven't seen the house yet?" Corwin asked.

"We arrived late today," I responded. "But we'd like to

look at the floor plans with you before final payment is released."

"If you wish," Killiner said and placed his glass of wine on a table. "Shall we take a walk to my office?" he said, gesturing to the side.

"Would you join us, Miss Nuwart?" I asked, looking at her. She stared at me suspiciously. Shit. Was that too brazen? "We have some last minute requests only you can fulfill."

Justine nodded once hesitantly before she and Killiner began to lead the way out of the ballroom. Damn. The money Gyllian had paid this pair sure lit a fire under their asses to do our bidding.

We were taken to the elevator at the end of the hall which Roy and I had come out of earlier. Gyllian and the others had better be ready upstairs. As we piled in, it was uncomfortably quiet, so much so that I began to sweat. Being in such a confined space with two Demons didn't help. Clearly noticing that I was on edge, Roy rested his hand on my lower back. He kept it there for a moment as a gesture of comfort before sliding it down the back of my dress and grabbing another handful of my ass to keep up the possessive pretense of a Demon.

The elevator gave a resounding ding when we reached the fourth floor. As we stepped out into the hallway, the whole floor felt heavy, like it was holding its breath. It was as if the house knew a trap was waiting for its master and was trying to give a warning. Panicked thoughts started to run through my head. What could go wrong? What might I do if it did? How would I be able to protect Gyllian and the others?

We stepped into the outer office and Killiner took out a set of keys to open the main office. "I trust you'll find the plans are to the specifications you requested," he said.

"They'd better be for what we're paying you," Roy said coldly as Killer inserted the key.

I smirked, pleased with his act. I noticed Justine staring at me, not looking pleased at all. I raised a brow, silently asking what her problem was, but she just looked away.

The office door swung open, and as soon as Killiner stepped through, I heard the electric buzzing sound of a spell that had been cast over the doorway that specifically targeted

Bishop Demons. Killiner convulsed briefly before he was face down on the floor and out cold. Justine had enough time to look at me before my elbow slammed into the side of her neck and she went down just as hard. She was still a human, thus susceptible to being rendered unconscious by a sharp blow to her carotid artery.

Gyllian appeared in the doorway. "Let's go," he said to Roy and me.

24

Fox grabbed Killiner and Gyllian grabbed Justine, tossed them over their shoulders, and brought them into the office. I stepped through in a hurry to see what they'd done, and felt a little skeptical. I wasn't sure how well this was going to work.

The plush chairs and furniture of the office were all pushed off to the side, and in the center, were two soundproof clear glass boxes side by side—our own little interrogation rooms. Each had a glass door and a single wooden chair sitting in the center. Booth's main ability was being able to create and shape matter out of nothing. It was represented by a tribal-looking chain tattoo on his back connecting the eight symbols of the elements. Earth, air, fire, and water were the main ones, but he could also manipulate subgenres of the elements like metal, ice, glass, and nature such as wood and plants. With a different ability, Booth could also infuse Holy energy into matter he created, as well as matter that already existed. Those two glass boxes were as Holy as a Catholic altar right now, and Demons didn't do very well with Holiness. The glass walls, the floor, the chairs, and even the ropes we were tying them down with were infused with the power.

I tried to talk my companions out of having the interrogation here because Killiner's office would throw a wrench into my work. There was a reason interrogation rooms were small with four blank walls. The room itself was used as psychological manipulation. The whole point of an interrogation room was to make the suspect feel uncomfortable. It emphasized the suspect's helplessness and powerlessness, and in that type of situation, people were more likely to talk, if only to get out of the room. Killiner's office was big and decorative and full of beautiful paintings and vases and Persian rugs familiar to him, which would negate the uncomfortable feeling the interrogation room was supposed to impose. In this environment, Killiner could sit there and smile at me for days and still not say anything.

Gyllian explained, however, that Demons had a much different threshold of what made them uncomfortable than humans did, and that the power of Holiness would do its work. Not only would it make the Demons crazy, but it would also suppress their powers, if not eliminate them. But it depended on how powerful each Demon was.

I decided on glass boxes for two reasons. First, in an effort to intimidate them into talking, I wanted the Demons to see us, the children of the Archangels. Second, I also wanted the Demons to see each other as I questioned them, because if one Demon started talking, the other might talk even more to cover his or her own ass. It worked when perps were told, or lied to, about a partner flipping on them, but I wasn't sure it would work on Demons. The best I had to offer, unfortunately, was only what worked on humans. These were the only ways I could come up with to try and knock the Demons off their game and get my friends the information they needed. But I was in uncharted territory here and wasn't sure what to expect.

Gyllian put Justine in the glass box on the right, while Fox put Killiner in the left. Both Demons were placed in the chairs facing each other and tied down. Another chair was waiting for me off to the side. Then they both pulled out long thin chains from their pockets with small bottles dangling on the ends and put them around Corwin's and Justine's necks.

As they made their way out of the boxes, Booth took hold of my wrist and my white evening gown faded away into the black uniform and long coat I'd worn when meeting Kye. I felt the material crawl over my exposed skin and take form. I knew the change was coming but didn't expect it to feel like that. He took Roy's arm next and changed his clothes as well.

Gyllian and Fox took positions beside me. Roy and Booth were behind and between us. We all crossed our arms and stood together, looking fiercely into the glass. We also tapped into our enhancement abilities to turn our eyes Angelic to add to the intimidating image.

"Booth," Gyllian said, and with a flick of his fingers, Booth made the corks in the little bottles vanish.

Justine and Killiner got one whiff of the frankincense, the holy herb of deity, and they jerked awake. It only took a split second before they were screaming and struggling against their ropes. Their screams defeated the soundproofing of the glass—not enough to alert the party downstairs, but enough to reach my ears and awaken that primal fear that made me want to run to save my life. But I stayed still. I didn't even allow myself to flinch. The sounds were something straight out of a nightmare, low, guttural, and animalistic, like a lion's roar only rawer, deeper, and more evil. As my throat went dry, one thought settled around me, they were Demons. I was about to get into a little glass room with fucking *Demons.*

"Steady, Bay," Gyllian said calmly, obviously picking up on my struggle.

The Demons made the creepiest movements, jerking violently, or stretching their joints too far for a human's capability before they snapped back to normal. My heart was pounding so hard I thought it was going to burst out of my chest like something from *Alien.*

"Do not lean on your own strength," Booth said gently beside me. I looked at him over my shoulder as casually as I could, and his Angelic eyes turned to me. "You know what I mean."

I glanced at my four companions. They were completely unfazed by the sounds of the Demons. I looked into the glass again and turned my thoughts to those beautiful, innocent children at the orphanage. I needed the intel these Demons had, and I needed it right now. For Dante, Richard, Samantha, Elle, and all the other kids in the path of Hell rising. Faith. My friends were strong because they had faith.

"God," I said. "I need your help."

Something suddenly bloomed to life inside of me, almost overfilling me with courage, peace and strength. I felt it pour into me from an endless wellspring I didn't understand. I would have gasped if I wasn't concerned with appearing intimidating. Suddenly, the sounds of the Demons became irritating more than terrifying.

I am with you, I heard him say.

"Thank you," I whispered.

When their screams quieted to growls and groans, I opened Justine's box and stepped inside.

"You bitch!" she screamed as I closed it. It was the strangest sound, a human voice mixed with a deep, wet growl lingering behind it.

I casually spun the extra chair around and straddled it backwards, letting the silence stretch for a moment before I finally spoke. "I know what you are."

"You," she said, and a small amount of yellowish spittle landed on her chin, "have no idea what you're dealing with."

"Oh, I know exactly what I'm dealing with, a Rook Demon." I smiled humorlessly and allowed a flash of satisfaction when she looked surprised. I guess some Demons didn't know I had an ability that could penetrate their disguises. "Only you're not a physical Demon, are you?" Her face contorted into a vicious, wild snarl as her breathing took on the same guttural growling sound as her voice. "See," I went on casually, "my friends and I there"—I pointed out the glass toward the others— "have these special abilities, numerous ones actually. One of them is that we can spot Demons in all sorts of disguises. Angels too. Since you're just a Demon spirit"—I leaned over the back of my chair and smiled— "we can exorcise your ass back to Hell."

Justine started vibrating so fast she became a blur. Her mouth started opening wide, like a python unhinging its jaws, stretching way beyond a human's physical capability. The corners of her mouth split open, causing streams of blood to run in down her jaw and neck.

I quickly stood and slapped her hard across the face. She went back to normal except for the low growl, and slowly looked back at me. "Down girl," I said without emotion. I came out from behind my chair, gripped the arms of hers, and put my face directly in front of her eyes. "Here's how this is going to work. I'm going to ask you questions, and you're going to answer them. And you'll do so without convulsing, yelling, spitting—"

Suddenly a stringy stream of yellow and red spit shot from her mouth toward me, but it came impossibly slow. It practically hovered in the air. I knew Gyllian wasn't messing with time because I didn't feel the heaviness that accompanied his ability. I had to be moving too fast again. I had more than enough time to move out of the way before the orange goo hit the glass wall behind with a splat. Then things went back to normal.

I locked eyes with her. The evil I saw there pissed me off! I slammed my hand over her mouth and shoved her backward, bringing her and the chair to the floor. "I told you no spitting!" I dug my fingertips hard into her face in case she tried to bite me or expand her jaw again. "Are you going to play nice, or are you going to give me a crack at your buddy across the way?"

I took my hand off her mouth, only to hear her say in a crackling, wet-sounding whisper, "Fuck you."

I shook my head. "Last chance."

Justine started vibrating again, which drew a forlorn sigh out of me. I should have known my psychological manipulations wouldn't work. A new strategy came to mind, one that was better tailored to Demons: appealing to the instinct of self-preservation. I began to recite the Latin incantation I'd memorized during my library binge that would exorcise the Demon spirit out of her. If Killiner saw me exorcise Justine, he'd know I wouldn't hesitate to end him, too. Maybe that would get him to answer my questions. Justine's vibrating got worse to the point that I had to tap into my enhanced strength to hold her down as I said the spell through gritted teeth. As soon as I said the last word, Justine jerked once and was still.

I raised one thigh and rested my arm across it as I looked down at her. I would have thought her dead, but the rising and falling of her chest allayed that fear. I slowly turned to look through the glass at Killiner. His eyes were wide with fear. Good. I got to my feet and left Justine's box. With only a glance at my companions, I went into Killiner's.

"You're wasting your time," he panted, sounding normal without a horrible growling sound in his voice. "You'll get nothing from me."

"Really?" I said casually as I spun the spare chair around under my palm before straddling it. "Do you think it's wise to underestimate me?" I tilted my head. "You don't know me."

He gave me a wolfish smile with his teeth fully bared. "You'll be in for a long night if you try to break me."

A strange spark, like arrogant self-amusement, flew

through his eyes as he said that, as if he knew something I didn't and he loved it. I took mental note of it to address later. I'd been doing interrogations long enough to know what to pay attention to.

I smiled at him and hooked my heels behind the cross bar at my feet, making myself more comfortable. "Okay, but tell me something bub. You—"

"I'm not telling you shit!"

I looked at him curiously. "Well, you're a Demon aren't you?"

His expression shifted into one of contempt. "Are you fucking retarded?"

I shrugged. "You're the one who can't answer a simple question."

He bared his teeth again, which were starting to sharpen and turn black. His skin was also turning an ugly pale gray color. He was trying to change into his Bishop Demon form.

"I only ask because I'm wondering if all Demons are utter pussies." His eyes darkened and vanished as they started to become the burned-out holes of his Demon form. "I mean, come on! You have to admit, being the Angels' bitch, that's…" I looked at him with exaggerated false sympathy. "That's pretty pathetic, man."

None of the fierceness left his face as his head struggled to grow and elongate, but the Holiness of the confinement was doing its job.

"Explain something to me," I went on. "Off the record if you want, but don't Demons scheme and connive and usurp by nature?" I let him seethe over that for a moment before giving him a disdainful look. "But you bow to fucking Angels? Seriously? I thought Demons were supposed to be badass. Now you're doormats to those halos." He released a rolling guttural howl that somehow still had a piercing edge, like metal grating against metal. I smirked at him. "I touched a little nerve there, did I?"

Suddenly his neck started stretching toward me. I could hear the popping of his joints as it lengthened unnaturally, and he brought his face closer to mine. Veins of red streaked down the sides of his neck as his skin tore like wet paper, exposing the muscle underneath. "I am going to suck your heart up through your throat, so you can watch it beat in my teeth."

I leaned toward him in turn, and my tone became severe. "You don't scare me, you pathetic, pansy-ass sellout."

A sound suddenly exploded in my ears and the glass box completely shattered. I ducked, covering my head with my hands as shards of glass rained down around me. My first thought was that I was dead. I'd taken my eyes off Killiner and he was eating my heart right now! But the small flashes of pain, cuts from the falling glass were the only injuries I could feel.

"Bay!"

"Bay!"

I looked up to see my companions running toward me. Through adrenaline-fueled clarity I saw past them. Standing and shoving Gyllian aside when he blocked my view, I saw a woman in a black evening gown. She was crouched on the sill of an open arched window, with black smoke swirling up from her index finger. I looked at Killiner, who was clearly dead, and sticking out of his chest was a black dart, which evaporated into smoke. I looked over at Justine and saw the same black dart evaporate from between her eyes.

When I looked back at the woman, I suddenly recognized her. It was the same woman that had been sitting alone at the club, leering at Gyllian in a way that had made me uneasy.

"Sorry Gilly-baby," she said in a low, seductive voice. Gyllian snapped around facing the windowsill. "But I'm the only one you get to come to for information." She released the ledge and dropped backward out of the window.

I started after her, but Gyllian grabbed my arm. "Bay, don't!" I turned back to him so fast, I hurt my own neck. "She's not a priority."

The controlled terror in his eyes made my insides shake. "Is that her?" I asked, pointing at the window. "Is that the fucking Demon that tortured you?"

He swallowed. "Yes. But we can't deal with her right now."

Some deep, feral instinct rose inside me. Looking into Gyllian's bright amber-brown eyes seemed to fuel the fire. Flashes of him being strapped to a post and abused repeatedly by that bitch made me wild with rage.

"Bay," he said, but I snatched my arm out of his grip and ran to the window.

Without even touching the ledge, I dove headfirst out of it, plummeting to the ground from four stories up. My senses seemed to expand beyond me, and I could feel my surroundings like they were a part of my body. I knew exactly how fast I was going, and how far the ground was, and exactly what to do when I reached it. Just as the lawn became all I could see, I flipped myself so I landed on my feet in a low crouch. Dirt and grass exploded around me as I zeroed in on the Demon cunt by the tree line and slowly straightened to my full height.

"Impressive," I heard her purr as she stepped out of the shadows. The early dawn made her snug black evening gown glitter like a disco ball. "What's the matter, puss?" she asked, putting on a pout. "Are you upset about what I put Gyllian through?" A smile spread across her face. "He came to me, you know."

My fist clenched around the hilt of my father's sword in my chest. I took it out and pointed the blade at her, allowing myself a moment of triumph as a look of terror flashed across her face. "You will *not* touch him again."

She forced a smile. "Oh, jealous, are you? Well, if it's one thing I know from experience, it's that Hell hath no fury like a woman scorned." She hunched down, and a pair of black leathery dragon wings tore from her back, sending a spray of blood and flesh flying through the air. She flapped them, lifting herself off her feet, and gave me a self-satisfied smile as my arm slowly dropped to my side. "I gotta fly, toots. Tell Gyllian I'll see him soon. I have a special new toy to try out on him. Don't worry"—she winked— "I have some really juicy information to go with it."

My shoulders were heaving with every breath I took. She would not hurt Gyllian again! Not while I had life in me. I would protect him with everything I had. I would protect all of them. I loved them.

I resisted the urge to flinch, as that thought settled around me. I wasn't even sure I was *capable* of loving anyone. But there it was; I loved them.

And this is my prayer, God's voice boomed out of nowhere, *that your love may abound more and more in knowledge and depth of insight.*

It was a Bible verse about love bringing knowledge. Suddenly, like a warm liquid seeping from some subconscious part of me, came incredible Angelic knowledge. Everything pertaining to my father flowed effortlessly though my memories. I felt the battles he'd fought as if they were my own. I knew how to use every weapon in existence, supernatural and manmade, and I knew how to use them well.

And I knew how to use my wings.

Glaring at the beast above me, I summoned my wings out. They kicked up a plume of dust as they emerged with force, and I stretched them wide to my sides. The Knight Demon gasped in terror as I slowly raised my sword again and pointed it at her. "So fly, bitch."

She spun and took off over the trees toward the lake. I ran, flapping my wings once, which lifted me off the ground. I flew flush with the tree trunks before bursting over the canopy, where I spotted her soaring over the water. I flew over the treetops before diving down and leveling out over the water as well. I was on her heels in about four seconds. I couldn't help being a little surprised because I was barely in first gear, while she looked like she was flying with all her might at top speed. I dove under her, spinning myself around so I was facing her while keeping course. She had just enough time to gasp before I shoved my father's sword up into her chest. Her face went slack as her blood ran over my hand and dripped down my arm. I grabbed a fistful of her hair, and slowly turned until we both hovered vertically over the water.

"I told you," I managed through clenched teeth, as her wings gradually went still, "you will *not* touch him again." With a sharp thrust upward I split her chest cavity open and let her fall from my hand, my sword sliding out of her chest as she dropped like a stone toward the lake.

My wings kept a rhythmic, whooshing beat as I put my dad's sword away in my tattoo. Pressing my lips together, I sighed softly and began to relax. Gyllian was safe.

I concentrated on the feel of my wings beating and the fact that my feet weren't touching the ground, and I smiled. I did a graceful back flip, so I was flying face down toward the water. Stopping just above the surface, I submerged my blood-soaked hands to clean them off. Flicking off the excess water, I looked up at the sky. It was now a dusty light blue as the sun breached the horizon. I closed my eyes and, pumping my wings, lifted myself in a slow spiral so I could feel the air all around me. What freedom. I could feel every temperature variation, every micro air current that wrapped around my feathers. Each little sensation culminated into one vast array of feeling that really made my wings an extension of my body.

As I spiraled up, I found myself thinking about my dad. He'd done this all the time. He'd flown with ease when he was an Angel, but he'd never been able to enjoy it as a human. With that new rush of knowledge, I realized that humanity added beauty and quality to life that immortals were not capable of grasping. Flying was a regular occurrence for my father, as simple as walking was for me. As a human though, flight was glorious.

"Bay!"

Gyllian's voice startled me. I halted my upward spiral and looked over my shoulder. My heart instantly liquefied. He stood in his black uniform on the opposite shore I had left from. The sun could just be seen coming through the trees behind him in a fiery glow that matched his eyes. Tilting forward, I flew the short distance to shore and lowered myself to the ground in front of him. Folding my wings behind me without putting them away, I held my head high as I braced myself for him to start in on me about killing his informant.

But he didn't jump down my throat. Instead, he took a careful step forward. "Are you all right?"

I nodded as an unbelievable longing to touch him came over me again. With his wavy black hair and orange eyes, the sight of him made my heart swell and my knees shake.

"You didn't have to do that," he said gently.

I stared at him without flinching. "Yes, I did."

Suddenly he was pulling me into an embrace. "Thank you."

My heart was pounding as I rested my cheek on his shoulder. He surprised me by pressing his face firmly into my hair and tightening his arms around me. I closed my eyes and inhaled him. He smelled exactly like he had in the hospital room, only with faint traces of gunpowder and leather from the weapons and holsters he had on. I couldn't remember when anything in my life had felt so good and so peaceful.

"You were beautiful," he muttered into my hair.

My heart exploded with more emotions than I knew what to do with, more emotions then I thought it possible to feel. I couldn't speak. I didn't trust my voice to work. I didn't even know what I could possibly say. *Thank you?* It was so weak compared to what I was feeling.

He eventually kissed the side of my head and pulled away. "Come on," he said, smiling ruefully. "Some of us have to get some sleep before work tonight."

25

I wiped down the bar absentmindedly. My mind and my heart were all on Gyllian. I slipped into daydreams of him without even realizing it. I hated that. I couldn't focus. I couldn't concentrate. I found myself glancing up at him in the balcony all damn night just for the sake of looking at him. I had to scold myself to pay attention to my patrons every time it happened.

"Stop it!" I muttered to myself for the two hundredth time. "Just stop! Damn it."

I turned my mind to this morning's interrogation. I'd gotten nothing out of those Demons. I shouldn't be surprised. They weren't prone to the same manipulations humans were, the same fears. That Knight Demon showing up, though, had me concerned. How had she known where to find us? It wasn't clear exactly what the Demons and Angels knew about the five of us—did they all know who we were, or did only some of them? And if either of those were true, why hadn't they spread the word and ended us?

Every time I thought about it, I heard God's words to me as loud and clear as if he were speaking them again: *"There is a purpose for what I allow to happen."* Everything happened, or didn't happen, for a reason. That was a concept that still made me uneasy. I suppose that's where faith came in, trusting him blindly, and I wasn't doing a great job with that.

"Bay," Roy called. He approached with a tray full of empty glasses over his shoulder. "Can you grab the guy on the far end? I'm slammed with a party of twenty."

I nodded. "Sure."

"Thanks," he replied and continued on his way to the dish room in the back.

I looked after him briefly. I was going to have to talk to him. He liked me, but I couldn't reciprocate it, not with the way I felt about Gyllian. I was really reluctant to hurt him, though. He was a good friend, probably my best friend, and a good man. Lord only knew what would happen to the team if I upset him. I'd have to deal with it later.

I headed to the far end of the bar, only to stop dead in my tracks when I recognized the solo patron at the end.

"Porter," I said softly.

It was my old boss. It was hard to look at him because he was entirely sloshed. I knew he'd been sober for fifteen years, eight of which I'd known him, so I'd never seen him as a drunk. It was sad to witness it now. He was never the most happy-go-lucky guy to work for, but he was reasonably pleasant. I'd seen him a few times when a case got him down in the dumps, but this looked nothing like that. Something was wrong. I activated my flaming eye tattoo to make sure he was still human, ignoring the abundance of Demons in my peripheral vision. Porter was fully human.

I looked back at the stage and didn't see Fox yet, so I went down the bar, passing Roy as he came out of the dish room. "I need to leave the bar with you."

"What? Bay, I'm already in over my head."

I continued toward the backstage area, addressing him over my shoulder. "Get one of the waitresses to help you."

"Bay? Bay!"

I ignored him and pushed open the door to the bustling backstage area. The dancers were all rummaging through costumes, or frantically putting on makeup, or adjusting their hair. All of them were talking a mile a minute or shouting. A few girls roamed around completely naked while they went on about what costume combinations they could come up with and if they wanted to paint their bodies tonight. I weaved and dodged through them, looking for Fox, until finally finding her at the back wall near the shoes.

"Hey Fox," I called.

She spun at the sound of my voice. "Bay? Bay, what's wrong?" she asked, coming up to me with her Angelic eyes full of concern.

"Nothing, nothing, but..." I glanced around and realized no one was close enough to hear. I doubted anyone would hear me anyway over the noise. "I need you to take my disguise off."

Her eyes went wide. "But Bay, there are creatures out

there."

"I know. I know but"—I pressed my lips together as I resigned myself to what I was about to risk— "someone at the bar needs me right now."

She shook her head. "You'll be a mouse in a snake pit."

"I know, but…" I shrugged helplessly. "A friend needs me."

Her brows dropped. "What if the Demons attack?"

I shook my head. "Then we'll deal with it. But if they recognize me, I doubt they'll interrupt their business discussions to confront me. We're not a threat to them, remember?" I couldn't keep the bitterness out of my voice.

Fox sighed, contemplating it before she gave me a small nod. "Okay. But I'm going to keep your tattoos hidden so you're not a glaring beacon. And that is *not* negotiable," she said firmly.

I nodded. "That's fine."

She pressed her lips together and sighed. "Go into the bathroom and close yourself in a stall for a minute or two until the girls cycle out so they won't notice the change."

I smiled. "Thanks," I said and headed to the bathroom door behind her.

I slipped in and quickly jumped into an empty stall. I waited for the constant traffic of women to change over before I came out again. Looking in the mirror, I smiled at my own reflection and washed my hands. It was good to see me.

I left the bathroom without a glance at Fox and continued back into the club. I felt the energy drop slightly as I passed the busy table section. Some of the Demons likely recognized me. I didn't bother looking around, but I couldn't help stealing a glance up at Gyllian. He was already watching me with wide, horrified eyes and gripping the bar of the balcony so tightly his knuckles were white. I looked ahead again and continued toward the end of the bar where Porter was.

"Well, look at what the cat dragged in," I said, clapping him on the shoulder.

He turned his head as I sat down beside him, but his drunken stupor delayed his recognition for a moment. As soon as it clicked, his face brightened. "Bayyyy," he said and attempted to embrace me, nearly falling off his stool in the process. I had to grab hold of his shoulders to steady him while he gave me a limp, lopsided hug. He was saturated in the sharp, sour smell of old b.o. and it was all I could do not to gag.

"Well shit, boss," I said, steadying him on his stool. "How the hell are you?"

"Ahh, I got fired, Bay," he blurted out.

My eyes went wide. "What? Oh man, I'm so sorry."

"No big deal," he said dismissively with a wild wave of his hand. "Hey kid! Fill me up again, would you?"

Roy came over and poured him another shot of our top shelf whiskey. He gave me a lingering gaze as he filled the glass, clearly annoyed with me. But he pulled a second glass from under the bar and put it in front of me, pouring me my own drink so I fit in as a regular patron.

"When did this happen?" I asked.

"Oh, it's been about"—he squeezed one eye shut and gazed up at the ceiling, trying to figure out the time frame—"twelve days ago? No, ten. I think."

"What happened?" I asked, absently spinning my glass on top of the bar.

"I screwed up a case," he replied and then threw back his whiskey.

My brows dropped. "That doesn't sound like you."

"I know!" he said in an angry burst, nearly falling backward off the stool as he threw his arms out to his sides. "You know why?" He leaned close to me. I had to back away to spare myself the smell of his breath, which was pure ethanol. "Because I *didn't* screw up a case." His expression suddenly softened. "Ohh, you look so good, Bay." He leaned in with his mouth wide open in an attempt to kiss me.

"Whoa, whoa!" I said and held him back with little effort.

He barely noticed and turned his attention to Roy, who had moved down the bar. "Hey kid. Gimme another."

Roy looked in our direction, and I shook my head. "All right, champ," I said and stood. "Time to go home."

"Nooo. I don't wanna lea'f, Bay. I din' haf enouh."

"Come on." I took his jacket off the back of his stool and

put it over his shoulders. "I'm taking you home."

His face brightened as he looked up at me. "Slip ovh?"

I jerked my head toward the door. "You're going to have to come with me to see if I sleep over, aren't you?" An expectant grin spread across his face.

Sex with Porter wasn't about to happen, but I *was* going to sober his ass up and get more info out of him on this case he supposedly screwed up. It sounded like some high-level meddling to me. It was a long shot that this could be Demon related, but I knew two things for certain: I knew Demons could position themselves in high ranking government jobs, and I knew Porter wasn't one to screw up a case. He was too much of a perfectionist and often got made fun of for it. Even the *suggestion* that he'd screwed up a case made no sense and needed to be looked into.

Roy came to stand across from me. "What are you doing?" he asked quietly, trying to hide his urgency so the Demons wouldn't think we knew each other.

"Put whatever drinks he didn't pay for on my tab," I said and started to leave the club, guiding Porter by one arm. I thought I'd sneak another glance up at Gyllian, but his eyes were already on me as he watched me leave.

"I'll drif," Porter said when we reached the parking lot.

"Right," I said flatly and reached into his pocket, pulling out his keys.

"Bayyyyy," he groaned, making a lame attempt to take them back. I easily pulled them from his reach. "Imn fihn!"

I guided him to the passenger side and opened the door for him to get in. As I climbed into the driver's seat, he was smiling at me drunkenly. "What?" I asked.

"I din know yohu cahred."

I smiled a little as I put the key in the ignition and started it. "I didn't know I cared either," I replied, more to myself, but he didn't hear me anyway.

There was a time, not long ago, when I would have let Porter wrap his car around a telephone pole and not cared less. People hadn't mattered to me. I sighed as I pulled onto the street and headed toward Porter's apartment. My four new friends sure had done a number on me.

Porter finally started showing signs of life late the next morning. I closed the copied file I'd had my nose in all night, and tried to keep my own emotions in check. This whole venture with my four new companions had just become very real. The case Porter was blamed for screwing up was definitely Demon related, and it was catastrophic. Porter had to have stolen these copies, too, because there was no way the Bureau would have let this information out of their sight. Hell, the NSA wouldn't have let this information out of their sight.

I made my way over to Porter's bed. He was still in his clothes from last night, lying face down with barely enough strength to move his eyes. I crouched down in his line of sight, and they went a little wide.

"Bay," he said, not bothering to lift his head. "What are you doing in my apartment?"

Obviously he'd been too drunk to remember I'd brought him home. "I found you at Placids last night."

He squeezed his eyes closed and brought his hand up to his forehead. "Did I get hit by a truck?"

The comment made me grin. "Close. A fifth of whisky."

He dropped his hand onto the mattress. "That'll do it." I chuckled as his eyes shifted over to me. "You helped me?"

I shrugged. "You needed *someone's* help." I looked at him seriously and held up the file. "You didn't screw up this case, Porter." A little bit of life returned to his eyes, and he lifted his head slightly. "I can prove it, too, if you let me take this to some friends of mine."

He propped himself up on an elbow and looked at me with groggy skepticism. "You serious?"

"As a heart attack."

He sat himself up, putting his feet on the floor. "You'd do that?" His expression shifted to one of regret. "I can't get you your job back. Not anymore."

I smiled and stood. "Don't worry. I have a new job I'm pretty fond of."

He looked at me curiously. "Where?"

"I could tell you, but then I'd have to kill you."

He smirked. "Oh really? CIA? NSA? Homeland

security?"

"Do you *want* me to put a bullet in your brain?"

He managed a hollow laugh. "Maybe. Are you armed now?"

I shook my head, realizing sadly that was basically a suicide request. I reached down and took his chin in my fingers. "I'll help you on one condition." The humor dropped from his face. "You start taking care of yourself again."

A genuine, soft smile came to his face, and he nodded. "I can do that."

I nodded and dropped my hand. "Are you okay financially until I can get you cleared, and maybe get you your job back?"

I could tell from the shift in his shoulders and the barely noticeably twitch in his face that he was about to lie to me. "I should be fine."

"Don't be prideful right now, Porter. Are you really okay?"

He swallowed heavily. "Maybe. I might…I could use some help, I guess," he said in a small voice.

I nodded. "Go take a shower." I indicated his bathroom on the other side of the bedroom. "I'll make you some breakfast and call a friend of mine."

He stood up as I pulled out the new burner phone Fox gave me before we'd left for Virginia. "Um, Bay," he said cautiously. "This friend of yours—they'll help me legally, right?"

I nodded. "His methods are…strange, but legal."

He nodded warily before walking around his bed to the bathroom. When he closed the door, I punched Gyllian's name on the contact list. He picked up before the first ring. "What's going on?"

"Gyllian, I have something you need to see. Can you come to—"

"I know where you are," he said and hung up.

I had enough time to give my phone a dirty look before a knock came on Porter's door. I couldn't help the grin that came to my face as I tucked my phone away. Forcing the smile away, I answered it.

"How exactly do you know where I am all the time?"

Gyllian stepped past me into the apartment before turning around. "I can locate any of you whenever I need to. What's going on?"

I took a moment to appreciate his appearance. He was freshly showered with the tendrils of his wavy black hair styled back against his head. He had on a dark red V-neck sweater with a gray t-shirt peeking out from the top and bottom and a pair of dark blue jeans. The man took my breath away.

I cleared my throat and handed him the file. "We've got a serious problem."

He took it and went to the kitchen table, sitting on the edge as he flipped through the papers. I quietly took a seat in one of the chairs, but hearing the shower running, I recalled that Porter needed to eat. I stood as nonchalantly as I could, hopefully without alerting Gyllian to how much he distracted me from the immediate world, and went to Porter's fridge. Rummaging through, I found some eggs and scraps of ham that hadn't yet spoiled. As I brought it to the stove, I glanced at Gyllian and saw his expression had become grim.

As the pan heated up, he tossed the file across the table, sending it spinning, before closing his eyes and pinching the bridge of his nose. "Shit," he muttered.

"Yeah," I reluctantly agreed and focused on the stove.

Porter was not only my unit director, but we were also teammates in the Critical Incident Response Group. CIRG was like the Special Forces team of the FBI, with special weapons and tactical training. They responded to events like hostage negotiations, abductions, or mysterious disappearances, as well as domestic and international crisis management. The troubling case file that had cost Porter his job was a CIRG file that involved the disappearance of some nuclear warheads from Egypt, fifteen to be exact. It was called The Inferno Core.

A single missing warhead in the Middle East was bad. The Inferno Core missing was a global crisis.

To make matters worse, according to Porter's report, there was no evidence to be found. No video, no footprints, no fingerprints, and no busted locks. The electronic doors to the vault where the Inferno Core had been kept, hadn't even been *disabled!* The transponders on each bomb *were* disabled, however, which was supposed to be impossible. Nothing could happen in this world, least of all fifteen fucking nuclear weapons going missing, without something, even trace evidence, being left behind. Zero evidence meant that Angels had to have taken them.

Gyllian blew out a breath and crossed his arms as he stared out ahead of him. "Well, at least we know how Hell is going to rise. I suppose that's some good news. Now we just have to figure out when and where."

I kept my back to him as I tried to find the right words for this atrocity. "They're going to blow a hole to the surface."

"Yeah," Gyllian said.

I couldn't say anything as I flipped over the omelets I was cooking. I just kept picturing a nuclear explosion being set off underground. *Underground!* Nukes were devastating enough when they were detonated on the surface. Fifteen detonated underground? Everything above could be obliterated for nearly 300,000 square miles, and the Demons would pour through like water from a busted dam. Hell was in another dimension, but its walls were the solid rock of the Earth's core.

God could stop this. Why *didn't* God stop this?

"Hey," Gyllian said as he came beside me. "Are you okay?"

"No," I barked a little harshly, trying to keep it together. "Nuclear bombs, Gyllian?" I said, wishing he could say or do something to make it not true. "*Fifteen* nuclear bombs?"

"Hey, hey," he said and pulled me into an embrace. I pressed my face into his shoulder and tried to calm down. "We're going to stop it."

I sighed heavily and tried to let that promise settle me down. A moment later a soft clearing of a throat drew our attention. Gyllian and I looked up to see Porter standing outside the bathroom door in a loose pair of pants and partially buttoned-up white shirt.

Gyllian pulled away and went to him with his hand out. "Hey. My name's Gyllian. I'm Bay's boyfriend." My heart jumped up into my throat at that.

Porter cautiously took Gyllian's hand, glancing at me a

little suspiciously. "Oh. Hey. Nice to meet you. Sorry. Bay didn't tell me she had a boyfriend."

I gathered my emotions and approached Porter. "Gyllian is also the one who can help you."

Porter's face brightened a little. "Oh great. Thank you."

Gyllian looked at me with his brows drawn. I hadn't told him how he was going to help Porter yet. "Come on," I said. "I made some breakfast."

Porter followed me into his kitchen. "You never struck me as the Betty Crocker type," he teased.

I smiled and pulled out a chair for him. "I have a few things I can do pretty well. But I think it's a safe assumption you'd probably eat dog food right now if it were available to you."

"Cat food, maybe," he said with a smile and sat down. "Never dog food."

I laughed, recalling the old joke our unit had pertaining to a confidential informant we relied heavily on. It was a homeless guy, clearly with some mental issues, who found cat food delicious. We tried to bribe him once with dog food and he pitched a fit for the record books.

I went back to the stove and began to fill two plates. "Hungry, honey?" I teased, looking back at Gyllian.

A slightly devilish smile came to his face. "Starving," he replied and took a seat across from Porter. "Waiting up all night for your girlfriend to come home tends to make a man famished."

I placed a plate in front of Porter and met his gaze. He was upset I didn't go home last night.

Porter cleared his throat uncomfortably as I placed the other plate in front of Gyllian. "That was my fault. Nothing happened between us, but I"—he glanced up at me shamefully— "I got a little too sloshed at Placids last night. Bay found me there and took me home."

"I understand," Gyllian said. "I just wish she would have called me."

A storm erupted inside of me as I went back to the stove to fill my plate. I wanted to tell him that I didn't have to answer to him, but the fact that he cared enough to worry about me like that clashed with those emotions. I didn't know what to do, so I stayed quiet.

"A small piece of advice," Porter said out of the blue. Hearing the slight edge to his tone, I looked and saw him glaring at Gyllian. "Don't get possessive of Bay. She can take care of herself well enough."

Gyllian looked stunned for a second, and then his expression shifted into a glare, too. "That's a hell of a way to talk to someone willing to help you."

Oh, this could end badly.

Porter dropped his fork on his plate. "I don't want your help if it means Bay has to silently obey the whim of a dominating asshole."

"Hey!" I yelled and slammed both my hands down on top of the table, silencing them. "Put the rulers away, boys." I looked at Gyllian. "Porter's right, I didn't have to call you last night when I was busy helping a friend." I looked at Porter. "And Gyllian doesn't dominate me. I'd kick his ass if he did, and you know it." I glanced between the two of them. "Now shut up and eat, both of you."

Both of them went back to their plates as I sat down at the head of the table with mine. "You've got your hands full with this one," Porter said suddenly.

"Yeah, tell me about it," Gyllian replied.

I rolled my eyes, relieved. "You guys are dicks." Both of them laughed. After it died, I held up the file of the missing nukes. "Porter." He looked at me. "What the fuck?"

He closed his eyes and shook his head. "I know."

"Headquarters must be losing their minds!"

"Bay," he said, still slowly shaking his head as he dug into his omelet. "If you can envision what a mass riot looks like within FBI ranks, that's what's happening."

I shook my head and slapped the file down on top of the table. "What's being done to find the Inferno Core?"

Porter shrugged. "Nothing *can* be done. There was nothing to find, I swear. We combed the place top to bottom. The Egyptian officials were just as baffled as we were." He sighed. "You know how it goes after that. One accuses the other. The other gets offended and accuses the other. Then all hell breaks loose."

"Shit," I said, bowing my head and slowly shaking it. He

had no idea how accurate that statement really was. "Has World War III begun yet, or what?"

"Pfft. It's on the brink. Egypt is losing their minds, too." He shook his head. "I'm telling you, they looked just as terrified as we were. Hell, they were the ones who informed us the Inferno Core was missing."

I looked at him, utterly dumbfounded. "How did you get away with just losing your job? How are you not in prison for treason?" I tapped the file. "You should be in jail just for having this."

He shook his head. "My reputation, my job, my *life* was on the line. I wasn't going down without a fight. So yeah, I stole it." I sighed. "My only saving grace in the case was the corroboration of the lab that there was *literally* nothing to find at the scene. We had the best technical analysts in the world looking for those transponder signals for days; they're probably *still* looking. We even stooped to freelancing some notorious, but genius hackers to try to find them. There was nothing in Egypt but an empty, underground warehouse."

"Fuck," I sighed.

"Look," Gyllian piped in. "I don't know how much we'll actually be able to help you, but if you let me take this back to our team, we'll try. This is big, though, so I won't promise you anything."

Porter nodded. "That's fine. I appreciate that." He shook his head and looked back at me. "I didn't screw up the investigation."

I nodded. "I know."

"We believe you," Gyllian said.

Porter glanced between the two of us a little suspiciously. "*Why* do you believe me?" Gyllian and I unwittingly glanced at each other, which, judging by his expression, Porter picked up on. "You know something, don't you?"

Gyllian sighed. "Nothing we can tell you."

"Porter," I said before another pissing contest could erupt between them, "you're just going to have to trust us."

"I trust *you*," he countered. "I don't know about your boyfriend here."

"Then trust me," I said, trying to keep things calm.

Porter pressed his lips together and finally nodded.

Gyllian took a bite of his eggs. "Bay mentioned you'll need financial help until we can get this squared away."

I looked at him confused. How did he know? I hadn't had a chance to tell him Porter needed money. Shame instantly consumed Porter's features and he lowered his eyes, pretending to concentrate on his breakfast.

"It's not a problem," Gyllian said lightly.

"I don't usually need help. I've taken care of—"

"Porter," Gyllian interrupted gently. "It's fine. Give me your checking account number and you'll have what you need before noon."

Porter drew his brows together and glanced at me. I gave him a small, reassuring nod. He reached for a nearby pen and wrote his checking account number on the file.

"Who *are* you?" he asked Gyllian, mystified.

Gyllian smiled. "Just someone who wants to help."

Porter hesitated a moment before sliding the file over to Gyllian, and then looked at me. "You sure you know what you're doing getting into bed with this guy?"

I tried not to blush at the thought of getting into bed with Gyllian, and failed. "I'm sure," was all I could manage before taking a bite of my omelet.

"Well, thank you. Both of you."

We finished breakfast with little more conversation. When we were done, I gathered the dishes and piled them into the already overflowing kitchen sink. I was half tempted to wash them. Hell, I was half tempted to clean Porter's whole apartment.

Before I started, he came up beside me with a smile. "I've got this."

"You sure?"

He nodded. "It'll help me get out of the funk I've been in."

"All right. Well, Gyllian and I are going to go see what we can do about this."

"Thanks, Bay."

I smiled and headed toward Gyllian, who was already standing by the door. I turned to face Porter again. "You remember to take care of yourself, okay? Keep your promise to me and"—I glanced at Gyllian before looking back at Porter— "we'll do our best to help you."

He nodded again. "Thanks."

Gyllian pulled open the door and we started out, but I paused a moment and faced Porter one more time. I knew Gyllian, and I knew he was going to give Porter more than enough money to take care of himself for a good long while.

"Porter?" He looked over his shoulder at me. "After you check your bank account"—I smiled a little mischievously— "take a vacation. You look like shit."

He gave me a curious stare and then smiled. "Copy that, Kennedy."

I smiled in return before Gyllian and I headed into the hallway, closing the door behind us. I looked up at him curiously. "How did you know he needed financial help?" I asked as we made our way down the hall.

"The man lost his job. It makes sense."

"Yeah, but how did you know I volunteered you to help him?"

"Because I know you," he said with a tone of finality that made it seem like the most obvious answer in the world.

"You know me?" I dared venture.

My words might have come off a little too sentimental, or desperate, because he looked down at me quickly as if my tone concerned him. He studied me for a moment before his face softened, "Yeah, I do."

He opened the door leading to the stairwell and we headed down. Halfway, Gyllian put his arm around me, and the world went watery and he teleported us back home.

26

When everything cleared, we were on the stairs leading down to the bunker. He pulled open the round door, and I thought it would be a fast sprint to the intelligence room with the file. Instead, he stopped in the hall, and crossed his arms with it tucked tightly to his chest.

"Listen," he said facing me. "We're going to be leaving for some travel soon."

"Travel?" I asked, crossing my arms, too.

"Three times a year, Fox, Booth and I visit my international nightlife establishments."

"International? You have clubs outside the United States?"

He nodded. "We'll be gone two months." My eyes went wide. "I have thirty buildings to get reports from, so I spend about two to seven days at each."

I ran my fingers through my hair and brought it over one shoulder before crossing my arms again, feeling uncomfortable with this news. "What kind of reports?"

He shrugged. "Unusual activity like increased crime rate, new mob or criminal bosses on the rise that I need to investigate, reports from my prostitute rings on unusual behavior, or comments from their clientele. I also have to check the underground stuff I have set up that keeps me on top of seedy human and Demon activity."

"What do you think you'll find?"

"Honestly?" He shook his head. "I don't expect to find much in my lower ranking slums and bars anymore. Based on this"—he tapped the file— "the Demon activity is way too advanced for them to be working their way up ranks trying to become influential. They already *are* influential. If they could do this…" He shook his head again and let the rest of that sentence die. "I don't know why I wasn't warned about it, but I need to kick over every stone I can at this point."

"But if you don't think you'll find anything, why go?"

I saw the hint of a smirk on his face. "I own more than a few dive bars, Bay." My eyebrow cocked up. "I have some high-end clubs that should be buzzing with Demon activity."

My heart was fluttering. This was the most I'd learned about Gyllian's underground operations since I'd gotten here. "How high end are we talking?"

"Twenty to thirty grand a head."

My eyes bulged. "What?" He smiled. I blinked. Those were clubs for people on the wealthiest end of the top one percentile! "How many of those do you own?"

"Three. Las Vegas, Los Angeles, and Miami."

I was taken aback. Clearly he had money, and a ton of it if he could build this bunker and twelve satellites for his personal use. But to add *three* nightclubs that charged thirty grand *a head*? He wasn't just a millionaire; he was likely a *billionaire*.

He watched me react with a hint of amusement on his face. "Wealthy people are influential," he said. "Influential people make things happen and have the means to cover bad things up. I had to get as close to those kinds of people as I could, in a loose social setting, with a wide range of alcohol available. That kind of environment helps me keep close tabs on the untouchable ranks of the Fortune 500."

I cleared my throat a little uncomfortably, trying to wrap my head around this. "So you're thinking the higher end the establishment, the more influential the Demons?"

He nodded.

I shook my head in disbelief. "How? I don't understand how you pulled this off in just ten years."

He shrugged nonchalantly. "God can make anything happen if it's for his purpose and will."

I raised a brow. "God made you a successful nightclub owner?"

"And criminal." My eyes narrowed. "It worked. My success has let me penetrate every level of the first-percentile cliques and criminal underground. It's how we've gotten every shred of intel we have on the Demons and Hell rising so far."

I found myself about to ask why he needed to get this intel on his own, but I already knew what he'd say: "It's not my place to question God." Blind faith. It was fucking bonkers.

"How come Roy doesn't go?"

"He minds the club for me here. The intel we get at Placids is too substantial to ignore for any length of time. That's why I settled here permanently in the first place."

I pressed my lips together and sighed, coming to a decision he probably wasn't going to like. "I want to go."

Gyllian shook his head. "No."

"Why not?"

"Because I have to act a certain way when I'm on these trips. I have to be the typical pompous asshole billionaire and crime lord while I'm dealing with people." He shook his head and glanced off to the side. "I don't want you to see me like that."

I had a difficult time coming up with an argument. I wasn't sure I wanted to see Gyllian like that either. Worse, though, would be not seeing him at all for two months. "Why do Fox and Booth go?"

"Booth acts as my bodyguard. Typical pompous asshole billionaires usually have one. Fox disguises us and protects us if we get into scrapes. She also kills herself putting reports together while I'm busy getting as much information as I can. Her ability to multiply herself comes in handy. Plus, she acts as my escort since typical pompous asshole billionaires usually have one of those, too."

"How about this? I'll be your escort so Fox can concentrate on the reports and keeping us disguised?"

His body sagged. "Bay," he said his voice almost pleading. "Please."

My heart was pounding, and I shook my head. "I probably know the criminal mind better than the four of you anyway, so I should come."

His eyes pleaded with me to reconsider, but he asked, "Are you sure?"

Seeing the way he was looking at me, unguarded for a moment, practically forced my response. "Yeah."

I expected him to give me hard time but he said, "Okay," brusquely and started down the hall toward the intelligence room. I followed.

I couldn't conceive of not seeing him for two months. I also couldn't conceive of being left behind during an expedition into what he actually did among the criminal underground. I was rabid with curiosity and eagerness to be a part of this with him. I was surprised, though, that he hadn't totally shot me down.

Fox, Booth and Roy were already working as Gyllian and I entered the intelligence room. "We know how the Demons are rising," he called, holding the file over his head.

"What?"

"No way."

"Praise the Lord."

Gyllian slapped the file down and pressed his palms into the table top, leaning heavily over his arms as the others gathered around. "Fifteen nuclear warheads known as the Inferno Core went missing from Egypt."

"What?" Fox gasped and snatched the file up to start reading. Roy and Booth gathered behind her. She flipped through it for a moment, getting the gist of the issue at hand. "Holy gracious, God," she finally said, looking up at Gyllian and me. Roy took the file from her, and he and Booth continued reading. "Gyllian…" her voice trailed off, as concern and devastation erupted in her dark blue eyes.

"I know," he said with a stiff nod.

She sighed heavily and pulled out a chair to sit, prompting me to crouch next to her and take her hand. Her gaze was turned away and far off, like I wasn't even there. She probably was doing what I'd done, picturing the explosion in her mind.

"Damn," Roy said and looked at Gyllian. "Gyllian"—he shook his head— "we have to find them *now*."

"I know," Gyllian said. "We will. Finding this out now will help narrow our focus during the club tour. We know *how* Hell is going to rise. Now we can concentrate on *when* and *where*."

Roy smiled at me, probably thinking we were going to be left alone for the next two months. "I'm going, too," I said before he could get too excited. His hopeful smile dissolved, and my heart broke.

"Really?" Fox exclaimed, coming back to life. She

looked up at Gyllian. "Is she going to help me?"

Gyllian nodded. "She'll be my escort so you can concentrate on the reports."

"Hallelujah!" she cried, jumping to her feet. "Oh Bay"— she took my elbows and guided me to a stand — "I can't wait for you to see some of Gyllian's clubs. They are beyond stunning! You'll need to wear some of my evening gowns from Paris, and you *have* to let me do your hair and makeup."

I chuckled, though it was a little forced with Roy on my mind. "That's the only way I'd want to be seen in public."

She let out a very girly squeal and embraced me. "I am so excited!"

Gyllian was gazing at me with a smile and a touch of excitement. He looked like a teenage boy about to show off his new car to a girl he liked while still trying to be cool about it. Suddenly, the door to the intelligence room slammed. Fox jumped out of my arms, and all of us turned in the direction of the sound.

Sure enough, Roy was gone. Shit.

Gyllian and I looked at each other, our gazes locked, and then I took a deep breath and went after him. It was now or never. I didn't want to hurt him, but he wasn't giving me much choice. I opened the door and saw him heading down the hall toward the gym.

"Roy!" I called and started after him.

He faced me. "Oh! I'm worthy of your attention now?"

I sighed as I approached. I needed to fix this. If I didn't, this team would disintegrate before it even had a chance to fight Hell. But I didn't know how. "I'm sorry."

"Sorry for what? Sorry for how you can barely look me in the eye? Sorry about how you get doe-eyed every time Gyllian glances at you? Sorry for lying to me?"

I looked at him confused. "I never lied to you."

"Yes, you did," he said matter-of-factly. "When you let me kiss you in the hospital room. When we danced together at the club and at the manor. When you told me about your wings. Every time you looked in my eyes, you lied to me." He glared at me. "Every interaction we've had has been honest on my part, because I *can't* lie!" He yelled. "But you?" he said more softly. "You're a liar, Bay." He started walking away again.

I stared after him, astonished. My whole life I'd never really cared about hurting other people's feelings, because I didn't care about people. The problem here was that I cared about Roy. I cared what he thought of me. I cared that he was mad at me.

"You want honesty?" I yelled after him. He turned to face me again. "I looked at you the way I did, danced with you the way I did, told you about my wings the way I did because I *trusted* you!" I shook my head. "You have no idea what it took for me to do that, to let you in like that. No idea! It may not have been a lot to you, or what you wanted, but it was *everything* to me!"

I was shaking with anger and fear that I'd just lost the first man I'd ever fully trusted in my life. Someone I could talk to, open up to, be myself with. Someone who didn't make me crazy like Gyllian did.

"Would that have been better, Roy?" I went on. "If I didn't trust you?"

He glanced away, and a weird detachment came into his eyes. He was shutting down. Even now, as I poured my heart out to him, he was detaching himself from caring about me. He was dismissing the vulnerability I was allowing him to see. I was putting my trust in him right now, and he wasn't letting himself care.

A strange desperation to not lose him welled up inside me. I needed him to understand what it took to let him even an inch near my heart. I needed to show him what he actually meant to me, even if I wasn't in love with him. I rested my hand on his cheek and pondered how to explain this, and debated if I should even reveal this part of myself to him. But he needed to see the kind of men I had known, the kind of men I was used to, and what they had done to me. He needed to understand why trust was such a fragile thing for me to extend.

I was about to speak when my hand started to burn! It felt like a tattoo was activating, but I didn't have any tattoos on my hands.

Roy's eyes suddenly went wide and his jaw dropped. I stared in horror as his face got red like he was in incredible pain. I tried to take my hand away, but it wouldn't come off his face! My heart seized in panic as he started sinking to his knees, and I bent down with him. I yanked on my arm like I was yanking on a stubborn car door, but it wouldn't come off! "Roy? Roy!" I screamed in panic.

I heard a scream from the direction of the intelligence room and snapped my head around.

"Gyllian!" I cried, yanking on my hand again.

When I looked back at Roy it finally came free, sending me flying into the wall, and Roy nearly went forehead first into the floor. I jumped and caught him in time. "Roy?" I said, checking his pulse and looking for any damage.

Fox threw open the door to the intelligence room and came toward us. "Go," she said, thrusting her thumb back. She took over caring for Roy as I ran down the hall. Inside, Gyllian was on his knees clutching his right shoulder with Booth holding him up.

"Gyllian?" I fell to my knees next to him. "Gyllian?"

"It's okay, Bay," he said so calmly that the world didn't make sense for a minute. "Roy and I aren't in danger."

"What?" I looked back into the hallway and saw Fox and Roy softly talking. Fox eventually helped Roy to his feet, and they both came back toward the intelligence room. I looked at Booth and saw calm resolve on his serene face. I appeared to be the only one panicking.

"What memory did she give you?" Gyllian asked as Roy and Fox approached.

"Her childhood," Roy responded. I could have sworn his eyes were red and glistening. Gyllian nodded without a word.

I glanced between the two of them. "What just happened?"

Gyllian looked at me with a small, pleased smile, and then started to pull up his sleeve. He brought it all the way up to his shoulder and pointed to one of his tattoos. It depicted two faces, both with closed eyes that looked like they were merging into one face in the middle. "This ability allows me to manipulate memories. I can extract them from myself, or other people, and project them into another person." He glanced at Roy. "You just used my ability on Roy to make him see your childhood."

My eyes went wide as I looked at Roy. I was completely unprepared to address that level of exposure. I was going to *tell* him about my childhood, not show him.

"So…what?" I looked back at Gyllian. "We can use each other's abilities?"

Gyllian stood and held a hand out to me. I took it, and he helped me to my feet. "The Angels," he began, and started pulling down his sleeve, "with their kind of power individualized equally, became arrogant. That arrogance made them turn against God." He looked down as he pulled his sleeve to his wrist. "Instead of repeating that with us, God broke up the Angels' abilities between the five of us. None of us, individually, can have the power of an Angel. But together we do."

I shook my head. "That doesn't make sense. That weakens us…considerably."

Booth shook his head. "We each have different abilities so that we need each other to do together what one Angel can. Needing one another, depending on one another, allows us a better chance of not assuming the same level of arrogance as the Angels. If we stay in need of each other, we stay humble and compassionate."

My eyes widened as I envisioned the abilities I'd already seen—Roy's Holy Fire blades and healing, Gyllian's time manipulation, Fox's self-replication, Booth's matter manipulation, my wings. To be able to do all that and more was insane! I couldn't help imagining the possibilities if we ever got to that point. Damn, we might actually stand a chance at stopping Hell from rising.

I sobered quickly, though. "But I heard you scream."

"Because it hurt," Gyllian said, chuckling, which immediately coerced a grin out of me. "Small price to pay, though, to have you do that. You're the first one of us that's been able to use one of the other's abilities."

"But I don't want to if it hurts you, *any* of you, or *me* for that matter."

Gyllian shook his head. "It will get easier."

"The more we work together," Booth said, "the closer we come to reaching the point of using each other's abilities with ease. God created us to exceed the power of the Angels, but only together."

I rubbed my forehead with my fingertips. This was nuts. I couldn't even believe such an extraordinary possibility was in front me.

"Try to think about how you did it," Gyllian said. "What was going through your mind to trigger it?"

"I…" I glanced at Roy.

"What was your dominant feeling just before it happened?" Gyllian asked.

I kept my eyes on Roy. I really didn't want to show any more vulnerability than I already had, but it was vital that they knew. "Desperation."

"Desperation?" Gyllian asked.

I nodded. "Losing you, Roy. Having you dismiss me. Having you not care about me." Tears filled my eyes, and I tried to force them back by looking up at the ceiling. "I was desperate for you to know how much you mean to me, even if I don't feel the way about you that you wish I did." Fighting my tears was futile. I could tell by how fast they filled my eyes. So I just let them fall as I looked back down at him. "Desperate for you to understand what it took for me to extend the amount of trust toward you that I had." I swallowed down my sobs. "You mean a lot to me, and I don't want to lose you, any of you." I wiped my sleeve across my cheeks. "You're all I have," I croaked, silently begging my tears to stop. "And the four of you are all I want in the world anymore."

They all gazed at me, with unbarred compassion.

I forced a smile as I dabbed my eyes. "You're not going to get all mushy on me now, are you?" I asked in a stuffy voice.

"I am," Fox said and came forward to embrace me.

I allowed myself to sink into her arms, resting my head on her shoulder. It felt really good to be held by her, to be cared for. I actually had people in my life I could call friends, people I could trust to have my back through anything, even the apocalypse. For the first time, I had people in my life I feared to lose.

Fox pulled away with tears in her own eyes and smoothed down my hair without a word. Her eyes said more to me than words really could anyway.

"Desperation?" I heard Gyllian say to Booth.

Fox and I faced them with our arms around each other.

Booth shook his head. "I don't believe it was the desperation itself that allowed her to use your ability. I believe it was the fierce desire not to lose one of us." He smiled at me. "Something I very much doubt she has felt toward anyone before."

I smiled a little and wiped the last of my tears away. "All right, so if using each other's abilities depends on working closer as a team, then I don't think Roy should stay here during the club tour."

"Bay, I have to," Roy said.

Gyllian nodded. "I agree. The intel is too rich here to leave it unattended."

"Don't leave it unattended. Get Porter to watch it."

"Porter?" Fox asked.

I nodded. "James Porter is my former boss."

Gyllian gave me a wary look. "I don't know about that, Bay. We'd have to tell him everything— about us, about Hell rising, and he'd have to be okay with letting crime go unnoticed in his presence."

"He was the Executive Assistant Director of four separate units at the Bureau, he's a former member of CIRG, and he's done plenty of undercover work in his career. He'll do it. Especially if he knows what's at stake."

Gyllian eyes narrowed curiously. "You trust him that much? With something this big?"

I nodded. "I do. If Roy stays here, we waste two months of time in which we could have all been together." I shook my head. "With the Inferno Core gone, I'm not sure we have that kind of time to lose. I think Hell might be closer to rising than you think, Gyllian. We have to stay together."

It was quiet a moment, and I thought for sure that Gyllian was going to shoot me down. In fact, he looked about ready to, but then Fox timidly held up a finger. "Roy could help me with the reports. You know how the old saying goes: two heads are better than one." She smiled. "We have a better chance of narrowing down time and location if we both work on it." She nodded toward me. "I think Bay is right. We don't have the kind of time we used to."

"I feel it too," Booth piped in. "A quickening of my spirit is the best way to put it. With those weapons missing, Bay joining us and tapping into your abilities, the excessive Demon activity, it feels like a clock is ticking down. We need to start narrowing our parameters quickly."

Gyllian sighed and nodded. "Okay. Let's go. All of us." He looked at me. "I'll talk to Porter." I nodded. "Let's start packing and getting ready to go. We leave for Florida tomorrow."

We all nodded, and everyone headed off in different directions except Roy and me.

I turned to him. "I'm sorry," I finally said. "I didn't mean…" My voice broke. "I didn't mean to hurt you."

He nodded and swallowed heavily. "I'm so sorry," he whispered emotionally. He still, unbelievably, looked on the verge of tears. "I'm so sorry for what you've been through," and then his tears fell.

I froze and watched them fall down his cheeks. He was the second man in my life to cry on my behalf. My father had been the first. We embraced each other tightly, and my heart swelled with affection for him. He was a good man and, of the others, my best friend. Gyllian was something else I didn't quite understand yet, maybe I never would, but I'd opened up to Roy first in ways I'd never opened up to anybody. I did love him, just not the way he wanted. I hoped that would be enough.

27

Our first stop had to be Gyllian's high-end club in Miami, Florida. The other two, Las Vegas and Los Angeles, would be later since we figured the Demon activity would be thickest there. But the Miami club was the first he owned, and he was due for a visit. Unfortunately, Gyllian had started running this club before he found Fox, who could change his appearance, so we wouldn't be disguised tonight. She was only going to hide our tattoos. I just hoped the Angels and Demons were too busy with the Inferno Core to pay attention to us, or better yet, still didn't know what we even looked like.

Fox and I were in her bedroom in a penthouse suite, and she was holding up two different dresses to my neck. Both were small, tight cocktail dresses, one hot pink and the other black. She had already straightened my hair and put it back in a high ponytail, wrapping a thick section around the hair tie to hide it. My makeup was light but dazzling, with dark eyeliner and a variety of pinks, including hot pink, over my lids. I never thought I'd see a day where I would wear hot pink eye shadow.

"Ugh," Fox said and deflated a little, her arms dropping heavily to her sides. "Gyllian!" she called. A moment later I heard him coming up the stairs.

When he turned the corner into the room, I stopped breathing. His hands were in the pockets of his black dress pants. His shirt was a steel-gray button-up with black pinstripes, and he had the sleeves rolled up to his elbows. A long pink necktie rested on his chest, and his wavy black locks looked slightly wet and were styled to perfection. He looked like a magazine model. If I was staring at him in some stupid way, which was likely, he pretended not to notice.

"Okay," Fox said.

Gyllian's brows dropped curiously. "What did you call me for?"

"I couldn't decide which dress to put on Bay, so I wanted

to see what you were wearing. Your pink tie gave me the answer." Gyllian looked down at his chest, seeming to suddenly question his choice. "No no," Fox said, as if reading his mind. "You look fine." I saw her brow cock up as she shamelessly checked him out. "Mighty, *mighty* fine."

Gyllian grinned and rolled his eyes before leaving.

Fox shook her head and faced me, her attention on the dresses again. "That man is a stunner."

I couldn't help the clench of my heart at hearing that. Fox was this side of inhumanly beautiful, someone I could see Gyllian with, and that hurt in a way I had no right to feel hurt about.

She held up the hot pink dress to my throat and gave a jerky nod, "This one."

I slid it on. Not much more than a body stocking, it had a high neckline which crossed just under my throat, and full-length lace sleeves. It came down just far enough to cover the bottom curve of my ass, but not by much. Fox also handed me a pair of hot pink matching platform heels with a half a dozen straps crisscrossing halfway up my calf. I hoped I wasn't expected to dance in these things because I wouldn't survive.

"There," Fox said admiringly. "You look perfect."

"I look like a hooker," I said flatly.

Fox shrugged her shoulders high and smiled, her dark blue eyes shining. "At least you look like an expensive one."

I threw my head back and laughed. That was the truth.

I grabbed the matching clutch off the dresser before we made our way down the stairs to the living room and kitchen area where Gyllian, Booth, and Roy were already waiting by the front door talking.

I rolled my eyes as I approached. "If one of you says a single word…" I began. They all turned to face me. "I'll crush your testicles with my bare hands." They remained quiet, but I could feel the weight of their stares on me. I sighed heavily and planted my hands on my hips, waiting for their jabs.

"Is saying you look immensely hot out of the question?" Roy asked, and both Booth and Gyllian chuckled.

I glared at him playfully. "I have fingernails now, pal," I said, brandishing the new white-tipped acrylics that Fox made me get yesterday. "And I'll use them."

The three of them laughed. "All right, let's go," Gyllian said, placing his hand on my lower back.

Booth opened the door, and we made our way down to the lobby where a white limo was waiting outside. I'd never been in a limo before, so I was intrigued, but I couldn't let my guard down. Gyllian was about to enter the lion's den of the criminal underbelly. My adrenaline was pumping and my senses were firing on all cylinders. I had to be careful, though. I couldn't *look* like I was searching for a threat around every corner. Since this club was one of Gyllian's high-end ones, Demon activity would be thick here. If I was truly honest, though, the thing that made me the most nervous was seeing what he would become. The man I knew, the brave, self-sacrificing hero, would likely become a stranger to me.

When we got into the limo, I made sure my back was stiff and my ass was the first thing to touch the leather, mimicking the rigidness of rich people. "Club Zyrca. Step on it," Gyllian commanded the driver. His voice was gruff, abrupt, and harsh, and I already had to remind myself it was just an act.

"Yes, sir," the driver replied.

Gyllian was immediately pulling out his phone and dialing. "Liam. Yeah, I'm on my way." Pause. "Blame my woman." Pause. "You know, have to have every eyebrow hair in place before stepping out in public. I should be there in fifteen minutes as long as my driver isn't a useless moron." He hung up without a goodbye and dialed another number. "Natalie. Drop them off at midnight." Pause. "Mr. Hoybur can have Shara as long as he needs, I'll get hers later. Just have the rest packed up and ready for me." He hung up again and dialed again. "Mr. Kasata..." Gyllian carried on a conversation in Japanese, which impressed me considerably. I didn't know what he was saying, but my character wasn't supposed to care. All I had to concern myself with was looking pretty to impress Gyllian's clients and patrons and anyone else he dealt with.

When we pulled up in front of the elaborate Zyrca Club, Gyllian looked at me with no warmth, and a superiority that made my skin crawl. "Let's go."

Holy shit, this was a bad idea. No. I had to remind

myself again that it was an act, a cover. Gyllian was not this…*person.*

The driver opened our door, and Booth stepped out first. He scanned the crowd briefly for potential threats before giving Gyllian a subtle signal to step out. Keeping my back straight, I gently placed my hand in his and slid out of the car. People were all around the club, mostly tourists who were gazing in awe at a club they could only dream of entering since the cover charge was $26,000 a head. A few celebrities posed for the dozen or so paparazzi near the entrance. Gyllian and I were ignored. No one cared who we were, and we were okay with that. The last thing we needed was our real images plastered all over some tabloid.

When the large, glass double doors opened, my jaw dropped. I wouldn't have to fake a reaction to what I was seeing. It was a small place, but stunning and elaborate without being gaudy. The ceiling was absolutely amazing. Thousands of soft glowing colored lights were hanging down covering the entire thing. The way the orange, pink, green, and yellow colors were displayed, it was like looking at a vast rainbow through the haze of a dream. The colors blended together and stood out in stunning and wild harmony. A long, marble, dark-gray bar was at the back, with a grid pattern shelf system for its booze up the back wall. Each cubby of drinks had a different color bulb backlighting it. There was a small dance floor in the middle of the room, but gray and white long couches and love seats mostly filled the space.

"Mr. Gabriel," a pleasant voice called.

I resisted the urge to rib Gyllian for using his Angelic dad's name as an alias. It was adorable, though.

"Liam," Gyllian said, and the two shook hands.

Liam was a short, thin man with very tan skin. He had blonde hair slicked back and hard, like a helmet, and dull, blue-gray eyes. He approached with four other men in suits. "It's good to see you, sir."

"Same. Everything ready?"

"Yes, sir."

"Good." Gyllian kissed my cheek. "Have fun. I'll be late, so call the limo when you want to go."

"I'll be fine, babe," I said and headed toward the bar,

swinging my hips a little more than normal.

It was a good thing the bar stools were padded and comfortable because I had a feeling I'd be parking it here for a while. I ordered an Amaretto sour from the bartender, turned toward the room, and activated my flaming eye tattoo. I saw a few Pawns and Rooks and one Bishop Demon, but they weren't paying a suspicious amount of attention to me, Booth, or Gyllian. I deactivated it and scanned the room one more time looking for potential human threats and shady characters, but no one jumped out at me to keep an eye on.

By the time the bartender dropped off my drink, I had strangers migrating toward me. Word must have gotten around that I was there with the club owner because soon I was surrounded by over a dozen brownnosers. After doing another quick sweep with my flaming eye tattoo and seeing that everyone around me was human, I allowed myself to relax a little and slip into my role.

I'd never socialized with the rich and affluent before, and I discovered quickly that it was draining. A look of bewilderment often crossed my face, which I would hastily correct, as I wondered how these people could live such materialistic and meaningless lives. An hour into feigning interest in them, I was exhausted. It was all sex, drinking, partying, hair, makeup, clothes, cars, and other toys. Every time I tried to work an intelligent angle into the conversation, someone would interrupt with something else, usually negative. "Oh my God, did you see what Keira Knightley was wearing at the Golden Globe Awards? She looked like a cow." I wanted to knock every single one of them out. They were hateful little people. It was disturbing my soul and numbing my brain dealing with them.

One redheaded woman suddenly started bitching about having had the worst hangover ever last Friday. "My God, it was unbearable! You've never had a hangover like this one. I guarantee it. I just thought I was going to die! But I don't regret the party the night before," she said, followed by a high-pitched, shrill laugh. The laugh killed me. I was done.

I plastered a false smile on my face. "Excuse me," I said and picked up my drink. I waded through the small crowd and headed toward Booth, who stood guard outside the VIP area where Gyllian and the suit pack were meeting.

"Am I allowed in there?" I asked softly, keeping the fake smile on my face. "Because if I have to listen to one more manicure horror story, you and Mr. Gabriel will be scraping my remains off the sidewalk after I throw myself from the fucking roof."

Booth pressed his lips together trying not to laugh and then quickly cleared his throat and looked behind him in the VIP area. "Mr. Gabriel, Jocelynn would like to join you."

Gyllian glanced up from the portfolio he was nose deep in. "Fine," he said shortly.

I nodded to Booth, strolled up the two steps, and made my way to a long, gray couch to the left of the oval table everyone was sitting at.

"Everything okay, babe?" Gyllian asked without looking up.

"Fine," I replied as I lounged on the couch. "These crowds just bore me to pieces."

"Well, just a few more hours and it'll be just you and me."

"Sounds good," I said and went quiet so he could continue conducting business.

Now this was stimulating conversation! I tried to appear uninterested as I listened intently to the details of Gyllian's underground smuggling rings. Drugs were the hot topic here—it was Florida after all, easy access to the ocean. Gyllian's operation was a daring and incredibly profitable one. He smuggled drugs inside hollowed-out cars. Thousands of kilos of cocaine and heroin were packed in trunks and wheel wells, under hoods, and even sewn into the seats. On top of that, he could get about four hundred cars across the border in a month. A month! No one I'd ever heard of succeeded so long at such a brazen operation because cars were searched across international borders. But apparently Gyllian was paid up with the right people, so he could practically come and go as he pleased with his merchandise. He covered his tracks well, too, because if the FBI had a clue someone like Gyllian, or "Mr. Gabriel" existed, I would have heard of him. Headquarters would have been abuzz with the name, and he'd have earned the top slot on our America's

Most Wanted list real quick.

Hours passed, and I could tell Gyllian was disappointed. Drugs were not his focus right now, weapons were. He needed to find the Inferno Core, and his Florida drug rings had nothing on the matter. When they finally got to discussing weapons, there was nothing significant to report. From the sound of it, it was just usual shipments to other criminal bosses and mob families. Nothing as momentous as a nuclear weapon was even hinted at.

At midnight, an elegant black woman in a long black dress came to the VIP area. She spoke with Booth briefly before she was able to approach the table. She stopped in her tracks when she saw me, and slowly smiled. I got the distinct feeling I was being checked out. Demon? Maybe. I nodded to her in greeting. She returned the gesture and headed around the opposite side of the table. Only then did I notice the large case she was carrying. It looked like a cross between a lockbox and a briefcase.

I was close to raising an alarm when Gyllian spoke. "Natalie."

My body relaxed. He knew her. Gyllian stood from his chair, and they kissed each other's cheeks like they were old buddies.

"This is all of them," Natalie said, handing Gyllian the case. "Mr. Hoybur left Shara early, so hers are included."

"Perfect. Thanks, love."

"Anything for you." Natalie nodded in my direction. "Is that a new girl?"

I pretended not to hear her, focusing on Liam, who was having a side conversation with someone else.

"No," Gyllian said. "She's mine."

"Damn," Natalie said, sounding genuinely disappointed. "She would have brought in some serious business. Put that body on a street corner, and I'd have *the cops* tripping over themselves for a night with her."

I looked down at my drink and took a long sip.

"All right gentlemen," Gyllian said. "Let's call it a night."

Goodbyes were exchanged, hands were shaken, and then Gyllian led me out of the building. As we made our way to the limo, he became tense and distracted. I glanced at Booth, and even he looked preoccupied. Something was wrong.

"Where to, sir?" the limo driver asked once we were in.

"Pier 37."

Even though I was sitting right next to Gyllian, he suddenly had a wall up around him a mile high. Staring out the window in silence, he completely refused to look at me. Across the way I managed to catch Booth's eye for a brief second before he, too, looked away, avoiding my gaze.

My finger was instantly on the button that raised the tinted barrier between the driver and us. "Excuse us, Dennis," I said with a sweet smile.

He met my eyes in the rearview mirror and touched the rim of his hat. "Yes, ma'am."

"What is it?" I asked once the divider was up. Both of them stayed silent. "Hey," I said to Gyllian, trying to catch his gaze as he stared out the window, but he adamantly avoided it. I rested my hand on his arm. "What's wrong?"

"Bay," Booth said gently, drawing my attention. "This is where it becomes hard for Gyllian to do what he does as an undercover crime boss."

I looked at Gyllian and saw his eyes were squeezed shut. My heart clenched. "What do you mean?" I asked as the car slowed down.

"Someone," Booth said heavily, "went to the FBI about him, about Mr. Gabriel and his illegal activities." Booth looked at Gyllian. "And now he has to deal with it as a crime boss would."

My eyes went wide as the car stopped. Gyllian was going to kill someone. Every single mob hit photo I'd ever seen in my career flashed through my mind. They were all blood, blood, and more blood. Hands cut off. Eyelids cut off. Twenty-dollar bills shoved down slashed throats or up rectums. Torture evident before each kill. Gyllian was a crime boss. But…he wouldn't do that, would he?

"Stay here," he ordered as Dennis opened the door and he stepped out.

I reached for him on reflex, to snatch his arm or his sleeve, and drag his ass back in the car and take him away from here, but I only caught air. Booth seized my hand. I looked at him in horror. He gave me a sad smile and then kissed my knuckles before he, too, got out of the car. Dennis closed the door, leaving me alone in the backseat trembling.

Gyllian wasn't capable of that kind of brutality, was he? No way. Not him. Not the man that would subject himself to Demonic torture to get intel on how to save humanity. But, at the same time, I'd *seen* what Gyllian was willing to do to get to the bottom of Hell rising. He would do *whatever* it took. Gyllian *would* torture someone, he was probably doing it right now. As my stomach flipped and spun, I found myself saying again that Gyllian was not what he pretended to be. He was not! But now it seemed like I was just trying to convince myself. He'd been at this for ten years. Who knew the things he'd done in that time, especially to become as successful a criminal as he was? The ladder that led to the top of the criminal underground was slick with blood.

I waited in the car chewing on my acrylic nails for over an hour before Dennis finally climbed out of the driver's seat. I watched him as he approached the back door, pulling it open. Gyllian and Booth climbed in a moment later, and I examined them both silently. I couldn't see any blood on them but I could smell it, the leftover coppery tang of a long and heavy torture session, and likely a murder.

Dennis pulled onto the main road, and every instinct in my brain and body was screaming at me to get away. But looking into Gyllian's eyes, I saw a self-loathing he was barely able to contain. He wasn't a psychopath or sadist. He hated himself for whatever he'd just done. Buried under the madness, I could still see the hero there. That's who Gyllian was, who he *really* was.

I rested my hand on Gyllian's forearm. He jumped and jerked it violently out of my reach and looked at me. His eyes were wide, as if he couldn't believe I was touching him, and my heart crumbled. Keeping my face carefully compassionate, I took his hand and slowly moved it to rest on my cheek. I stared at him, making sure my eyes told him that I wasn't repelled by his actions, and that I cared about him. His guard came down and he surprised me by lowering his forehead onto my shoulder. I quickly embraced him. He returned the gesture, wrapping me up tightly in his arms.

I looked over at Booth at one point and saw his eyes glistening with unshed tears. He gave me a subtle nod and mouthed, "Thank you," before pinching the corners of his eyes.

We stayed like that until we got back to the hotel. As soon as the car stopped, though, Gyllian pulled himself together. I guess he was used to turning it off like a light switch or risk blowing his cover.

Fox and Roy were both still up, sucking down coffee and going through the stacks of papers they'd brought from home. "How'd it go?" Roy asked from the couch as we entered.

Gyllian headed to the kitchen and put the metal briefcase on top of the dining table. "Nothing here," he said and started pulling at his tie. "Just the usual drug trafficking. I need you two to start going through the wiretaps."

"Sure," Roy said, standing and making his way over.

"Wiretaps?" I asked, heading over, too.

Gyllian glanced at me before he started unbuttoning his shirt. "I have my prostitutes put them in rooms when they take highly influential johns. It's for 'blackmail purposes' as far as they know, but we use them to listen to any odd supernatural or Demon talk." He pulled off his shirt, leaving him in a snug white sleeveless tank, and headed for the stairs with his hands in his pockets. "Everyone get some sleep." He hurried up to his room like he couldn't wait to be alone, and I couldn't really blame him.

Later that night, I was sitting on the edge of my bed with a heavy heart and slumped shoulders. I had a better picture now of what the next two months were going to be like. This was going to be rough on so many levels, for everyone. I was more worried about Gyllian than anyone. That defeat, that madness, it was unfathomable, and this was just stop number one.

28

After Florida, we headed straight into the Middle East—Saudi Arabia, Iran, Iraq, and Pakistan. Fox had packed burkas and saris that, according to the dress code of each country, I needed to wear.

Gyllian owned several small slums throughout these countries. He said these places used to be a wealth of intel and activity when Demons were just starting to organize, because what better place for them to hide than within the ranks of Al Qaeda and ISIS? There were still some low-level criminals left in these areas, but his clientele was mainly comprised of impoverished people just trying to escape their reality. There weren't even any rumors here about where the Inferno Core could have been moved, or shipped, or distributed.

Gyllian owned several more bars in India, from Jaipur down to Goa. All we found there was the same kind of stuff as in the Middle East. There was some excess drug trafficking, but that turned out to be a result of human, not Demon, exploits. It was nothing apocalyptic in nature, so we didn't spend very much time there. Fox did take some time to visit her human father's extended family, though, so Roy took full responsibly for the reports for a few days. Fox came back positively alight with peace and contentment. She hadn't seen her family in a while because she was always so busy on these trips.

Gyllian's buildings in South America and Canada were a step up from the slums, looking more like regular bars and mediocre clubs. But these didn't provide much information either, just the usual drugs and violence that was typical in the world today. We visited Africa and Russia, too. Africa's intel had dried up as well, but at least Booth was able to visit extended family, though only briefly because Gyllian's aliases couldn't go long without a bodyguard.

I was happy for Fox and Booth, but it kind of felt like they were saying goodbye to their families. I guess the clock ticking down was weighing on all of us.

Roy didn't have any family left in Russia, so he and Fox just continued working on reports about local criminal activity, and trying to discern what was relevant to Hell rising. Here, Gyllian owned a string of theaters, bars, and nightclubs between St. Petersburg and Moscow. Before this trip, the term "billionaire" seemed a lucrative, far reaching anomaly to me. But here Gyllian's wealth really started to take form. These buildings were three or four stories and packed. His theaters were vast and luxurious, and they were all his. Even at these establishments, though, there wasn't much intel for us to gather.

It seemed more and more likely that the Demons had advanced themselves enough to be sitting pretty among the ranks of the rich and influential. It was discouraging because there had been no hint, no warning, to such a rise. My four friends had been keeping a close eye, gathering information everywhere they could for ten years. Now they were discovering that everything they'd been watching for, and working so diligently to detect, had already been happening under their noses.

Gyllian was the most frustrated. I could tell from how he periodically closed himself off and spent more time by himself. He had this constant look on his face that asked, "How had I not known?"

We were in Italy tonight as that question rolled around in my mind, making me toss and turn in bed. I began to wonder about God's role in all of this. Why had he not warned Gyllian? Why had he allowed the rise of the Demons?

Sleep was impossible, and I eventually sat up with a sigh. It didn't make sense. It was torturing Gyllian, too, and there was nothing I could do about it. I got out of bed and headed for the living area downstairs, thinking I could go through some of the wiretaps we had gathered.

As I passed Gyllian's room, though, I noticed the light was on under the door. He was awake.

I stared at that bedroom door like it might come to life and swallow me. I wanted to see him, to make sure he was okay, but I wasn't sure I could be alone with him in a bedroom without things getting out of control. I weighed my options and wondered about my own willpower. Could I see him without losing it? It was a bad idea in every possible way, so of course I knocked on his door.

"Come in," he said softly.

I turned the knob and pushed the door open. My heart burst at the sight of him, like it usually did. Oh gracious, the man was beautiful. His body was lean and muscular, his orange eyes were bright, and his black hair was a soft backdrop for his face. He was sitting up on top of all the bed covers in only a pair of black sweatpants with a few books around him, and one open in his hands.

"Hey," I said.

"Hey."

I crossed my arms and leaned a shoulder against the doorframe. "I saw your light on and wanted to see if you were okay."

"I'm all right," he said and nodded to the place beside him.

The ache in my chest burned as I made my way to him. He moved the books aside, making room for me to sit. Trying not to lose it, I sat on the edge of the mattress and looked at him over my shoulder.

He rolled his eyes and smiled. "I'm not going to bite you."

I grinned and slid back until I was beside him resting my legs parallel to his. I thought that was as close as we were going to get, but then he lifted his arm and put it around me, pulling me against him until my head rested on his bare shoulder. I relaxed and allowed myself to snuggle next to him. I was surprised how content that made me. I thought for sure we wouldn't be able to get into bed together without our passions going crazy, but I was glad to be wrong.

"What are you reading?"

"Ah, just a book about my dad," he said and tilted it up in his hand.

The picture he was evidently using as a bookmark caught my eye. I sat forward and lifted it off the pages before settling against him again. It was a perfectly square photo, faded a little, with slightly worn and wrinkled edges. A stunningly beautiful man was on one knee on a well-manicured grass field with a little boy, obviously his son, wrapped snuggly in his arms. The man had a smile that melted my heart, and the light in his eyes lifted my spirit. Both had soft-looking mops of wavy black hair and the unique cognac eyes.

My eyes went wide, and I looked up at Gyllian, only to see him already smiling down at me. "Yes, that's my dad."

I quickly looked back at the photograph. That was the Archangel Gabriel! I stared at it forever. He was beautiful. It was still strange to know I was looking at an Angel in a photograph. He looked so normal, handsome.

I smiled up at Gyllian. "You look like him."

He laughed softly. "I know I do."

I placed the picture tenderly back down on the pages and closed the cover to keep it safe.

Gyllian rubbed my arm affectionately. "How come you're up? I know you're due for sleep."

I sighed and rested my head on his shoulder again. "Just questions plaguing me."

"What kind of questions?"

"I don't know. About everything," I replied, not wanting to tell him the truth. "And I was worried about you."

He started running his fingers through a thick strand of my hair. "I'm all right."

I shifted so I was looking up at him, my chin still resting on his shoulder. "I know you're not, Gyllian."

He smiled. "And I know you're dodging my question."

I couldn't help but grin. I wanted to kiss him, but I didn't dare. I didn't want to ruin this moment, so I just shifted my head back down and looked at the book on the mattress. "Do you remember your dad?"

"Mm hmm."

"What was he like?"

Gyllian made a curious humming sound. "Getting a little personal, Bay?"

I snapped to look up at him in a panic, wondering if I'd crossed some line. Maybe discussing his dad was off limits. But the panic dissipated quickly when I saw him peering at me with a playful smirk.

I grinned. "Shut up," and then rested my head on his

shoulder again.

He chuckled. "I remember he was really energetic. In just about every memory I have of him, he was chasing me around some playground or park, or playing a game with me and the neighborhood kids. That picture was actually taken at one of my youth games. Soccer was his favorite. He was pretty good. He was fast!" Gyllian said with gentle enthusiasm.

"Did you play with him a lot?"

"All the time," he replied and rubbed my arm. "I loved my dad a lot."

"How old were you when you lost him?"

"Seven."

"Your mom?"

"Three. Before I could remember her."

"So you're a victim of the system, too?" I asked, even as I hoped beyond hope that his experience had been better than mine.

Gyllian shook his head. "No, I was lucky. A good family from the United States adopted me from Australia. Very devout Christians who didn't know the details of what I was, but took my magically appearing tattoos as a sign of God's divinity. They were far more kind and patient with me than they should have had to be."

I grinned broadly. "Were you a rebel?"

"Hell, yes," he replied, which made me laugh. "My adopted dad was a military guy, the complete opposite of my Angelic dad. Gabriel was way more playful and loose about things. My adopted dad was a good man, but rigid, and all business, and work, work, work." Gyllian shook his head. "Just not the way I was raised. So, I did everything I could to make their lives miserable." He sighed. "But they never gave up on me. They prayed with me every day, took me to church and Bible studies, and always talked about my dad so he was included in my life in some way, even though he was gone." Gyllian paused and said thoughtfully, "That was probably the best thing they could have done for me, talk about my dad. I never felt like I had to pick a side or exclude such a huge part of my life in order to be loyal to them." He went quiet for a moment, so I just waited and listened to his heartbeat under my ear. "I didn't get my head on straight and really appreciate them until the year I left for boot camp."

"Where are they now?"

He sighed. "They were killed while I was being held in Afghanistan." I squeezed my eyes closed. "Suspicious car accent, likely caused by Demons or Angels searching for me."

"Shit." I lifted my head and looked at him. "I'm so sorry."

He gazed at me as he ran his fingers through my hair again. "Thanks."

Just one kiss. Could I pull off one kiss without things getting out of hand? I didn't take much time to debate it as I lifted myself up and kissed his lips quickly but firmly.

When I pulled away, his eyes opened and his expression softened. "Thanks. I needed that."

I snuggled back down next to him, and he pulled me closer so my head was on his chest. I suddenly realized this was what emotional closeness was. It was something I never really experienced before. Sex was physical closeness and, for the first time in my life, I could make the distinction.

"So, what questions are keeping you up?"

I sighed. "God questions."

"Do you want to talk about them?"

I shook my head. "I'm not sure you're going to be much help." I met his eyes. "The questions I have are the same as yours."

He pressed his lips together and didn't say anything for a beat while I watched the sadness cloud his features. He finally sighed and rubbed my arm. "Have faith, Bay."

I rested my cheek on his chest again. "In what?"

"In God. His timing. His plan."

I sighed. "I'm not sure I can. Knowing he's real is one thing. Having faith in him, in his plan, is something else."

"How come?"

"Because he didn't warn you about the Demons' rise in power." Gyllian sighed softly. "Because he could stop Hell from rising, but doesn't." I shook my head. "I don't know what he's doing or what his plan is, so how am I supposed to trust it?"

Gyllian kissed my forehead. "By faith."

I sighed again. "Like I said, I'm not sure I can do that."

We stayed quiet for the rest of the night until I woke up the next morning, and we were still holding each other. It was a good thing that we managed to get some sleep, because we still had a long way to go on this trip.

We went through the rest of the clubs Gyllian owned in Europe, and then the couple he owned in China, but things were quiet. With all of us in agreement that our time was short, we headed back to the states. We still had two high-end clubs in Las Vegas and Los Angeles to check, and any Demons there would be the ones we'd need to talk to about the Inferno Core.

29

The hotel room in Las Vegas was basically a mansion. The whole atmosphere of the penthouse was warm and cozy with soft golds, browns, and tans with a few splashes of deep reds and orange. The living area on the first floor was vast, with the back wall made entirely of windows that offered a magnificent view of the strip. Three master bedrooms were down a hallway on the right. Above the windows was the balcony of the second floor that had two master bedrooms which Fox and I claimed.

We were in her room staring at the most elaborate evening gowns I'd ever seen laid out on her bed. I'd never worn an evening gown before. I'd never had an occasion to do so. My blonde hair was in a pile of loose curls on my head with a few soft tendrils falling down. My makeup had taken over an hour as Fox did things like "contour" my skin, whatever that meant. She had three dresses she could match to my makeup and was having a hard time deciding which one I should wear.

"Fox! Bay!" Gyllian called from downstairs. "We have to go!"

My heart swelled a little at hearing his voice. I wasn't sure I was emotionally prepared to see him in his custom-tailored tux.

"Gyllian," Fox said casually, but loudly, without taking her eyes off the dresses. "You know better than to rush me on girl things."

Gyllian chuckled softly. "Hurry up, we're running late."

"You can't hurry perfection, sir." I was grinning. "All right," Fox finally said and picked a dress up. "This one."

It was the most stunning gold, cap-sleeve gown with a heart-shaped neckline, and a bodice that sparkled even as it lay on the mattress. One side of the bodice came down over one hip, while the gold skirt dropped in glorious layers of chiffon and silk, which floated elegantly to the floor. I slipped it on carefully and Fox zipped me up before helping me with my shoes. As a final touch, I put on diamond teardrop earrings, a diamond necklace, and a diamond tennis bracelet.

"There," she said, examining her work with affection. "You look perfect."

I smoothed out the dress. I felt weird wearing it, but it looked amazing. I'd take this any day over the pink tube sock in Florida.

"Girls!" Gyllian called. "Come on!"

"All right, all right, we're coming," Fox responded. "Go," she said softly with an eager smile.

I grabbed the gold clutch off the dresser and headed into the hallway with the hem of the skirt floating gracefully around my ankles. I felt really beautiful, and I hated the fact that I wanted the guys to think so, too. I would be devastated if I didn't get some kind of reaction out of them after the effort that had gone into this.

The balcony outside my and Fox's rooms allowed a full view of the living area downstairs. Roy was sitting on a couch with headphones on and his back to the stairs, listening to the wiretaps. Booth was in a full tux, waiting by the door while he watched a baseball game on television. Gyllian was at the bottom of the stairs, looking at his watch. My breath rushed out of me at seeing him. He was in a full tux, with a two-button black vest under a custom-cut black jacket. Every piece of the ensemble accented his perfection. I legitimately became afraid I would fall down the stairs as my legs went weak, and gripped the banister until my knuckles were white.

Blowing out a nervous breath, I tried to compose myself and started down the stairs. Gyllian's eyes came up, and for a split second I felt panicked that I didn't look right. But his expression changed to sheer, uncensored amazement. I felt myself blush, and my anxiety lightened a little.

"Whoa," I heard Roy say.

I saw him snatch the headphones off his head and turn around to kneel on the couch facing me. I'd even diverted Booth's attention from sports. I smiled, happy to have gotten a reaction out of them.

The silence dragged on as I reached the bottom of the stairs, and I gave Gyllian a teasing smile. "I thought we were running late."

He flinched like he'd just woken up. "Uh yeah," he said, his voice cracking. I had to bite my bottom lip to keep from laughing. He cleared his throat. "Yeah," he said stronger. He held his arm out to me, and I laced mine around it as we headed for the door. "We'll probably be back late," Gyllian said, looking at Roy and then at Fox, who was smiling on the balcony.

"We know," she said. "We'll wait up."

Gyllian nodded, and the three of us headed into the hallway. Booth had barely gotten the door closed when Gyllian faced me. "Before you become nothing more than an arm trophy for me, I want you to know that you look absolutely stunning."

I smiled and reached up to unnecessarily straighten his collar and his bowtie. "So do you."

"I mean it," he said seriously and looked at me with a mix of deep longing and compassion. "You took my breath away." His eyes became a little sad and he swallowed heavily. "You still are."

A burst of emotion erupted in my chest making me feel hot all over. "Thanks, Gyllian," I said softly.

He leaned down and kissed my cheek tenderly, lingering a moment before he offered me his arm again. I threaded mine through his once more, and we made our way down the hall. The feelings I had for this man were going to kill me or drive me insane. I wondered which would come first.

After another quick limo ride we were outside of the gold-plated double doors of his Las Vegas club, Astrotec. When the doors opened, gold filled the entire horizon of my vision. Large gold lamps hung down from the gold grid beam ceiling. Gold mesh and gold cloth curtains decorated the walls and columns or were strategically placed on the walls. Gold plush couches were arranged in square meeting areas around short gold-and-tan marble tables. A gold gazebo was at the back, housing an elaborate bar with a drink shelf that reached the ceiling. The only thing that broke up the gold atmosphere was the circular blue pool built into the floor at the center of the club.

"K.J.," Gyllian said, and he led me over to the group of

suits waiting for him. At the front was a man in his late thirties with wavy brown hair, cold blue eyes, and a small scar above his lip.

"Mr. Debour," K.J. said politely.

The two shook hands firmly before K.J.'s gaze fell on me. I knew a sexual predator when I saw one. He leered at me hungrily before reaching for my hand. "This must be the new Mrs. Debour," he said and kissed the back of it.

As creepy as this guy was, I had to put on my bubblehead show.

I held my left hand up with one of Fox's massive diamond rings on it and wiggled my fingers. "Goin' on three months now," I said in my best valley girl accent.

K.J.'s eyes lit up with heavy lust, something a real bubblehead wouldn't pick up on. "You're a lucky man, Shaun. She's beautiful."

Gyllian patted my ass. "That's why I picked her. And this," he said, indicating my body with a gesture of his hand, "is all real, my friend."

"I believe that," K.J. commented, licking his lips as they unashamedly washed down my body.

I wanted to clean this scumbag's clock. Instead, I struck a pose, popping my hip out, and flipped some tendrils of my hair. "Eat your heart out, boys."

"Oh, I definitely want to eat something out," K.J. stated.

Bile rose in my throat as everyone, even Gyllian, erupted in laughter. Every fiber of my being was screaming to get away from these pricks, but Gyllian's cover was more important. There was a bigger picture here.

I playfully pushed K.J.'s shoulder and giggled. "Well, sir, that is no way to talk to a lady," I said flirtatiously as I linked my arm with Gyllian's. "Especially a happily married one."

He smiled wolfishly, wrinkling his nose. "My apologies, Mrs. Debour."

When my foster fathers and brother used to look at me like that, I'd always known I was in for a rough night. My blood went ice cold and my core started shivering as those memories surfaced.

"Darlin'," I said to Gyllian, trying to keep it light. I had to step away for a minute or I was going to lose it. "I think that pool is callin' my name. I'm going to head up to our room and get into that slinky little gold bikini you love."

Gyllian sighed heavily like he was annoyed and looked at K.J. "Get everything ready. I'll be back down shortly."

"Yes, sir," K.J. said politely.

I didn't mean for Gyllian to come with me, but I had a feeling he already knew he didn't have to.

We headed for the gold elevators to our right, and few elderly men in suits left their couches to join us. "Mr. Debour," one greeted.

"Mr. Ruthmore," Gyllian responded, and they shook hands.

Gyllian introduced me and I kept it together enough to play my part, greeting them in turn, and then we all piled into one of the elevators. They talked some politics, which I cared nothing about, and some Wall Street business I'd never had a desire to understand—all within the thirty-second elevator ride to the club suite. Gyllian shook their hands again when we reached the top floor, and they went their separate way.

"No disturbances, Alec," Gyllian said to Booth.

"Yes sir," Booth replied and took up a post outside our door. I went into the room first with Gyllian right behind me.

"Hey, hey," he said compassionately when the door was closed.

"I'm okay. I just—"

Before I could even come up with an excuse, Gyllian enveloped me in his arms. I sighed and relaxed with my head on his chest. It felt so good to be held by him.

"I'm sorry. I just—"

"I know," he said gently.

I sighed again. It was nice not to have to explain myself when something felt wrong. To know it was okay to *not* be okay was the safest feeling I'd ever felt. A man I cared for had my back, even though I could have blown his cover.

I blew out a breath and met his eyes. "I'm sorry," I said, having composed myself.

That's when the desire erupted in his eyes and my breath caught in my throat. I quickly looked down at his chest to try and break the spell, but I had a feeling it wouldn't be enough.

We couldn't be alone. The temptation for intimacy was too strong.

"Okay," I said, trying to stay cavalier as I pulled out of his embrace and went to our suitcases that the limo driver had brought up, giving the appearance we were staying here for the night.

I pulled mine up on the bed and opened it, refusing to meet Gyllian's eyes because I knew how he'd be looking at me. Knowing he had his promise to keep, I couldn't bear to see that look in his eyes. I rooted around for the gold bikini Fox had packed. It was a racy little number that left just about nothing to the imagination, but it was exactly what my bubbleheaded character would wear in a place like this.

As soon as I pulled it out, I felt Gyllian's fingertips on my lower back.

I froze. I squeezed my eyes shut as he got behind me with his chest against my back and slid his hand around to rest on my stomach. His warm breath caressed my ear and neck, and suddenly the fiercest battle of my life was taking place inside me.

I fought. I wrestled. I was not strong enough to resist him. There was no way. I wanted him too much. My entire body begged for him to touch me with every part of him, his hands, his mouth, everything. Where his breath wafted over my skin, hot sparks of desire erupted that nearly made me moan. Every particle of me, inside and out, ached to feel his body on top of mine. I wanted him, but I didn't want him breaking his promise. But was I responsible for his promise?

God, I prayed silently from out of nowhere. *Give me strength.*

I didn't say what for. I wasn't specific in any way. But strength suddenly bloomed to life inside me. "Don't," I said, spinning to face him, keeping my eyes on his chest. "I can't let you do this." My whole body trembled. "No matter how badly I want you, too." I forced myself to look up at him. His orange eyes were searching my face, looking for an explanation. "You have to keep your promise. I *want you* to keep your promise." I swallowed down the lump forming in my throat. "That's more important to me than being with you this way. *You* are more important to me than being with you this way."

He stared at me, and I could see the battle erupt in his eyes, too. I didn't know what God would do if Gyllian broke his promise, but I didn't want to find out.

"This," I said tapping the bed behind me, "would be a temporary thrill." I swallowed again. "It's not worth the regret I know you'll feel after." I shook my head, fearing he would hate me forever. "I won't do that to you, Gyllian."

He suddenly crushed me against his chest. As we held on, I felt him clutching at my dress, pulling on the material in trembling fists like he wanted to rip it off, but he didn't. He was battling.

"Why are you making this so hard?" he whispered. I wasn't sure if he was talking to me or praying. Maybe both.

While he railed against the temptation, I just held him, and a strange peace settled around me. This was right. This was the right decision. I held onto him until his shoulders loosened and his breathing went back to normal.

"I'm sorry. I'm sorry," he said, shaking his head and pulling away from me. His eyes were filled with regret and longing, but he was calm.

"It's okay," I said and rested my hands on his cheeks. "Someday, after we've saved the world, we can figure this out. Okay?"

He nodded.

I smiled. "Now come on," I picked up the gold bikini and matching silk robe. "Let's get to work." Then I went into the bathroom to change.

———

Gyllian, Booth, and I were back in the club in no time. Gyllian kissed my cheek then he and Booth headed to the private table with the suits while I went to the pool. I slid off my robe, placed it on one of the nearby gold hooks, and sat on the edge, sticking my feet in. The water was warm.

At first, I watched Gyllian for a while. He and his crew passed around clipboards and portfolios and paperwork and briefcases, examining and discussing each paper intently. I couldn't watch him for long, though, because eventually the brownnosers converged around me. They talked about the same trivial things as did the other rich folks I'd encountered during this trip. The only thing that made this one more bearable was the distraction of the pool. People weren't just sitting around me drinking and droning out meaningless talk; there was fun to be had, and most people indulged.

At about eleven, Gyllian and his crew got up and left the table. Everything seemed ordinary and boring like the last two months had been, and I began to think that even Las Vegas would be a bust…until an hour dragged by and something started to feel wrong. I wasn't sure why. It wasn't like Gyllian never left my sight during these meetings. He sometimes went to check on a product, or oversee a small shipment, or conduct a transaction. However, the uncomfortable stirring got steadily worse as another twenty minutes passed and I finally couldn't ignore it. Something was wrong.

"Well," I said in my little accent and stood. "I do believe it's time to find my husband and retire for the night." I gathered my robe from the hook and threw it on. "Have a good night, ya'll."

The people in the pool gave me a halfhearted response before I headed in the direction Gyllian and the pack had left in. I probably moved too fast for my cover, but urgency pounded in my chest like a rabid beast.

While on my way, the bad feeling somehow took on a weird physical manifestation. I could feel a distinct pressure in my hand, and then I was being guided in certain directions by the shift in the pressure. It felt like an invisible person was holding my hand and pulling me. I didn't know this club from a cat's hair, but I maneuvered back hallways and stairs like I'd been raised here.

I eventually found myself standing in an empty hallway that looked like a supply corridor with yellow lights. The pressure took me to the first door on my left. My cover completely forgotten, I threw it open and two dozen people spun to face me. They were lit only by the hall light behind me and the moonlight that came through a thin line of windows on the far wall. My heart seized when I saw Gyllian at the center of them. He was in a chair, shirtless and barefoot, with his arms tied tightly behind his back. Covered in sweat, he had patches of large black bruises on his entire left side and over a hundred small cuts on his shoulders and arms. Blood ran freely down the swollen left side of his face and dripped to the floor.

"Bay," he panted.

I didn't even have the presence of mind to draw a weapon as I ran to him. The people surrounding him tried to stop me, but I was too fast. I ducked and twisted out of their reach until I was on my knees beside him. "Gyllian," I choked out as I tenderly cupped his jaw in my hands.

"You…" he said, "you have to get out of here."

I shook my head as tears blurred my vision. "I'm not leaving you."

"Bay," he said a little stronger, "You have to…"

An arm hooked around mine, and then another. The other people tried to pull me away from him, and I flailed like an animal! "No! NO!" I screamed, twisting out of their grip, and dropped back on my knees beside him. His feet were bruised completely black, and I saw a bloody hammer on the floor behind the chair.

The others redoubled their efforts, and several grabbed my arms pulling me away. I struggled as best I could, but I was eventually flung into a chair across from him. My arms were tied, but I could see him so I didn't care. I scooted my chair forward even as they tied me down just to get that much closer to him. One guy noticed and slammed his hand on the back of it to keep it still.

"Well," a vaguely familiar voice said, one I had heard earlier in the night. "What do we have here?" K.J. rounded my chair coming into view. My tears evaporated under the heat of my hatred. "Michael's Daughter, I presume? Well, isn't this pretty," he said, crouching down in front of me.

The idiots hadn't tied my feet down yet. I kicked K.J. in the groin first. As he doubled over in pain, my knee came up, connecting with his nose. His head jerked back, and I lifted my foot, driving my heel hard into his face. His nose broke with a satisfying snap and he went flying, the back of his head hitting the edge of Gyllian's chair. A few of the others came to their senses and held my legs down while they strapped my ankles to the chair.

Blood dripped over K.J.'s lip and down his chin as he picked himself up, staring at me with dangerously wide eyes. "You bitch!"

"You," I growled at him, "have no *fucking* idea." For a moment K.J. seemed daunted. "You're dead," I hissed and started to activate my heightened abilities tattoo. I'd break their necks, all of them!

Nothing happened.

I froze. My tattoo didn't warm up!

I tried again.

Nothing!

A self-satisfied smirk came over K.J.'s face. "Having issues, doll?"

Panic began to creep up. I jerked on the ropes holding me, and only then did I feel the weird energy emanating from them. I looked across at Gyllian, who was already looking at me, defeated.

"See," K.J. said, sauntering over.

"Don't touch her," Gyllian said, even as blood continued to steadily drip down his face.

K.J. looked over his shoulder and shrugged. "She crashed *our* party. She only has herself to blame." He crouched in front of me again. "See, our Angel pals stole these ropes from Heaven's own weapon storage." He tapped on the one around my right ankle. "They render everything, including Nephilims, powerless." He started lightly dragging his finger up the inside of my leg. "They're infused with God's power." He smirked when he reached my thigh and slid his finger up under my short gold robe. "And nothing beats God." His fingertip rested over my clitoris and there was nothing between my flesh and his except the thin silky material of my bikini bottoms. "Now let's try this on for size."

A horrific burning sensation suddenly erupted under his fingertip. I gasped from the pain. He held his finger there for a short span, but I quickly started to tremble with the effort to not scream. I wouldn't give him the satisfaction. *I refused!*

K.J.'s teeth clenched forming a hateful smile. "Come on," he said. Then he started dragging his finger slowly down the inside of my thigh.

The burning sensation suddenly shot through my entire

leg, and I screamed.

"Louder!"

He added pressure and the white hot pain shot up my spine to the back of my skull. I screamed with such force the chair shook under me. He was ripping my skin off! Blood flowed freely, pooling under my leg. I could smell it.

"I warned you," Gyllian suddenly said.

He said it so quietly, but his voice cut through every other noise in the room, including my screams. It was enough to make K.J. stop torturing me and look over his shoulder. Trying to focus through the pain, I looked past him at Gyllian and saw his eyes were Angelic!

K.J.'s face flooded with fear. "You...you can't!" he stammered.

The wounds on Gyllian's face started to fade. The bruises vanished. Even the blood disappeared. He was healing! He was using Roy's ability! When he was fully restored, Gyllian stood up as if he hadn't been bound at all, and my eyes went wide when suddenly a pair of black wings sprouted from his back—*my* wings!

They stretched wide to his sides, and for a second, I thought I was looking at a real Angel, or some sort of beautiful Demon with those black wings and black claw-mark tattoos on his right side. The sight made me feel lightheaded, but that could also have been from blood loss.

Gyllian's hands were then on K.J.'s face, and after a quick spin and a loud snap, his neck was broken and Gyllian let him drop to the floor. His silvery Angelic eyes scanned the room, and panic set in. The others raced for the exit as fast as they could go, shouting and trampling each other in a fit of madness to try and escape, but the door didn't budge. They piled up against it, banging on it and the wall, trying to get out.

I could have smiled at the sight, but something slapped down on my thighs, making me jump. When I looked, Gyllian's face was inches from mine. He was bent over, gripping my legs. I wasn't sure what he was doing until the pain started to fade. He was healing me. When it was gone, he pulled the ropes off me with an effortless tug and took my hand, helping me stand. My legs stuck to the seat from my own blood, and the hem of my robe was saturated in it.

I looked down at the puddles that had accumulated on both chairs and the floor, and something flipped inside of me. It was something hard and unwavering that went through my entire system like adrenaline in my veins. I turned my eyes to the two dozen people trying to escape and activated my flaming eye tattoo. A mix of Rook and Bishop Demons were before me and one single Knight. My teeth clenched. They had hurt Gyllian for the *last* time!

As I made my way toward them, the world slowed down in the way that meant I was moving too fast. I pulled my father's sword out of my chest and longed for another blade to make this quicker. The moment the thought crossed my mind, a gentle burning sensation erupted around the circumference of my hips. Immediately following that, my skin started to hum with a strange energy.

No, several strange energies.

Wait.

I concentrated a little on what I was feeling and realized that there were nearly a hundred different energy spots humming on my skin. My brows dropped a moment. It was magical energy.

Grazing my awareness over them, I felt the most unreal and vast array of abilities. There were enhancement abilities, mental abilities, manipulation and telekinetic abilities, incorporeal abilities, vision abilities, materializing abilities, precognition abilities, shifting abilities. It was an insane mix of powers that was awe inspiring and terrifying.

I didn't dare activate any them. I honestly thought I might combust or implode if I did. But in one pocket of energy on my back, I felt a pair of Holy Fire blades. Suddenly, I realized these spots of energy were all of our abilities! Roy's, Gyllian's, Fox's, Booth's and mine!

Too enraged to ponder it farther, I reached behind me and took hold of one of Roy's katana blades and pulled it out, only a little surprised when it took form. With his flaming sword in one hand and my father's glass sword in the other, I cut across the Demons at the back of the pack before they even had a chance to turn around. My father's sword sliced clean through the stone and plaster of the wall, leaving a streak of yellow light coming in from the other hallway. The creatures went down in halves. The only thing on my mind was what they had done to Gyllian.

They—I cut across the throat of a Rook Demon—would not—I sliced backwards loping off the head of a Bishop—touch him—I brought both blades forward like giant scissors and cut off the head of another Rook—again! I plunged both swords into the Knight Demon's chest, driving them in so deep, the hilts were flush with its skin and the blades went clean through the wall behind it. It was pinned so efficiently that when I took my hands away, the Demon stayed upright as the Holy Fire slowly consumed it. Unfortunately, it was too slow for me. I punched the Knight hard in the face for good measure, the force of its head leaving a dent in the stone wall behind it.

My adrenaline and energy suddenly drained out of me, and the buzzing of the others' abilities left my skin. My legs turned to liquid, and I just managed to get my arms under me before face-planting into the cement. Roy's katana blade vanished, but my father's sword kept the Knight pinned to the wall, and it continued to burn in the Holy Fire.

"Bay?" I heard behind me.

I tried to turn, but a dizzy spell claimed me before I could. Gyllian suddenly appeared, crouching next to me with a hand on my shoulder. I could focus enough to see that my wings were gone and his eyes were a sunset orange again. Still wearing only his dress pants, he looked clean and beautiful, his skin smooth and unmarred by the Demons' torture.

"Are you all right?" we both asked, drawing a small smile from each of us.

Booth suddenly stepped into view looking downtrodden but completely in one piece. There wasn't so much as a snag in his suit! If I'd had the strength, I would have stood up and busted his lip.

"Where the fuck were *you?*" I yelled.

"Bay, stop," Gyllian said gently. "This wasn't his fault."

"The hell it wasn't!" I cried. "He was supposed to protect you!"

"I told him not to." My mouth snapped shut and my eyes went wide. "This was my idea."

311

My brows dropped. "You *planned* this?"

"Improvised."

"What are you talking about? For what?"

He pressed his lips together. "Why do I ever subject myself to torture?"

"For information." He nodded. "On what?"

He sighed softly and tenderly kissed my forehead. "Let's get out of here first, huh?"

I shifted my legs to try to stand, but it was clear that they couldn't hold my weight. I wasn't sure why. "I might need a minute. Something is—"

Gyllian suddenly swept me up into his arms, making me gasp, before looking at Booth. "As soon as we get back, infuse every single wall, floor, ceiling, and door of the hotel room with Holiness. Roy and I will put up some Demon warding." Booth nodded and rested a hand on Gyllian's shoulder.

"Wait!" I called.

Gyllian looked down at me, and I looked over at the Knight Demon pinned to the wall. I reached for my father's sword pathetically, even though I was five feet away, but Gyllian understood and walked me over. I took hold of the hilt and tried to pull it out, but whatever this weakness was, it defeated me. I pulled and pulled but only managed to slightly jiggle the pinned Demon. Gyllian's hand then wrapped around mine. When I looked over at him, and our eyes met, emotions overflowed into every crevasse of my existence. His eyes were like warm honey, flooding into every particle of my past, present, and future, making this moment, right now, make sense in every aspect of my world.

I eventually looked back at my dad's sword, and with Gyllian's hand wrapped around mine, both of us pulled it out. The Demon crumpled to the floor. I put the blade back where it belonged, and the world went watery.

30

"Shit!" Roy exclaimed. He and Fox ran to us as soon as the hotel room became clear. "Where is she hurt?"

"What happened?" Fox asked.

"I'm okay," I responded.

Booth pressed his palm into the door, and a ripple of energy spread from his hand, traveling out to both sides of the wall before stopping at intersections on either side. He then took off across the room to the windows overlooking the strip and did the same.

"Fox," Gyllian said and handed me to her. Her eyes went Angelic, and she took me in her arms with ease. "Get her cleaned up. Roy, help Booth and me ward the room."

"What happened?" Roy asked as he and Gyllian both ran off, pulling small knives out of their back pockets so they could draw blood sigils to ward off Demons.

Fox hurried in the opposite direction to the master bathroom on the first floor. She quickly placed me on the toilet seat before she, too, pulled out a knife from her back pocket and cut a small nick in her index finger. Standing on the edge of the tub, she drew a Demon warding symbol on the wall above the shower.

"I'm sorry," I heard from the door. Booth quickly came in, touching the floor, ceiling, and all four of the walls of the bathroom, making them ripple with energy before quickly leaving and closing the door behind him.

Fox stepped down from the tub. "What happened?"

I looked up at her. "I killed a lot of Demons."

"Good," she responded without even flinching.

"I *slaughtered* them, Fox."

"Good," she said again.

I smiled a little, but it was gone quickly. "Something weird happened, though."

"What?" she asked and started helping me take off my bloody robe.

I gave her a quick recap of what had happened, finishing with the way all their abilities had left me once the last Demon was dead. "I don't know why I'm weak, though. It's like all that magical energy sapped my own out of me."

She squatted down. "That might explain this."

I looked where she pointed and saw a new tattoo had appeared. "What the hell?" It sat low on my hips, just above the rim of my bikini bottoms. That explained the burning sensation I'd felt there. It was of chain-shaped links that looked made of rope with a small knot low in the front. There was also a knot on my right and left hip. Fox stood and looked behind me.

"Two knots on your back," she said, crouching again. "Five knots which likely represents all of our abilities converging onto you."

"Jesus," I muttered. "It…" I shook my head, recalling the unstable feeling of their magic all over me. "It was too much. I thought I was going to implode or explode or something if I touched them. I don't want your abilities."

Fox chuckled. "Oh, my dear Bay," she put her hand on my cheek and looked at me with her eyes full of sincerity and sympathy. "That's exactly why *you* have access to them."

"What?"

"You're…" She paused, her hand dropping, and her lovely face softening. "I'm only supposed to tell you that you're clean."

"What do you mean I'm clean?" I asked, feeling oddly offended, probably because that was a lie if I ever heard one. "Who told you to tell me that?" She just smiled gently and knowingly. "God?" I barked. "So God gave me this ability because I'm cleaner than the rest of you?"

Fox nodded. "Yes."

"Bullshit," I replied abruptly. Her gentle smile vanished. "Gyllian, you, and the other two are God's champions here. Gyllian is the *most* passionate about fighting Hell out of any of us, and he's been at it for ten years. If anyone is 'clean,' it's him."

Fox's gaze lingered on me a moment before she stood and went to the bathtub, turning on the faucet.

My shoulders drooped. "I'm sorry."

She looked back at me with a soft smile. "It's all right."

"No." I shook my head. "It's not. I didn't mean to go off like that. I just…" My sentence died there and I looked down at the floor. I wasn't sure what to say. She didn't say anything either, so it stayed silent. I distracted myself with other thoughts. "Hey Fox."

She looked back at me again, and something in my expression caused her to look concerned. "What is it?"

I shriveled inside myself. This was embarrassing. I tried to think of something less personal to ask her but…no, I needed her help. "Have you ever been in love?"

Her expression unexpectedly turned deeply sad, and she looked down at the filling tub to avoid my gaze.

"Oh Jesus," I said, shaking my head. "I'm sorry. I shouldn't have asked."

She forced a smile and looked at me again. "It's all right," she said lightly. The tub was full, so she turned the faucet off. "Yes, I have been in love."

The guilt made my heart sink to the floor. "I'm so sorry. You don't have to talk about it. I didn't mean to—"

"It's all right, Bay," she said, helping me get my bikini off.

Her eyes went Angelic again as she picked me up and brought me over to the tub. She gently lowered me into the warm water and it turned pink immediately. Kneeling on the floor, she gazed at the beautiful henna pattern tattoo on the back of her left hand.

"I was married once."

My heart stopped. "Oh God," I said, closing my eyes, knowing from her tone how this was going to end.

She gently started scooping some water up onto my shoulders, which weren't fully submerged. "After my sex trafficking ring was broken up, she found me wandering the streets—"

"She?" I blurted out before I could stop myself.

Fox looked at me, and my cheeks flushed, afraid I had offended her. Before I could utter an apology, she smiled. "Yes, she."

I couldn't help my amazement. I'd always thought the religious fanatics of the world were full of shit—the ones claiming God hated homosexuals—and I'd been right. Here was a woman, one of God's most exclusive and elite warriors, one of five to ever exist in the history of mankind, and she was a lesbian. With a small smirk, I mentally flipped off every single bigot that had given God such a bad name with claims like that. At the same time, my respect for God blossomed a little.

Fox reached under the sink and grabbed a white pitcher out of the cabinet. "She found me on the streets begging for rupees that I could put toward my next fix of crystal meth"— Fox shrugged deeply— "and she decided to take me in." Tears suddenly filled her eyes. I wanted to say something, but wasn't sure what. "We were together for a year, married for three months, unofficially of course." She gave me a pained smile since same sex marriage was illegal in India. "I never got fully clean while I was with her, but she loved me more than I deserved, and more than I thought possible." Fox sniffed and gently poured some water over my shoulders and back. "She pulled out all the stops, and gave me chance after chance to get free of that hateful drug. I tried a few times, even made it a full month once. But one slip up"—her voice became passionate— "just *one* chance run-in with a girl I had been trafficked with, and I was an addict again." She chuckled gently and unexpectedly. "Lord only knows why that woman loved me at all, but she did, and I was safe and happy for the first time since my dad had died."

"I am so sorry," I whispered.

"Her name was Myra," she said, gazing down at the tattoo on her hand again. "I was out meeting with my dealer when she was killed by Demons who were looking for me."

I chewed my bottom lip nervously and searched her face to see if it was okay to ask my next question. "What did it feel like? Loving her?"

"Oh honey," Fox said dabbing her eyes with the side of her wrist. "There is nothing like it. It's insanity. Pure insanity that takes over your entire being."

I smiled a little as I looked at the opposite wall. "Yeah. That sounds about right."

"Bay?" She rested her hand on my shoulder. I looked over, and she studied my face a moment before giving me a tiny smile. "It's Gyllian, isn't it?" I quickly looked away. Fox was quiet until I glanced at her again and saw her smiling. "He loves you, too, you know."

I felt heat erupt in my cheeks and looked down at the water. "I don't know about that."

"It's true." I didn't argue because I wanted to pretend for a moment it could be true. Fox caressed my arm. "What is it, honey? You don't seem very happy for a woman in love."

I shook my head. "I don't know. I just…" I sighed. "I don't know how to love people." It wasn't really what I'd meant to say, but it was true enough. "Gyllian deserves someone who knows how to love him."

I glanced at Fox and saw her gazing at me with sympathy and compassion. "That's for Gyllian to decide, not you," she declared. "You don't get to choose who you love, Bay. Nobody does. Not you, not Gyllian. You don't get to tell Gyllian he can't love you because you don't think you're good enough. That is for him and him alone to decide. Don't you dare try to take that away from him."

I was grasping at straws. "What do I do then? How do I act?"

Fox took up the pitcher again and poured some water higher onto my back. "Take each moment with him and enjoy it for all it's worth, whatever that means, in whatever situation you find yourself in with him." Her face became serious and she shook her head. "Don't throw love away because you think someone deserves more than you can give. Because you don't know what you can give"—she pinched my chin affectionately— "until you give it all you can in the first place."

I smiled, feeling oddly comforted.

While Fox washed me up, I slowly felt my strength return. By the time she was massaging some luxurious conditioner in my hair, I could stand and finish it myself. "All right," she said, drying her hands with a towel. "I'm going to talk to the boys and see what's happening, if we're staying or going. I'll bring you some clothes, too."

"Thanks, Fox," I said as she started to leave. "And," I said, making her pause in the doorway, "thanks for listening."

She smiled. "I'll be right back."

She left and closed the door behind her while I finished my shower. I was drying my hair when she came back with a set of clothes.

"We're going to talk and see what our next steps should be."

I nodded, turning the hair dryer off. "I'll be out in a second."

She headed for the door. "I told them about your new tattoo. Gyllian wants to ask you about it."

I nodded. "I figured he would."

With a smile, she left the bathroom. I threw on the clothes she'd brought, a simple pair of jeans, a white tank top, and a loose light blue duster without sleeves. I took a deep breath and looked in the mirror, very aware that I was bracing myself to go see Gyllian. Before I could chicken out—and I really thought I might—I pulled open the bathroom door and headed to where they were gathered in the living area.

Gyllian was standing in front of the windows with his arms crossed, staring out over the strip below. He had changed into a pair of dark jeans and a snug black t-shirt. Roy and Booth stood from the couches when I appeared, Booth still in his tuxedo. Fox was standing next to another couch with her arms crossed, and one knee resting up on the arm.

Gyllian came over as soon as he noticed me. "Can I see it?"

Before showing him anything, he had some explaining to do. I crossed my arms. "First, you need to tell me exactly what happened tonight."

He sighed and jerked his head in the direction of the couches. "Come on."

We headed over and I sat next to Roy with my feet folded under me while Gyllian sat next to Booth across from us. I looked around the room and noticed blood sigils on every wall. I even saw some on the windows, as well as the balcony.

"How are you feeling?" Roy asked.

I nodded. "I'm okay," then looked at Gyllian. "So what happened?"

Gyllian sighed. "Booth and I had to improvise an interrogation of the Demons I was dealing with tonight."

"Gyllian," Fox gasped.

"Without proper planning?" Roy asked.

"And without us?" Fox added.

"Look, look!" Gyllian said, silencing them. "It was an emergency."

"Uh," I interrupted. "You were *bound* to a chair. I saw your injuries. What I walked into was not an interrogation of Demons. They were interrogating you."

Gyllian shook his head. "You don't understand how Demons work."

"Enlighten me."

He met my gaze directly. "Why do you think I let them torture me when I want to get information out of them?"

I shook my head and shrugged. "I figured it was part of the deal. They love to torture. You offer up yourself in exchange for information they have."

"Partly," he said. I raised an eyebrow. "But Demons also have a blind spot when it comes to torture. Every ounce of pain they inflict is like an orgasm for them. They lose track of what they say and often don't *care* what they say as long as they can keep inflicting the pain."

I recalled the ecstasy K.J. seemed to be in as his finger trailed down my leg and he ripped open my skin. I reflexively rubbed my thigh, recalling the unbelievable pain he'd caused me. Unfortunately, Gyllian saw me do that and his expression flooded with regret. Thankfully he didn't say anything, though. I didn't want the others to know about that.

"Why didn't you tell me?" I asked.

"Because you would have tried to stop me."

"You're right."

"That's why I didn't tell you." He met my gaze, and gently shook his head. "I hadn't counted on you showing up. I didn't think you'd find us. I'm so sorry."

I shrugged it off like it didn't matter, but his apology meant a lot. At the same time, though, I also felt a little ashamed. I thought I had rescued Gyllian. So much for that. He hadn't wanted to be rescued. He'd probably been upset that I interrupted what he was doing. The way he was looking at me now, however, told a different story and made it impossible to talk, so I didn't.

Luckily, Fox filled the silence. "What was Booth's

role?"

That brought Gyllian's attention to her. "Once I picked up on their suspicious behavior, I had Booth 'secretly' consort with K.J. during the meeting and express concern about me. They decided to question me after that, and Booth agreed to jump me once they got me alone. He was also my rescue plan for when I'd gotten all the information I could, or if they were about to kill me."

I pressed my lips together and looked at Booth. "I'm sorry," I said, drawing a small smile of understanding from him. I shook my head. "I didn't know."

"It is all right, Bay," he said kindly.

I shook my head and looked at the floor. He shouldn't have had to understand my harsh words. I should have trusted him. I should have known he wasn't turning on us or abandoning us. As if she knew how lousy I was feeling, Fox moved to sit on the arm of the couch I was on, and put her arm around me.

"What brought on an emergency interrogation?" Roy asked. "Just their dodgy behavior?"

Gyllian tented his fingers in front of his mouth. "Two other things. First, a rising star in the criminal underworld on the West Coast." Anticipation erupted silently in our hotel room. Gyllian stood, put his hands in his pockets, and then sat on the arm of a chair diagonally from him. "While we were going through my weapon-smuggling numbers, K.J. mentioned an offer that had come his way from this up and comer. She wanted to use my Las Vegas ring to transport a very large shipment."

"The Inferno Core?" I asked, my eyes going wide.

Gyllian nodded. "The operation would have been worth upwards of a billion dollars for me. No normal shipment is worth that much."

My heart started pounding at the prospect that we might have found the Inferno Core. If we could intercept the shipment through Gyllian's smuggling rings, we could stop Hell from blowing a hole to the surface. Who better to intercept a shipment than the boss himself? We could actually do this!

Then something else he said registered. "What do you

mean 'would have been'? K.J. turned it down?"

Gyllian shook his head. "Turns out this rising star, Grace Admiral, pulled out of the deal."

My heart sank. "What? Why?"

"That's why I needed to interrogate them."

I pressed my lips together and sat back with my arms crossed when it dawned on me. "You think she caught wind of who you were."

Gyllian nodded. "From the way they were acting they *all* seemed to be on to me—but I wasn't sure if it was only me. That's the second reason I needed to interrogate them. I needed to find out what they knew about us." Gyllian gave a resigned sigh. "They know who I am at least."

"Shit," Roy said, sitting forward and rubbing his hands over his face. "How much do they know?"

Gyllian shook his head. "More than we thought. What I look like, most of my aliases, and what most of my aliases look like."

Fox bowed her head, and a sense of defeat suddenly loomed in the air. "No wonder she pulled out of the deal."

Gyllian nodded.

"What about the Angels?" Roy asked. "Do they know?"

"They know as much as the Demons."

"Fuck!" Roy cried and quickly stood from the couch. He stopped a few paces away with his back to the rest of us and his hands on his hips. "So it's game over?" he asked, facing Gyllian and shaking his head. "We're not ready for a confrontation with Hell."

"I know," Gyllian said and sighed. "I have one idea."

"What?" Roy asked.

"For now, we go home and regroup."

My heart clenched. "What do you mean go home? This Admiral woman has the Inferno Core! Hell will blow it if we don't stop her!"

Gyllian met my gaze. "There is *nothing* we can do," he said slowly and patiently. "We aren't ready."

The unspoken meaning behind that stabbed me in the heart. "Because of me." No one said anything. I stood and went to Gyllian. "What about this?"

I held my shirt up and pulled down my pants slightly,

exposing the rope-chain tattoo low on my beltline. Gyllian crouched down, taking a hold of my hips to look at it while I tried to ignore the hot flames erupting from his touch. "When this activated, I felt the energy, the magic, of every single one of your abilities humming all over my skin." Everyone but Fox, who had already seen it, moved in for a closer look.

"Turn?" Gyllian asked, and I did, putting my back to him.

I looked down at Roy. "I was able to use one of your Holy Fire blades." He glanced up at me and smiled, though it seemed a little forced, before looking back at my tattoo.

"When did you get this?" Gyllian asked. "Before or after your wings appeared on my back?"

"After. It happened just before I slaughtered that horde." I looked down at Gyllian behind me. "Why?"

He looked at Booth. "It *is* desperation that lets us use each other abilities." Booth nodded. "It's how I was able to use Roy's healing and Bay's wings to intimidate them. But I don't know what this is," he said, looking back at my tattoo. "Can you activate it now?"

I grimaced. "Do you really need me to?" He looked up at me. "It felt really weird, bad weird, and I'm pretty sure using it turned me into the wet noodle you had to carry back here."

Gyllian shook his head and looked back down at it. "No, you don't have to."

"Thanks," I said, lowering my shirt and turning. I tried to back away from him nonchalantly and stumbled over my own feet. Making it worse, Gyllian quickly grabbed my upper arms like I might fall. "Um," I said, placing my hand on my forehead and avoiding eye contact with him. "Sorry. I guess I'm not quite 100% yet."

"It's all right," he said and guided me to sit back on the couch.

Once I was seated, I looked up at him as he sat on the arm of the chair closer to me. "How did you get out of those ropes without your abilities?"

"The ropes were made by God."

"And nothing beats God. So how did you?"

He smiled. "It's easy when God is on your side."

My eyes narrowed. "So you could have gotten out of those ropes anytime?" He nodded. "Why couldn't I?" His smile vanished quickly, and I understood. "Oh," I said with unbarred shame. "Because of my lack of faith."

Gyllian simply pursed his lips and bowed his head. I sighed and rubbed my eyes. Faith. It was fucking bonkers.

31

I didn't sleep, but I didn't need to. I wasn't due. I was left brooding with my thoughts all night and resisting, fiercely, the urge to pray and ask God what *exactly* he wanted from me. My thoughts were consumed by how I was letting my team down, my friends, and how I was letting Gyllian down. He'd been diligently working to stop Hell from rising for ten years, suffering immensely for that cause, and here I was, a faithless rookie, disrupting his plans.

A knock came at my door. "Bay?" Fox called.

"Come in," I said and propped myself up on my elbow.

She poked her head in. "We're meeting downstairs. Gyllian is going to teleport us home."

"What about Los Angeles?" It was our last stop, and close to where that Grace Admiral woman was.

Fox shook her head. "That's going to have to wait. Gyllian's alias might be compromised there."

I sighed and sat on the side of the bed, pulling the jeans on that I'd thrown to the floor last night. Standing, I noticed for the first time that Fox looked distracted. Her mind was somewhere else and the small crease in her forehead meant it wasn't good.

"Hey," I said, going to her. "What's wrong?"

She shook her head. "Nothing."

"Fox."

She met my eyes and sighed heavily. "I'm just frustrated. We all are."

I looked at her helplessly. "With me?"

She looked surprised. "What? No, no. Of course not. This will click for you in due time."

I flinched at the dismissiveness of that. It was as if my lack of faith was a non-issue. It seemed like a big deal to me if it was stopping us from intercepting the Inferno Core and keeping Hell from rising. She was talking like we had *time* for me to come around in "due time."

"Roy and I have just gone through everything," she went on. "Every wiretap, every piece of paper, every sticky note—but still there is nothing. No overtly suspicious transactions or payoffs from any known crime lord, terrorist, or billionaire in the entire *world* that could fund the move of the Inferno Core." She sighed and rested her head against the doorframe. "But Angels could have just taken it right to its destination." She fell quiet, and all I could do was rub her back in a silent gesture of comfort. "At this point," she looked at me, "we're just spinning our wheels. Burning up the tires, sure, but getting absolutely nowhere." She shook her head. "We're not going to get the location or time of Hell rising by any practical means. We need a miracle."

I desperately fished for a way to comfort her. "Maybe we'll get one."

She nodded. "That's the only hope we have left at this point." She forced a smile on her face and patted my shoulder. "Now come on. Let's go home for a bit where we're safe. Oh, I miss my bed and my room…" Her voice trailed off as she continued down the hall out of earshot.

I smiled and closed the door, then finished getting dressed. Soon I was heading down the stairs where the four of them were already waiting in the living room area of the penthouse. The blood sigils hadn't been wiped clean. As much as that was going to suck for the cleaning staff today, I understood why we couldn't take them down; we needed to stay hidden.

"You all right?" Gyllian asked as I approached.

I nodded. "Let's just go home."

"I believe we can all second that," Booth said.

He looked exhausted. His pale green eyes were heavy and nearly half closed, his face drawn. Booth's condition prompted me to gaze at all my other friends, and I really noticed how hollowed out they seemed. The last two months had taken its toll. They were utterly drained.

"Come on then," Gyllian said.

Each of us reached out and touched Gyllian, and the world went watery as he teleported us back home. Focus returned, and we all appeared on the stairs leading down to the bunker. Gyllian pulled open the round concrete door and we headed inside, dispersing without a word. Roy and Fox headed down the vertical hall toward the intelligence room while Booth took a right toward his room at the end of this hall.

I looked up at Gyllian, who stayed behind with me for a moment. "I'm going to lie down," I said, though I really didn't need to at all.

Gyllian nodded but made no move to head anywhere else. I turned toward my bedroom a little nervously, wondering why he was just standing there. I didn't have long to worry about it because when my bedroom door opened, my jaw hit the floor and I gasped. It was my room, but it wasn't!

"I knew you liked purple," he said behind me.

My room was fully decorated, bright and stunning! It wasn't the brick wall dungeon with brass candle stands anymore. White wallboard was up, and the wall behind my bed was painted a beautiful rosy purple color. Four separate picture frames, different sizes, were side by side with a picture of a purple flower across a white background, looking like one connected picture. On the left was a series of irregular white cubbyholes, all different sizes and shapes, with the same rosy purple back splashing the inside of every box. Each cubbyhole held a different silver, white, or purple piece of art or beautifully dried flowers in vases. My bed was huge, with a decorative silver frame of vines and leaves. The purple pillows and comforter matched the back wall. The floor was covered with wall-to-wall white carpet, with a shaggy, deep purple area carpet under my bed. A few silver oil lamps, all burning with white fire, were evenly spaced around the ceiling, and there was a white vanity table to the right of the room with a stool that had a plush, deep purple seat to match.

I looked back at Gyllian who followed me in with a soft smile. I'd never had anyone give me something so beautiful. As he sat on the edge of my vanity table, I walked up to him and pressed my face firmly into his chest, and he gathered me tightly in his arms.

"Thank you, Gyllian," I said in a shaky breath.

"You're welcome," he said, burying his face in my neck.

When I pulled away, he looked at me with a tenderness and benevolence that made me have to count my breaths. "I thought you were upset with me."

His brows dropped. "Why would I be upset with you?"

I shook my head. "Because I'm stopping you from intercepting the Inferno Core. Because I'm keeping you from saving humanity."

"Hey, hey," he said, taking hold of my hips. "This isn't your fault."

"What do you mean? It's *all* my fault."

He bowed his head and shook it before looking up at me again. "No, it's not. You want to know what faith looks like? It looks like this: I know you're struggling right now, but I'm not mad at you for that. I don't blame you for that. None of us do." He dipped his head to hold my gaze when I tried to glance away. "Because I have faith that this is happening exactly as it's supposed to. I have faith that God knows what he's doing. I have faith that his timing is perfect and you'll understand this in his time, not mine, not the world's, but in *God's* time, which will *be* in time to stop Hell from rising."

I couldn't believe I was hearing this. "But you don't *know* that."

He shook his head and looked at me with what I swore was a little amusement. "No, I don't. But if I *knew* any of this, I wouldn't need faith, would I? Faith is believing in the things you *cannot* see."

I was flummoxed. "That doesn't make sense."

This time Gyllian grinned broadly. "Faith rarely does."

I didn't know what to say, so I just rested my head on his shoulder, and we embraced each other. It seemed so foolish to bet the fate of the world on something as invisible and ridiculous as faith. But then again, if an all-powerful God was behind the faith, perhaps faith wasn't as fragile as I assumed.

"I did my room too," Gyllian said.

I pulled away with a smile. "Can I see?"

He nodded and took my hand and led me next door to his room. My jaw dropped again as he opened the door. The back wall was his favorite color, a deep steel gray, but the other three walls were a beautiful red and gray color marble. Light wood paneled flooring brightened up the room as much as the red marble did. A long abstract painting on the back wall looked like a jungle scene made from a child's finger-painting, which was actually very charming. The bed frame was a rich, shiny, dark cherry wood that looked like it would weigh a ton. He had the same kind of dark shiny wood for his dresser, end tables, and a tall, full bookshelf to the left that almost took up the entire wall.

Gyllian leaned against the edge of his short dresser and crossed his arms. "I scheduled the contractors and decorators before we left. Same ones I used to build the bunker. I left the doors open, and they came right in."

I sat on his dresser, close enough so that our shoulders touched. "What brought this on?"

He got unexpectedly sad. "I don't know."

"Hey," I said, linking my arm with his. He looked over at me. "Tell me."

He took a deep breath and sighed heavily as he looked over his room. "I held off decorating it because I felt like if I did, I'd be admitting defeat. If I did, I was admitting we were going to fail, and Hell was going to rise, and we were going to be stuck down here." He shook his head. "With us coming up so empty handed at such a dire time, I don't know." He shrugged. "I guess I've lost some hope. If we're going to be stuck down here, at least we'll be comfortable."

"Hey," I said, jiggling his arm. "What happened to faith?"

He smiled at me. "I never said it was perfect." I laughed. His gaze went over his room again. "Humans often find faith challenging." He shrugged. "And I'm still half human."

"Well," I said, scrambling for a way to comfort him. "At least we know one thing." He looked at me curiously. "We know Hell is going to rise stateside." One brow went up. I shrugged. "We came up empty handed internationally, so we know we can concentrate our focus and efforts here instead of spreading them all over the world."

Gyllian's face brightened like a thousand-watt light bulb. "You're right. Come on," he said and started out of his room. I quickly followed. "Booth went to rest, but the rest of us can start narrowing everything down."

"All right. How?"

"I want to give the intelligence room an overhaul. Pack

up, delete, and get rid of everything we think we can on international Demon activity. I want to turn our focus to here and only here."

I smiled. "Okay," I said, and we made our way to the intelligence room.

Roy and Fox were both in there already, sitting at the table and looking horribly defeated. When Gyllian shared my idea, they lit up like firecrackers, and all of us excitedly got to work. We cleared out, deleted, and put away anything having to do with activity outside the United States. I discarded piles of files of Middle Eastern terrorists and focused on the domestic ones. Any kind of criminal muscle outside the United States, I cleared out. I kept the international bankers in play, though, because money could cross borders way too easily to count them out. About 96% of ten years' worth of work was junked. Fox got busy deleting records of international seismic activity. Roy destroyed all his international biological results and samples. Gyllian did the same with international meteorology records and turned all twelve of his satellites onto the United States. White boards were cleared and cleaned and new notes put up. Booth joined us a few hours into it and also enthusiastically got to work. He created boxes with his ability of matter manipulation, and we packed them full of everything we didn't need and stacked them in the hallway. Fourteen hours and over two hundred boxes of paper later, we all basically collapsed around the dining table, but we were smiling. The lists were smaller, the boards and walls didn't overflow, and we were thrilled about it. Our focus was narrowed.

We'd sat down for only a minute or so when Gyllian's cell phone rang. He dug it out of his pocket. "Hello?" Pause. "Hold on, Porter. Let me put you on speaker." Gyllian hit a button and fuzzy club music filled the quiet intelligence room.

Gyllian told us that Porter hadn't taken the news of Hell on Earth very well, nor had he been thrilled about the idea that the five of us were half Angels. But after Gyllian had demonstrated some of his abilities and dropped two and a half million dollars into his bank account, Porter warmed to the idea of heading up Placids while "Dimitri Dinahe" was away on business.

"Hey," Porter said, sounding tight lipped and nervous. The others picked up on this as well, and we all glanced at each other. "Um, listen, I'm not sure if this is the type of thing you're looking for, but I just heard one of your working girls talking, and it sounded a little serious."

"What's going on?" I asked.

"Oh hey, Bay," he said, still sounding uneasy. "I heard one of them talking about how one of her regular johns was committed to an asylum this morning."

"A nuthouse?" Roy asked.

"Yeah. That would be an asylum," Porter said flatly. "I don't know. Is that the type of thing you're looking for?"

"Damn straight it is," Gyllian said. "Who are the girl and the john?"

"I didn't hear any names, but it was a pretty black girl with a red streak in her hair."

A wave of heat swept through me as a memory came flooding back from the first night I worked at Gyllian's club. Something I should have told them but I'd ridiculously forgotten!

"Robyn," I whispered at the exact moment Gyllian said her name. He looked up at me quickly, and my expression must have spoken a thousand words because his eyes didn't leave my face. "Thanks, Porter. We'll be in touch." He hung up. "Bay?"

"Shit. *Shit!*" I said and stood from my chair. I was an idiot!

"Bay?" Gyllian said standing.

"I'm sorry," I said shaking my head. "I'm so sorry. It was before I knew any of you and really got this gist of what you do and…shit!"

"Bay!" Gyllian grabbed my shoulders. "What?"

I met his fiery amber eyes and felt my insides shrivel. "José SanSosa." He waited quietly for more. "I was talking to Robyn the first night I worked the club. She said one of her regular johns was deathly afraid of his boss. That he would jump at shadows like his boss was listening through the walls or watching him or something. I meant to tell you, I swear. I just…" I had no good excuse. "I forgot. I didn't understand…"

Gyllian let go of me and went straight over to a computer. Bending over the back of a chair, he began to type furiously. I looked at the others helplessly. Fox and Booth both gave me small encouraging smiles and then went to stand with Gyllian. Roy was the only one who approached me.

"It's okay, Bay," he said quietly. "There's a reason this wasn't revealed earlier. Gyllian knows that."

I nodded as he went to stand with the others. After a forlorn sigh, I joined them, staying quiet while I watched Gyllian attempt to locate this man. The screen showed all sorts of different computer mumbo-jumbo I didn't understand. Several windows opened and moved, showing different codes and things. Finally, it seemed to settle on one screen.

"Got him," Gyllian said.

I found myself gazing at a personal email exchange between SanSosa's sister and his wife. My eyes went wide. He'd just hacked their personal email accounts.

"José SanSosa was admitted to Chicago Mental Health Center this morning. Room 213." He started typing again until another screen popped up. He straightened, and his eyes unexpectedly flashed Angelic before he looked at us. "Let's go," he said as he headed for the door. Fox and Booth moved behind the chair to look at the computer screen, their eyes flashing Angelic as well, before following Gyllian.

"What? Go where?" I asked Roy.

"Come on," he said, looking at the computer screen. His eyes flashed, too, before he looked at me. "We're going to talk to SanSosa."

"Why are your eyes flashing?"

He smiled and nodded toward the computer screen. "Memorizing."

On the screen were the blueprints of the mental hospital SanSosa was committed to. "Blueprints?" I asked, looking at him again. "You want to breech the building?" He didn't say anything, but suddenly it dawned on me. "You think it's a trap."

Roy nodded. "And SanSosa's the bait."

"Shit." I sighed and leaned over the chair, examining the blueprints closely. If this was a trap, we'd have to sneak in to get to SanSosa. I obviously knew how to breech a building—it was standard FBI training—but there were too many unknown variables to make clear decisions. We needed to examine the situation. What kind of equipment were we going to use? Were we going to extract our target or subdue the total threat and interview him on site? But to do that we'd have to know how many threats were *on* site. A tactical initiative like this took hours to plan, even with preliminary information, but we had no preliminary information. Maybe I could get a basis to start from once I had some questions answered. First, I found room 213, and then I looked for the best entry points and the safest paths to the room. I tried to commit to memory the stairwells and closets and –

"Bay," Roy interrupted, making me look at him. He was smiling. "Just take a picture." My brows dropped. He tilted his head toward the screen again.

I looked back at it. Curious, I activated the Hebrew symbols down the middle of my back. They flashed to life for a moment, and instantly I had a perfect mental picture of the blueprints, one I could stare at in my mind and study for as long as I wanted.

"Whoa," I said, straightening.

Roy chuckled. "Come on. We'll come up with a plan when we get there."

We headed to the bunker's armory even as I continued staring at the blueprint in my mind. I could picture myself on all the routes we might take, and alternate routes, and I could see secondary entry points. A plan already started forming in my head, but I needed more intel to properly assess the situation.

In the armory, Gyllian, Fox, and Booth were getting their black clothes on and grabbing handguns off the walls and out of drawers. Our new Aeternum bullets had their own special drawer, which everyone eventually huddled around. Booth got 150 bullets out of the water like I suspected, but it was spread thin through a few different calibers. He concentrated his efforts on the handguns, the .9 millimeters, .45s, and .22s, since that was primarily what we used.

As I was distracted by the activity, the blueprint in my mind vanished. In a moment of paranoia, I tried to recall the image, worried it would have degraded somehow, but it hadn't. I could pull it up again and still see every measurement in the margins and every sprinkler head on the page. Confident I'd be able to recall the image when I needed it, I changed into my black clothes and started loading my magazines.

32

Gyllian teleported us to an empty dirt lot across the street from the mental hospital. The building was just about the only thing in an empty space for at least four blocks. It was five stories high, a fat pinnacle of black against the night sky, and was disturbingly creepy.

Lovely, I thought.

It wasn't in bad shape or run down; in fact, it looked very well maintained. But it was a mental hospital at night. To the left, about two blocks down, was the only other building in the vicinity, a short, stout little office building that looked abandoned this late. The rest of the surrounding area was open and vacant until the tree line rose up a half a mile in the distance.

In the armory, Gyllian had told me to think his name once we arrived. It would activate his mindreading ability and start a party line for all of us to communicate.

Gyllian... I thought.

Here Bay, came his response, which made me jump a little.

I didn't hear him with my ears; it was like hearing him from a memory. When recalling a memory, people don't actually hear the sound of what was said, but they remember what was said.

All right, came Roy. *What do we have here, folks?*

Looks like a big ugly scary looking building to me, Fox said.

I glanced at her beside me. Her mouth was twisted in a sour frown, and I smiled. I was glad I wasn't the only one creeped out.

We need to assess the situation thoroughly, I chimed in, as my mental and emotional gears shifted into special weapons and tactics mode. *One of you has some sort of x-ray vision, don't you?* Everyone but Gyllian looked at me, a little surprised. *I felt it when all your abilities were on me,* I explained.

I do, Gyllian said in front of me.

Well? I said. *Use it. Tell us what you see.*

He was quiet, leaving me staring at the back of his head. *How about you try to use it?* he finally said.

I sighed audibly. The first time I'd accidently triggered Gyllian's ability, it had hurt him. But I sealed my resolve. If I knew anything about Gyllian, it was that he was willing to risk pain to get intel he needed, and, like it or not, we needed the intel SanSosa could have.

I'll try.

I tried to put myself in a place of desperation like I had experienced when I activated his ability before. Nothing happened. Waves of nervous heat rushed up to my face. I couldn't screw this up. Not tonight. I needed to protect them!

Suddenly, the walls of the hospital vanished before my eyes, and I flinched. I was now looking at a perfect cross-section of the building. I could see the lines of each individual floor and wall—plumbing, storage areas, medical supply cabinets, and offices were all laid bare. I supposed it *was* desperation that allowed us to use each other's abilities. Each situation in which we managed to do so seemed to call for it.

I thought I saw some unmoving silhouettes hanging out in rooms like sentries. No, that wasn't suspicious at all. Most of the beds looked unoccupied, but I wasn't quite sure. From here, I could only make out shadows. I needed more variables so I could figure out how to get into the building safely. Then I recalled another ability I'd felt on my skin in Las Vegas.

Which one of you has infrared vision? I demanded. Before anyone could answer, the building erupted into various spots of color and my eyes went wide. "Whoa!" I whispered out loud.

That would be me, Roy said.

His voice, even in my mind, was tight. I looked over and saw his face twisted in a grimace of pain. *Am I hurting you?* I asked, panicked, and started to cut myself off from his ability.

Don't you dare stop, he said, meeting my eyes fiercely. His Angelic eyes practically glowed. *Don't you dare. Get all the information you can.*

Chewing my bottom lip, I looked back at the hospital.

There were a lot of blue and green cold spots that suspiciously took the shapes of people, with a few red hot spots mixed in.

Do Demons burn blue? I asked.

Yes, Roy responded. *They are cold blooded. Drakes burn red, though. They get their warm-bloodedness from their human half.*

My eyebrow cocked up. *Well then, boys and girls, we've got a serious problem. There are at least two hundred cold spots on the second floor.* Everyone was quiet. *I see a few dozen hot spots, which are likely Drakes.*

It was quiet for a beat. *They could be hospital staff or patients,* Fox offered.

I shook my head. *I doubt it, since every other floor is devoid of color.*

All my friends deflated slightly. In a place like this, the patients and night staff should be burning red on all floors. The lack of heat signatures meant they were missing or dead, likely the latter.

I pulled in a deep breath. My friends desperately needed to see what I could see. Roy hadn't seen the explosion of blue and green for himself because he'd needed Gyllian's x-ray vision to take the walls away first. I started shaking my head. I understood that God had separated our powers as a precaution against us becoming assholes like the Angels, but the problem was that all of us needed these abilities to be an efficient team.

Something came to mind. Activating my chain-rope tattoo put all their abilities on me, and we needed all our abilities tonight. Curious—and strictly acting on the kind of faith Gyllian was talking about this morning—I activated it. Immediately I felt the drain on my own strength as the spots of energy started to tingle on my skin. I nearly deactivated the tattoo, deeming it useless, when suddenly I felt something else.

My eyes went wide.

Invisible tethers of energy were stretching from me to each of my companions. It was like I was standing in the middle of a four-pronged web. Suddenly I understood. I wasn't supposed to use all that magic myself...but I could share it with my friends.

With a smile and a gentle sweeping hand gesture, I pushed the hot energy of the two active powers through the tethers. The tethers acted as a conduit to pass abilities through, and I felt the energy of the x-ray and infrared visions go. As soon as they reached the others, my strength was restored.

All of them reacted with a different kind of surprise when they could see the cross section of the building and infrared spots. When they turned to me with wide eyes, it was all I could do not to break into hysterics.

My chain-rope tattoo lets us use each other's abilities without desperate circumstances, I explained. *And without pain.*

They all quickly looked back at the building. I felt like I was walking a tightrope of hysterical joy and deep reverence. God had made me the conduit to hold our abilities because he trusted me enough to share them, as opposed to taking them all onto myself and becoming like the Angels. I was both humbled and excited that he trusted me like that. I'd never expected that.

Well, I said, looking at the others with a smile and drawing their attention. *We're the ones who are supposed to stop Hell from rising, right?* I took out my .9 millimeter sidearm and drew the slide back; the sound of metal scraping on metal and the click of a bullet moving into the chamber filled the silence of the clearing. *So let's fucking stop it.*

All of them grinned and looked back at the building. *Got an entry plan?* Gyllian asked.

I shrugged, feeling an odd confidence that came with the awareness that God was on my side, and pulled out a .45 from another holster. "How about the front door?" I asked out loud.

God wanted to see me have faith? Here it was—walking into a highly dangerous situation completely unprepared.

Gyllian grinned at me over his shoulder. He was raring to go. Hell, we all were. It had been a long, frustrating two-month search for a lead, any kind of lead. Now we finally might have one. Nothing was going to keep *us* out of that building.

Thunder rumbled as the five of us started across the street. I took it as a sign that God was letting us know he had our backs; I hoped I was right. My companions each pulled out their weapon of choice. Fox and Booth took out handguns. Roy took out one Holy Fire blade and a handgun. Gyllian opted for two silver crescent blades that he put on his hands like brass knuckles, the sharp edges of the blades facing outward. I realized absently that those were the weapons he'd used to kill Sari. His hands were left free to also pull out two handguns. Thunder rumbled again, and the first fat raindrops began to fall as the five of us crossed the front lawn toward the main entrance.

I activated my flaming eye tattoo and passed the energy of the magic to the others. At the same time, I felt Fox activate an ability of hers. I wasn't sure how I could tell it was Fox. I just knew. It was like knowing the difference between my own abilities. I just felt her essence in it. Focusing lightly on it, I realized it was the ability to phase through solid objects. I passed that ability to the others as well, and the five of us walked right through the glass doors of the lobby.

A Rook Demon behind the front desk and was on her feet immediately. Her face contorted, her mouth opened too wide as she prepared to alert the others, but before a sound could escape, Gyllian took aim and fired. A rosebud of red bloomed in her forehead, and she went down. We took a stairwell on the left and started making our way up to the second floor.

We weren't in proper formation. We weren't even trying to be quiet, and it was oddly thrilling. Humans needed formations and protocols as a safety measure. The five of us? We didn't need safety. I wasn't even being careful, and that was a new feeling.

When the second floor landing came into view, the door suddenly burst open and a Bishop Demon charged down the stairs toward us. The air went heavy with Gyllian's time manipulation, which stopped it right in its tracks. Gyllian raised his gun and put an Aeternum bullet between its eyes.

As soon as he started time again, though, suddenly a flood of Demons started pouring into the stairwell.

I activated Gyllian's time manipulation myself, stopping them, and glared at the horde. We were about to be overrun, and I had thirty-five seconds to do something about it. Staring at the faces of those Demons, and feeling all that power on my skin, an odd confidence burst to life in me.

With a determined twitch of my lip, I activated every, single ability on me. I would go weak, I might even explode, but I'd take the Demons with me. God would protect the others because they still had work to do.

As I activated all that power, I expected perhaps a bright flash of light and then nothing, but instead the world went surreal. I became radiant with a bright white-gold light that nearly blinded me, and I felt the weight of eternity drop on my shoulders. It was like the entire sky was on top of me. Somehow, some way, I could hold it. It was heavy, but not impossible.

"Gyllian," I said, my voice echoing eerily. He looked back at me as time returned to normal, and his eyes went wide. "Move."

Without a word, he pressed his back against the wall, keeping his eyes on me as I climbed up to the landing. The light emanating from me touched the Demons as I neared, and they dissolved into nothing without a move on my part. Dust wasn't even left behind.

Only man shall return to dust, oddly came to my mind.

I waded through the Demons until I was through the doorway, moving slowly, being careful with the weight that was on me. Every creature in the immediate vicinity evaporated in the light coming off me. In this state, I could see the beginning and end of everything that ever existed, so I knew the precise location of every other Demon on the floor, actually in the entire building, the entire world, and then all of them in Hell.

I was about to clear this entire floor myself when suddenly the heat and the weight became too much. My insides were cooking, and my blood was boiling. My human half couldn't handle it. I dropped to a knee, catching myself with one hand as eternity started to crush me like an aluminum can under a hydraulic press. I wouldn't be able to clear the floor. But I needed to protect them!

"Bay!" Gyllian appeared by my side.

I looked up at his face. "I need...to protect you."

He gave me a wry smile. "We can protect ourselves, thank you very much." Concern filled his eyes. "It's okay. Let it go."

I was trembling, and I wrestled briefly with whether I really wanted to let it go or not. The power was so tempting. No wonder the Angels had turned into such dicks. Absolute power corrupts absolutely, and this wasn't even all the power. I still had my human half to contend with. The Angels didn't have that limitation.

I blew out a breath and deactivated my tattoo. I felt normal again right away, but it was a conundrum. I felt so small and insignificant, yet at the same time I knew I had the ability to touch that power again. To be honest, I kind of wanted too, but my humanness wouldn't allow it. I found myself impressed by the wisdom of what God had done. He had made the five of us all-powerful, but limited. Just like the way he cultivated compassion from brokenness. He had a talent for taking two ends of a spectrum and tying them together to make it work.

Gyllian took my arm and helped me to my feet. I was relieved when I could stand. I wasn't sure why I didn't remain weak. I could only figure that God was giving me strength because our mission here wasn't complete yet, and I needed to be able to walk.

I noticed that all my friends except Gyllian were looking at me with wide eyes. I shook my head. "I'll explain later."

They nodded a little warily, and then we looked around, examining our immediate surroundings. A small waiting room was to the right, and a nurse's station was to the left. Two security doors were on either end of the hall where the patients' rooms would be. The only light was the dim one of an emergency generator, and it was deathly quiet. No one was panicking or running. No security was being called. It was just silent.

I activated my rope-chain hybrid tattoo again and passed Gyllian's x-ray vision and Roy's infrared to the others once more. There were still a hundred and fifty or so temperature signatures on this floor, with the heaviest concentration down the right side of the hall. Pulling up the blueprints in my memory, I knew SanSosa's room was right where the biggest cluster of Demons was. Why weren't they attacking us if this was a trap? Weren't any of them keeping watch? Weren't they wondering where the horde was that I just eliminated?

Split up, Gyllian said in our heads. *Based on the blueprints, this hallway comes full circle. Fox, Roy, you come with me to the left and clear the floor. Booth and Bay, wait here until I give the all-clear then go to the right and we'll meet at room 213.*

Booth and I nodded, and the three of them phased through the security door on the left. I looked down the other hallway at the temperature signatures. As I readied myself for Gyllian to give the all clear, I realized instantly the quick adjustment I would have to make when I headed down there. I could see cold spots through the walls, which meant I had to be careful when I took a shot, lest I aim for a head and hit a support beam. I attempted to turn down Gyllian's x-ray vision and was startled when it worked. He actually had varying degrees of x-ray vision. The walls came into a fuzzy focus like I was adjusting a camera lens. Now I could see which cold spots I had a clear line of sight to.

I heard gunshots on the other side of the hallway and braced myself for the Demons to charge our way to investigate, but none of them moved. I didn't even see a head turn. More gunshots, and the Demons stayed still.

Why are they just standing there? I thought, forgetting everyone could hear me.

Because they can't hear the gunshots, Booth replied next to me.

I gave him a slight scowl. *What do you mean they can't hear it? How can they—* Booth's serene smile cut me off, and it dawned on me. *Because they can't hear it,* I said.

God had deafened their ears to us. That's why they weren't aware of our presence yet. I couldn't help the small smile that came to my face. The things we could do with God backing us were astonishing.

I focused on room 213. Hot and cold spots filled the room and overflowed into the hallway. Picking up on some repetitive motion near the floor, I adjusted my sight to try and make it out. I turned up Gyllian's x-ray vision, clearing the walls completely again, and turned off Roy's infrared. On the outside of my right thigh, I felt Fox's ability to zoom vision, and did. When I saw what was happening, bile rushed up my throat in a sickening wave.

SanSosa was sitting on the floor with his back against the wall while a King Demon forced its dick down SanSosa's throat. The King was moaning like a whore, his head lolled back with a hand behind SanSosa's head, keeping his face flush to its skin. I doubted SanSosa could even breathe, but he didn't struggle. His hands were clenched into tight, trembling fists at his sides. The other creatures in the room, a mix of Kings, Queens, and Knights, male and female alike, stood with pants around their ankles or skirts hiked up around their waists and were masturbating while SanSosa was being violated.

I looked up at Booth. He was already staring down the hall. *Gyllian,* he said, sounding uncharacteristically lethal. *Hurry up.*

90 seconds, Gyllian replied as more gunshots sounded around the back of the hallway.

Booth looked at me and we shared an unspoken decision. *Gyllian,* I said, keeping my eyes locked with Booth's. *We're going in. Stay out of the back hallway so you don't get caught in our crossfire.*

I almost expected an argument. *Copy that*, was all that came.

I turned on Roy's infrared again, and Booth and I phased through the solid aluminum security door. Every demonic head turned in our direction, and I accessed Gyllian's time manipulation as we took aim.

Pop! Pop!

Pop! Pop! Pop!

The hallway became a targeting range, and my world became a blur of gunshots and blood as Booth and I repainted the white sterile walls with thick dark red Demon blood and gray matter. The crowd thinned out considerably by the time we were in sword range. I tucked my guns away and pulled out my father's sword. These Demons had no idea what they were getting into with us. It almost wasn't fair—but then I remembered they were Demons.

After the last Knight Demon fell, time returned to normal. The hallway was quiet, and Booth and I stood in a pile of bodies as tall as our knees and as wide as the hallway.

Blood dripped down the walls and formed puddles on the floor.

The King Demon that had been assaulting SanSosa sauntered into the hallway. He looked surprised to see us standing in a pile of Demon bodies, likely because he hadn't heard anything happen. His expression quickly melted into a snarl.

"Well, well, well," he said in a voice that sounded like a car slowly rolling over wet gravel. "Michael's Daughter and Jophiel's Son. I've been waiting for—"

I pulled out a gun and put an Aeternum bullet between its eyes at point-blank range. The back of its head exploded and splashed against the wall behind.

Booth, Bay, Gyllian said. *We're at the back of the hallway.*

You're clear, Booth replied. *We're nearly done.*

I slowed time down again and whirled into room 213. Another King Demon was forcing himself down SanSosa's throat, so I put an Aeternum bullet in the back of its head, and then popped a few more rounds off into the Demons that were enjoying the show. I watched each of them slowly crumble to the floor before I returned time to normal.

SanSosa took in a long, heavy gasp of air, then doubled over and threw up all over the floor. Hurrying to him, I crouched by his side, resting a hand on his back, and couldn't help noticing the color and smell of the spew. There was no food in it, just cum and stomach acid. He vomited again then gasped violently, trying to breathe while the others dragged the Demon bodies into the hallway.

"This floor is clear," Roy said.

Booth's Angelic eyes turned up to the ceiling. "Above is not."

I looked up as well, and through Gyllian's x-ray and Roy's infrared I saw a few dozen more colored spots on the floors above.

Gyllian jerked his head to the others. "Go. Be back here in three minutes for extraction." They nodded and took off to clear the floors above. "Bay. Door," he said.

I nodded and took up position just outside the door to keep watch. Between glances of the hallway and the room, it was easy to see SanSosa was out of it. He sat on the floor in the same place, only now with his legs crossed, staring blankly ahead.

Gyllian carefully approached. "José?"

José focused on Gyllian, and then terror consumed his features. He scrambled to his feet, crawling over his bed, and pressed himself as far back into the corner of the room as he could. "I know you can dish it out. I know you can. I know you can! I see you. I ssssee you!"

"José," Gyllian said, approaching carefully again. "My name is Gyllian. Do you know where you are?"

"I see you, Gabriel's Son." Gyllian and I looked at each other nervously. Only Angels and Demons called us that. "I ssssee you. I see you!" José screeched at the top of his lungs like a trapped animal.

"José, do you know where you are?"

José was like a car wreck. I didn't want to look because I should be keeping guard, but I couldn't look away from him. I wasn't sure if it was more concern or curiosity, but either way I was sucking as a guard.

José glanced around the room in odd jerky movements. "Crazy house. Nut house. Safe house. I like it here. She's not here. I don't think she is. I haven't seen her."

"Who?" Gyllian said. "Who haven't you seen?"

"Her! Her! Her!" José cried, holding his hands up as if to ward off an attack.

"Her? Who is her? What is her name?" Gyllian asked, taking a step forward.

"Get away! Get away! Get away, Gabriel's Son! Get away!" He cowered, pressing himself even more tightly into the corner. "She's after you. I know what you are! I ssssee you. I ssee you. I seeeeeee you!"

José's eyes seemed to suddenly focus on me with some lucidity. He got on his hands and knees on the mattress and leered at me with lustful eyes. "Hey, you're pretty. I have money. How much?" He straightened and reached into his hospital-issued pants and pulled out his dick. "I can get it nice and hard for you," he said as he started rubbing it. "How much? I'm rich, you know. A banker. How much?"

"Shit," I said and looked back in the hallway. "We're

not going to get anything out of him." I glanced at my watch. "Two minutes," I said, indicating when Roy, Booth and Fox would return.

"José," Gyllian said, but José was already breathing heavily. I could feel his eyes burning into the back of my neck. "Do you know anything about the stolen nuclear weapons?"

It got quiet, so I looked back to see José had stopped masturbating and was staring at Gyllian as if stunned into reality for a moment. "The Angels can't move it or won't. She's not sure. She needs to move it. And she's angry. Oh, she is angry. But she's always angry. I'm not telling you shit! You're in for a long night, a very long night, Gabriel's Son." He looked back at me and placed one foot on the floor, keeping his other knee on the mattress, and started rubbing himself more vigorously. "Will you suck my dick? Please? It's hard for you. It's been a while, a long while, and I like your lips. Your lips would feel good around my cock. Please?"

He suddenly ran toward me, but Gyllian's forearm shot out, clotheslining him so hard that he landed flat on his back at Gyllian's feet.

José moaned, and I thought it was from pain, but then I saw he was still rubbing himself. "Pretty lips. Pretty lips. Pretty lips around my cock!" His body went stiff and he gave a loud yell as he ejaculated all over himself. After relaxing he was still whispering, "Pretty lips. Pretty lips. Pretty lips."

"José," Gyllian said, sounding dangerous as he got down on a knee next to José's head. José looked up at him, and suddenly Gyllian sliced a shallow gash across José's chest with one of his crescent blades. I jumped, and José screamed in agony. "Where is she?" Gyllian yelled.

I looked at him in horror. This man had just been violated by a pack of Demons! Now Gyllian was torturing him. As if he hadn't been through enough!

José's eyes widened on Gyllian's face. "I see you, Gabriel's Son," he whispered. "I see you."

"Where is she?" Gyllian yelled again and sliced another gash across José's chest, leaving another long line of red blood seeping through his white shirt. José screamed again.

I was trembling. I wanted to stop him, but I wasn't sure

how! I couldn't turn on Gyllian, but Gyllian shouldn't be doing this to him!

José stared up at Gyllian's face with dead eyes, like a doll's. "I see you, Gabriel's Son. I see you."

Gyllian slashed across José's chest again. "Where?" Gyllian screamed.

I watched, frozen in horror. This was not my Gyllian. This was the dark, dangerous Gyllian. This was the Gyllian that my Gyllian hated.

"Pretty lips…" José moaned pathetically.

Gyllian slashed him again. "Where is she, SanSosa!" he screamed.

José had another moment of clarity as he looked up at Gyllian. "I…don't…maybe…maybe California? I think, maybe. Please…" José's face twisted until he was openly crying, tears running over his temples into his hairline. "Please don't hurt me again," he said in a soft whimper. "She hurt me a lot. Please, please…"

José sounded so small and childlike, begging Gyllian for mercy. Unable to stand it, I abandoned my watch of the hallway and dropped to my knees beside him. Resting my hands on José's chest, I used Roy's healing ability.

José looked up at me with tears still glistening in his eyes as his wounds closed. "Thank you," he whispered. "Thank you, Michael's Daughter." He smiled sweetly. "I see you."

Three minutes were up, and Roy, Booth and Fox came back into the room.

"Did you get what we needed?" Roy asked.

"No," Gyllian responded tersely and went to the others.

I couldn't even look at him. Seeing him torture a human…my mind and emotions were all over the place.

"Bay," Gyllian barked, making me jump.

Keeping my eyes on José, I rested my hand on his head and leaned down to kiss his forehead. He smiled up at me. "Goodbye, Michael's Daughter."

I pressed my lips together in a weak smile and deactivated my chain-rope tattoo. I stood and went to the group, reaching my hand out to rest on Gyllian's chest but keeping my eyes on the floor. The hospital was drowned out, and we all appeared again on the staircase of the bunker.

Well, almost all of us.

33

Gyllian was gone.

I swiveled my head, looking for him, as the others went down to the bunker like nothing was amiss. "Hey," I called. They all looked up at me as I held my hands out to my sides. "Where's Gyllian?"

"Where he always goes when he gets too close to the dark," Roy replied somberly. I jerked my hands in irritation, waiting for further explanation. "To the orphanage." He pulled open the heavy round door, and they all headed inside.

"But it's the middle of the night."

Roy looked up at me again and nodded. "We know." Then they disappeared through the door.

I bowed my head and rested my hands on my hips. I finally understood what I'd only caught a glimpse of in Florida. I'd witnessed him torturing a human. It was comforting that he needed the company of the kids right now, even though they were sound asleep at this hour, but I couldn't shake the darkness I'd seen in his eyes. It was so deep and hard. I shouldn't go after him. I shouldn't comfort him. But he might need someone right now.

I looked up at the bunker door standing wide open, waiting for me, then went down and slapped it closed. I activated my chain-rope tattoo, feeling the invisible tethers to my four friends. Sure enough, one was stretched far into the distance. I tapped into Gyllian's teleporting abilities and followed it.

When I appeared behind him, I found him sitting in a plush brown armchair. A dim floor lamp illuminated him, but most of the room was dark. His elbows were on his knees, and his mouth rested against his interlaced fingers. Four beds were in front of him with little lumps of sleeping kids snuggled under the covers. Gyllian made no indication he was aware of my presence, so I waited and watched him. He fidgeted and sighed, rubbing his eyes and face a lot. Seeing him practically writhing in agony broke my heart. Unable to stand it for long, I stepped forward and rested my hand on his shoulder.

He jumped to his feet, and spun to face me. When he saw me, his expression unexpectedly twisted in disgust. "What are you doing here?" he snarled quietly.

My brows dropped. "I was worried about you."

He looked at me with such hatred I felt like I'd been stabbed. "Don't be!"

Oh, the agony of those words was something I'd never experienced in my life, and neither was the accompanying desperation to keep this man in my life. The sudden knowledge, the awareness, of how much I felt for him was something out of the Twilight Zone. I needed him in a way I'd never needed anybody. I needed him in a way I'd never *wanted* to need anybody.

I marched up to him and grabbed his coat collar in a fist, and then teleported us to an empty office building across the street. I knew I was going to yell, and I didn't want to wake the kids. Flinging him into the nearest room, which was some sort of filing room, I closed the door behind me. "Where do you get off talking to me like that?"

"Get away from me, Bay," he said with an edge of warning.

"Not until you tell me what your fucking problem is!"

"Bay…"

"No!" I barked. "Tell me what's wrong!" I watched despairingly as his guard started to go up. He was going to fight me. "I love you, Gyllian!" I cried with a piercing edge of desperation I'd never heard in my own voice. "Talk to me!"

He stood there frozen for a long span of a few seconds, and then suddenly he was stalking heavily toward me. For a moment, I thought he was actually going to fight me, but instead he pressed his mouth against mine with such force that I hit the wall behind me with a soft bang. He started tearing off my black trench coat, dropping it to the floor, and his own quickly followed. His breath was so hot and he smelled so good that the notion to resist him didn't even enter my brain. One hand was instantly up my tank top, cupping my right breast over my sports bra for only a quick moment before he slid it up underneath to cup my flesh. He rubbed his thumb over my nipple, and I moaned when it instantly got stiff, to which he responded by pinching it and rolling it between his fingers. I gasped around his mouth and inadvertently dug my fingernails into the back of his shoulder, taking a fistful of his tank top in my hand.

"Gyllian," I panted when he moved down to kiss my neck.

Before I could say another word, he slid my shirt and bra up around my throat, exposing my breasts completely. As soon as they hit the cool air, his hand cupped one and his mouth covered the other, suckling and licking. I gasped through clenched teeth, making a sizzling, hissing sound as his tongue circled my nipple.

I couldn't think. There was no resistance. None.

His mouth briefly came off me, and he pulled my bra and shirt up over my head before taking off his own. As soon as they dropped, his mouth was on me again. I clutched a fistful of his hair, feeling what his mouth was doing to my nipple while his thumb erected the other. He pulled away and came to my eye level as he slipped one hand down my pants. With a small jab upwards, his fingers were inside of me. I gasped again. He was looking at me with wild scrutiny, studying my face to make sure I was enjoying myself. He finally gripped the waist of my pants and pulled them down, allowing him better access to get his fingers deeper inside of me. I was already soaking wet when his thumb started circling my clitoris, and then my knees went weak. I nearly fell, but Gyllian swept me up in one arm and pinned me between his body and the wall. With his free hand, he pulled down his own pants, letting them drop to the floor. I felt the arousing hardness of him as he flattened himself out against me.

Somehow, with zero conviction, I managed to say in a breathless whisper, "Your promise."

He crushed his mouth to mine before pulling an inch away from my face, enough to look into my eyes. "Fuck my promise."

Then he slid inside of me with the ease of a serpent through a river.

———

Dawn broke as we lay together on the floor of the room, covered only by the scraps of our discarded clothing. He was on his back with an arm around my shoulders, while I was curled up by his side with my head resting on his chest. We'd been silent since finishing. I feared what would happen when the fog of desire and passion lifted and he realized what he'd done. Would he hate me? Would he blame me? His blaming me was what I feared the most. I could have stopped him, I should have stopped him, but there was nothing in me that wanted to. Was I at fault for this?

He finally took in a breath, and I thought this was it. It was over. "I love you," he said.

My heart exploded. Heat radiated off my face in burning waves that he must have felt since my cheek was on his chest. I was fairly certain I missed a breath, but I was too overwhelmed to notice or care. I turned so I was looking at him. His amber-brown eyes met mine with such conviction that my heart fluttered and stopped all at once.

Suddenly regret filled in his eyes. "But I've done things," he said quietly. "I've done"—he took a deep breath like he was bracing himself— "evil things." He swallowed heavily. "José is not the first person I've done that to. And I've done worse." I started to feel my pulse in my ears, though I didn't allow myself to show a reaction. "I've climbed the ranks of the criminal underworld for years. The whole time I've had to build my reputation as a person to be respected and feared. I spent a lot of time with Demons when they started to rise. I did their bidding, for years, and I was okay with it. I was good at it. I told myself it was for the greater good, it was for the salvation of humanity." His throat bobbed in another heavy swallow. "Eventually it got easier. It even became routine."

A part of me wanted to silence him, if only to spare him the agony of what he was saying, but it was also something I needed to hear.

He shifted his eyes to his fingers as he tucked some hair behind my ears. "And then you came along." His eyes met mine again. "You are the best of all five of us. Roy, Fox, and even Booth all followed me into the darkness wholeheartedly without even raising an eyebrow, telling themselves the same things I did when I started out." He tenderly rested his knuckles against my cheek. "You didn't. You have fought me at every turn, or begrudgingly joined me, which jarred me out of the apathy I'd fallen into about what I'd been doing." He swallowed again. "And I hated you for that." I was stunned. "Because since we found you, you've made me feel unclean." I opened my mouth to apologize, but before I could, he tenderly took my chin in his fingers. "Because I *am*."

Hearing these words was so unreal that I was hardly able to process it. But at the same time, every word bled into my soul, into the very essence of my entire being. First, they curled up in my heart, leaving a hot brand in their wake, before they spread like a wild blaze of emotion and affection through my system.

"You reminded me what it was like to be appalled by people like me, because people *should* be appalled by people like me." He took in a shaky breath. "Your light, your cleanliness, was always there, all the time, chipping away at the darkness I'd encased myself in since the Taliban captured me. Even your subtle dirty looks when we entered one of my bars and clubs chipped away at it. Every glimpse I got of your light made me hate you"—he sighed— "and love you at the same time. And last night…" He shook his head. "I didn't think twice about torturing José. It's who I was, who I've *been*." His eyes traveled over my face like he was committing it to memory. "But when I saw the look on your face, that look of horror, like you were staring at a stranger, your light broke though completely and I really saw what I'd become."

It was madness to hear this, to hear these words for real, to hear them from the lips of a man I loved.

"I couldn't stand myself," he went on. "I felt every damn second of the last ten years I had lived this way, and my soul felt saturated in evil." He paused and tucked more hair behind my ear. "I left last night because the kids usually help me with that. They remind me why I live with this darkness." He shook his head. "But then you showed up." I held my breath. "Your cleanliness against my filth made a tidal wave of shame wash over me. I was drowning in it." He looked at his hand as he brushed some of my long hair off my bare shoulder. "Then you tell me you love me." He met my eyes again and ran his knuckles lightly down my arm. "And I let myself think that maybe if someone like you could love someone like me, there was hope for me."

I stared at his face, seeing truly, for the first time, how broken he was.

"Gyllian," I said, rolling over and putting myself on top of him so I could stare down into his face. "You, Roy, Fox, and Booth are the best people I have ever known." He ran his fingertips down my back, and a glimmer of hope started to shine in his eyes. "Don't you dare belittle yourself, or the others to me, because I'll defend you until my last breath." I saw him swallow heavily again. "Your unyielding passion to save humanity, no matter the cost, including any and all association with the Demons, you've done with a noble goal. That was something I didn't have before I met you all. You think I'm 'cleaner' than you because I didn't enter the darkness so willingly?" I ran my thumb lightly over his lips. "I think you're the clean one for having the bravery and conviction to do what you've done for humanity."

He stared at me for a long time before his arm draped behind my neck and he pulled me down to kiss me. When we disengaged, he nuzzled his forehead against my cheek. "I love you," he said softly.

I kissed his cheek and jaw and he pet my hair and nuzzled my neck. "We'd better go," he said softly with clear regret.

I looked down at him. "What about your broken promise?" I asked, wary about bringing the subject up, but feeling like I had to.

Gyllian sighed and ran a thick strand of my hair through a loosely held fist. "I'm human, even if just half human, and God forgives humans if we ask. He always has."

He was talking about faith again. He had faith he'd be forgiven, but that wasn't a guarantee. I let the subject drop, though, and kissed his lips. "Okay. Let's go."

We hastily threw our clothes back on, and Gyllian teleported us back to the staircase of the bunker. He opened the door for me and we went in. Pausing outside his bedroom, he stared at the floor before meeting my eyes. "I'm going to try and get some shut eye."

I nodded. "You haven't slept for a full day."

He smiled weakly before pressing his lips firmly to my forehead. With a lingering gaze, he headed into his bedroom and closed the door.

With a sigh, I went into my beautiful purple room, my gift from Gyllian, and shed my filthy black clothes before jumping in the shower. I still had blood on me from the battle at the hospital and, though I didn't usually sweat, Gyllian sure knew how to change that. When I was clean and dry, I put on a pair of light blue jeans and pale orange V-neck shirt. I piled my black clothes into a corner for laundry later and headed to the kitchen in the back hallway. I was starving. I couldn't remember the last thing I'd eaten, or when. I wanted to head into the intelligence room afterwards to see if I could get some work done on figuring out when and where Hell was going to rise.

Reaching the kitchen, I was surprised to see Roy already in there. They'd gotten in at three in the morning, so I thought for sure he, Fox, and Booth would be sleeping in until noon. He was sitting at the high top counter wearing a white tank top and thin, light blue pajama pants, poring over a few files. He was concentrating so hard he didn't even hear me come in.

"There'd better be some food in here," I said as I passed behind him.

He jumped a little and spun to face me as I made my way around the other side of the counter. "Don't do that," he said, making me smile. "I think there's some cereal in that cabinet," he said, indicating the general area with the back of his pen before looking down at his work again.

I pulled down a box of Special K, reached into the refrigerator pulling out the milk, and searched for a bowl and spoon. I sat on a high chair across from Roy and put my small meal together. "Still spinning your wheels?" I asked.

He sighed and sat back on the stool, raising his arms and clasping them behind his head in a small stretch. "Yeah," he said, staring up at the ceiling. "Did SanSosa give you anything?"

I scoffed. "You mean before or after he started jerking off in front of me and asking how much it would cost to suck his dick?"

"Shit," Roy said, his face twisting in disgust. "Seriously?"

"Dude," I said, shaking my head. "The guy was off his rocker."

Roy tossed his pen on top of the file and blew out a long breath with a look of utter defeat. "So we've got nothing. All of that was for nothing." He shook his head. "Figures."

I had no words of comfort for him. Fox was feeling the strain of having no leads, too, and I wanted to help them. I ran the brief conversation Gyllian had with José through my mind, and the strangest thing stuck out. I tried to pass it over and turn to the rest of the conversation, but it stayed for some reason.

"You're in for a long night, a very long night," I whispered distractedly, wondering why that particular phrase would stand out.

"What did you say?" Roy asked all the sudden.

I looked across the counter at him. He stared at me with his eyes so large that my heart jumped into my throat. "Huh?" I hadn't realized I'd said it loud enough to be heard.

"What did you just say?"

I shook my head. "Something SanSosa said, but…" My voice trailed off as I sat in thought a moment. "I think I've heard it before."

"So have I!" Roy exclaimed. He gathered up the files and started out of the kitchen at a run.

His excitement was contagious, so I abandoned my breakfast and ran after him. If anyone was going to pick up on something small, it would be him or Fox.

Roy headed toward the intelligence room. Throwing open the door, he took a quick peak inside. "She's not here." We ran down the hall toward our rooms and stopped at the fourth door, where Roy knocked loud and fast. "Fox? Fox, are you in there?"

Fox opened the door, seeming to have just woken up, but still looked stunning. She stood in a small silky red tank top with no bra and a pair of black lace panties. Her black hair fanned out over her shoulders like a smooth, silken cape.

"What is it? What's wrong?" she asked, rubbing her eyes.

"Nothing. Nothing," Roy said, oblivious to the incredibly sexy woman standing barely clothed in front of him. Even my fantasies were aroused looking at her. I noticed for the first time that her tattoos were concentrated only along the outer edges of her body. The front of her was completely void of ink. They decorated the outside of her arms, her entire torso, and down the outside edges of her legs. Her filler tattoos were gorgeous henna designs like the one on her left hand. "In the wire taps, did anything stand out to you?"

"Um." She rubbed her eyes again and looked at the wall, deep in thought. Her grogginess faded a bit. "Why? What did you hear in yours?"

"I don't want to tell you and bias you. What do you remember?"

"Um, let me..." She glanced back into her room and opened the door, waving us in. "Let me get dressed. My notes are in the intelligence room."

Roy and I stepped in, and my eyes went a little wide. It looked like the entire spectrum of color had thrown up sheer beaded curtains in her room. They were draped down walls, and some hung from the ceiling creating pathways, like one from her bed to her bathroom. Three walls were painted light pink, while the wall behind us was a pretty burnt yellow color. Her large bed was covered with a colorful patchwork silk quilt, with a matching area carpet underneath it. A bright orange curtain was suspended from the ceiling and draped beautifully across her headboard like a lover's arms.

I found myself drawn to her headboard and footboard, which were the most extraordinary things I'd ever seen. They were made of thick heavy looking light oak, but on her footboard, was a stunning carving of the Last Supper. No color, just wood. The detail was sensational, like Leonardo da Vinci would have carved it himself if he'd ever dabbled in woodwork. The headboard was tall, higher than any I'd seen, going almost halfway up the wall and covered with artistically carved words. I stared at them, transfixed for a moment, and realized it was a verse from Psalm 91.

I'd read the Bible sure, when I had to or risk punishment from my fanatical foster mother. But I'd never taken it to heart. The words carved into that headboard, though, seemed to come alive somehow and speak directly to me. They were words I hadn't even realized I'd desperately needed until that very moment because of how accurately they spoke to our current situation.

You will not fear the terror of night, nor the arrow that flies by day, nor the pestilence that stalks in the darkness, nor the plague that destroys at midday. A thousand may fall at your side, ten thousand at your right hand, but it will not come near you.

"Disaster will not come near you," I whispered to myself. Safety. Safety in God's hands.

I placed a knee on Fox's bed and reaching out to touch the carving. I half expected the words to pulsate with life. They were filling me with hope and confidence and fearlessness, not of myself, but of God and his protection. These words were a promise from him that we were safe. His warriors, those that followed him, were safe. *A thousand may fall at your side, ten thousand at your right hand, but it will not come near you.*

My eyes moved to the first line again. *You will not fear the terror of night.* That line was like a nail into my brain. Terror of night. Long night.

"You're in for a long night," I said aloud, and my eyes went wide. "Killiner," I said in a breath.

I spun to face Roy and Fox. Fox was now fully dressed, and both of them were staring at me with deep affection, as if they'd been there for an hour. The memory of my brief interrogation of Killiner exploded profoundly in my mind.

"You're in for a long night," I said as I walked up to them. "Killiner said that to me when I interrogated him. And SanSosa said it last night."

Roy nodded. "That's exactly what I heard in a lot in the wiretaps. I didn't think anything of it until you repeated it from SanSosa in the kitchen."

Fox gasped and gripped Roy's shirt in a fist. "That's one of the side notes I made. I often heard the vilest johns saying that a long night was coming. I didn't think much of it either."

"Okay. Okay," I interrupted before the spike of energy and excitement could cause us to lose focus. "So, long night. What does mean?"

They glanced at each other, and then looked at me, clueless. "Booth would know," Roy said. "He's the astronomer."

"Find him," I ordered. "I'm going to wake Gyllian. Meet in the intelligence room in five minutes."

We all dispersed in a hurry. Fox and Roy headed next door to Booth's room while I jogged down the hall to Gyllian's. I knocked quickly but didn't get an answer. I figured he was asleep, so I pushed open his door and went in, closing it behind me. He was sprawled on his stomach on top of his covers in a pair of black silk boxers, deeply asleep. Tenderness washed over me as I looked at him. He looked so peaceful, and I regretted having to wake him. Once I did, the burdens he carried would remove the softness I now saw in his face. In an effort to delay waking him, I crawled onto his bed and sat down tight to his side, curling my legs under me. I smiled and lightly started to trace the lines of his hourglass tattoo with my fingers.

Finally, I leaned down and kissed his back gently, making my way up his shoulder and to his neck, until he stirred. His eyes opened into slits and, seeing that it was me, he propped himself on one elbow while the other hand went behind my back.

"Bay, what's wrong? What is it?" he asked groggily and rubbed his eyes.

I smiled. "We might have a lead."

He looked up at me quickly. "What? What are you talking about?"

I patted his back purposefully a little too close to his ass. "Get dressed." I got off the bed. "We're meeting in the intelligence room."

Gyllian got up quickly, throwing on a pair of dark blue jeans and an olive green, long-sleeved jersey shirt with a V-neck. He pulled the sleeves up to his elbows and headed for the hallway barefoot. I paused, admiring him a little inappropriately from behind.

When I didn't follow right away, he stopped and looked back at me. "What is it?"

For some reason, at that moment I wanted to see him smile—a real, genuine smile that I so rarely got out of him.

"You know, you're *really* hot, Gyllian."

He gave me a playfully annoyed look, and then rolled his eyes before grinning, which made me laugh. "You coming or not?" he asked. I walked up to him, still smiling, and he greeted me with an arm around my shoulders and a firm kiss on my forehead. "What's the lead?"

I shook my head. "We're not sure if it's significant yet, but it's something. And something is more than we had before."

He nodded. "We'll find out."

We didn't even make it halfway up the vertical hallway toward the intelligence room before Roy, Fox, and Booth were all running toward us from that direction. "December 21st!" Roy screamed.

Gyllian's whole body went rigid, and he left my side quickly to meet them. "What?"

"The Winter Solstice," Roy said. "The longest night of the year. December 21st. That's the deadline when Hell is going to blow those bombs."

"How do you know? What happened?"

"It's all over the wiretaps," Fox explained. "Johns with terrifying sounding 'bosses' mention it constantly. 'The long night is coming,' or 'the long night we're in for' and so on."

"SanSosa mentioned it, and so did Killiner," I explained. "Long night."

Booth stepped forward. "Roy and Fox came to me with the news, and I made the connection right away. It is the Winter Solstice. December 21st."

"Shit," Gyllian said, his eyes widening. "That's only two months away. We still need a location."

"We know," Roy said, and as if by silent command, we all started walking toward the intelligence room. "We've already gotten to work trying to narrow the locations."

"What have you got it down to?"

"Too many still," Fox said. "But we're trying."

"What does the list of the most promising look like?"

"Over seventy possible locations."

"How many of those are in the west?"

Fox shook her head and looked off in thought. "Maybe forty or fifty. Why?"

"Focus there. SanSosa was a rich bank manager, so he would be someone useful to Demons, likely driven mad by his terrifying boss. He said she might be in California. She might even be that Grace Admiral woman who wanted to use my Las Vegas smuggling rings to move the Inferno Core. Whether it's two separate people, or one, they are likely major players. Even if they're not, I want to talk to them."

As we entered the intelligence room, the place seemed to buzz with life, and electricity had nothing to do with it. It buzzed with hope. Hope that we might actually be able to stop this disaster from occurring.

Gyllian looked at his watch. "Okay, listen," he said. "I can keep my original appointment for tonight at my Los Angeles club."

"I thought all your covers were blown," I said.

"Most of them are, but I think my West Coast alias is still okay."

"You think?" I asked. "That's very promising, Gyllian."

He shrugged. "It's a risk I've got to take."

I shook my head helplessly, conceding his point, though I wasn't thrilled about it. I just had to hope he was right.

Gyllian addressed everyone. "Gather everything essential you need to keep narrowing down the location. I don't care if we have to teleport the entire damn room to our hotel. We have to find these bitches."

"She might be waiting for you," Roy said with a glance at me, clearly sharing my worry.

Gyllian just nodded sharply. "Then she'll be easy to find." His eyes passed over all four of us. "We're in the home stretch. So let's get to work."

34

Concerned about how little Gyllian had slept over the past two days, I practically had to force him to take a nap when we arrived at our penthouse suite in California. Even he couldn't deny how exhausted he was, so he ended up listening to me. He would only get about two hours before we had to leave, but it was better than nothing.

The suite was currently alive with computers and makeshift labs and equipment and my companions and I were already narrowing down possible locations. Coffee was brewing and delicious. None of us really needed it, but it was a warm, soothing drink that helped us focus. Papers and files were laid out on the tables and floors, photographs and charts were on the walls, and several white boards stood at five respective work stations.

"Bay," Fox said from behind her computer. "Go upstairs and shower. You've got to get ready for tonight. I'll be up in a bit."

I nodded and put down my coffee mug. I'd made a few more notes on my whiteboard of where Hell could rise based on local profiles and criminal activity and some of Roy's biological samples that drew his attention to the same areas, but so far, I'd come up with nothing. I reluctantly placed my marker down and, with a sigh, headed up stairs.

As the hot water ran down my back, my mind drifted. The words in the Psalm carved into Fox's headboard were sticking with me, filling me with confidence and, dared I even believe, a sense of freedom. If God had my back like the Psalm said, everything was going to be all right.

But the plaguing question that still lingered was, *Why did everything even need to be all right?* Why did we have to make it all right? Why couldn't God? My thoughts also lingered on the very real fact that, as Nephilims, this was it for us. It was stopping Hell from rising or bust. And the "bust" plagued me, too. Were we ready? What if we failed?

I got out of the shower and thought about Gyllian, and Roy, and Fox, and Booth as I wrapped a towel around myself. I saddled myself with the decision that if we failed in stopping Hell rise, all five of us were heading down into that bunker. Not one of them would be absent from that. I sealed it with the determination of that Psalm on Fox's headboard. *You will not fear the terror of night... A thousand may fall at your side, ten thousand at your right hand, but it will not come near you.*

And it would not come near *them.*

A soft knock came on my door and Fox popped her head in. "Ready?"

I nodded. "I'm ready."

"Well, let's go, silly," she said, coming into my room. "My hair and makeup stations are all set up. Gyllian is due at the club at eight."

I nodded again. "Is he up?"

She tugged at the corners of my sheets to straighten them. "I just woke him. He's in the shower."

"Is he okay? I mean, did he look rested?"

She smiled up at me. "He looked fine, Bay. Now come on. I already have your dress, hair, and makeup picked out. Tonight, we're going with simple elegance," she said, taking my hand and towing me into the hallway toward her room.

By eight o'clock, Fox had me dressed in a long, figure-hugging, velvet and silk purple gown. It had an attractive beaded decoration starting at the top of the heart-shaped neckline above my left breast and scooping down under my right breast. Then it wound around the small of my back before it appeared again in a line down my left hip. The beads stopped at the tip of the thigh-high slit in the skirt. She only made small alterations to my face, but the biggest change was turning my hair a beautiful, rich chestnut brown. She left it down and straightened it for the look of simple elegance she wanted.

We stepped out of her room to find Gyllian already waiting at the end of the hallway. I wondered if there would be a time when looking at him would not stop my heart. He was in a well-fitting gray suit with a snug, matching vest. His pocket square, necktie, and textured silk scarf were the exact same purple as my dress.

362

He eventually smiled. "You look beautiful."

I smiled in return. "Thanks. You do, too."

He held his arm out to me, and we headed down the stairs. Down here, among our makeshift intelligence room, everyone gathered around Gyllian. For a moment, we all just looked at each other. I also conjured an image of the innocent children in the world in my mind. Not just at the orphanage, but every child I had encountered in my life and career. I called to memory all their faces and let them fan the embers of determination in my chest. Hell would not get them.

"This is it," Gyllian said somberly. "Whatever happens now is going to decide the fate of the world. Are we ready?"

Everyone affirmed that we were, but there was sadness behind the eyes of each of them. Sure we wanted to be ready, and we were going to do the best we could, but the fear was very present that it wouldn't be enough.

———

The entire interior of Gyllian's Los Angeles club was purple. It had light purple walls and floors and a dark purple curtain that looked like a stage curtain taking up the whole back wall. The light purple couches had perfectly flat seats, with cushiony pillow backings arranged in about fifty perfect squares around the room. A single, low silver table was in the center of each one. It gave the club a sleek, sharp, clean look. But because it was entirely purple, it didn't have a sterile feeling. The purple gave it a fun atmosphere, but it was definitely lower key then Vegas.

It looked like Gyllian's West Coast alias, Damien Toro, was safe after all because the night wore on uneventfully. My heart started to sink with dread. If Gyllian didn't catch a whiff of the women, or woman, that we were looking for here, we were going to be in for a world of hurt. I'd thought for sure we'd be ambushed here or something, but it was business as usual—which was the worst thing that could happen right now.

When 3:00 am rolled around, Gyllian and his cronies stood and started to shake hands. Shit. They were calling it a night, and nothing of significance had happened. I sighed internally as he and Booth started making their way toward me.

"Well," I said, placing my cosmopolitan down on a short silver table and addressing the group that had gathered around me. "Looks like I'm about to retire. Goodnight," I said and stood.

Gyllian put his arm around my back and we headed to the elevators. He was walking a little faster than normal, and my heart started pounding. Maybe he'd caught a scent after all. A few people joined us in the elevator, meaning we couldn't talk freely, so I just hung on Gyllian and went into a useless monologue about what a good time I'd had and what a gorgeous club this was and how I *had* to see this one woman at a local nail salon who was supposed to be "just magic" with acrylics. We stepped out of the elevator and still weren't completely alone, so Gyllian and I beelined to our room with Booth close behind.

As soon as we were all inside, I spun to face him. "What is it?"

Gyllian tore off his blazer and headed straight to my suitcases on the bed. He pulled out a more casual, but still ridiculously fancy, outfit for me. "Put this on quickly."

I grabbed the set of clothes and started to peel the purple dress off me. "What's going on?"

He started taking off the rest of his suit while Booth paced nearby, looking oddly distressed. "Just get dressed."

I did so as fast as I could. The outfit consisted of tight, shiny white leggings, a silk purple tank top, and a short white jacket. A shimmering purple scarf matched the snug top and velvet stiletto heels.

Booth approached Gyllian stiffly. "I don't like this."

"Have faith," Gyllian said as he put on black V-neck t-shirt. "Let Roy and Fox know." Booth let out a frustrated sigh as Gyllian took his arm, and he faded from sight.

"What did you find out?" I asked and sat on the bed. I lifted my foot onto the mattress, trying to buckle the seven straps of my shoes.

"Grace Admiral is here," Gyllian said, then sat down and started strapping them for me. I couldn't even say anything as I gazed at him helping me with my shoes. When he finished, he quickly put on an electric blue blazer. "Marcel caught wind of a big weapons deal going down in this area, a contract I should have been offered but wasn't."

"Almost like Vegas," I noted, wondering if his alias here actually had been compromised. I doubted it, though, because we surely would have found ourselves in a battle by now if it was.

Gyllian nodded. "Almost. But Marcel went to ask why this person hadn't enlist the help of the most successful weapons smuggler on the west coast, only to find out she had bought the loyalty of 70% of my own smugglers." My eyes went wide. "She's taken over my West Coast ring." He pulled on a pair of electric blue pants that matched his jacket. "She's called me to a meeting to discuss her position which, in the criminal underworld means…?" He paused to let me answer.

"She wants to ensure your loyalty to her and will kill you if you don't comply."

Gyllian nodded. "Exactly. So naturally, the boss, me, wants to go since she cost me over a billion dollars in a weapons transfer and has taken control of my operation."

"Why isn't Booth coming?" I asked, draping the scarf around my neck. "This seems like it's going to require all five of us."

"He can't."

"Why not?" I asked and stood.

He shook his head. "You and I need to do this alone."

"Why? I'm just playing your empty-headed girlfriend. What good am I going to be in a territory war between two crime bosses?"

"Would you rather I go alone?" he asked, tucking in his t-shirt.

"Hell no, but I think Booth needs to come, or one of the others."

"Bay," he said, taking my upper arms. "I need you to trust me. This is something only you and I are going to be able to do."

I couldn't help feeling something was wrong. Staring into the layers of Gyllian's eyes, I saw something there. He looked away from me the second I picked up on it, and it took every ounce of my willpower not to scream. Gyllian was avoiding eye contact with me which was not good. Liars avoided eye contact.

"Gyllian," I said. He hesitantly looked back at me. "What are you not telling me?" He opened his mouth to reply, but I cut him off. "Don't bullshit me," I said, slowly shaking my head. "Just don't."

He searched my face for a second, seeming to be looking for an answer, and let out a breath. He sat down heavily on the bed, bowing his head between his shoulders. I sat down beside him and threaded my arm through his.

"Are you afraid?" he asked after a moment.

We looked at each other, and his eyes swept over my face in a sweet, sensitive way that made my heart beat faster. I thought about it for a second and was surprised that I had an answer. "No."

"Why not?"

I sighed and gazed at the floor. "Maybe because I know all of you and trust you. Maybe because I found a little trust in God." I shrugged. "Maybe both?"

When I looked back up at him, he kissed my lips quickly. "I meant what I said," he declared out of the blue. "I love you. You believe me, right?"

Seeing this much emotion from him would have been nice under any other circumstances. Something about this was off, though.

"Gyllian," I said, "what are you not telling me?"

He cupped my face in his hands, and my breath caught in my throat when I saw the beginning of tears forming in his eyes. "Just know that I love you. No matter what you see, or what happens tonight, just know that. Can you do that?"

"Gyllian, what—?"

"Can you do that?"

I swallowed, searching his eyes. "Yes," I said. I was surprised at that answer, too.

He pressed his forehead to mine and squeezed his eyes closed. "Thank you." He lifted his face and kissed my forehead, my cheek, and then my lips. "Let's go," he said standing.

We went back down the elevators and through the club. Outside, waiting for us at the valet parking, was a stunning white Jaguar convertible with the top down. Black leather covered the entire interior and the computer dashboard looked like it could launch a rocket. Gyllian started her up, and the engine purred in a way that would turn a woman on even if she knew nothing about cars.

He pulled out onto the road, and I struggled with my trust in him. If this ended badly, it would destroy me. Questions were already starting to circle my brain. Had I put too much faith in them too soon?

Amid this, Gyllian gently took my hand. I turned and saw him pleading with his eyes. I could practically hear him begging me not to give up. I interlaced my fingers with his and forced a smile. I had to trust him.

Gyllian made a few turns, and the buildings started to gradually change. They went from his heavily lit, $31,000 dollar-a-night club, to the dark streets of $50-dollar-an-hour motels and projects. Hundreds of people, teen and twenty-something boys and a few scantily clad girls, were hanging out in groups on the streets, watching the pretty white Jaguar pass by. I could practically read all their minds: "Dibs." This place was as bad as the streets of Chicago. The difference was, I knew those streets. They were familiar, like an old friend. I'd had plenty of confidential informants that looked a lot like these kids. In Chicago, though, I hadn't been by the side of a handsome billionaire, pretending to be his airheaded arm trophy.

Gyllian pulled down a dark alleyway, where a sinister black SUV and matching van were waiting, and I found myself thinking about the ridiculous predicament I was in. Shit. I really, *really* hated undercover work.

My heels. How fast could I run in these stupid shoes? Maybe I could break the heels off. Would I have time? I could fly, but that would blow our cover. I would risk that. Could I use my strength to lift Gyllian take him with me? Gyllian could teleport, though. Every possible negative scenario flew through my brain in a nanosecond. On the streets of Chicago, as an agent, it was easy to be brave when you had a badge and a gun. This? This was bullshit. I was dressed stupidly and was unequipped and unprepared for this. What had Gyllian been thinking? He could have at least warned me! Maybe this was what he was so upset about, knowing the disadvantage he was putting us both at.

Two people got out of the van, and four got out of the SUV. One of them was a beautiful, tall, slender woman. She had very tan skin and short, wildly spiky fire-engine red hair. Her eyes were large and light brown. She stood in a full black leather getup with her arms crossed, a hip popped out, and no smile on her face.

"Come on," Gyllian said tersely through thinned-out lips, and we both got out of the car.

I wasn't sure how I was supposed to act. Did "Mr. Toro's girlfriend" know about his underground criminal activities? Was I supposed to act appalled? Nervous? Indifferent? He hadn't told me!

Jesus, Gyllian! I cried in my mind. *Why didn't you prepare me better?* He didn't answer.

The woman came strolling up to us as we rounded the hood of the car and stood in the headlights. She looked me up and down, scrutinizing what felt like every detail of my body and appearance. Then, without a word, she took my upper arm and started leading me toward the black van.

Oh, hell no!

I snatched my arm from her grip. "Get off me, bitch!"

The woman paused and looked back at me with a raised brow, as if she was surprised that I hadn't just let her herd me away. She looked behind me, and I didn't even have time to turn around before Gyllian twisted my arm behind my back and gripped a fist full of my hair. I screamed in pain and shock as he forced me toward the van where two beefy men were waiting.

This was not happening! This was *not* happening! Rage erupted inside me, and all my muscles coiled to get ready to fight him. I knew how to get out of this hold, a hard kick into his kneecap and then an elbow once or twice up into the bridge of his nose to break the bone and blind him.

Trust him, came God's ethereal voice in my head just as I lifted my foot to kick him.

I paused in shock as Gyllian shoved me into the arms of the two men outside the van. A black bag was put over my head and then a cloth was over my nose and mouth. I could smell the chloroform. I held my breath, but I knew I'd already inhaled enough to make me pass out. Only I didn't pass out.

Act. Go limp, God said in my head.

I hesitated. Was he seriously asking this of me? To play along with this terrifying kidnapping?

There is a reason, his voice said in an almost pleading tone.

I felt like I was on the edge of a proverbial precipice. All at once, I had a very important decision to make, probably the most important decision of my life—to trust God to guide me over the cliff, or fight my way out of this and never have anything to do with him or Gyllian or the others ever again.

It felt like time stopped. Maybe it did, as both choices swam in and out of possibility and I considered the consequences of each.

Fighting back meant Hell would rise. It meant those kids would die. I knew I couldn't stomach that. I also knew the other Lights meant too much to me to abandon them. They needed me, and I vowed to protect them with everything I had and everything I was. I couldn't do that if I escaped here and fled.

But trust in God was a leap I was unprepared for.

It was do or die this second. Fight and flee forever, or trust an invisible being I didn't know and had hated my entire life.

The lines of the Psalm carved into Fox's headboard came to me like a whisper; *You will not fear the terror of night, nor the arrow that flies by day, nor the pestilence that stalks in the darkness, nor the plague that destroys at midday. A thousand may fall at your side, ten thousand at your right hand, but it will not come near you.*

So I went limp.

35

I was caught before I hit the ground. My wrists were zip tied behind my back, and I was placed on the floor of the van.

"Nice offering," I heard the female say outside.

"Nothing is official yet," Gyllian replied sharply.

The van bounced a little as people climbed inside, and the door slid closed with a slam. I thought about using Gyllian's x-ray ability to see what was happening around me, but decided to wait until I really needed my magic to do something. God wanted me in this situation, so I would be in this situation. *Trust him. Trust Gyllian*, I kept telling myself.

I kept careful track of time because the amount of chloroform I breathed in, based on my particular body mass, would wear off in about a half hour. Just fifteen minutes later, the engine died and the van door slid open again.

Hands started dragging me out. "Back up!" Gyllian said harshly, and the hands were off. "You fucks aren't getting near her until we reach an agreement. You got that?"

"Whatever you say, boss," a male voice said condescendingly.

These people, whoever they were, had no respect for Gyllian, certainly no fear. Gyllian threw me over his shoulder like a sack of potatoes with my head near the small of his back and started to carry me away.

This was going to end badly. So what was the purpose? There was always a purpose for what Gyllian did— information. This Admiral woman had information Gyllian needed, something vital if he was willing to take this kind of risk with me.

Comfort Gyllian, God said. *He is stressed and needs to know you are okay or he won't be able to concentrate during the meeting.*

I didn't even question the request. I deliberately pressed my chin into Gyllian's back and slowly moved my head back and forth so he could feel me. I felt his entire body nearly liquefy with relief. Then he rubbed the back of my thigh in such a subtle tender way I barely felt it. But it was there.

We went from outdoors to indoors. The sound and smell of the place we entered made me think it was concrete or brick. A warehouse? Basement? It was definitely empty. I heard about two dozen footsteps marching, maybe a few more. Shit. We were incredibly outnumbered.

No, you're not, God said to me.

Hearing that, something burst to life in me. Not only was I not alone, but I had God with me, the Alpha and the Omega, the beginning and the end. Nothing defeated God, certainly not these specks of existence trying to be big scary badasses. Even Angels were like dust particles compared to God.

As I basked in this revelation, I felt the weights of trepidation, fear, agitation, and foreboding—a lifetime supply of them—drop off my shoulders and land on the floor behind Gyllian's heels. I smiled under the hood.

Suddenly I felt a hand, an enormous hand, pass through my entire body and hold me gently and firmly. There was a deliberate gentle pressure all over me, and I knew God was gripping me tight, letting me know he was here. It was so distinct, so vivid, that I could feel the cracks between his fingers.

I will never leave you, nor forsake you, his voice came softly.

I couldn't help the tears that welled up in my eyes as an unreal peace and love filled me. I had never been laid so bare before, but I didn't feel exposed… I felt light. I felt free. Free of shame, hurt, longing, pain, and I was just loved, heavily, by the Almighty God.

His hand lifted off me as Gyllian turned left. I felt another doorway enclose around us before moving into open space. After more footsteps, a door closed, and things slowly went quiet. Through the hood I could smell musty stone and wet wood like in a basement. Then there was a soft scraping sound like something dragging across a stone floor. Gyllian walked toward it and set me down on a hard wooden chair. He kept his hand on my shoulder, steadying me as my head hung limp. I felt the skittering of hands as I was zip tied by my ankles and wrists to my seat. The hood was ripped off, and a dim yellow light appeared on the other side of my closed lids, while a ball of cloth was forced into my mouth and tied behind my head.

"Wake her up," the female voice said. "Let me see those pretty blue eyes again."

I was about to ask God how I was supposed to act, when I suddenly knew. I didn't even need to hear his voice. I could just feel what he was asking of me. A sharp smell came under my nose. My head jerked back and I opened my eyes. I looked around, seeming confused, before acting like it was dawning on me what my predicament was. I pretended to struggle against the zip ties and started to cry and scream, though it was muffled by the rag in my mouth.

I looked at Gyllian. The change in him was astounding. This was the Gyllian I'd seen torture SanSosa. His expression was so dark it was difficult for me to look at him. His eyes were so mean and hateful it did something to my insides, like a small uncomfortable twitch deep inside my chest. Seeing what he was portraying made me want to drag him out of here just to soften his beautiful features again into warmth and kindness.

Struggling in the ropes, I saw the shift in his face. I knew what was coming next, and I was ready. Gyllian marched toward me with heavy, threatening steps and punched me right across my face with all his 6'4", 200-pound weight behind his fist.

"Shut the fuck up!" he screamed.

The chair was knocked violently to its side and slid half a foot across the stone floor, but Gyllian might as well have punched through me. There was no pain. Not even in my shoulder, which had scraped across the floor. I squeezed my eyes closed anyway and started to softly cry and whimper.

"Now, now, Toro," the woman chastised, holding the same condescending tone as the male had. She came into view and lifted me and the chair up properly. "Don't damage my property."

"She's not yours yet," Gyllian argued with horrible distain. "Now what the fuck do you want?"

The woman, Grace Admiral, held her hands out to her sides. "Nothing," she said with false innocence. "I just wanted to meet the West Coast head honcho."

"Bullshit," Gyllian spat. "You said you had information that would cost me my woman. Now spit it out."

"Tsk tsk tsk," she chastised. "I said it would cost you a human. You're the sick psychopath who chose your woman."

"Fuck you."

"Oh no," the woman said, caressing my cheek with the back of her finger. I drew away from her hand as much as I could and whimpered. "That'll be her job later."

"Are you trying my patience? Because trust me, that won't end well for you."

"All right," the woman conceded, throwing her hands up as she walked toward her twenty cronies gathered on the left side of the room. "We'll get to brass tacks and all that." She faced Gyllian with a graceful swinging spin.

Gyllian looked so lonely on the opposite side of the room, but he still cut an imposing figure with that regal frame of his shrouded in the countenance of evil.

"I wanted to tell you that it's time for you to step down."

"What?" Gyllian asked.

"Actually, more like, it's time for you to step down and away and"—she paused— "really just disappear, Toro."

Gyllian gave her a vicious smile that didn't reach his darkened eyes. He looked like a wolf about to tear the throat out of much bigger prey. "You try to get into a territory war with me, you fucking cunt, and you'll find yourself strapped nice and tight to a Spanish donkey with concrete bells dangling from your ankles. Believe that." He pointed venomously to himself. "I run the West Coast!"

She clicked her tongue and cooed seductively, which sounded more like a moan, "Temper, temper."

"Now do you have anything important to say, or are we leaving?"

"Actually, I do have something important to say," the woman went on with a slight edge to her tone. "I'm not giving you a choice in the matter."

Gyllian flashed a grin that bared his teeth. "I'll take that as a no, so bye."

"Actually," the woman said, holding a finger up. "I was just doing you a courtesy by letting you know you'll be stepping down. See, I have a very large, and very important shipment coming down the pike of your smuggling ring, and you're going to stay out of my way while I get it to where it needs to be."

The Inferno Core!

"The thing is," she gave an airy laugh. "I've already turned most of your smugglers into mine, so you really don't have much of an operation left, do you?" The smile melted off her face and she gave him a severe look. "You're not in charge anymore, Toro. I am."

Gyllian's teeth clenched. "We'll see about that. My ring spreads to places I doubt you've even dreamed of looking." He took a few steps toward her. "Tell you what. I'll do *you* a courtesy, and let you know what's happening next." He continued slowly toward her. "I'm going to round up my loyal laborers, I'm going to find whatever you're trying to sneak through my territory, and I'm going to intercept it and bring it to its destination myself." He stopped in front of her and his 6'4" frame suddenly looked even bigger against her 5'6" one. I wanted to grin fiercely at this woman in pure satisfaction, but I had to concentrate on looking afraid. "Then I'm going to annihilate any taint of yours in my ring."

The woman shook her head. "I don't think you're going to do that," she said with dead calmness and a confidence I didn't like.

"Oh no?" Gyllian challenged her, just as calmly.

As he said that, my left shoulder suddenly got warm. A tattoo was activated. It took me a moment to recall which one it was, but the memory came quickly enough. It was my truth tattoo. Suddenly, with unmistakable clarity, I knew. I knew! I knew where Hell was going to rise! I saw it all in my mind like I'd seen Gyllian's torture from the Knight Demon with upsetting detail. My eyes went horribly wide, though, because I saw that the Inferno Core wasn't "coming down the pike" as this woman claimed. It was already at its destination!

"No," the woman said. "See, because you were a dumbass and came alone, like I told you to."

She smiled, and suddenly her appearance began to change in the most horrifying way. The skin on her face and arms started to melt off in bloody globs and chunks, like wax from a huge candle. They plopped to the floor with sickeningly heavy splashing sounds, until a King Demon formed. Without a word, she pointed a glowing orange finger at the twenty minions behind her, and they started changing in an even more horrifying way. Their skin started splitting open. Long red cuts opened up along their arms and necks and faces while they writhed and screamed in pain. The King was forcing them to change! The sound was as bad as the screams at Killiner's manor, a mix between grating metal and an arena of burning children. The sound awakened that deep primal fear, as the Demons "hatched" out of their human forms with pieces falling to the floor like broken ceramic. When the change was done, a bunch of Queens stood behind the King, and the two largest stepped up to either side of her. Two beings, however, at the very back of the pack, didn't change at all. For some reason, that seemed worse.

"See," the woman said, her voice now a deep guttural echoing sound like it was coming from the depths of a pit, "there's more than one way to eliminate the competition."

I looked at Gyllian, and he nodded his head so casually, that I smiled behind the rag in my mouth. My Gyllian was back, Gabriel's Son, the half Angel who hated evil and fought it with the very flesh on his back and the damning of his soul.

"You're right," he said. Then in one swift move, his arms went up and wide to his sides, slicing off the heads of the two Queens with the crescent blades on the back of his knuckles. Their heads landed hard and rolled wetly away, and every being in that room looked at him in wide-eyed terror. Gyllian's brow cocked up. "But you're not the only ones who can disguise yourself as human."

Fox, Booth, and Roy all appeared in full black uniform behind him, and I took that as my cue. Tapping into my enhanced strength, I stood from the chair, snapping through the zip ties just by moving. I tossed aside the rag that had been in my mouth and stood beside Gyllian.

The King's alarm melted into a vicious snarl as the fiery blood running under her skin seemed to brighten. "Maybe," she said, "but you don't have Angels on your side."

The two beings at the back stepped forward. Their arms were crossed, and while their faces were set and hard, there was sadness to them as well, perhaps even regret. The King Demon and her posse vanished, leaving the five of us with the two Angels.

"Please," the male on the right said, genuinely pleading, "try to understand."

He had short sandy blonde hair, big sapphire-colored eyes and soft looking peach skin. He wore jeans with a green button up shirt and a dark brown leather jacket. The female was a tall, thin beautiful black woman in a dark business suit, with soft looking tendrils of spiral-curled black hair.

"You know," Gyllian said as his black uniform started appearing over his skin, oozing all over him and taking shape. "I never could understand genocide." I soon felt my own black uniform oozing over me as Booth made them appear. I instantly felt more confident when those stupid purple heels melted into black combat boots.

"Please," the woman said. "You are all so rare and utterly beautiful. Don't make us destroy you."

"Don't view it as genocide, Gabriel's Son," the male Angel said. "It is a cleansing. Humanity will not evolve any further, so they have begun to devolve into disarray and darkness. Their time is up."

"They can be saved!" Gyllian countered passionately. "I've seen it!"

"The children," I piped in, feeling very out of my depth but unable to keep silent. "There's hope there."

"There is no hope, Michael's Daughter," the female Angel said, shaking her head. "Not anymore."

"You are the babies of our brethren," the male stated. "It was foolish of them to Fall as they did. Don't martyr yourselves as well."

Gyllian's jaw clenched. "I will stop you," he said. "At whatever cost." He looked so confident that I actually felt bad for the Angels in front of us.

"Ask yourself this, Gabriel's Son," the female said. "If you are correct in your actions, and God still loves humanity, why have we gotten as far as we have in helping Hell to rise?"

"I don't know," Gyllian replied without missing a beat. "How far *have* you gotten?"

The female gave a gentle patient smile. "Far enough to

know that you will fail in stopping us."

"The weapons are already in place," the male said.

Something warm was in my hand. Squeezing it, I realized it was my father's sword. I didn't even recall reaching for it in my tattoo. Then my mouth started moving with words I hadn't thought to say. "Our Angelic parents sacrificed themselves for a cause they believed in," I said. "A cause strong enough to compel them to leave everything that they had ever known, to lose everything that mattered to them, a cause they were willing to die for." As both Angels turned their attention to me, I thought about the conviction it took for my father to do what he did, to Fall, to risk mortality and death after an eternity of existing. My voice became dangerously low. "Whether we fail or not, that sacrifice *will* be honored by us."

Pity and regret took hold of the Angel's features. "Then I am sorry we must destroy you," the female said.

"Before you do," I said. "There are a few things *you* should ask yourself." The Angels waited. "If God is 100% on your side, then why did he allow our parents to Fall and create us to stop you?" The Angels paused. "Consider this, too. You haven't been able to find us, have you?" The two of them glanced warily at each other. "You couldn't even find our house. Why do you think that is?" I asked, feigning curiosity. "It's almost like…like we were protected, isn't it?" I felt a flash of triumph when the Angels' throats bobbed in nervous swallows. "You also might want to think about why you had to resort to human smuggling rings to get the bombs where you wanted them. You're Angels. Why couldn't you just deliver them?" I glanced between the two of them. "Did something more powerful than you stop you? And geez, there's only one being I can think of that is more powerful than you." I smiled without mirth. "While you're at it," I added finally, holding up my father's sword like a mother holding up a finger to chastise a child. "Tell me why you can't call down a Heavenly host right now to deal with us. Go ahead," I egged them on. "Give it a try."

Both the Angels dropped their eyes closed. My heart seized in panic as I wondered if that had been too bold. I wasn't even sure I was correct in claiming that God was protecting us this whole time. If these two Angels did call down a Heavenly host, we were screwed. It was by faith, and faith alone, that I made the claim that they wouldn't be able to, and I was terrified to be proven wrong. But when their eyes opened and no back-up arrived, my heart calmed, while at the same time brimmed with joy. Not only because I was right, but because God really was protecting us. We were not mistakes. We were not accidents. We were not the product of a rebellious act on our Angelic parents' behalf. God meant for us to exist.

"Now, tell me," I said, "because I'm really curious to know." My eyes narrowed. "How does it feel to be the Demon's bitch?"

Rage blazed in the Angels' eyes, and suddenly the woman was at me while the male went for Gyllian. Without even flinching, I swept my father's sword out to the side, and from it came a shimmering wall of white and gold light. It filled the space in front of us from floor to ceiling, and both Angels crashed into it before they got near us. The woman looked at me stunned, her hands splayed flat against a wall she couldn't penetrate.

I tipped my sword toward her, and it passed through the wall like it wasn't even there. "Still think God is on your side?"

Her eyes went wide as I plunged my blade into her throat. Gyllian held a gun out as far as his arm could stretch and fired, putting an Aeternum bullet between the eyes of the male Angel. Both fell dead at our feet. After that, the light absorbed back into my father's sword.

Gyllian turned to me, and he didn't even have to ask. "Sedona, Arizona," I said.

The last piece of the puzzle. The location of where Hell was going to rise. This had been Gyllian's plan. To chat up a high-ranking Demon, getting me close enough where I could extract the location from her with my truth ability.

"You could have told me," I said.

Gyllian's hand went behind my head, and he pulled me forward to kiss my forehead once, before his lips lingered a good half a minute for the second one. Then he smiled at me. "I know you hate undercover work."

The comment made me grin. I'd needed to be surprised about my kidnapping so I would act correctly; that's why he left me in the dark about it. Gazing at him, I couldn't believe what I was seeing. There was a light in his orange eyes that I so rarely saw. It was as if the sun had come out from behind thick storm clouds to light up his features. Looking at the others, I saw the same thing — light, and hope, and genuine joy.

A reverential silence came over my little group. Ten years' worth of work had culminated in this moment. Ten years of fighting, ten years of fear, ten years of darkness and stress, and it was about to happen. We were about to go to war with Hell with time to spare.

"So, what's the plan?" I asked.

"We head to Hell and get those nuclear weapons back," Gyllian said.

"Don't we need a strategy?"

"We have one," he said, still grinning. "God's here."

I smiled. Yeah. That was all we really needed. Blind faith, it really was fucking bonkers, but it was strong with God behind it. "Well, lead the way."

Gyllian shook his head. "*You* need to lead the way."

I flinched. "Me?"

Gyllian tapped the broad side of my father's blade with his fingernail. "You unlock the door."

Then I recalled a chapter I'd read in my father's book during my week-long library binge. When he had cast Lucifer out of Heaven, the power within his sword is what had locked the door behind him so he couldn't resurface. Lucifer couldn't use the door, so he found a way around his confinement by going through the walls.

Looking down, I examined my father's sword with new affection. It was beautiful. Glass so clear I could see the floor through it, yet strong enough to imprison a creature like Lucifer for tens of thousands of years. This is what opened the door to the prison.

I looked up at Gyllian. "How high can you get us?"

"High enough."

I smiled. "Then let's go."

36

After the watery effect of Gyllian's teleportation faded, my eyes went wide, as did everyone else's but Gyllian's. Apparently he'd been here before.

It wasn't so much the sight—truth be told, there wasn't much to see. It was the overwhelming feeling of...wholeness? Or perhaps Holiness. I couldn't really describe it. Everything good a human being could possibly feel filled me up until it overflowed out of me. I was one with the entire area, and it made me feel almost not there, if that even made sense. Everything was a smoky white. There seemed to be no beginning and no end, but I could see layers and layers of unfathomable depth. Under us, the "floor" gently shifted and swirled like clouds, but our footing was solid.

"What is this place?" I asked.

"It's high," Gyllian answered.

"Well, thank you for clearing that up," I chuckled, which made everyone laugh in return.

"Think of it as the front yard of Heaven," he said.

My eyes went wide. "Heaven?" I asked, looking around. I needed height to open the door to Hell, and Gyllian had delivered. "Geez, Gyllian, are you sure you got us high enough?" I said, making everyone laugh again.

We'd had our share of good times since I'd joined the pack, but this was different. Their laughter came so easily. Their burdens were gone, their exhaustion, their fear. I think a part of it, too, was the knowledge that, whatever happened now, we'd done everything we could to fulfill our purpose, our duty, in the time allowed to us. It was the knowledge that our parents' sacrifice was about to be honored by us.

"We'll see Lucifer, won't we?" I asked.

"Likely," Gyllian replied.

I nodded, then my eyes narrowed curiously. "How come I'm not afraid?" It sounded like a stupid question, but I was genuinely curious. I *wasn't* afraid.

Fox smiled at me. "It's the confidence that comes when you put your faith in God." She narrowed her eyes in pleasant determination. "*Nothing* scares you then."

I took in a breath and sighed. "Well, my dad beat him before, right?"

"Yes, he did," Gyllian answered.

I nodded again. Even with a war in Hell in front of us, I was okay. Here, with my friends and with God, I was okay. This was right.

"I love you all," I said. Their smiles brightened. "The four of you saved my life and then changed it forever." I smiled. "I'm a better person because of you. I hope you know that."

They were quiet for a moment. "All right," Fox said, waving her hands toward herself. "Bring it in. I know it's silly, but I'm calling for a group hug."

With all of us laughing, we gathered together, putting our arms around each other. We absorbed each other's company and strength. I prayed silently for courage to do what I was about to do, and I was sure the others were saying their own prayers as well. When all of us were looking up at each other again, we smiled.

"Let's go save the world," Gyllian said.

We all nodded and dispersed, lining up in formation. Gyllian was behind me to my right, Roy behind me on the left. Booth took position behind Roy, and Fox was behind Gyllian, forming a perfect V-shape with me at the point. My eyes went Angelic, and my father's sword began to glow with that familiar white and gold tinged light. I had to smile a little because the last time it was used like this, to imprison Lucifer, it had been in my father's hands. That thought made me feel incredibly close to him.

When I squeezed the hilt, my determination was ignited. With my dying breath, I would defend those children from the Demons of Hell and nothing, not even the Devil himself, was going to stop me.

With that, I plunged my father's sword into the smoky floor, going down to one knee behind it. A moment later a fissure opened up before me, the edges dropping like silent waterfalls, and the beautiful sprawling red rocks of Sedona,

Arizona were revealed far below. Standing again, I went to the edge and hopped off like an infantry solider from a plane. Face down, my team and I plummeted to the Earth. I could keep my eyes open and breathe, but my hair tore away from my face and my black trench coat flapped like a superhero cape as we fell.

After a sixty-second freefall, I brought my arm in front of me and pointed my dad's sword toward the ground. A blast of white light erupted from it as precise as a laser. The continuous blast hit the Earth and expanded outward over the ground like white lava from a manhole. My heart started pounding as we got closer to it. I kept imagining myself hitting the ground and being reduced to a bloody pile of mush, but we dropped into the roaring, white maw of light without any impact.

Rock and stone whizzed by as we fell deep into the Earth as quickly as if we were still falling from the sky. The stone around us shivered the entire way down, getting more violent with every second we got closer to our goal. Miles and miles passed above, until the white light pooled together on a perfectly square slab of stone in front of us. I watched that slab as cracks of orange fire started to form, like a brand coming through the opposite side. Burning depictions of Demons, and warnings in a language it was probably better I didn't understand, covered the entire thing. Such menacing evil and hatred in glowing Hellfire made my insides shrivel, as if my soul were being squeezed into useless pulp by an invisible fist in my chest, and we were falling right toward it.

Then, like cleansing water, the white light traveled over the fiery orange, extinguishing it, and took a different shape. The writing now appeared in my favorite ancient language, the beautiful lost symbols of Atlantis, which read, "Stay Steadfast in Faith, Dear Children, as You Enter Here." My heart swelled when the Demon heads changed into images of full-bodied Angels—the five Archangel's to be exact. The glowing white image of my father was in the top left corner, his wings splayed wide with one over the top of the door and the other down the left side. His face was turned inward so that he was looking at the center of the door, like he'd be watching over me as I entered. Beautiful Gabriel was in the opposite corner, splayed in the same manner as my father, and smiling brightly. Raphael, Uriel, and Jophiel took up the entire bottom with their wings wide and their heads tilted up to the center as well. The idea that their images would be watching over us made me smile, as we finally fell through the door.

The world went blinding white once we entered, and everything went utterly still. We weren't falling anymore; we were floating. It was like being submerged in water but without the feel of water surrounding us. It was also utterly silent. In that light, a blue print of Hell entered my mind with an old fashioned 'x' marking the spot where the Inferno Core was. I realized we were going to have to fly through here. I activated my chain-rope tattoo and passed the ability to my team before summoning my wings out. As soon as I did, a soft ringing sound came to my ears. As it faded, so did the white from my vision.

Suddenly the most horrifying screeches and screams erupted all around me, drowning out every other sound, and making me want to curl into a ball with my hands over my ears. We were hovering inside a massive rock cavern in a place I couldn't have imagined in my worst nightmares. An expansive lake of orange lava was in front of us that went on forever into the horizon. There was no sky, just brown stone as far as the eye could see. Thousands, maybe millions, of naked, bald and black charred bodies thrashed in the lava that came up to their shoulders. The sound they made was something not of this world. It was a loud, maniacal clamoring of pure pain, panic, and chaos, all wrapped up in one bloodcurdling sound echoing off the walls and ceiling. It seemed to take on a physical layer that beat me all over my body, especially my ears.

The worst part was knowing that these were not Demons. They were human souls.

Some creatures tried to pull themselves up onto narrow shores to the left and right, but anything that touched the shores was still set ablaze. Besides the physical agony they were in, the shore was psychological torture—relief that was right in front of them, but unattainable. The ones that made it still writhed as they burned in fire anyway. None of them, not one, burned up completely. Many of them even ran headlong into the rock walls, or bashed their brains in repeatedly, trying to end their suffering. They only succeeded in causing themselves more pain. Some skulls were completely broken open, yet they still lived, and they still tried.

When they caught a glimpse of my companions and me, their screams changed. The sounds became louder, more high-pitched, and they waded through the lava in our direction with their hands above their heads, reaching for us. Everything inside of me wanted to fly over that orange lake and pull those souls out. I even started angling myself down to do so, but before I could, their actions in their human lives invaded my consciousness. I saw child molesters. I saw sadistic serial killers who had tortured their victims in brutal ways. I saw people who had murdered defenseless families, babies, and toddlers for fun. Every ugly action that a human being was capable of, assaulted my senses, and my pity vanished.

I tore my eyes away from them to look up at the rock walls rising on either side. Four black gaps were a hundred yards above us—two on the right, two on the left, each leading to different torture chambers.

"Bay," I heard to my right.

I glanced over at Gyllian. My black wings gently flapped on his back, sending a cooling breeze in my direction that made strands of my hair dance. He didn't say anything, just pressed his lips together in a sad but encouraging smile. I returned the tightlipped smile and nodded. Angling toward the second gaping hole on the right, I started to ascend toward it.

As soon as we entered the gap, the darkness swallowed us. There was no fire light in here, only a gray ambient light that originated from places unknown and likely magical. Chains grimly decorated the gray stone walls, hanging across the open air at odd angels and random zigzags. Slick spots of blood blackened the walls where someone had recently been skinned alive for perhaps the fiftieth time in an hour. The sounds in this chamber were different. They were low, defeated mournful groans. This chamber held the souls that had given up trying to reach the shore. Muscles were torn apart here, bones were broken, and human souls were turned into marionettes. This was where devices like razors, stretching racks, and crosses were used.

When the gap behind us was the size of a softball, the souls became visible. Hundreds of them were hanging by meat hooks across the chains with gruesomely torn open carcasses. Some were so damaged that they could only twitch in their imprisonment. Every one of them, though, had an odd clarity in his or her eyes, a clarity that told you they were all aware of how much pain they were in. There was no anesthesia here. No passing out from blood loss. It was just constant, conscious pain. Below, the stone floor looked like a graveyard with crosses lined up in neat rows, each with a crucified soul mounted on it. Crucifixion, the worse torturous death mankind ever conceived because of the length of time the victim suffered before he or she died. Relief came with death, but in Hell, none of them could die.

I flew faster to get through this place quickly. Two miles ahead, a massive black fissure opened up in a quarter-mile maw, stretching an unfathomable length to each side. It was like looking down at a black Grand Canyon, and I dove into it. The darkness enveloped us so completely that it constricted around the blazing white power of my father's sword like a living thing. The light was only able to reach a few inches into the dark, not enough to see by. Not wanting to activate any magic yet, conserving my strength for the main battle, I held confidence in God, telling myself that he would guide me through open air, and I wouldn't fly into anything.

The maniacal screams of the souls condemned to this chamber rose up like a horde of rabid bats on each side. This chamber was for pure mental torture. Things happened to people in eternal darkness, insanity of a level I doubted humans were capable of while alive. The light from my sword was likely the only light they'd seen in a thousand years or more. Their wild screams almost drowned out the rushing stampede I heard as they converged near the light from places unknown. But they must have been confined somehow because the sounds stayed distant and they didn't touch us.

At last, a pinpoint of light formed in the distance where the Inferno Core was. My heart started to burn with anticipation, and my fist clenched around the hilt of my dad's sword as I raced toward it. The light became the size of a baseball, then a Volkswagen, then a four-story building. The battle cries of the Demons grew closer, rising from a gentle rumble of thunder to the crescendo of a baseball crowd whose home team had just hit a grand slam in the World Series. They were ready, and, I hoped, so were we.

Finally, we were flying through the opening. I stopped quickly midflight, barely catching myself before I plummeted to the floor.

Lucifer was there.

At the center of the back wall, in this vast room, he sat in a throne of white stone over a thousand feet high. Lucifer himself was over five hundred feet tall, his little finger about the length of my whole body, and he was glorious! The long blonde hair that cascaded across his shoulders looked spun from golden silk and sunshine. His face was a level of perfection no human being could match. He had prominent cheekbones and a strong but elegant jawline, and his eyes were as blue and clear as aquamarine gemstones. A crown of flickering silver fire sat upon his brow, and he wore white silk robes loosely draped over his left arm and shoulder, exposing the right half of his chest and a well-defined muscular right arm. He looked like a Greek god, and he was the most beautiful thing I'd ever seen. I was completely transfixed by him.

Where was the beast of Biblical lore? Where were the horns, forked tail, and red skin? I supposed though, looking at him now, it had been stupid to believe that imagery. Lucifer, after all, was an Angel.

His throne room was completely made up of white stone and silver adornments. Beautiful, decorative stone balconies circled the rim, going up for miles into the ceiling until the details were obscured from the sheer height. A thousand stone archways scaled the walls like palace windows. White light burned from at least a million and a half torches along the walls. The floor, about a half a mile below where we hovered, was made of shining white marble with swirls of silver that flashed in the torchlight like liquid. The only thing that marred the pristine perfection of this room was the three million snarling Demons waiting at the foot of the throne.

Lucifer looked at us without saying a word, and any confidence I had drained out of me. We were supposed to stop *this* being? It was madness! The five of us could fit in the palm of his hand and be crushed. My father's sword, the tool that had cast this creature into the depths, looked like a sewing needle against him. I doubted it would even draw blood if I stuck him. Unworthiness and self-loathing assaulted me. I was not fit to carry my father's sword. What had we been thinking trying to take on the Devil? How insane were we to even have come down here?

Lucifer's eyes went Angelic as he stood from his throne. I stopped breathing, positive his wrath was about to rain down on us. He lifted a foot, and in the middle of a single stride that put him in front of us, he suddenly became aflame with silver fire. It consumed him, then imploded in on itself and shrunk until hitting the floor. When it did, a small portion rose back up and took Lucifer's form again, only now he was human size. His eyes faded back to blue as he gazed up at us almost curiously, and I wondered if he was waiting for us to go down to him.

I started to lower myself to the floor when Gyllian grabbed my arm. "No," he said, shaking his head.

"Let me go, Gyllian."

"His words are poisonous," he hissed. "He corrupts everything just by whispering in ears!"

I met his eyes. "Then come with me."

"Why?" he barked softly. I didn't have an answer. He studied my face and then started shaking his head. "Don't give up, Bay. Please don't give up."

I mustered a small, resigned smile before gently removing my arm from his grip and started lowering myself to the floor. I landed in front of Lucifer and folded my wings behind me without putting them away. Gyllian landed beside me, and I couldn't deny the small bursts of joy I felt when I heard the others land as well. Lucifer's eyes settled on my father's sword first, and a deep darkness came over them. It seemed like the only thing he could see in that moment. The palace faded, Hell faded, and I faded for a moment as he stared at my blade. Then, just like that, the light came back when his eyes panned over my little party.

"So, you are the ones who are supposed to stop me?" he said in a surprisingly soft and gentle voice. "You. Among all of humanity, you five have chosen to save it."

"Yes," Gyllian said. "After all your attempts to make us hate humanity, we—"

"Shh," Lucifer said, closing his eyes and touching a finger to his lips. Suddenly Gyllian's voice was gone. Lucifer looked at him with a terrifying look of detachment. "I'm speaking now."

He took one step toward Gyllian, and my blade was between them. "Stay away from him," I said slowly.

I don't know where the courage came from, but I turned the blade so the tip pointed at Lucifer's chest, and eased him away from Gyllian. I tried not to let surprise register on my face when he actually backed up.

"Where are the bombs, Lucifer?"

"They are already in place, Michael's Daughter."

"Where?"

Lucifer looked up and casually examined the fathomless ceiling. "Far, far above." I almost glanced up, but decided it would probably be wiser to keep my eyes on him. "I was going to wait until the Winter Solstice to detonate them since my Demons draw power from the night. But seeing as how you have annoyed me..." Lucifer suddenly grabbed my wrist and twisted it until the point of my father's sword was aimed at my chest. I screamed in pain and thrust my free hand against my own arm, trying to keep the sword at bay. "I believe I will detonate them slightly ahead of schedule."

Lucifer looked positively bored, as if I'd interrupted him during a good book rather than while he was trying to end the world. He wasn't strained or trembling as he inched the blade closer to my chest. I dropped down to a knee in front of him, trying to keep it away from me with all my enhanced strength. I glanced over at Gyllian and saw him frozen in mid-motion, halfway between pulling out one of Roy's Holy Fire blades and having it form in his hand. Lucifer had stopped time around him. I didn't even have to look at the others to know they were in the same predicament.

"What were you thinking, coming down here?" Lucifer asked, mildly curious. "Only God can kill me, you disgusting creature." His lip curled slightly with barely controlled disdain. "He wouldn't kill me the first time he had the chance, and he won't kill me now." The tip of my sword rested on my skin. "I'll tell you something, though," he said as it slowly started to pierce me. I gasped. "His love for humanity made it even more fun to corrupt them." My wings vanished as I put all my strength into trying to stay alive and keeping the sword back. "It was pathetically easy. Humans," he shook his head. "They will do anything to get what they want, with no regard for others. They will rape, they will murder, and they will sell their souls to have their way, because they believe the universe owes them something." I screamed through clenched teeth as the sword dug deeper and blood started dribbling down my chest. "How a Holy being like God could love something as disgusting and corrupt as mankind is beyond me. I stopped trying to understand eons ago."

I became dauntingly aware of the fact I couldn't really die down here. Hell was eternal. I could have no blood in my veins, no skin on my back, be as broken as a glass marionette found in a trash compactor, and I wouldn't die. Looking at my father's sword, though, as it slowly stabbed me, I knew I'd done the best I could. I'd done everything within my power to…wait. Not quite everything.

God, I found myself praying. *Protect my friends. Please,* I thought. *Get them home safe. Don't let them die down here.*

With that, my strength gave out, and my father's sword plunged into my chest. I gasped as white-hot agony filled my entire body, and I heard a sickening *thunk* as the hilt banged against my breastbone. The glass was so cold against my hot blood and innards that it felt like I'd been stabbed with an icicle—an icicle that was coming out of my back. Lucifer released me, leaving the sword in my hand, and I dropped to both knees. My eyes found the horde of gleeful Demons howling for my death, and I fully realized that we'd failed.

"AWAY FROM HER, LUCIFER!" came a voice so huge that it felt like it reached the other side of the universe.

Lucifer spun toward the sound with wide terrified eyes. Seeing the Devil afraid brought me a measure of satisfaction, and I smiled slightly. Off to the side, a white light tinged with moving watery gold appeared, blocking out the entire left wall of Lucifer's throne room. From within, a gold shadow was coming toward us. It was enormous, at least as tall as Lucifer had been when we arrived, but with six massive gold wings on its back, which were three times as wide as the shadow was tall. When the being emerged, my eyes went wide.

"Dad," I whispered in astonishment.

I suddenly realized my pain was gone. Glancing down, I saw that my father's sword was no longer in my chest, but in my dad's hand, and it was now two hundred feet long. Slowly getting to my feet, I looked at him in glorious terror, trying to comprehend what had happened. He hadn't drawn it out of me, or healed me, but I was whole. A more pressing question came to mind then: How was my father an Angel again? A thousand possibilities and scenarios ran through my mind, each one making less sense than the last. I could only sum it all up one way: nothing was impossible with God.

"Michael," Lucifer gasped in astonishment, and then started shaking a fist at my father. "You can't!" he screamed, getting childishly defiant. "This is my time! I was told!"

"SILENCE, BEAST!" my father bellowed, that powerful voice likely making stars tremble even from down here in the depths of Hell.

Lucifer, as if against his will, was suddenly pushed face down into the pretty marble floor. He was moaning but could not, or *would* not, raise his eyes to my father again.

My dad turned his Angelic eyes on me, his expression brightening with the tenderness of a father seeing his child. My insides liquefied, and suddenly I wanted my daddy. No sooner had the thought crossed my mind than he erupted into a mass of gold sparkles. They imploded in on him until they hit the floor. When they rose again, they reformed him whole, only at regular human size.

"Bay," he said affectionately, his eyes fading back to blue.

That was all it took for me to run to him. If he weren't an Angel, I likely would have knocked him down from how hard I slammed into him. As it was, he caught me and held me in an airborne hug. The two of us could have squeezed the life out of each other from how tightly we embraced. I allowed myself a few moments to hold him. I made sure to touch his golden wings, which were softer than mine, and relished his strong arms wrapped tightly around me. I even allowed myself a little time to imagine what it would have been like growing up with those arms around me. God, how things would have been different. I would have given anything to have been raised by my father, but I did understand why I needed to go through the foster care system the way I did.

I reluctantly pulled away from him but kept my hands on his shoulders. "Dad, how…" My father's body suddenly jerked and he nearly fell. I grabbed his shoulders to steady him. "Dad?" I cried in a near panic. "What's wrong?"

His blue eyes rested on my face, and they glistened with unshed tears. "Say it again, please," he said in a soft breath.

"What?"

"Call me that again. Please."

I smiled. "Dad?"

This time he dropped to a knee, as if he couldn't hold his own weight. I was on my knees in front of him, trying to keep his forehead from striking the marble floor.

I couldn't help but laugh a little. "Dad, you're acting like you've never heard me call you that before."

He looked at me and shook his head. "I haven't."

My brows dropped confused. "What? What do you mean? On the Riverwalk in Chicago. We–"

"I am not in your time right now."

"What?" I ran my eyes over him, wondering if I was dreaming or just going insane. "What do you mean?"

"This is a meeting place where my current time meets yours, and your current time meets mine, no matter how far apart they might be."

"Oh," I said, trying to wrap my mind around that. "So, *when* are you?"

He caressed the side of my head. "In a time about fifty years before the Fall."

My eyes went wide. "You haven't Fallen yet?"

My dad shook his head. "This is the first time, in my eternity, that I've seen you." Tears dropped down his cheeks, looking like drops of water with gold glitter in each one. "My daughter," he said almost choking. "My child."

Seeing my father crying from just looking at me made

me tremble. I rested my hands on his cheeks and said with as much seriousness as I could muster, so he would never forget it, "I love you, dad. Forever."

He pulled me against him. "Lord God. Thank you for such a blessing as this, to have a daughter, to *meet* my daughter. This one instant has brought me more joy than an eternity of existing. Thank you for letting me become a father," he whispered, clutching me to him.

A few moments passed before I heard a soft spoken, *Michael*, come from the expansive light behind him.

"Yes, Lord," he said and reluctantly pulled away, his cheeks wet. "Forgive me," he said as he took my hand and we both got to our feet. "Emotions are not something I'm well acquainted with and these are"—he swallowed—"overwhelming."

I smiled. "It's okay, Dad."

He smiled. "Come. God wants to see you."

My eyes went wide as I glanced nervously into the glorious white light. "What? Why?" Then it dawned on me. "Lucifer killed me, didn't he?"

My dad laughed, a soft melodic sound, like music coming from his inner being. "Not at all, but God does want to speak with you."

A ball of fear formed in my chest and squeezed tightly. Every mistake and dirty thing I'd ever done exploded in my mind like a cracked spider's nest, scattering across my awareness, making me feel disgusting. Amidst the spiders, I tried to think about how things had changed since I'd met the other Nephilims. I'd done well, hadn't I? Maybe not.

"Did I...do something wrong?" I asked nervously. "I didn't mean to, if I did."

"Bay," my dad said, tenderly holding my hand to his chest. "Don't be afraid."

I swallowed heavily and let my father lead me into the light. It looked like we had a long, long way to go. I looked back at my friends, wishing they could come with me. They were all still frozen in mid-motion, each drawing a weapon, ready to come to my defense. As I moved deeper into the tunnel, the edges of light framed them all, making them look like an epic piece of artwork. I kept my eyes on them, hoping this wasn't the last time I would see them. And more so, hoping they would be okay if it were.

37

When I turned around, someone stood twenty feet in front of me, making me stop in my tracks. He was of Middle Eastern descent and exceedingly handsome physically, but with a beauty that went far beneath skin deep. He had large, light eyes of bluish-green, which were striking against his dark tan skin, dark beard, and windswept dark hair that framed his face like a lion's mane. He wore long white robes with a purple sash across his chest and brown sandals.

I recoiled against my father when I realized who it was. It wasn't the kind of fear that made me think I was in danger, but fear of who he was. I knew enough Biblical lore to know this was Yeshua, or Jesus as he was more widely known. I felt so filthy next to the beauty and purity of him. A big part of me wanted to run in the other direction but, oddly enough, my feeling of unworthiness diminished the longer I stood in his presence. I quickly found myself wanting to run to him and embrace him, but doubts plagued me. Was I allowed to do that? Would it be disrespectful? Could I even touch this man without burning where I stood? I was shaking with emotional conflict and overwhelming sensations I couldn't even define.

"Bailey," he said.

Hearing his voice, that gentle, kind voice I'd only heard in my head periodically since Gyllian found me, sent a bolt of shock through me. The voice had a face now, and that face was smiling at me. Everything inside of me ached to be held by him, to be cared for by him, to be known by him. Still, I hesitated, desperate not to be disrespectful or make him angry. But when he held his arms open to me, it was like hearing the shot of a starting pistol, and I ran. I trembled, barely able to stay on my feet, until I threw myself in his arms. He gathered me up and held me close and tight against him, gently laughing. Everything vanished. Everything dark and ugly about me and my past vanished in the embrace of this man.

As he held me, suddenly, everything in the world made

sense. Things made sense that I hadn't even known needed to be understood. Other things I never really needed to understand became common knowledge. Some questions that had nothing to do with me, and some that had everything to do with me, were all answered.

My contentment was short lived, though, because in this place where everything made sense, it dawned on me why I was brought there. I pulled back and met Yeshua's clear blue-green eyes, which now radiated unfathomable grief amongst kindness and love.

"I knew it," I whispered, resting a hand on my stomach and feeling ill. It wasn't the kind of illness associated with a cold or flu, but an illness in my soul. "Oh God, I knew it."

Hell was meant to rise.

Yeshua and I stared at each other for a moment, before he guided to me to sit down on a white bench nearby. It had a sprinkling of white grass, and a few white flowers under and beside it, almost like we were in a park. I sat down, and for the first time in my life, I grieved for humanity. I knew allowing the world to continue as it had been was a mistake. I'd felt it in my bones, even before I'd allowed myself to trust God. I thought it had just been my own hatred for humanity I was wrestling with, but it wasn't.

Lucifer's words to my father came to my ears again. "It's my time! I was told!" He'd been told by God that it was his time. The prophesized Great Tribulation was about to come to pass, and Hell would rise.

Yeshua sat down beside me, and I almost wanted to blame him for this, but mankind had been making choices of their own accord for eons, and this was the consequence. They'd chosen self-gratification, murder, rape, and abuse in a pursuit of all that was greedy over all that was good, clean, lovely, and kind. Gyllian had told me when we first met, "This day in age, Hell is a myth to people, a scary story. Without a fear of Hell, humans don't think there are any consequences for their actions, least of all eternal ones."

Yeshua's head was bowed low. The pain of what was about to come to pass was not just in his expression, but in his entire countenance. Grief penetrated the very essence of his being. He, the Almighty God, looked exhausted with sorrow.

This was his last opportunity to save humanity. He needed to show them that they needed to fear Hell, show them what an eternity there would be like, so he was going to allow it to come to Earth. I imagined the stars and the suns of the entire universe were crying with him over this choice. In fact, I was certain I could hear them wailing from where I sat.

"Is there no other way?" I asked. "Any other way?"

"I prayed for one, knowing already that we'd exhausted every other avenue over the history of mankind."

I almost asked, "We?" but here where everything made sense, I recalled the Trinity. Father, Son, and Holy Spirit…he was talking about God, his Father, whose eyes I felt on me as much as I felt Yeshua's.

"Oh God," I whispered, clutching my stomach again as my insides burned with agony and fear for the human race. The Demons were going to rise, and humanity was going to suffer.

"I see the beginning and end of every person, Bay, from the past to those who are not yet born. My children," Yeshua said, "have done everything they possibly can. They have done everything they were destined to do. They have been spent, they have been sacrificed, and there is nothing more that can be done. There is no one left who will come home to me as things are. Not one more child born will come to know my name. Not one more soul. If I want to save my children, this is the only way."

A vast hollowness threatened to overtake me, and questions plagued my mind. *Then what was the point of this? Me? The other Nephilims? The Fall? If Hell was going to rise anyway, why did you create us in the first place*? No sooner had the questions passed through my awareness than they were answered without a word needing to be spoken because in this place, everything made sense. I understood, but I wasn't sure Gyllian or the others would.

"What about your people on Earth now?" I asked. "Will they be spared?"

Yeshua nodded with his eyes downcast. "I will take them home when you leave here."

"What about the children in the world who may not know you?" I asked, daring to put an edge in my voice, as if

God should be threatened by me.

His gentle blue-green eyes came up and held mine. "Do you trust me, Bay?" As soon as he asked the question, I knew I did, and I knew he was going to spare the children of Earth from Hell's wrath.

I sighed heavily and took hold of the edge of the bench with both hands. I glanced at the ground before looking across at my father. He was giving me a sad but encouraging smile. I bowed my head and stared at my feet upon the white grass. "So what do you want me to do?"

I felt Yeshua's hand gently rest on the back of my head, and he began to stroke my hair. "Take the others home, and wait until it's time."

With a heavy heart, I sighed and nodded. Yeshua leaned forward and kissed my temple, sending a burst of warmth and light through the cold despair that was consuming me. I knew I was about to leave soon, so I looked up at my dad, only to see him already leaning down to kiss my forehead. I closed my eyes and brought my hands up to rest on his cheeks in a lame attempt to keep him there with me. But when he pulled away, my eyes opened, and I was back in Lucifer's throne room.

Lucifer was still on his hands and knees, and my friends were still frozen. I bowed my head a moment, resigning myself to what I needed to do next. Then, taking a deep breath, I summoned my wings out and started running toward Gyllian. Just as his movement resumed, I grabbed hold of him and instantly appeared back inside the bunker. The world didn't need to go watery because I'd used God's will to teleport us, which meant things went a lot quicker. Gyllian spun around, confused, but I was already back in Hell, grabbing Roy. In the bunker again, the pair of them had enough time to look at each other in confusion before I was gone to get Booth next, and then Fox.

Once the four of them were safe, I went to Hell one last time.

The throne room was now empty except for Lucifer, who stood at his full five-hundred-foot height again. His arms were crossed, and he was glaring at me. He couldn't touch me and I couldn't touch him, and we both knew it.

"I win, Bailey," he said confidently.

I nodded. "For now," I agreed. "But I want you to know something."

With that, I called upon my Angelic power. It was something completely separate from the abilities in my tattoos and something I hadn't been aware of until being with God in that place where everything made sense. I became enveloped in something that looked like black sand with twinkling white lights mixed in, like stars on a clear night. The pretty substance circled around me in a gentle tornado before it was all I could see for a moment. When the sand cleared again, I was nose to nose with Lucifer at his full five-hundred-foot height.

"When this is over," I said as Lucifer staggered backwards, "and your time is up, I'm going to be the one who throws you into the lake of fire for eternity."

"You think so?" he said, trying to remain unaffected, though his eyes were wide.

I leaned forward and looked him square in the eye. "I'll see you soon, Lucifer." I wanted him to fear those words until the day came. Even the Devil had to bow to God's timing. Lucifer would only be allowed to run amuck on Earth for a short time. He knew that as well as I did.

I spread my wings and leapt into the air, lifting myself toward the endless ceiling above. For miles I flew, increasing my speed until the wind blew my hair back. When I finally reached the stone roof, I phased through like the rock wasn't even there and emerged above ground in Sedona, Arizona. I could have teleported out, but there was a certain freedom in flying that I loved. I also could have gone back to the bunker, but I wasn't ready for that yet. I wasn't ready to explain.

I looked around at the peaceful stunning red rock landscape below, knowing full well that Lucifer's finger was on the Inferno Core's detonator. A few people milled about, walking dogs or coming home from school. They wouldn't have seen me rise from the ground in this form, and couldn't see me now hovering in the sky. People rarely saw Angels, and I was in full uniform at the moment. A divine perception filter automatically activated when an Angel was in their full glory like this, making me invisible to them, something I had learned in that place with God where everything made sense. Watching the people below, my heart seized in dread, because all of them were about to die. All of them.

A black sedan rolled lazily along the curvy blacktop through the center of town. Looking inside with x-ray and zoom, I saw a baby asleep in a car seat. My heart started pounding in my temples as I waited for him to disappear, to be safe like God said. God said he would spare the kids! He said he would! But there were only seconds left!

I started panting and prepared to return to Hell to try and kill Lucifer before he could detonate those bombs, but God's soothing voice came to my ears. *Do you trust me, Bay?*

I closed my eyes and bowed my head, my wings flapping, keeping me hovering where I waited in the sky. I tried to force down my panic and fear for the child in the backseat. *God is good,* I told myself. *He keeps his promises.* "Yes," I said in a breathless whisper.

In my mind's eye, I saw Lucifer's hand rest on the launch button.

At the exact same time, tiny white lights rose up all around me as far and as wide as my eyes could see. They looked like little shooting stars coming from the Earth toward the sky. Children's spirits. It was all across the world. I could feel their sparks of life and energy like I could feel raindrops on my skin during a storm. He was keeping the children safe. A tiny spark of light flew up within a foot of me, and I knew it was the baby from the car below.

I watched them all disappear out of sight, and then the nukes went off.

38

It started as a low rumble deep beneath the ground. I took one last look at the picturesque landscape. Small, fragile houses embedded in hillsides and sitting on street corners. Tall, masterfully crafted red rock formations of God's own handiwork. By the time the five of us would come out of the bunker, the world would never look like this again.

I bowed my head in grief as the first cloud of red smoke erupted under me. The entire ground, every square inch within my sight, reached toward me like a drowning victim about to go under. The mushroom cloud of red dust and debris passed right through me as if I was a ghost. It was hard to watch, but I made myself do it. I was going to need this vivid reminder of the devastation and decimation wrought today to get through the wait time until we could surface again. After one explosion, the ground was gone. Looking up, I couldn't see the sun either, just red smoke in every direction like I was on Mars. My wings flapped slowly and somberly, sending a few tendrils of dust swirling away from me.

Only fourteen bombs to go. I wouldn't be able to stomach it though. It was done.

I took a deep breath and steeled myself against the reaction I was going to get from my companions. With a burdened heart, I transformed to normal size and teleported back to the bunker.

———

Inside, I found Gyllian throwing himself violently into the doorway that led to the house upstairs. His knuckles were bruised black, and bleeding from repeatedly punching the concrete door trying to open it. They all spun to face me as soon as I appeared.

"Bay!" Gyllian cried in relief as his eyes faded back to sunset orange. "Thank God!" He came toward me and crushed me to his chest. "Thank God," he whispered again and started kissing across my cheek until his lips rested on mine. I savored the feel of his mouth since it would likely be the last affectionate exchange between us. When he pulled away, he rested his forehead against mine. "We thought we'd lost you."

"I'm okay," I replied, though that wasn't completely true.

He kissed me one more time before moving aside so Roy could embrace me. I worried for a moment what his face would look like, but his expression was of pure relief as he embraced me, too.

"I'm so happy you're okay," he said softly.

"Bay," Booth said in a breath and came to hug me as well.

"We thought you were stuck in Hell," Fox said and fiercely embraced me last.

"We all appeared here somehow," Gyllian said when she released me. "Then the door sealed itself."

"We tried *everything* to break it down," Roy added. "All four of us with all our strength couldn't budge it," he concluded, showing me his bloody knuckles. Fox and Booth's knuckles were also bruised and bleeding.

I braced myself a moment and finally took a breath to speak. "That's because God sealed it."

Gyllian's bows dropped. "What?"

I swallowed heavily. "And Lucifer detonated the Inferno Core."

All their eyes went wide. "No," Gyllian whispered. Tense silence filled the bunker. "No!" He screamed, and then spun around, banging his fist on the door again.

I watched helplessly as he pounded on it with every particle of strength he had. Booth and Roy tried to pull him away to no avail. Fox tried to talk to him to calm him down. I waited, quietly, as tears started running down my cheeks.

His strength was finally sapped, and he fell to his knees in front of the door with Booth, Fox, and Roy tending him. Suddenly aware of my silence, Gyllian looked back at me over his shoulder. "Bay?" He said with a dangerous edge. "What are you not telling us?"

I started shivering, like I couldn't keep warm, and my

hands became like ice. "This was God's plan all along, Gyllian."

He stared at me a moment before slowly getting to his feet. "What are you talking about?"

I looked at each of them in turn and gently shook my head. "We were never meant to stop Hell from rising." They remained silent. "God intended for it to rise all along."

None of them moved, until Gyllian started shaking his head. "No," he said. "No. You're wrong. You know how I know? Because God told me his plan!"

I swallowed heavily as my eyes went to the floor. I was expecting this. "What exactly did he tell you about his plan?" I asked.

"That we would fight Hell and save humanity!"

I nodded and finally looked up at him. "And we will. But not yet."

"What do you mean?" Roy asked placing a comforting hand on Gyllian's shoulder.

"We were never humanity's defenders," I swallowed heavily again. "We are their rescuers."

I saw realization, and agony, and disbelief dawn on the faces of the other three. Fox began to cry as she pressed her face into Roy's chest. Roy, with mouth a gap, gathered her tightly in his arms. Booth's head was bowed solemnly.

"No!" Gyllian cried. "Step by step I followed his instructions, with blind trust I didn't even know it was possible to conjure! Everything God has had me do for the past ten years was to *stop* Hell from rising!"

I remained silent.

"Tell me something," he went on, holding a finger up at me. "If you're right, then what was the point of this, huh? The Fall? Us? If Hell was *meant* to rise, why did he create us? What was the fucking point?" he screamed.

I swallowed. These were the questions I had been waiting for. "Everything God has done with each of us was to build our trust in him, to stretch our faith, and to ensure we would be ready when the time came to deliver humanity from Hell's hands." I met his eyes. "I was in no shape to want to save humanity when you all found me, and you know that. None of us were, after what we'd been through. That needed to change, and it has." I nodded as a little confidence crept its way into my heart. "We will fight Hell, and we will save humanity." I shook my head. "Just not yet."

"When?" Booth asked quietly from behind Gyllian.

Gyllian looked back at him in disbelief he was encouraging this conversation.

"I don't know how long," I responded.

"Well, that's just perfect," Gyllian spat. "You seem to have all sorts of new information except how long we're going to be stuck down here!"

I turned my eyes to the floor. I would rather have shriveled into a ball and cease to exist than have Gyllian in so much pain. He knew. He knew what was happening up there, better than any one of us.

"Everything God does," Booth interjected gently, drawing my eyes up to him. "Everything he allows to happen is for his love of mankind, and his desire to bring them home safely to him."

I nodded gently, half in disbelief, half in gratitude. I was thankful beyond words for his calm voice of reason. I was also grateful that he wasn't looking at me scornfully the way Gyllian was.

"How is letting Hell rise saving humanity?" Gyllian yelled at him. "Do you know what those fucking Demons are doing up there right now? Well, I do!" He screamed, pounding his fist against his chest.

Booth didn't take his eyes off me. "God can see the beginning and end of every human life." I nodded again as he started to recite God's exact words to me, the exact words I had been planning to say to Gyllian. "He knows there is no one left on Earth that would come home to him if things remained the way they were."

Realization finally dawned on Gyllian's face, and he staggered back a few steps, bumping into the door, as if his legs had gone numb.

"You told me when we first met, that Hell was just a scary myth to people," I nodded. "You were right." Gyllian looked at me in wide-eyed horror. "The human race has no fear of Hell, even though it should. And you know as well as I do that God doesn't want anyone to go there." I glanced back at the floor. "So this is his final, desperate attempt to get them to come home safely to Heaven, by showing them that Hell is real, in hopes that they won't want to spend eternity there."

Gyllian's expression didn't budge as he turned his gaze down the hallway toward the back of the bunker. He slid his trench coat off and let it float silently to the floor before he headed in that direction without another glance at me. Roy and Fox took his exit as their own cue to start down the hallway to their rooms. Booth was the only one who stayed.

"Thank you," I said in a shaky whisper as I wiped the tears from my cheeks.

"I had a feeling this is what was meant to be." I looked up at him surprised, and he forced a small, sad smile. "I had hoped to be wrong, though."

I nodded. "I wish we were wrong, too." My eyes went to the floor again. "They're going to hate me forever, aren't they?"

"For a while, perhaps," he replied and his words stabbed me like a knife. "But they would be in the wrong if they did."

I looked up at him again.

With a sympathetic smile, he rested a hand on my shoulder. "This is not your fault, Bay," he said gently. "For anyone, including our dear companions to think otherwise, is to take the power out of God's hands. It shows their lack of trust in his wisdom and his will in allowing this to happen. That, my darling, is on them." Booth stepped forward and embraced me. I gratefully accepted it and rested my cheek on his chest. "Give them some time," he said with a squeeze. "They lost much of their faith today. They will be questioning their purpose and likely spending many agonizing hours in prayer while shaking their fists at the sky. Have patience, and they will come around."

I nodded. "Thanks, Booth." He kissed the top of my head and pulled away. When he did, I saw a flash of devastation come into his eyes. "What is it?"

He sighed. "I am thinking about Neesa. The children..." his voice drifted off as he bowed his head.

I rested my hand on his forearm. "They're okay." He looked up at me quickly, and I nodded. "God took all of his children out of the Earth before the bombs went off."

Booth nearly collapsed in relief, and I reached out to steady him. "Thank you, Lord Jesus," he said in a breath. "Thank you, thank you, thank you." After a few moments, he straightened and took a deep breath. "I believe I will be doing some praying of my own, thanking God for his goodness." He leaned forward and kissed my forehead.

I watched him head down the hall and enter his room. Alone, I stood there for a while, not sure where to go. Gyllian was down the other hall somewhere, and I knew I was the last person on Earth he wanted to see. But, like it or not, we were stuck down here together for only God knew how long. We had to find a way to coexist, or else get to work on a rotating schedule of common areas so we could avoid each other. I needed to know which one he would prefer.

I activated my chain-rope tattoo, bringing to life the four-pronged web of energy, and felt the whereabouts of the others. Fox and Roy were together in Fox's room. Booth was in his room. Gyllian was somewhere else, and his location felt odd. Not threatening odd, but odd nonetheless.

I took off in a run down the hallway. Grabbing the corner of the wall, I slingshot myself around it and ran to the very last room on the left, which was the kitchen. Sure enough, the refrigerator had been shoved aside, and the escape hatch in the floor leading down to the natural cave was wide open.

Gyllian was trying to escape the bunker underground.

I jumped into the darkness, grabbing hold of the fifth rung of the ladder, and shimmied down by my hands, saving time by not bothering to place my feet. This was one of several escape hatches in case the bunker ever became compromised. The idea was to use our heightened Angelic senses and abilities to escape through the caves, since the only opening to the outside world was an eleven-mile swim through a maze of rock islands and other cave formations.

The cave below was unexpectedly well lit even without my abilities active. Ambient blue light shimmered off the brown stone like the sun reflecting off the surface of water, but there was no way the sun reached down here. I could just see the island of stone beneath me in the faint blue iridescent light, and released the ladder, landing easily on my feet. My eyes went wide as I glanced around because the blue light wasn't the sun reflecting off water, but a wall of pure blue magic encircling the escape hatch in a ten-yard circumference. It waved and shimmered like vertical water from the ceiling to down deep beneath the depths, until the light couldn't even be seen anymore.

We couldn't get out, so God was going to make sure nothing could get in either.

At the edge of the blue wall, mostly in shadow, I saw Gyllian's silhouette. He was sitting on a rock island in the corner with his knees drawn up. I dove into the water and swam to the island he was on. Pulling myself out, I got on my knees in front of him. He was barefoot and soaking wet and I just wanted to hold him. I didn't dare try, though, not yet.

"I can't get through it, Bay," he said, still shrouded in shadow. He lightly banged his head against the blue light beside him, and it made a low thumping sound as if it were a solid surface.

I pressed my palms into my thighs to keep them from shaking. "God doesn't want you to, Gyllian."

He turned and pressed his forehead into the blue light which now illuminated his face. His eyes were closed and his expression was drawn with desperate sorrow and exhaustion. A few minutes passed before he slowly, with his eyes still closed, leaned forward until he was on his stomach with his head resting on my lap. I leaned over him, wrapping him up in my arms as best I could from this position, and kissed his temple.

"How long?" he asked in a small voice.

I smoothed his hair back so I could see him better. "I don't know. God didn't tell me."

He was quiet for a while before I realized his breathing had become steady and he was asleep. I sighed and continued to pet his hair.

The five of us only had each other left and the hope of when we could rise and deliver humanity from the jaws of Hell. The optimist in me hoped that once mankind got a taste of Hell, they would never want to have anything to do with that place ever again. That they would want to come home and be safe in God's arms. But the realist in me knew that human beings were survivors. They were adaptable, and it was very hard for them to learn lessons if it meant admitting, even for one second, that they could be wrong. Hell rising would be God's fault in many eyes. *He* would be to blame, not them. Not their own greedy, murderous, abusive ways. Too few would be able to view it as a last-ditch effort on God's behalf to save them.

I feared to see where the chips would fall in each category once we did surface.

Don't miss the EPIC sequel…

Continue reading for an exclusive look at Lights Rise.
(Coming soon!)

1

I could still taste the beautiful red rock in my mouth, my last sensation above ground, as fifteen nuclear warheads had reduced Sedona, Arizona to dust. Seven years had passed since Hell had risen from the depths of the Earth. We thought we were supposed to save humanity by stopping it; we were wrong. My powerful companions and I would have to wait.

Humanity had become so uncaring about the consequences of its actions, with no fear of Hell whatsoever, that just about its entire species was headed in that direction. But God truly loved mankind and wanted people all home safe with him. So, as much as it had pained him, he had given Hell temporary run over the Earth to remind mankind why Hell should be feared and avoided. So we waited.

Gyllian had had the hardest time accepting God's reasons for letting Hell rise. He'd been a prisoner of war in Afghanistan many years ago and had later endured torture from a Knight Demon to gain information on the Demons' activity to prevent the apocalypse. It was his own suffering in those situations that had put him on the determined path to try to stop Hell from rising and save the humans, so they'd never have to go through what he did. Unfortunately, he hadn't known Hell was *meant* to rise—none of us had. Over the past seven years, I'd seen his guilt get heavier and heavier. Now it was at the point where he had no energy. He slept all the time, at least fourteen hours a day, sometimes more. He hadn't been to the gym once in the past two years. He barely even left his room. Occasionally he'd go to the library, but whenever I found him in there, he was just staring at the wall with big eyes and no book. I'd been trying to take care of him, but I doubted I was doing much good. Sometimes Gyllian was so far beyond consoling that all I could do was sit quietly with him in his room.

That's where I was now. He had fallen asleep again. I sat beside him and caressed his back, letting him know in a small way that I was here. His face was turned toward me, and I sighed at the sight of how pale he looked. We were all pale. We'd been underground for seven years, so it was expected, but it hurt me to see Gyllian looking as ill as he was. Lowering myself onto the mattress, I brought my face close to his and gently ran my fingers through his black hair. It had gotten long again. I'd have to talk to Fox later about cutting it. I leaned down and kissed his cheek, lingering a moment before kissing it again, and then left his room.

The bunker was quiet. It was always quiet in an uncomfortably eerie way. As I made my way down the hall, the silence made the air feel heavy, and it pressed in around me like it wanted to choke me. The sounds of my footsteps were even swallowed up. I wished Booth were in the library playing his oldies records too loudly again, anything to break this oppressive silence.

I passed our four monstrous storage rooms. Each one was about the size of six aisles in a grocery store but taller. God always gave us exactly what we needed, and in seven years, the five of us had barely put a dent in our supplies. It made me wonder fearfully how much longer we had down here. I crossed my arms to keep from trembling, and hurried past them as a tension headache came on. I was getting those a lot lately. I was pretty sure my worry for Gyllian was the root of them. The past seven years had already been hard on him and, looking at those four full storage rooms, I wasn't sure how much more he could take.

I quickly made my way toward the gym to go for a run or something. That usually took care of my headaches. I stopped in my tracks, though, when I saw Roy in there already. He was in a white tank top and dark blue sweatpants with boxing gloves on, wailing on one of our heavy-duty punching bags. His brown hair was sopping wet with strings of it sticking to his forehead, indicating he had been at this for at least six hours. Our endurance for physical activity was incredibly high because we were Nephilims—half human, half Archangels—so it took quite a bit to make us sweat.

Seeing me come in, Roy paused his workout. "Hey," he said, glancing down at his gloves.

"Hey." I dipped my head toward his appearance and

smirked. "You trying to prove a point or something?"

He grinned broadly with a smile that still melted my heart. "Nah." He glanced down at his gloves again. "Just killing time."

I nodded. I really wanted to be alone and kill six or seven hours of my own, but the way he looked at me, with reserved affection, I couldn't bear to leave him like that. So I smiled and went to the glove rack. "Up for sparing with something that can hit back?" I asked a little playfully.

He smiled again and he gave me a jerky nod. "You know it."

I tossed my gray hoodie to the floor, which left me in a white tank top and my blue and purple flannel sleeping shorts. I threw my hair back into a ponytail before putting my gloves on.

"How's Gyllian?" Roy asked as I adjusted the straps on my wrists.

"Same," I replied, keeping my voice carefully neutral. If I let any emotion slip in my response, Roy would likely ask what was wrong. If he did that, I was going to break down and never recover. "He'll be okay once we get out of here."

Roy nodded, and then we tapped gloves and our hands were up.

"Any idea how long it will be yet?" Roy asked as he tried to throw a right jab at me which I jerked away from.

I shook my head. "No," I said and tried a right hook, left jab combo, which he dodged.

Our sparing match started light and casual, but it escalated. It quickly became emotional, and both of us started throwing faster, harder punches. We started using moves and combinations that would be illegal in regular boxing rings. Soon, it became a kickboxing match. Finally, the gloves came off, and it became a full-on ultimate fighter match. It was surprisingly cathartic for me, and probably for Roy, too. The way the match evolved, or devolved rather, was a clear expression of both of our frustration. Not necessarily with each other, or one particular thing, but the general stress of being locked down here while Hell ran amuck on the surface. It also helped me with the stress I'd put on myself to take care of Gyllian.

Our fight became intense. Roy had healing abilities, so we could wail on each other within an inch of our lives and be put back together in two seconds. I never thought it would feel so damn good to have my jaw cracked so hard that I tasted blood in my mouth. My nose was broken. Roy's left cheekbone was shattered and bleeding. Both of our knuckles were red with blood. Since we'd been sealed down here, everything always stayed within the realm of safety, and we put respect and caring for each other above all else. But we were warriors, atrophied warriors, and today Roy and I threw politeness and common courtesy out the fucking window which felt great. We had been idle and stuck down here for seven damn years! The fight was a welcome reprieve from the walking death that had become our life. I beat on Roy like I wished I could beat on the silence that constantly pressed in around us.

I spun away from an attack of his and, with my back to him, brought my right foot up and stomped down hard onto his thigh. His femur bone, the hardest and thickest bone in the entire human body, cracked so loudly that the break echoed down the hallway. Roy screamed and was down on his back, gripping his thigh. My eyes went wide. Before I could get down by his side to help, his eyes turned the silvery gray color with a pinpoint black pupil, a clear indication he was using one of his abilities. His body relaxed then he suddenly grabbed the back of my ankle and threw my foot forward so hard I was thrown onto the mat beside him, hitting the back of my head. Both of us lay next to each other panting heavily.

"There's something wrong with us," Roy said.

I nodded. "Who gets pleasure from beating the absolute shit out of their best friend?"

Roy's panting gave way to laughter. It was contagious, and I started laughing as well. Soon we were both roaring. Lying on the mats, both of us beaten to absolute pulps, we clutched our stomachs in hysterical laughter.

When the laughter died down, Roy got to his feet in one smooth movement and held out his hand out to me. When I took it, he pulled me up, and then pulled me into his arms. I hadn't been expecting that, but as he embraced me, I felt my whole body start to uncoil. I sighed as I let myself relax against him. Roy eventually pressed his lips firmly to my forehead, and his healing magic spread throughout my body from that spot. My injuries faded, and the pain vanished.

I looked up at him and saw he'd fully healed himself too. Not one drop of blood was left on our faces. "Thanks," I said.

Gyllian, Fox, and Booth suddenly rushed into the gym in full black uniform and armed. My eyes went wide when I looked at Gyllian. It was the most fire I'd seen in him since the door was sealed, but it wasn't the controlled fierceness he used to have; it was wild murderous rage. He looked like he didn't know where he was, blinking a lot and glancing around in search of something.

Fox and Booth deflated a little while Gyllian's rage seemed to build. "What the fuck is happening?" he screamed.

"Whoa dude, calm down," Roy said, facing Gyllian with his hands up.

"We heard a crack and you screamed!" Gyllian cried. "It echoed through the whole bunker!"

Roy glanced at me, and I allowed the worry and fear to creep up into my eyes as I looked back at him. What was wrong with him?

Roy faced Gyllian. "Bay and I were just sparring. It got a little out of hand, and she broke my femur." He forced a smile. "That shit is no joke. It hurt. But I healed myself, and everything is fine."

Gyllian was visibly trembling. "There's blood everywhere."

Roy nodded. "Like I said, it got out of hand."

Gyllian glared at him. "You beat each other hard enough to draw this much blood?"

Roy hesitated to answer a moment, not sure how Gyllian was going to react, and then nodded carefully. "Yeah."

A shiver seemed to run up Gyllian's spine. His whole body jerked, like his strength was yanked out of him, and he sunk against a wall, catching himself by his elbow, before sinking to his knees.

"Gyllian!" I cried and ran to him.

His eyes closed. "I…I can't," he panted as I dropped to my knees in front of him, and crushed him to my chest. "I can't, Bay. I can't anymore."

My heart was broken. I squeezed my eyes closed and pressed my face firmly into his neck. "I know, sweetheart," I murmured. "I know."

Fox, Booth, and Roy all ended up getting on their knees around us, trying to offer their comfort. All of us were sad. All of us wanted out. All of us were helpless. None of us spoke. None of us needed to. We just drew strength and comfort from each other.

God, I prayed as my eyes turned upwards. *How long?*

There was nothing formal about it. It was a desperate plea on behalf of the humans we knew were suffering on Earth, and the man I loved.

Go now, children, came his voice.

All of us heard it, and life seemed to jump into every one of us as we looked up.

It's time.

Suddenly a loud sucking noise and a soft bang from the other side of the bunker echoed down the hallway. Our eyes snapped in that direction.

"The door," Gyllian said in a breath. "It's unsealed!"

All of us were instantly on our feet and running down the hall. Our steps echoed through the entire bunker, giving more life to this place then it had had since we'd come down here. There was urgency. There was excitement. There was relief. There was hope.

I fired up my chain-rope hybrid tattoo around my hips, using one of my abilities that linked all our abilities together, and activated Booth's ability of matter manipulation. I change me and Roy into our black uniforms, clothing made of flexible, absorbent black material, long black trench coats, and heavy black boots. I also filled our numerous weapon holsters using Fox's object relocation ability to magically raid our arsenal.

Soon we were standing in front of the door to the bunker that used to lead up to Gyllian's house. It was not only unsealed, but standing wide open. Unable to believe it, we stood there a moment, just staring. We were free. The humans were going to be saved.

Proceed with caution, children, God said to us all. *The world has changed since you were in it.*

After a glance around at each other, all of us pulled up the hoods of our trench coats and drew out our weapons. It was time to go to war.

Other ways to contact the Author:

Twitter: @Nichelle_Writes
Facebook: www.facebook.com/NichelleRaeAuthor
Email: Nichelle_Rae@yahoo.com
Website: www.nichellewrites.com

Follow Nichelle Rae on BookBub:
https://www.bookbub.com/authors/nichelle-rae